Isa

Claiming Destination, Volume 3

Colleen A. Parkinson

Published by Sepia Tree Publishing, 2025.

ISA

First edition. November 16, 2025.

ISBN: 979-8993369303

Written by Colleen A. Parkinson.

CHAPTER 1

OUT OF THE TAINTED SOIL

During the past week, Isabelle had snuck into Dillon's room a number of times when he was asleep and left behind little gifts for him. Usually, it was candy. Occasionally she left something more nutritious: a small box of raisins. Other times she left him items of comfort: a tiny stuffed angel bear that once served as a Christmas tree ornament, another time a small stuffed tiger, a discard from an old fast food kids' meal promotion. The day before, she had left him a homemade card she had created herself, a red crayon drawing of a daisy with the words, *"plese fel bedder sone!"* in blue crayon scrawl. He appreciated her efforts and placed the card upright on his bedside table for all to see.

Last night, he prepared a gift for her, a pencil drawing of a little girl with angel wings. He made certain the little girl looked just like her.

This morning, the drawing was gone, and a coloring book and crayons sat in its place on his bedside table. Her persistence and thoughtfulness made him smile. While he waited for someone to bring his breakfast, he began to color. It had been years since he had done such a thing, and he found it strangely therapeutic.

The person who brought his breakfast tray was the shortest and youngest nurse he had ever seen in his life. Today she was wearing a faded pink dress with a floral pattern of yellow roses with leafy, curly green stems.

"Day th-said I could bing it to you," she announced as she set the tray on his hospital table. She promptly climbed up on the bed with him and sat across from him near the foot. "I bot my food, too. Okay?"

"I guess," Dillon replied. He was not sure if he welcomed the intrusion or not. He had become accustomed to eating alone.

"Tankoo fo' da pitty dwawing. Was dat me?"

"Yeah. That was you."

She smiled a big smile, "You dwaw good!"

He returned her smile without restraint.

She pointed to the two plastic juice bottles. "Do you want appoo or gape?"

"Apple."

"Good. I like gape bettew."

Dillon looked over the meal. Two slices of toast, two scrambled powdered eggs, hash browns made with real potatoes, and some kind of mystery meat he assumed was Spam. A very small container held a few teaspoons of grape jelly. Miniature plastic shakers held salt and pepper. Both his meal and Isabelle's were identical.

"Do you like hath bowns?" Isabelle asked.

"Yeah." He took a forkful and inquired, "What's your name, kid?"

"Isa." She pronounced it the Spanish way, *Eesa,* the same as Unkaduffy, Unkabowis and Dockitew Mean pronounced it. Then she added, "Wanna know aw my names?" She did not wait for his answer. "Isabew Rosa Maria Rodriquez." She rolled the R's impressively from years of practice, and pronounced *"Rosa"* as *"Rrrote-za."* With a grin and hardly a breath, she asked him, "What's yoze?"

"Dillon."

She tried to pronounce it. "Di...yon" Oh, those pesky L's! She could pronounce the L's in some words, but in most words, her mouth simply would not work right.

He sounded it out for her, "Dil-lon."

She nodded, "Din."

He made a face at her, trying not to laugh. "Not *Din*. Dil-lon!"

She looked at him with all sincerity, "Dat's what I th-said. *Din*."

"No..." Dillon persisted, "You gotta pronounce the L's. Dil-lon."

She tried again. "Din."

"Good grief..." He chuckled.

"Unkadin!"

"No! I ain't your uncle!"

Isabelle felt hurt by this. To her, all male friends were uncles. "Why not?"

"'cause I ain't related to you."

"Unkas aw fwends! Fwends to me. You be fwend, Din?"

He gave up, "Eat your slop, rug rat."

"Is not sop. Is good food!" She bit into her toast and eyed him over the crust. "Be fwend wiff me, Din?" Crumbs flew when she said, *fwend*.

She reminded him of his little sister when she was that age, although his sister was Scandinavian blond. Little Isabelle had the same friendliness, persistence and cheerfulness. He wondered how she could be so cheerful in such a fucked-up circumstance.

"You got folks?"

"No mo'. Maybe faddoo. He's in dale."

"Dale?" He couldn't resist tacking on, "What's dale? His boyfriend?"

The black eyebrows came together as one perplexed line. "Huh?"

"Never mind." He thought it was fun to get her all confused. It was something he used to do to his sister all the time.

"Day tookim to dale. He got mad an' s-thot a guy."

"Good for him." When she pouted, he changed the subject. "Thank you for the coloring book."

"You like cuwoo?"

"Yeah."

"Me, too. Did you eat thuckoo?"

"Yep. Thanks for that, too."

She grinned. "Hep you feeyoo bettew."

"How'd you get here to this place?"

"Unkaduffy an' Unkabowis."

"Friends?"

"Uh-huh. Day hep me."

"Are they here?"

The little girl nodded. "Uh-huh. Duffy got awthwitis. Unkabowis take bud wiff needews. He wook hew, now." She smiled, her love for them evident. "Day hep me get bettew. Day hep you, too, if you want."

Dillon was not certain he wanted to get well. Being chronically ill had proven an ideal way to get out of chores at this place, and he knew they would assign him to some shit-work if he were healthy. Staying sick had its advantages. He decided to skirt the issue and bring up her comment about her health. "You were sick, Isa?"

"Yeah. I had biting sick."

"Biting sick? You mean like all those infected pusses that are eating people?"

"Yep."

He found this frightening and, at the same time, improbable. As far as he knew, the disease was incurable. "No way!"

"Uh-huh!" she insisted, "Da mean dockitew put me inna cage."

"What mean *dockitew*?"

"Da gway-haihwed goo. Ode. See hoot me!"

He remembered the caged mords at Baker Creek. He remembered the scientists with a mixture of grief and anger. Could the doctor be the same woman? "Did she have long gray hair?"

"Uh-huh."

"Did she hurt you while you were biting sick?"

"Uh-huh."

"Why?"

She laughed, "I twied to bite hoo!"

"Why?"

"Hung-ee." She laughed again, "Dockitew mell good! Make me hung-ee!"

"Aw, shit..." Dillon could not believe this. He wondered if she would have a relapse someday. "Do you still want to eat people?"

"No. Want good food. No peep fing." She dug into her eggs. They were cold by now, and she did not like cold eggs. Still, she was hungry enough to ignore that and eat them. She also appreciated the food. Unkaduffy said all food was a gift from Deezus. She would not waste a gift from Deezus, no way, no how.

"What's peep fing?"

She could not understand why no one in this place knew what peep fing was. The tone in her voice reflected that. "Peepo to eat."

He had just swallowed the last forkful of mystery meat on his plate. He hoped it was Spam and not something else. There was no telling what went on in the kitchen or where they got their food.

Just to be on the safe side, he asked her, "What do people taste like?" If she said *Spam*, he was going to puke.

She wrinkled her forehead, and her eyebrows met as she thought about it, tried to remember. After a minute, she gave up. She could not remember, and the entire episode was something she was glad to forget. "Don't know. Don't membew."

Dillon took a long look at her. Everything about the little girl seemed outwardly normal. "How'd you get cured?"

"Unkaduffy gib me weah food."

"That's all?"

She pointed to Dillon's IV. "Medsin, too."

"What kind of medicine?"

She shrugged. She considered that topic exhausted, and delved ahead to what was really important to her. "You fwend to me, Din?"

He liked her. She was fun in an innocent way, and she had gone to great lengths to befriend him. He did not know why she had chosen him out of all the other patients on the ward, but maybe she had already befriended everyone else and had gotten bored. Yet, it seemed important to her that *he* be her friend.

"I guess," he finally answered. "So long as you don't get all weird and try to eat me. You do that; I'll kick your little Mexican ass!"

This angered her. "I'm *Amewickan*!" With equal fury, she added, "An' I don't eat peepo no mo'!"

He had not expected her to react with such passion. "Okay, okay! Calm down! Don't get'cher cockles all tangled!"

She scrunched her face, pouted her full round lips, and the eyebrows came together again, "What?"

He cast her a friendly grin. "Don't get so mad. I was just kiddin'."

"You my fwend, Din?"

"Yeah."

"Okay." She stood up on her knees. "Gib me yo' head."

"Huh?"

She took his chemo-bald head in her little hands and bent it toward her. She kissed the top of his head and rubbed it briskly with her fingertips. "You good guy, Din!"

Dillon laughed.

CAROLYN PUSHED THE wheelchair for Natalie. She had taken it upon herself to give Natalie a tour of the hidden underground compound. Natalie gazed fascinated at the many different sections, most located in caverns. There was the little hospital, the huge dining room and kitchen, a section devoted to shops for ready supplies and gift items, the library, the conference room, gymnasium, indoor shooting range, main offices for staff and personnel, two giant barracks for male and female soldiers, a weapons storage facility, a giant facility for food and general supplies, and a residential area.

Carolyn casually pushed her through the residential area. This section resembled a very organized campground. Most of the residents lived in tents of different sizes and configurations. A number of small cabins, compact motor homes and camp trailers housed families.

Carolyn pointed to a tent that sat in the center of a charming fake yard carpeted with Astroturf, and decorated with plastic plants and flowers in little pots throughout. A pink flamingo added just the right amount of Carolyn-type whimsy. "That's my place up there. It's not much inside, just a cot and some plastic furniture to make it homey. I got a microwave and a coffee maker, too."

"Everyone's got electricity?"

"Yep. They generate it from the river. It's pretty cool, huh?"

"This is amazing!" Natalie said.

"They built the whole thing inside a lava tube. It took them ten years. Can you imagine that? We're inside a lava tube!"

"Are you telling me we're in a volcano?"

"It's a dead volcano."

"How'd they do it? Doesn't the government own the land?"

"Nope! James owns the land. Some guy he worked for deeded it to him. The guy, whatever his name was, planned it decades ago as a bomb shelter." She stopped in front of her tent and pointed, "How do you like my flamingo?"

Natalie laughed, "It's you, Care."

Carolyn grinned, "I thought you'd say that!" She gave the wheelchair a push and they continued on the tour.

"Does Ian live with you?"

"No. He lives with Joe and his family. They have a huge tent. Why'd you think he lives with me?"

"I heard you two are an item." She looked backwards at Carolyn to see her reaction.

Carolyn turned red and smiled. "Who's the bigmouth?"

"Joe."

"That figures."

"Good catch, there. Ian's a babe!"

Carolyn laughed, "Yeah... he sure is." She stopped the wheelchair at the community park area where there was an indoor fountain and a little pond. She took a seat on a bench. "So, Nat... Tell me the story about you and Harley Guy."

"There's not much to tell."

"Oh! Like hell! How'd he end up at *your* house?"

"My mom and dad. They'd been helping him."

Carolyn could not imagine hard-edged Harley Guy accepting help from Natalie's straight-laced parents. The combination seemed like oil and water. "Helping him what?"

"Get his life together."

Going on memory, Carolyn could see where Coltan could have used a lot of help. He seemed like the angriest person in the world, and also the saddest. And, then there were his parents. The thought of them sent a shiver up her spine.

Considering Coltan's standoffish attitude, she asked Natalie, "Did he let them?"

"Not only did he let them, he wanted them to." It was with sadness for him that she said, "He loved them. They loved him."

"Man..." Carolyn took note of her sadness. "I'm sorry about your parents."

Her eyes filled with tears, "Without Coltan, I couldn't have gotten through it."

"Are you in love with him?"

"It's beyond love. I can't describe it." She wiped her tears, "Remember how we thought he was nothing but trash? You can't believe how wrong we were. We were wrong about everything."

"He seems a lot different than he used to be."

"Oh! And, get this. The guy listens to classical music and opera! Can you believe that?" Natalie grinned and laughed, "He's an incurable romantic."

"Mister leather-clad bad boy on the Harley? Who would've even suspected? Now, I would've pegged him as a metal head." In the next breath, she became very serious. "I can't believe how he looks at you. And he sure holds you a lot."

"He wants to marry me."

Carolyn's expression darkened and then, as if aware of revealing her jealousy, lit up with feigned enthusiasm. "When?"

Natalie, too caught up to notice Carolyn's initial reaction, gushed, "As soon as possible. Can you imagine that? I never could."

Carolyn drew close to her and whispered, "Did you and him... you know?" After Natalie grinned and nodded, the next question spilled out, "How is he?"

She sighed; just the thought of his touch aroused her, "Incredible!"

"Ooohhh! You lucky dog! I knew it!"

Natalie giggled self-consciously. "Keep it down, girl!"

In a whisper, she kidded, "I can't help it. I think I just had an orgasm!"

The giggle gave way to laughter, "Stop it!"

Carolyn laughed with her, the two of them laughing softly and confidentially like old times. "By the way... Coltan doesn't know that I once—"

"I never told him. That's our secret, Care." Natalie then asked in a supportive tone of voice, "Say... what about you and Ian?"

"Just kissing. He's quite a gentleman. I like that. He makes me feel like a lady. I mean, remember those guys at school? The ones I let... well... I know I didn't mean a thing to them. I know they were just using me. Ian's not like that at all. You know something, Nat?

He's younger than me, yet he's more mature than any of the guys I knew. He's like an old soul in a young body."

Ian had impressed her the same way. "Yeah. I know what you mean." She offered her one good arm to give Carolyn a hug, "I'm happy for you, Care."

Carolyn hugged her, then stood and continued their journey, "I've got to show you Ian's indoor garden. It's fabulous. He's really got a way with plants. It's right down this corridor over here. Wait'll you see it."

DOCTOR QUIMBY SAT AT Coltan's bedside, the chart in his hand. Looking again over the test results, he could not fathom how Coltan had managed to survive so long with the virus in his system on top of the blood poisoning, liver damage and bleeding ulcers. "How are you feeling today, son?"

He was tired, in pain, and so weak he could barely lift his arms. "I think it's better than yesterday."

"Your temperature seems to be running from one extreme to the other. Has this been the case since you first became ill?"

"Yeah." He noticed the doctor's pursed brow plus the sympathy in his eyes. Caleb's gut twisted. "What's going on? Is it the dog bites?"

"You mentioned Natalie had given you vitamins and antibiotics. What kind of antibiotics?"

"I don't know. She mixed up a bunch of stuff. She was sure it was blood poisoning, and she said that they treat it with different antibiotics all at once." He tried to sit up a bit more, but it hurt to do so. "Was she right? Was it blood poisoning?"

"Yes, it was blood poisoning."

"What about my stomach pain?"

"I never saw ulcers as severe as yours. Your stomach was a mess." He referred again to the chart. Coltan's heartbeat sped in response to Quimby's growing uneasiness. The doctor sensed it and looked again at Coltan. "Do you know the dogs that attacked you were sick?"

"We had an idea. So? What did they give me?"

"No one's ever come up with a scientific name for it. We just call it the *dog virus.* "

Coltan had never heard of it, but he knew it had to be something serious. "What's that?"

"It's the canine equivalent of the mord virus. We never knew about it until some of our troops arrived with it."

He imagined himself waking up one morning to find he had eaten everyone in the hospital. "*What*?"

"Transmitted by dogs, it doesn't produce the same symptoms as the mord virus. That's the only good thing about it." Quimby paused and watched Coltan's face, anticipated a meltdown. In his experience, every patient reacted that way—with a hysterical meltdown. However, Coltan remained calm and waited for him to continue. He admired Coltan's courage. "The bad thing about it is it attacks the weakest part of the system first—in your case, your stomach ulcers—and then moves on to attack the liver, spleen, kidneys, lungs and then heart, before it finally settles in the brain where it wipes out the nervous system."

"You're telling me it's gonna kill me slowly." Coltan sat back and his first thought was not for himself, but for Natalie. How would she handle this news?

"However," Doctor Quimby said, "This is where your case is unusual. Your body has been trying to fight it off. We think the blood poisoning might have had something to do with it. Your body is trying to fight off both diseases and, in the process, is creating some rather unusual antibodies we've never seen before."

"Does that mean I'll get better?"

"We don't know at this point. The only thing we do know is you've managed to outlive every other victim of the dog virus. All of them died within a week of infection."

Coltan became frustrated. "So, are you telling me I'll still die of this thing? I'll just die slower?"

Doctor Quimby made it clear he was just as frustrated as Coltan. "We don't know."

He closed his eyes and turned away from the doctor. "Shit..."

"What are your symptoms today?"

Coltan took a deep breath. "The fever, of course. Every part of my body feels like it's on fire; I'm weak – can hardly move my arms and legs; I got a headache."

"How bad is the headache?"

"*Please cut off my head* bad."

"Is the pain medication helping with that at all?"

"No."

"We can up the morphine."

"Then I can't stay awake."

"It's a choice between that or the pain. What do you want to do?"

He considered it would be easiest to choose sleep over pain. Yet, how long would he have to keep making that choice? If Beverly was around, she would tell him to choose sleep and hope for a miracle. He decided he would do what Beverly would advise. Reluctantly he answered, "The morphine, I guess."

"Your liver has improved over the last few days. That's something."

It was not enough. "Sure." Coltan said.

Doctor Quimby set the chart aside and patted Coltan's hand, "Listen, Coltan. Morris is working on a cure. He's got an idea that perhaps Isabelle's blood may hold the answer. Do you know who Isabelle is?"

He had not met her. "Is she that kid that beat the mord virus?"

"Yes. Morris has tested her blood twice a week for the past month. She's still clear of the virus." He saw the doubt in Coltan's eyes. He squeezed Coltan's hand, "I don't want you to give up hope, son. Don't give up."

It was difficult not to give up when his life had been nothing but suffering until the last couple of years. Just when things had started to look up, the world fell apart, his surrogate parents died, and now he was dying, too. He could not fathom why God was allowing yet another catastrophe into his life. Coltan held back tears. He was not feeling sorry for himself; he was simply frustrated and angry.

To add to all that was his expectation of how Natalie would take this. She had struggled so to keep him alive through those dark days in the attic. He saw how she had psychologically shut down there at the hospital when she thought he had died. To go through the experience of his death twice would devastate her.

That is what hurt the most—what it would do to Natalie.

Coltan turned back to the doctor, "Please don't tell Natalie. I don't want her to know anything about this until we're sure I can't..." He trailed off, unable to say the words.

"You made it this far," Doctor Quimby reminded him. "You were barely alive when we found you. *God* has kept you alive, not us. Keep that under consideration."

"In all honesty, Doc... I don't know what to think or believe anymore."

"Don't give up!"

"I'd like that morphine now."

AS TWO MORE WEEKS STRETCHED into a third, Coltan became much stronger and the episodes of fever came to a halt. He was still unable to walk any great distance, and relied on a wheelchair to escape the room for a while. Bored and needing a purpose, he prayed for Jesus to show him what he could do for both himself and his fellow residents at the refuge. As he patiently awaited the answer, he resumed his Bible studies where he had left off before the dogs got him.

IN THE MEANTIME, TREVOR and Isabelle nagged a very stubborn Dillon out of his bed. The two accompanied Dillon as he struggled with his daily walk to the gardens outside the compound. Once Dillon became stronger, he asked for fishing poles and led Trevor, Isabelle and Guffy to the edge of the riverbank and taught them how to fish. Not only did the sunshine and fresh air prove beneficial to all of them, the Army of Christ received the fish to serve at mealtime. Through his passion for fishing, Dillon discovered a way to contribute that he actually enjoyed. That fact made it easier for him to desire a return to health. His days of escaping were officially over.

Isabelle waved an earthworm in front of Dillon's face, "Hew, fizzy, fizzy!"

Trevor watched amusedly as Dillon pulled her onto his lap and tickled the earthworm out of her hand while she giggled and protested. He dangled the earthworm over her open, laughing mouth, "Dinner, Isa. Here's your dinner!"

"No, no!" She giggled and squirmed, "You eat it! You da fith!"

"*Fish!* Not *fith!*" He hugged her to him, "Say *fish*."

"Fith."

"Fish! Fi-sh-sh-sh!"

"Fizz-z-z-z-!" She was too busy laughing to try.

Dillon chortled and giggled.

Trevor laughed with them. He was happy for Dillon. He had never seen the boy laugh as he did with the little girl. Isabelle was exactly the medicine Dillon needed.

Trevor accompanied them to the riverbank not to fish with them, but to protect them.

The chatter from Bonito Valle had trickled down to silence over the radio in the communications room. The last they had heard was a rumor some outpost in Siberia had been nuked, and the subject outpost had been an isolation camp that held suspected victims exposed to the mord virus. That made no sense to Trevor. It was very easy to eliminate the infected with a bullet; a nuke was overdoing it. However, the satellite image Mitchell brought up showed the evidence, the truth, in all its ugliness; someone had indeed nuked the outpost.

On the other side of the world, Americans were still suffering through the swift takeover of the country by the United Earth Federation. Acting President William Tewly, in his first television address since the death of President Alderton, announced the North American Union would remain under martial law until further notice. As the gargantuan task of re-building the cities and towns of America progressed, all able-bodied citizens were required to continue living in the rescue "centers" from which they would report for assignment each week. Under the current conditions, the President reminded viewers, it was against the law "for your own safety and that of your loved ones" to reside anywhere but in the rescue centers. Any citizens caught breaking that law would be subject to "swift and harsh" punishment. In addition, it was now against the law for any private citizen to own or possess firearms. Any citizens caught breaking that law would be subject to "swift and harsh" punishment. As Tewly droned on, it became obvious he deemed null and void the rights and protections guaranteed by the United States Constitution and the Bill of Rights. America was in a

State of Emergency, which gave him the right to suspend the rights of the citizens. The Canadian Prime Minister and Mexico's President broadcast similar speeches.

After viewing the three broadcasts, James remarked the once clandestine United Earth Federation had insidiously rescinded the rights of citizens all over the free world during the past few decades. It finally took a worldwide crisis in the form of the mord virus to give the UEF opportunity to pull the rest of the rug out from under the populace in one long-delayed and brazen sweep.

A bleak era had dawned on Planet Earth.

Trevor knew it was only a matter of time before the UEF got around to attempt to take out Alpha Base. *When* was the first question; *how* was the second question. He, James and Mitchell expected the attack would be by air, given the rough terrain at their position on the mountain.

Trevor made certain there were always trusted soldiers to monitor the skies and to watch over the residents who ventured outside the compound. Trevor also did his best to be available himself to stand guard. Ever vigilant, he eavesdropped on conversations and listened for anything suspicious. So far, he discovered no spies or suspected spies at Alpha. That did not mean there were no spies there; it only meant they had not blown their cover. With all of this in mind, he watched over the most vulnerable whenever he was available to do so. He considered Dillon, little Isa and Guffy among those most vulnerable, and even though the guards were nearby, he felt a need to be directly present with the three in case something happened.

Dillon was unaware of Trevor's concern as Guffy finally caught a fish and reeled it in. He unhooked it and proudly showed it to Dillon and Isabelle. Dillon congratulated him and added it to the cooler.

Isabelle trotted to the edge of the water and checked her line. She still had not caught a fish. She sighed with consternation and re-baited the hook, and then she cast out as Dillon had taught her. The little girl glanced over at Dillon and smiled.

"Nice cast!" Dillon called to her. One of the many things he liked about her was her willingness to learn. She seemed to have an intense desire to learn and experience new things, a trait they had in common.

He observed her as she stood there on the bank, resting her back against a tree as she peered out across the river in deep thought. He wondered what amazing images danced in that fanciful yet analytical brain of hers. As he wondered about this, he noted the serious contemplation on her face, and the confident stance of her body, even though her posture was relaxed. She appeared to be in another time or dimension at that moment, seeing not with her eyes but with her soul.

He wanted to capture this moment on paper, and he quickly reached for his ever-present sketchbook and pencils in his backpack. When he looked once again at her to begin his sketch, he found a creature surreal and compelling replaced the little girl who had been there a moment before. What stood there now was a beautiful woman attired in a patchwork military uniform. The woman carried a sword in a sheath attached to her belt diagonally across her left hip. She stood there and gazed both anxiously and hopefully into the distance, and she supported her balance upon a staff in her right hand, a staff shaped like a cross.

Dillon swallowed, gasped softly and blinked slowly in astonishment. In the very next second, the little girl returned to his eyes. She continued to peer across the river, peer across time and space into a world only she could see.

The boy drew in another breath, convinced himself his vision was only the result of too much time in the sun. Regardless, the image haunted him, and he immediately put his pencil to work.

When the mosquitoes emerged as the sun's descending rays

shimmered behind the darkening peaks, Dillon called an end to the day's fishing and everyone dismantled their rods. Trevor helped Guffy carry the very full cooler to the waiting golf cart on the garden path. From there, Guffy would drive it down to the garage and the kitchen staff would send someone to retrieve the fish from the cart.

Isabelle held Dillon's hand as they strolled back to the confines of the compound. She liked it when he held her hand because she knew it was his way of protecting her. Even when he bummed a smoke off one of the soldiers, he still held her hand. He introduced her to the soldiers by her full name. He never mentioned her bout with the mord virus to anyone, and she did not know why. However, she trusted him and trusted he had a good reason for not mentioning it. She followed Dillon's example and did not volunteer that information to anyone who did not already know about it. Just like in her former neighborhood, *silencio* seemed to be the best policy.

With Trevor occupied in conversation with the soldiers, Dillon led her to the smoking area off the gardens. She patiently sat with him while he stole a couple of forbidden puffs. The rest of the cigarette he would save for later when Trevor was not around to admonish him. Isabelle had already witnessed a few confrontations between Trevor and Dillon over the smoking issue. Although she did not understand what that was all about, she tolerated Dillon's rebelliousness.

He was lost in thought as they strolled hand-in-hand back to the lava tube entrance. At one point in their short journey, he glanced down at her and smiled, a strange mixture of appreciation and bewilderment in his eyes, as if he wanted to ask her a question. He looked away then, focused ahead to the lava tube. Isabelle got the feeling he decided to keep his inquiry secret for the time being, and she pictured him stowing his question into a bejeweled treasure chest for safekeeping. She trusted and respected his decision to save it for another day.

Dillon was her friend, and that was all that mattered to her.

CHAPTER 2

Mid-July brought thunderstorms and lightning to the mountain. The rains were heavy and almost killed some of the sun loving, drought tolerant vegetable crops in the garden. On the other hand, the vegetables and flowers that loved the rain grew healthy and happy. By the third week of July, summer returned in its full glory and all the heat tolerant crops perked up.

Coltan had perked up, too. It had been three days since he abandoned the wheelchair. The antibiotics had cured the blood poisoning, and the dog virus had weakened in the process. He knew it was a temporary respite from the disease. According to the latest blood test, the virus was still active in his system, and it appeared to Morris that it was regrouping for another assault.

Coltan did not know how much time he had left before the disease would lay him flat on his back again. He prayed about it with Morris, Ian and Joe, and afterward decided not to worry about it anymore. There was still the summer to enjoy, and God's word to nourish him.

He loved to sit outside under the shade of the thick pines. He missed the *berceuse* of raindrops, but he missed the luxury of basking in the warm fresh mountain air even more. There was no wind on this perfect day, only the slightest and warmest breeze. The warmth felt good on his body once ravaged by infection and disease. Coltan removed his thin outer shirt and sat on the ground against a boulder under a tree. Now that winter was far behind, he had returned to wearing his usual summer outfit, denims and a sleeveless undershirt. While in the confines of the compound, he only wore an outer shirt to be polite, also to conceal his scars.

Today was a perfect day, not only because the weather was fine and the air was clean, but also because the Bible studies he hosted for teens twice a week had attracted some new students. They met every Monday and Thursday evenings in the dining room, Coltan, Natalie, Ian, Carolyn and all the others. Last night, Dillon joined them for the first time at Ian's suggestion. Dillon's presence brought the attendance up to twenty, including Coltan.

All the teens in his group lost their parents and other family members during the mord plague and the subsequent takeover of North America by the UEF. They had consoled each other in their first months at the compound, but human sympathy and human words could only do so much. Coltan felt only God offered the consolation that ultimately healed the broken heart. It was with this in mind that he chose only certain Psalms for study and discussion for Monday night's lesson. The ones he had chosen were about disappointment, faith and God's promises to the grieving and suffering.

"Hey, dude!" Dillon, carrying his fishing gear, called to him as he neared the tree from a different direction. "You packin'?"

Coltan grinned and raised Clyde. "And, you?"

Dillon reached him quickly. He lifted a corner of his shirt to reveal a fat handgun tucked in his waistband. "Trevor finally decided he could trust me. I've only been shootin' since I was six years old!"

"I heard you were at the shooting range with him." Coltan scooted over to make room for Dillon beneath the shade of the tree.

Dillon sat and stretched out his long legs and turned the bill of his red *Peterbilt* cap (a gift from one of the nurses) to one side. "He thinks I should be a marksman."

Coltan shrugged, "Trevor's the best judge."

"When you goin' fishin' with me?"

"I can't, Dill."

"Why?"

"I don't like to kill stuff."

"If you don't like to kill stuff, why are you carrying a gun?"

"Protection. Just don't ask me to hunt and kill an animal. That's where I draw the line."

"Weeny sissy!" Dillon teased. "Where do ya think your food comes from?"

"I know, I know." He stuffed a loose sheet of notepaper into his Bible so he would not lose his place. "I guess I'd rather grow it than kill it."

"You must be a city boy." He said it with much disdain.

Coltan wanted to tell him the truth; that his crazy mother and her boyfriend, an equally crazy and twice as dangerous pedophile, raised him out in the boonies where no one could discover their abuse of him. However, Coltan was not ready to share that story with most people. He strongly sensed Dillon had his own sordid tale to tell, and that was probably why they took to each other so easily.

Dillon bent sideways and peered into his face. "Are you a city boy?"

"Uh-uh."

"What are you, then?"

"Just me. That's all."

"Come fishin' with me."

"You're not supposed to go out there alone."

"I ain't. I'm waitin' for Isa and Guffy. Trev's gotta teach a class, or he'd be with us, too." He tightened the reel when he noticed the line was slack on the pole. He continued speaking as he did this. "You don't have to fish. Just be with us. C'mon, man..."

Coltan peered at the edges of the compound property where twelve soldiers patrolled the perimeter. When a resident wished to go beyond the perimeter, as Dillon did in order to fish from his favorite spot, a few of the soldiers accompanied them and lingered nearby as protection. Coltan thought it would be safe enough to join Dillon's fishing party. He had been curious about the spot since Dillon described it to him, and he wanted to see it for himself.

"Okay. Thanks." Coltan said. He began to pack up his Bible and notebooks into the leather case Brian gave him.

Dillon watched for a moment before he spoke again. "How long have you been a Christian?"

"Almost three years."

"Why do you believe?"

"I've experienced the work of Christ in my life."

Dillon pointed to Coltan's many scars, "Is all that the work of Christ?"

"Of course not!"

"If Christ is the Savior, why didn't he protect you?"

It sounded like a question Satan would ask him. Coltan referred to scripture and pointed out the Apostle Paul's suffering. When God did not ease his suffering, Paul accepted it with faith that God had a very good reason for allowing it. In addition, Paul reflected his suffering kept him humble and strengthened his faith as well as his reliance on God. Coltan topped that off by explaining to Dillon the agony Jesus suffered, and that he had suffered it willingly in order to save mankind and complete God's work in the world.

Dillon lit a smoke and leaned back against the tree. "Sounds to me like God's a sadistic little tyrant."

"No."

He referred to Coltan's scars again. "Who beat you?"

"Why does it matter to you?" He zipped his Bible case, and faced Dillon squarely. "What should matter is the fact God delivered me from the effects of it. Three years ago, I would've beaten the shit out of you for asking about my scars. I would've put you in the hospital, and I wouldn't have regretted it for a minute."

Coltan was bigger and more physically fit than Dillon, so Dillon did not doubt the *hospital* reference. He observed a flicker of anger in Coltan's eyes. It was the same ember in the eyes of all the redneck, macho-man straight guys around Baker Creek. They were the eyes of his classmates. They were the eyes of the drunken jocks that beat him, the only obviously gay boy in town, just for fun. He had lost count of the number of vicious ambushes he had endured. He wondered if Coltan detected his secret.

Dillon removed his shirt and showed Coltan the history there of his own battles. "I took more than my share, man."

"Child abuse?"

"Jocks and Rednecks. There were also a few Bible Bangers in the mix!"

Coltan expressed his sympathy in his voice, "Gay bashers."

"So, you know?"

"I've known since the first time I saw you. You walk like a girl!"

Dillon laughed. "Shit..." He quickly and self-consciously put his shirt on as he asked, "I walk like a girl?"

"Yeah!" Coltan laughed a little. "You gotta use more shoulder and less hip action. Have you ever had a girlfriend?"

"Not really. Let's just say that once I *had* a girl. It was a disaster."

"Why?"

"She said I didn't know nothin' about pleasin' a girl. She said I was the worst lay she ever had. I didn't really like her. It was just an experiment."

"You probably made that obvious to her." Coltan paused long enough to take a drag off the cigarette Dillon offered him before he inquired, "How old were you at the time?"

"Twelve." He quickly implored as Coltan dissolved into a fit of belly laughs, "What?"

"At twelve, you don't know anything! At twelve, all you care about is getting your own rocks off. At twelve, you know nothing about the way a girl's body works, all you know is your own body."

"I knew stuff!" Dillon insisted defensively.

Coltan stopped laughing. "Dillon... was that the only girl?"

"Yeah." He felt Coltan was trying to belittle him, and that he was trying to invalidate his view of himself as homosexual. "I wasn't attracted to girls. It was the guys that did it for me."

"They did it, all right," Coltan said. "They did *you*. Once they did you, they threw you aside. Am I right?"

It was true. Back then, it did not matter. Sex was not only an experiment; it was an escape from a meaningless existence. He shot back at Coltan with an immature pout. "So?"

Coltan shook his head sadly, "And, I thought *my* self-esteem was low! All they did was use you, Dillon! Can't you see that?"

"So, what?"

"So, what? What did you get out it?"

"Pleasure. Money." Suddenly, he felt ashamed. It was not the fact he had sex with men, it was the fact he did it for money—that was the source of his shame. He looked away from Coltan and wondered why he should feel ashamed. The sex was usually fun, and the money always came in handy. But then the true root of his shame occurred to him: Evan had pimped him out, and Dillon being young, inexperienced and starved for approval and affection wholeheartedly allowed it. In a sense, he had traded his dignity for what he naively thought was love.

They sat in silence for a few minutes while Coltan pondered what little he knew about Dillon. He wondered what had happened to Dillon to make him think so little of himself. The only possible answer Coltan had to go on was his own troubled past. He asked Dillon, "What was it like at home?"

Dillon shrugged. There was no way to describe it. He turned the question back to Coltan. "What was it like for you?"

"It was ugly." Coltan waited for Dillon to ask another question. Dillon only gazed at him curiously and with a hint of sympathy.

Coltan pushed forward, "That ugliness caused me to become ugly, and I hated it. I hated what I'd become. That's when Jesus knocked on my door." He continued and spent the next fifteen minutes describing his past. He shared his testimony with Dillon, shared how Jesus forgave his many crimes and taught him how to love himself and others. He described how his life had gradually changed for the better, how he had changed for the better, once he turned control over to Jesus.

After listening to Coltan's story, Dillon bravely shared his own. He was convinced God had already reserved a spot in Hell for him because of his many sins, most of which he honestly did not regret.

For Coltan, it was an ideal springboard from which to witness to Dillon. He sympathized greatly with the younger boy's many conflicts, and completely understood Dillon's hunger for acceptance and guidance. They had both considered this hunger a weakness of character and had spent years denying it and hiding it from the rest of the world. It was something they had in common, and Coltan knew Dillon was ready to address it and accept it, just as he had done three years before.

Grateful for the God-given opportunity to bring another to Christ, Coltan discussed in depth with Dillon the subjects of sin, shame and redemption. He pulled out his Bible and referred to specific scriptures about Jesus' mission to redeem mankind who, without exception, were all sinners. He explained to Dillon that a new life in Christ was not a life of ease, but a life of continual learning, experiences and growth. Some of that growth would be painful, but it was necessary. It was the same as pruning a plant in order to keep it healthy. He referred to Jesus' testimony about the grapes, the vines, and the branches, and explained to Dillon what Jesus meant; that people can live in Christ, Christ can live in people and Christ lives in the Father in Heaven. When Dillon pointed out the scriptures in Romans that referred to the sin of homosexuality and how God saw it as an abomination, Coltan countered with Jesus' statement there is only one unforgivable sin; that sin being the rejection of the Holy Spirit. It set Dillon's mind at ease to know he was salvageable. It touched him profoundly when Coltan convinced him Jesus had brought him to Alpha Base because he loved him and wanted Dillon to accept him and love him just as much.

By the time Isabelle and Guffy finally emerged from the refuge with their fishing gear, Dillon had received Christ as his Savior. Coltan baptized him at the river with Isabelle and Guffy their joyful witnesses.

Yes. It was a perfect day.

TREVOR WAS IMPRESSED with Natalie's skill at the gun range. Even with only one good arm, she managed to hit her targets with amazing precision. The soldiers who had come by to practice had become her audience.

"Who taught you?" Trevor asked.

"My dad. He was a cop. He used to be in the Marine Corps, too." She locked Bonnie's safety and stowed the gun in her holster. "He also taught Coltan. Coltan hasn't been at it very long, and he hates to shoot anything. He's not as accurate, but he's pretty good. I don't think he's into it as much as I am."

A female soldier detoured on her way out and approached Natalie. She was older than Natalie, a tall girl with a muscular build and a square face full of freckles. "You should be a soldier," she said admiringly.

"I want to be a soldier," Natalie responded.

"We'll have to tailor a uniform small enough for you." She grinned and patted Natalie's shoulder. "There should be an extra somewhere." She offered her hand. "My name's Jill."

Natalie shook her hand. "I'm Natalie." She turned inquiringly to Trevor, "Can I join?"

Trevor's first thought was of Coltan. He knew Coltan would not want Natalie on the battlefield. So as not to begin a discussion in front of the soldier, he said, "We'll talk about it after your arm and your ankle mend."

"Good enough." Natalie responded.

Another female soldier called to Jill. Jill waved at her and said to Natalie, "I'll see you around, Natalie. Nice shooting!"

Trevor excused the rest of the soldiers for the day. It was well after five o'clock, and he was tired and hungry. He waited until the last of the soldiers exited before he turned his attention once more to Natalie. "I wish they'd observe high tea here in the States. I tend to run out of petrol before we run out of hours. Would you join me for a sandwich?"

"I should check on Coltan, first." She limped alongside Trevor, supporting herself with a cane. "Did Ian tell you about our Bible studies?"

He slowed his pace so she would not feel compelled to hurry on his account. "Yes, he did. He said Coltan has a gift for teaching."

"I think so, too. He studies all the time." She giggled, "He's become a walking encyclopedia of the Bible. No one can stump him."

"Stump him?" That was a new term.

"You can't ask a question about it he can't answer correctly."

Trevor smiled at this. "Apparently, the good Lord has gifted him to be a teacher."

"While we lived up in the attic, he studied every theology book we had."

"How long did you live together there?"

"Almost a year." They passed Carolyn's tent. Natalie pointed at the flamingo in the fake front yard. "How do you like Carolyn's pink flamingo?"

"Very *Floridian trailer park*." Trevor joked dryly. They walked on toward the dining room where afternoon sandwiches tucked in plastic bags awaited the late luncher. He had a good reason for asking about Natalie's home. Her skill with firearms caused him to speculate she and Coltan had left weapons behind in Bonito Valle. Alpha Base could use all the firepower they could get. He wanted to keep the conversation on track. "Did your father stock firearms at the house?"

"Absolutely. He knew this was coming. He even managed to get some military weapons. I shot a few of them. They came in handy when the mords invaded our neighborhood."

"Mitchell told me your father died. And your mother, as well."

"Yeah." Their deaths, especially how her mother died, still hurt.

"So, that left only you and Coltan?"

"Yeah." She stopped walking, which caused him to stop in mid stride. "What do you want to know, Trev? Do you want to know about me and Coltan? Or, do you want to know about the weapons? Perhaps, both?"

"You and Coltan are not my business." He faced her and said honestly, "We need all the weapons we can get. We need food, medicine, bedding—everything. If you and Coltan managed a year there, you must have had these things."

"We have an attic and a basement both fully stocked with everything you need. You're welcome to all of it. Just park a U-Haul in the garage and move the whole house! That's if the fascist scum in the valley haven't claimed it yet."

Trevor thought about it for only a few seconds. "We can scout the area before we move in..."

"Good luck!" Natalie laughed. "You might wanna ask God to put a force-field around you while you're at it!"

"Mitch and his team can zero in on it by satellite." He was completely serious. "We can also check it by telescope before we hit the foothills." She laughed and began to walk again, hobbling on her cane. Trevor caught up and intercepted her. "Mitch could not remember if your house had a full attic. He couldn't recall a basement, either. Are both rooms hidden?"

"Yeah." She could not believe he was serious about this.

He kept her stopped dead in her tracks. "Could you draw us a floor plan?"

"I can do better than that. I can go with you."

He was adamantly against that idea. "No!"

"Why not? It'd make it easier and faster."

His eyes were sad when they looked into hers. "There are too many memories there for you, Natalie. Think of it."

She nodded bravely. "I can handle it." She cleared her throat and began walking again.

"No, dear. I think not." He paced her. "Think of Coltan. Think of what he went through to bring you both here to safety. Would he want you to return there?"

This made her stop. Coltan would side with Trevor on this. They both viewed her as still emotionally fragile. "I can talk to him about it."

"He won't want you to go."

"He can't tell me what to do!"

"Do you love him enough to stay here? Do you love him enough to give him peace of mind, Natalie? Think what it would do to him if you returned there, even for one day. He isn't well enough to make the journey with you. If you went without him, he'd be overcome with worry. Do you want that for him?"

"No."

"Sketch us a floor plan." They reached the hospital, the only fully built and enclosed structure situated in the largest cavern inside the lava tube compound. He reached for her arm and stopped her at the hospital doors. "There is one other thing."

"What?"

"Are you certain you want to be a soldier?"

"Completely certain."

"How would he feel about that?"

"His nickname for me is *Commando Natalie*."

"That's all well and good, but how does he feel about you being a soldier? Have you ever discussed it?"

"No."

"Very well."

"Why?"

"If he joins us for dinner, I won't bring it up." He winked confidentially.

"Oh," she said softly. "Yeah... That might be a sore subject with him. I never considered how he might—"

Coltan's voice joined the greetings from Dillon, Guffy and Isabelle, "Hey, Nat! Hey, Trev!"

Dillon ran to Trevor and hugged him. "Guess what I did, Trev. You'll never guess!"

Trevor dodged the fishing pole over Dillon's shoulder. He stepped back from him and looked at him. He had never seen Dillon so excited and happy. In the next moment, he detected the telling light that glimmered behind his eyes, detected the brightness and clarity there. Trevor knew, and it caused him to grin from ear to ear with joy. "You accepted the Lord!"

Dillon nodded, laughing, "How'd you know, Trev?"

"You have his light within you! God bless you, Dillon!" He gave him a bear hug, lifted him off the floor in his arms. "Oh...! God bless you!"

Once Trevor set him back on his feet, Dillon pointed at Coltan. "He did it. He baptized me in the river, too!"

"Reverend Coltan!" Natalie blurted in a congratulatory tone.

Trevor went to Coltan and hugged him. "I don't know how you did it."

Coltan said simply, "God did it."

"I invited him fishing," Dillon interjected, "And, what'd he reel in? Me!"

Isabelle added, "He put 'im in da watoo, an' I saw Deezus th-smile happy!"

"Yes," Trevor announced to them, "There's a party in Heaven, as we speak!" He placed his arm around Dillon's shoulders. "Welcome to the Body of Christ, Dillon! Welcome to God's family!"

EARLY THE NEXT MORNING, Natalie, Coltan and Trevor met with Mitchell, Glenda and James in the communications room. The six of them crowded around the computer monitors as Mitchell brought Natalie's old neighborhood up on the satellite feed.

The area looked the same as when Natalie and Coltan left it. A wider view of the central and south areas of town showed military and civilians milling about. The military were the only ones manning vehicles, and the civilians were hard at work clearing and reconstructing the large number of damaged buildings. The soldiers had set up six gathering areas throughout the town where the people ate and checked in and out and received further orders. All of the gathering areas were equipped with chip scanners, and the soldiers scanned every single person as they reached the head of the line.

"You notice something?" Natalie remarked.

"What?" Mitch asked.

"There's no kids. I wonder where the kids are."

Trevor suggested, "Zero in on the schools, Mitch."

The schools were in session and very busy. The activity at the grade schools appeared normal, as normal as life was before the virus and the UEF takeover. However, on the athletic field at the high school, the soldiers were putting the students through a series of different military training exercises. Soldiers acted as instructors.

"There's your answer," Trevor said. "I bet they're indoctrinating the younger children with films and whatnot."

"God Almighty..." Mitchell moaned sadly. He typed in the coordinates for Natalie's east side neighborhood and returned there. "It doesn't look like they've dealt with the east side yet. I wonder why."

"It's nothing but wreckage," Coltan offered. "There's nothing they need there."

"They'll need homes for people, eventually," Natalie said.

"Not for a long time," James asserted. "They're keeping the people in the camps where they can control them. They won't trust any citizen on their own until they're certain the indoctrination is complete." He told Trevor, "We can go in. We can arrive at dawn. That way, we won't have to use the headlights and give ourselves away. It's far enough from the central areas to be safe."

"There's a lot of stuff at the house," Natalie told him. "You'll probably need to spend a couple of days there."

"Can a large truck and two jeeps fit in your garage?"

"Yeah."

James directed the next comment to Trevor, "We'll need a large team. At least twelve."

"Will one truck be enough?" Trevor asked.

"We're not taking furniture. However, we can use the mattresses, box springs and linens." To Natalie, he inquired, "Is there any camping equipment? Tents, sleeping bags, camp stoves, propane and all?"

"Both up in the attic and in the basement," Coltan answered. "There's also tools and some leftover building materials."

"What about food and medicine?"

Natalie and Coltan laughed, both thinking of all the summer canning Natalie had slaved over for weeks and all the journeys into town to collect everything else. Natalie answered, this time, "There's lots! You'll see." She told Trevor, "Say, Trev: When I mentioned parking a U-Haul, I wasn't kidding!"

James laughed, "That's what we got. A three-bedroom size U-Haul I bought at auction. Will it fit inside the garage with the door down? And the jeeps, too?"

She nodded. "Yeah. It's monstrous. Dad added on to it when he thought of getting a motor home."

"You got a motor home?"

"Not anymore. He sold it a long time ago, put the money into solar panels. You could use those, I bet."

Trevor grinned and rubbed her shoulders, "You're making our day, Natalie!"

"I still want to go with you." Natalie suggested.

A round of adamant *no's* answered her. Coltan shot her a *what the hell are you thinking* expression.

James inquired to Mitchell, "Can you monitor the place by satellite while we're there?"

"Definitely." Mitchell was already a step ahead. "We can radio you if there's any threat on the way. I'll set up a trunked frequency for all your radios. Sound good?"

"Sounds good!"

Trevor asked James, "When do you want to do this?"

"Tomorrow." James paused and took a sip of coffee while he thought about this new mission and their tight time frame. He considered that perhaps they were rushing things, but there was the weather—a storm on the way, plus the increasing number of UEF soldiers in the central suburbs of Bonito Valle his surveillance teams observed that made him feel it would be disastrous if they waited any longer. Additionally, they had to complete the mission invisibly, quickly and safely. "We'll bring a team together tonight. I want our sharpest soldiers on this, the strongest ones, too." To Coltan and

Natalie, he inquired, "Can you have the floor plans drawn by thirteen-hundred hours today?"

"I think so." Natalie said.

"Don't say you think so. We need them by thirteen-hundred." James reiterated.

"Dillon's the artist around here," Coltan said. "We'll have him draw them up."

"Have it in my office by thirteen-hundred, no sooner, no later. Is that clear?"

"Yes, sir." Natalie responded.

AFTER A LATE LUNCH, Natalie went out for a smoke by the gardens. She spotted Mitchell at the boulder circle, the area used by the few smokers in residence. Mitchell was enjoying his pipe and the afternoon sunshine. She sat beside him and lit her cigarette.

Mitchell narrowed his eyes at her. "When did you start smokin', missy?"

"When the world started to fall apart." She took a long drag, let it out, and said, "Don't rag on me, Mitch."

"Did Coltan get you started?"

"No, sir. I did." Natalie looked him square in the eyes. "Dad knew about it. He didn't approve, but he didn't give me grief about it, either. So..."

"Your father wanted me to look after you if something happened to him."

"I know."

"I guess you think you're too old."

"No, sir."

"What are you now? Fifteen?"

She chuckled. "I'll be seventeen in December."

"Seventeen?" He looked her up and down. She had such a tiny build. She could easily pass for fourteen. Yet, when he regarded her face, he noticed the maturity there, the loss of innocence. It was only last year at about this same time when they last conversed under semi-normal circumstances. That was at his electronics shop in Bonito Valle, the day she came by to pick up the scanners. She was cheerful that day, and she still had a slight lingering innocence of childhood in her eyes. That innocence was now gone. She had aged significantly in a short time. He felt sad for her.

"I want to go back to the house," she told him.

"It'd be a bad idea, Nat."

"I wanted to get Mom's and Dad's Bibles," she explained, "Dad wanted you to have his. He told me that once."

"Tell James. He'll see to it."

"I already did when I gave him the floor plans."

"Why didn't you bring their Bibles in the first place?"

"It hurt to see them, to touch them. Every page had their life energy. I couldn't handle it. Neither could Coltan. We hoped whoever lived in the house next would find them and be comforted by them. Maybe even come to the Lord, if that was the Lord's will." She paused and thought about Coltan. He was the reason she now wanted her mother's Bible. "Mom's Bible has all our family record. Now that Coltan and I are getting married, we thought we should have it. Coltan's got no family, you know."

"His parents didn't make it, either," Mitchell assumed.

"No, they didn't. Whether they did or not wouldn't have mattered, anyhow. His parents were never parents to him. They hurt him. They hurt him bad. Even when they were alive, he stayed away from them as much as he could. If you knew the whole story, Mitch, you'd understand. Coltan had been an orphan since the moment he was born. The only family he knew and loved, and who loved him, was mine." Her eyes were wet when she looked again at Mitchell.

"That's why I want him to have my mother's Bible. We'll enter our marriage into the family record. His name will be there as part of my family. The Danburys—we're his family."

Her sentiment deeply affected Mitchell. "I see..."

"I wanted to get Mom's wedding dress, too," she said without skipping a beat. "I told James where to find it. I want to ask you something."

"Yeah?"

"Will you give me away at my wedding?"

The hand that cupped his pipe paused halfway to his mouth. It hovered in mid-air for a moment before he brought it back down. He smiled at her, his eyes brimming. "Of course, I will. I'd be honored."

"And, one other thing, Mitch."

"Yeah?"

She earnestly told him, "I'll never be too old to need or want a Dad. If you still want the job, I'd be honored."

CHAPTER 3

Isabelle stood at the side of Dillon's bed as he sat at the edge of the mattress and pressed the control button to raise the headrest. Once the headrest was at the correct position, he checked the bed tray table to make certain all the *might needs* were accounted: one half-read sci-fi novel, one pitcher of water, one glass, one box of tissues and one kidney-shaped barf-basin. Today was his final round of chemotherapy.

He began to remove his slippers. Isabelle freed him of one while he got the other. She took both and set them neatly on the floor beside his bed. She helped him pull down the blanket so he could get under it, and she tucked it over him when he got comfortable.

"Thanks, Mom!" He kidded her.

Isabelle laughed at that. "Can I stay wiff you?"

He noticed her pronunciation of the letter S was better today. Guffy had informed him Isa's speech impediment became worse after she saw her brother Mario die. Under Dillon's tutelage, she was finally showing progress. "Yeah, you can stay with me," he told her.

"Is Bowis gibbing you da needew?"

"Uh-huh."

"Bowis does it widdout hoot. He's good at it." She climbed up on the bed with him and sat at the foot so she could face him. "Does chemo hoot?"

"Uh-uh."

She glanced at the barf-basin. She knew what that was for. Her gaze returned to Dillon, concerned for him. "But it makes you frow up, huh?"

"Sometimes." He smiled and winked at her to ease her worry. "Only sometimes."

"It make you seepy, too, huh?"

"Definitely!"

"Aw'l be vewy quiet, den. Okay, Din?"

"Okay, Isa." He was glad she wanted to stay. Somewhere along the line, he had grown used to her company. When she was not around, he found himself actually missing her.

She pointed to her coloring book and crayons on the table along the wall. "I can cowoo quietwee ovoo dehw. Okay?"

"That's fine."

Isabelle relaxed against the footboard and folded her hands in her lap. She gazed at Dillon comfortingly, as if to wordlessly tell him he would get through this with no trouble at all. Isabelle gazed at him so earnestly, so concernedly and comfortingly that it made him feel strangely vulnerable, as if he was her child. The sensation was too weird for him, and he sought to break the spell. He crossed his eyes and made her laugh.

"You teach me dat!" she commanded.

He laughed and opened his arms to her. "C'mere, you!"

She crawled over and rested her cheek on his shoulder. "You my fwend, Din."

"You're my friend, too," he said, "You're a good kid, Isa." He hugged her tightly. "Where's Unkaduffy today?"

"He wook inna nyebawwy."

"A *nyebawwy*? What's a *nyebawwy*?"

She flopped both hands out, palms up. "Da book pace!"

"Oh!" he exclaimed, "The *library*."

"Dat's what I th-said. Da *nyebawwy*!"

He chuckled and hugged her a little tighter. She stared up at him, her eyes wide and bright. Her eyes glistened tenderly with an infinite and enduring love for him, a love that invited his submission into its soothing depths. Dillon became so enraptured with the unsullied universe within her eyes that his own gaze came to mirror hers. For a few moments, they floated together in that place where there is only *being*, until a scuffing noise and a bump at the door brought them crashing back to the physical world.

Morris entered with his lab kit, the chemo bag and IV set-up. He asked Dillon like Dillon had a choice, "Ready for one more?"

"I'm good to go," Dillon replied. Their spell broken, he nudged Isabelle playfully. "So's my trusty sidekick here." He kissed her forehead. "Ain't 'cha, buddy?"

She grinned big at him. "Yep!"

Morris hung the bag and attached the intravenous tube. He paused at the side of the bed with the needle uncapped and ready. He gave Dillon a sealed alcohol swab to open. As Dillon opened it Morris said, "Choose your spot, Dill."

"Get a good bane!" Isabelle coached him. She bent and watched closely as Dillon chose a spot and applied the alcohol. To Morris, she said, "Wite dehw. Dat's a good spot."

"Why do you want to watch this?" Morris asked her.

"I don't know." It was the most innocent of replies. She really did not know.

Morris inserted the needle. Dillon winced. "Your vein jumped," Morris told him. "Try to relax." Dillon took a deep breath and looked away. He knew his veins were sclerosed from years of intravenous treatments. "Don't hold your breath," Morris advised him, "It makes you tense up. Breathe normally."

Isabelle realized this would not be so easy for Dillon. Although she did not understand why he experienced pain from Morris' unfailingly painless injection procedure, she accepted his pain as something unique and genuine. She detected the anticipation of more pain in Dillon's eyes. As a way to detract his attention from the IV site, she softly rubbed his other arm with her fingertips and told

Dillon, "Concentwate on dis. Put aw yo' feewing on dis uddew ahm, Din. Tink of ony dat."

He gave her an appreciative smile and took her advice. He was still too tense for it to work, and he bit his lower lip in frustration.

She gently patted his arm to regain his attention. "Do you know a th-song cawed *Itsy-bitsy Pidoo*?" After he nodded, she suggested, "Wets th-sing it toogeddoo."

He began to sing with her, and the combination of singing and her rhythmic feathery caress on his arm distracted him from the painful insertion of the needle that would allow advancement of the IV catheter. He closed his eyes when he felt Morris tape the tube down under a square of sterile gauze. The site was sore, but it was no longer painful. He sighed silently with relief as he sang the final lyric with Isabelle.

"All done." Morris patted his shoulder and nodded encouragingly. To Isabelle, he said, "You should get off the bed now, Isa."

"She can stay," Dillon said. "I'll tell her when it's time."

"I'll see you in an hour unless you need help. If that happens, send Isa." He gathered his lab kit and left the room.

"Thanks for helping me," Dillon told Isabelle.

She brightened and grinned at him. "We did good, huh?"

"We sure did! So... how'd you like to learn how to cross your eyes?" He crossed his own for her and made her laugh hysterically. Her laughter soothed him.

JAMES SEARCHED THE nightstands beside Brian's and Beverly's queen size bed. He found their Bibles easily, and a little something else, as well. He sat down on the bed and opened the two small ring cases. The cases contained their wedding rings. He surmised they both kept the rings at home because of their lines of work. He gazed at their wedding photograph on the bureau across the room, the young doctor in her wedding gown and her young handsome cop in his tux. It made him think of Natalie and Coltan and reminded him of Natalie's request to retrieve her mother's wedding gown. He went to the doctor's closet and searched the top shelf for the large box that contained the gown.

The bustle of many footsteps and voices, and the sound of items dropping into boxes drifted up the staircase. Sixteen soldiers had volunteered for the duty of supplies acquisition from the Danbury house. With Mitchell and his team watching the skies and the ground for them, the trip into Bonito Valle had gone smoothly. They reached the house and tucked the vehicles into the garage just when the sun peeked over the horizon. As Natalie assured him, all three vehicles fit easily.

Jill's voice echoed from the attic, "Man! It's hot up here!"

Sergeant Elmer's voice boomed from downstairs. "Only take the boxed foods."

"What about the medical equipment?" Jill's voice again.

"Well..." The sergeant thought for a moment, "Take the whole thing. We'll label the drugs as possibly compromised by the heat. The doctors can decide once we get it back there."

"Roger!" Jill said.

Sergeant Elmer spoke into his transmitter, "Conway and Reston, report to the attic."

James spotted a large flat white box under two smaller boxes on the top shelf. He brought all three boxes down and set them on the bed. The smaller boxes held dress shoes. The large flat box held the jackpot item. He took a moment to caress the satin material. Shiny white beads and a trim of lace embellished the bodice. It was a beautiful gown, and he pictured Natalie wearing it on her Big Day. He imagined the ceremony, the exchange of rings. It reminded him about her parents' wedding rings. James could not predict how Natalie and Coltan would feel about using those rings, but he decided to include them in the box. He thought about the white high-heeled pumps all brides wore, and he double-checked the shoeboxes. One pair of shoes was white satin. He assumed those shoes went with the gown. The only things missing were the veil and the garter. He returned to the closet and searched through a few more boxes until he found the veil and garter packed together in a sturdy pink box.

A search of the policeman's closet revealed the tux and shoes packed together in a protective garment bag. He was not certain if the ensemble would fit Coltan, but it would come in handy for any future weddings at the refuge.

James also found a spare .38 handgun and two ammo boxes of bullets, plus a double-barrel shotgun in a case behind a second garment bag in a corner of the closet. He discovered another box of bullets and a container of shotgun shells on the closet floor when he swept the garment bag along the rod away from the corner. He considered this find and the cache in the attic. Just the number of firearms alone had made this trip worth it.

He sat again at the edge of the bed and surveyed the room. It would be a good idea to take all the clothing and toiletries for the residents who needed them. Brian and Beverly's wedding photo stared back at him. He thought he should take it for Natalie, and he retrieved it and set it in the box with the wedding gown.

Conway and Reston paused in the doorway on their way to the attic. Conway, a muscular redheaded kid from the Montana compound, spoke to James.

"There's a computer and two shelves full of medical books in the office downstairs. Do you want us to take them?"

"Yes." James replied.

Reston, the lanky black kid who lifted weights in his spare time said, "We'll tell the sergeant." With that, both of them proceeded to the attic.

James heard the screech of the rusted doors of the tool-shed opening in the garden area below. He went to the window and watched two soldiers enter the shed with boxes. They had kicked aside the desiccated corpses of the dead dogs in front of it, and one of the soldiers commented about the stench that still hung in the air.

James recalled the day he and Mitchell had searched this house, they had no idea Coltan was up in the attic suffering through the effects of the dog virus. In the time since then, the story had slowly come together from Natalie, and also her recollection of her adventure at Swain's Pharmacy, the same place he and Mitchell found unlocked and waiting for them. It seemed like an act of God then, and he was convinced even now God's hand was orchestrating their movements. Why he had not revealed Coltan to them on that day was a mystery.

James decided to check the office on the main floor. He grabbed his lantern and made his way down the stairs, saw the soldiers were well organized and keeping to their tasks, carrying box after box to the van in the garage. Even with this many hands, the job of gathering supplies from this large house would take all day.

He expected they would bunk there overnight and head back to Alpha Base in the twilight before dawn.

MORRIS EXAMINED THE drop of blood on the slide from Coltan's latest blood draw. What his electron microscope displayed was disheartening. He called for Doctor Quimby, who was in the next room updating Dillon's chart.

Quimby could tell it was bad news the moment he saw Morris' face. "What did you find?"

"The dog virus is strengthening, increasing." He moved aside, "Come see for yourself."

The doctor peered through the lens at a horror show in progress. The segmented sheaths belonging to the unique bacteriophages resembling centipedes broke off into fragments, subdivided and then created new phages. They had increased in number and speed of reproduction since Coltan's last sample from the week before. The virus was devouring the few antibodies that remained in the current sample on the slide.

Doctor Quimby pulled away and grimly faced Morris. "Is he showing any new symptoms?"

"He hasn't mentioned anything."

"He's getting married on Saturday."

"I know."

"He told me they haven't had intercourse since before he came down with the virus. I don't know if he's telling me the truth. If he's lying, he's put the girl at risk. I want a semen sample and a urine sample. I also want to get a spinal fluid sample." The doctor looked around the lab, "Do you have his chart?" It was the only one on the table. Morris handed it to him. "Have Joe bring him in, stat." He sat down with Coltan's chart and began to write. As he did so, he wondered about Natalie. "I want the girl checked, too."

"We checked her when she first came in. She was negative."

"Check her again."

"Coltan doesn't want her to know about this."

"Tell her it's a routine pre-marital blood test." He stopped writing and gave Morris his full attention. "Have there been any promising results from Isa's blood properties?"

"No." Morris joined the doctor at the table, "There's some odd antibodies, but they have no effect on the dog virus."

"I'd like to interview her again."

"She's with Dillon right now."

"During his chemo?" He found that mildly alarming. There was no telling what Isabelle could expose to Dillon's fragile immune system. "She shouldn't be there."

"He wants her there." Morris smiled, "They've adopted each other. She's given him purpose. You've seen the change in him."

"Get her out of there. Limit their visits over the next few days. I want Dillon to have time to recover before he's exposed to any possible contagions."

"Okay." Morris expected that would not be easy. He would have to explain it to Isabelle. If she understood her presence might expose Dillon to even the mildest illness, she would cooperate in order to make him well. Dillon would have to understand and accept it, too. "There has to be something unusual about her system that helped her beat the mord virus. For the life of me, I have not been able to detect it."

"That's why I want to get another history on her. There's something she's not telling us, something she may not remember." He closed Coltan's chart and started back to his office. He told Morris, "Bring her to my office right away. I want to see Coltan, too."

MORRIS FOUND DILLON and Isabelle both asleep; Isabelle curled up against his chest. Dillon's arms were around her. He approached quietly and woke the little girl, and brought her to Doctor Quimby.

Quimby gave her a lollipop and began the interview. "I need to know some more things about you, Isa."

She asked as she unwrapped the sucker, "What tings?"

"What do you remember about when you were sick with the biting disease?"

"Unkaduffy nice to me."

"What about how you felt? Did your body hurt?"

"When da dockitew booned me wiff da hot ting."

"Are you talking about the cattle prod? The electrical shocks?"

"Yeah. Can't ponounce da wood. Sowwy."

"What about your life before you got sick?"

"Huh?"

"Tell me what happened just before the biting people hurt you. Was anyone in your family already sick? Were you sick with anything?"

Isabelle took a long time to remember it all. It was so long ago, and the chronology of every incident blurred into one. It required a lot of effort on her part to sort through it and recall the order of events. "Mama got hoot foost when Raul bit hoo fingoo an' see tew him ouda da house. Den a cop shottim."

"Who's Raul?"

"Awa neighboo. Mama got sick da nex day. See 'pit up bud, an' Diego yicked it up."

"Who's Diego?"

"Awa dog."

Doctor Quimby sat back in his chair. Isabelle had never mentioned a dog before. "Did Diego get sick?"

"Uh-huh! He bit me, an' Mama shottim!" Her eyes filled with tears. "Po' Diego...!"

"Where on your body did Diego bite you?"

"On my ankoo." She slipped off her sandal and propped her bare foot on the doctor's desk. She pointed to the scar surrounding her ankle. "Wite hew. Dat's wew he bit me."

"Did you get sick after the dog bit you?"

"Uh-huh."

"How soon after?"

"Dat night. By dat time, Mama too sick to bing me to dockitew. In bed... sick in bed. No move. I cwy fo' hoo. I sick aw night. Mama come in moning. Not Mama no' mo'." She broke down in tears at that point.

"I'm sorry, Isa." Quimby said. "But, this is all very important. Did your mother bite you?"

"Uh-huh!" She began to sob, "Den Mawio shotter! He twied to take me to dockitew. Deya woo biting peepo aw ovoo. We dwove to Bujja-Mot wew he wooked. Biting peepo deya, too. Day bittim. Day bit me, too. We hid in wah inna tore. We got biting sick at same time."

"Who is Mario?"

"My bwuddoo. He dead now."

Quimby took a moment to put all the pieces together. "So, you got sick from the dog bite, first. After that, while you were still sick from the dog bite, you got biting sick from the biting people. Is that right? Is that the way it happened?"

"Yes, dockitew. Dat's how it happened." She put the lollipop back in her mouth. It was more for self-comfort than for the flavor. "When can I see Din again?"

"Let's give it three days."

"Why?"

"To give him time to get stronger." He smiled warmly at her, "You love Dillon, huh? Does he remind you of Mario?"

"He not Mawio. Din jus' Din. Good guy. Fwend to me." She grinned through her tears, "Din hep me talk bettew. He nice to me, an' fun." Her expression melted to one of serious concern. "Wew Din get bettew?"

"Yes, he'll get better. He's a lot better, already."

"Wew his hahw gwow back?"

"Yes."

She suddenly looked up and sniffed the air. "Kotin hew."

This was something new. The doctor sat forward. "You can smell him?"

"He got dog 'mell in his bud. I had dat when I was sick fum dog."

"Can you smell other sicknesses in people?"

"Uh-uh. Just dog and biting sick."

"That's amazing!"

Isabelle shrugged her shoulders and stared at the doctor. "Deezus said it gift."

"Can you see and hear Jesus?"

"Uh-huh."

He was not so sure about that, but thought it was worth a shot. "What does Jesus say to do to heal Coltan?"

She silently asked him and waited patiently for the answer. After a few minutes, she relayed the answer to Quimby. "You got ansoo in you head. You aweady tink it. Dog kews biting an' biting kews Dog."

The doctor rushed to Morris in the lab. "Do you have any samples of the mord virus?"

"No. Why?"

"We need it for Coltan."

He thought Quimby had lost his mind. *"What?"*

The doctor quoted Isabelle, "Dog cures biting and biting cures Dog."

It was too incredible, and it did not seem feasible. "Even if I could get a sample of the mord virus, the combination would kill him!"

"Isabelle said Jesus told her." He persisted, "If we can get a sample of the virus, you can test it here in the lab before we treat Coltan. It's worth a try, Morris."

"And, where are we gonna get the virus?"

MITCHELL'S VOICE OVER his radio woke James.

"What's up, man?" James asked sleepily.

"How's it goin'?"

"It's all packed up, and we're gettin' some shuteye. We'll roll in around eight-hundred tomorrow. Everything okay up there?"

"We're fine. Say, Morris and Quimby got a big favor to ask."

James could not imagine what it could be. Whatever it was, it was important enough not to wait until morning. "Shoot it by me."

"Have you seen any mords?"

"Not a one. Why?"

"They want you to capture one and bring it back, if possible."

James sat up on the bed. "Hell no! Tell 'em I said *hell no*!"

"Coltan's getting sick again."

"Aw... dammit! What's that got to do with mords?"

"They think the mord virus is the cure."

"Where'd they get that idea?"

"Isabelle told them Jesus told her."

"Get outa here, man!" He would never trust the fantasies of a child to cure all the world's ills and sins.

"Well, James... they believe her. It turns out she had both viruses. That's why she survived. They think it's worth a try."

More than likely, all the mords were dead. On the slim-to-none chance they would encounter one, the risk of capturing it was too perilous for his troops. In addition, there was the very real danger the introduction of the virus into the compound could spell the end for all of them. One life was not worth the risk.

"Forget it!" James said firmly.

"They were afraid you'd say that." Mitchell paused, and then offered, "Here's Plan B: would you be open to the idea of snagging a tissue sample off a mord corpse?"

That idea was just as risky. "No."

"There's no Plan C, James! The kid's gonna die unless they find a cure."

"I ain't risking the lives of my troops for one kid. Tell those two mad scientists I'm sorry."

"Are you sure, James?"

James would have slapped Mitchell upside his head if he had been there to receive the blow. "I'm sure."

Mitchell thought of Natalie and how she would handle Coltan's death. His voice came over the radio to James as both disappointed and very emotional, "Okay, James. I'll tell them."

James regretted he had to be the hard-ass on this, but there was no other choice. He turned to the only consolation left in situations like this, "We'll pray for him. Over and out, Mitch."

COLTAN WAITED UNTIL Natalie was asleep before he left their tent and headed over to Morris' lab. Earlier that day, he had endured the pain of the spinal tap, followed that with the pleasure of supplying a sperm sample, and topped off the evening with a urine sample and a fresh blood draw. They had also drawn Natalie's blood, and had explained—lied—to her the procedures were a premarital requirement. Coltan was certain the results were in by this time. He was relieved to find Morris still in the lab when he arrived.

Coltan did not have to ask. Morris knew the reason for his visit. He hated to be the bearer of bad news, and he wished Quimby were still on duty to take the burden.

"Well?" Coltan said.

Morris motioned him to the table and they sat down together. "Natalie's blood test came out negative. As for you, the news isn't good, Coltan."

"Shit..." He had been ignoring the minor symptoms, had dismissed them as fatigue.

"I found the virus in all the samples."

"Now, what?"

"I'm still working on that. I think it's time you told Natalie."

"Uh-uh!" He shook his head fiercely. "I want her to be happy on our wedding day! She doesn't have to know yet."

"You can't consummate the marriage! If you do, you'll be spreading the disease to her."

"I can use a condom."

"Have you used one in the past?"

"No. But, we haven't had sex since just before I got sick. I promise you I'll use condoms from now on."

"Won't she be suspicious?"

"Probably."

"Is she on birth control?"

"She got some kind of injection to stop her periods. That makes her sterile until her periods start up again, right?"

"What kind of injection?"

"Something they give women troops."

"Have her periods resumed yet?"

"No."

"Well... that negates the birth control excuse. You have to tell her the truth."

"No. Not until we know there's no chance I'll ever be cured. I'm not giving up, Morris. Don't *you* give up, either." He gazed sternly at Morris. "It's killed everyone else quick, everyone but me. Why? Because God wants me to live, that's why. Maybe, like Isa, I can beat this thing. I can beat it like she beat the mord virus."

"She beat the mord virus because she was already sick from the dog virus. We learned that today."

"She had the dog virus?"

"Yeah."

"How'd you find out? Her lab tests?"

"It didn't show up in her labs. She told Doctor Quimby about it. We think the viruses killed each other warring for dominance in her body. We won't know for sure until we get a sample of the mord virus to test."

RESTON'S JEEP HEADED the pack. James' jeep was in the middle with Jill driving. The moving van brought up the rear. All of the vehicles were packed with supplies, and the weight of people and stuff made the engines labor as they wound through the foothills and into the base of the mountain range.

"It was a good haul," Jill remarked to James in the passenger seat. The sunlight hurt her eyes, and she dropped down the visor. "There was sure a lot of blood up in that attic. I'm amazed he survived."

"The girl had some basic medical training from her mother," James said.

"That's Natalie, right?" She did not wait for James to answer, "I saw her photo with the folks downstairs. Is she gonna be a doctor like her mother? She told me she wants to be a soldier. Could she do both?"

James considered that. Although Natalie had her heart set on being a battlefield soldier, it would be a perfect compromise to train her as a field medic. He thought it would be worth mentioning to Natalie once she and Coltan settled in to married life.

"Could she be a medic?" Jill asked.

"That's a good idea," James replied. "But let's not mention it to either of them, yet."

The front vehicle slowed at the junction and caused the two behind to slow. Reston's voice came over the radio, "There's something moving in the trees at the Baker Creek road. Should we check it out?"

"Naw..." James came back, "Keep going."

Reston replied, "Roger that." As soon as the convoy regained speed, the front vehicle screeched to a halt, causing those behind to do the same. Reston's voice came over again, "Shit! I just hit him!"

"Hit who?" James squawked into the radio.

"A kid! I think it's a mord!"

"Is he dead?"

"He's movin'. He's flat on the road, but he's still movin', tryin' to get up."

Another voice came over in the background, "I'll shoot him, bro!"

"No!" James yelled, "Don't shoot him!" He ordered Jill, "Take us around up front!"

Jill shifted, gunned the engine and came up around the jeep at the front. She braked six feet in front of the young boy sprawled in the road. She asked James, "What are we doing?"

For a few moments, James said nothing. It crossed his mind God had sent that mordant child as an answer to their prayers for Coltan. He did not like the idea of capturing the infected child and bringing him back to base, yet the conviction filled his brain that this was exactly what they should do.

In answer to Jill's question, he told her, "We're trusting God."

He readied his weapon and approached the boy, who was sprawled on his belly on the hot asphalt. The boy had shed all his clothing, and the bloody scars of many bites were plainly visible on his body. He hissed and growled at James as he drew near. He tried to get up on his feet, but could not; both his legs were broken.

All the troops in the first jeep readied their weapons.

James squatted a safe distance away. "Can you understand what I'm sayin' to you, boy?"

The boy grunted in response, his eyes full of pain and fear.

James estimated he was between eight and eleven years old. He was emaciated and obviously weak. The absence of blood residue around his mouth indicated he had not eaten anything, animal or human. "Can you talk?" James asked him gently.

"Wad..." the boy said with much effort. He reached out one hand and curled his fingers, and then he touched his mouth. "Wad...der. Wad...der."

"He wants water," Jill remarked to no one in particular. She offered James her water bottle and removed the cap.

"We oughta shoot him," Reston said. He aimed his weapon.

James took the water from her and set it close to the boy's hand. He took it and drank it all.

"Can you understand me?" James asked him again.

"Food!" The boy patted his chest.

"What's your name?"

The mord thought about it. He could not remember his name. He looked up at James with tears running down his face. "Legs! Ow...! Food!"

James called out to Conway in the back seat of his jeep, "Conway! You still got some of that beef jerky left?"

Conway tossed him the open bag. James offered a slice to the boy. He took it and sniffed it, made a face of disappointment. "That's all we got," James told him. "I ain't feedin' you no humans. You get that idea outa your head, boy. Get it outa there right now." The boy shoved the whole thing into his mouth and chewed it. James stood, "Alright, then..."

"I never saw one talk." Jill said. She left the jeep and approached James. "What are we gonna do with him?"

"Get the litter outa the back," James ordered. "We're taking him with us."

"That's crazy!" Reston yelled.

James was thinking about what Mitchell relayed to him the night before. He was certain God's hand was in this, and God was watching. He shot back at Reston, "We can save him. In turn, he can save others!" He briefed his soldiers then on his conversation with Mitchell about what the doctor and Morris had discovered. He reminded them God had not turned his back on them, or even the infected.

That inspired Reston to rethink the situation. "We'll strap him down to the litter. We'll gag him so he can't bite." He looked again at Conway. "Bring the litter over here." To another soldier he said, "Find some bindings and something we can use as a gag."

On the asphalt, and in great pain, the child cried out and began to sob.

Jill consoled him. "We're gonna help you. We're gonna try to make you well again. Would you like that?"

He nodded and sobbed painfully.

"Don't try to bite us," James told him. "If you try to bite us, I'll have to shoot you."

"No... bite... "

Once they secured the boy and resumed their journey up the mountain, James prayed. After he prayed, he realized something. If Morris and Quimby were correct, he would be delivering to Natalie and Coltan the best wedding present ever.

CHAPTER 4

Morris, Guffy, Quimby, Joe, Trevor, and Doctors Proust and Macky met the convoy outside and carried the litter with the boy into the examination room. By this time, the child had passed out from pain and exhaustion, which made him less hazardous to handle. Just to be safe, Quimby ordered Joe to inject a strong sedative to keep the boy out cold. Morris drew the boy's blood, and then Joe and Guffy transferred him, still strapped to the litter, to a gurney and took him to x-ray.

The blood tests confirmed their new patient was suffering from the mord virus and nothing else. Morris immediately went to work isolating the viral cells and preparing culture plates and slides for the task of crossing the mord virus with the dog virus. He could not anticipate the time it would take to see the results, but he was confident God would deliver it all soon.

As the doctors began to scrub in to perform surgery on the boy's broken legs, the boy died. They were unable to resuscitate him.

NATALIE AND COLTAN cuddled inside their tent. Coltan's favorite music filled the space from the disk player at low volume. Natalie loved the music.

"What is this one called?" She asked in regard to the violin piece.

"*Beau Soir*, by Debussy. Beau Soir means *Beautiful Evening*."

"That's my favorite one," she said. "How come all composers are men? You'd think a woman could—"

"Lili Boulanger," Coltan interrupted. "Her nocturne is here. You've heard it. She wrote a lot of pieces. Most of them were choral." He grinned at her and stroked her face, kissed her and hugged her to him, "There were a lot of women composers. Some of the best was written by women."

"I never knew." She rolled over on her stomach and kissed his lips, gazed into his deep blue eyes. She thought her heart would burst with the abundance of love she felt for him. That would be a glorious mess, to bathe him in a sudden deluge of love from her heart. "Grow old with me," she purred. "Grow old with me. We'll set our trifocals on the nightstand beside our dentures. We'll massage each other with arthritis ointment and make love every night. I'll still be mad about you even then, you know!"

He laughed and tickled her. "Two wrinkled up old coots still hot for each other! I'm there!" He stopped laughing and asked brightly, "How many kids will we have?"

She pulled back a little. "I don't want kids."

"Why not?"

"Do you really want to bring kids into this horrible world? I don't!"

He had not considered the sorry state of life on Planet Earth and the effects on the children until she mentioned it. All of the children at the compound were walking cases of intense PTSD, and some may never recover. It was hard to picture the future as anything better than what they had now. Yes, he decided, she was right. Then, again, it was ultimately up to God. Coltan decided he would abandon the issue for the moment.

"Whatever you decide, I'll honor your decision." He hugged her to him. "I'm happy so long as I have you, *mon belle ange*." Another piece of music began. "Ah! Here's Lili. Listen..."

"Tallyho!" Ian's voice outside their tent made them sit up.

"Come on in," Natalie said.

He entered the tent carrying a large flat white box. On top of that box, Ian balanced a shoebox. Over his shoulder, he toted a clear garment bag that seemed very heavy.

"I bring you tidings of a mission completed." He swung the garment bag toward Coltan, "Take this, will ya? Mind you, there are shoes at the bottom."

Coltan rose and took it. Through the clear plastic, he could tell it was a tuxedo. He sat down, unzipped the bag and caressed the material of the swank jacket. "Wow...!"

Natalie took the shoebox while Ian set the large flat box on their mattress. "For the bride and groom!" he announced with a wide grin.

"Have you thought it over?" Coltan asked him, "Will you be my Best Man?"

Ian answered without hesitation, "I think Trevor's your man. 'e's been the Best at many weddin's. 'e said 'e'd be honored if you chose 'im."

"Carolyn's still my Maid of Honor," Natalie said. She opened the shoebox and admired the satin shoes. She noticed they were a half-size too big for her feet, but figured they would do so long as she walked carefully down the aisle. That thought brought up the issue of the walking cast on her left foot. Her wedding would be in two days. The cast was big and clunky, and she would be limping like a gimp up the aisle. She wondered if Doctor Quimby could offer a temporary solution, perhaps a thin but sturdy brace of some kind. It was another task to add to her *things to do* list.

She spied the big box that held her mother's wedding dress. She knew the dress would be too big for her. However, Jill and Darla had offered to work together to tailor it for her.

"Let's see the gown," Coltan suggested anxiously.

She covered the lid of the box with her arms to protect it. "Not until the big day, mister." She stood clumsily, stumbled, and dropped the box. Coltan supported her until she caught her balance. "I keep forgetting," she told him. "I have to get the gown over to Darla."

Coltan and Ian stated at the same time, "I'll carry it for you."

Natalie grinned and laughed. "Such gentlemen!" She took the box from Coltan. "I can handle it, sweetie. Thank you for bringing it, Ian."

"Thank *James*." Ian replied.

"Of course I will," she said. "I'll be back in a while, Coltan."

"We got study in two hours." He reminded her. Coltan set the shoebox on top of the big box. "You might as well take the shoes, too."

"She's a stubborn one," Ian remarked after she left.

"Have a seat," Coltan said, "I can make us some tea."

"Try on the tux, first," Ian suggested. "Let's make certain it fits."

"Okay." He put the jacket on over his shirt.

Ian straightened it and buttoned the front. He stood back and took a good look. "It fits. It fits you perfectly. By Jove, as if it was made especially for you!"

Coltan ran his fingers over it and tugged at the hem. Everything about it felt right. However, something within the interior breast pocket begged for his attention. He unbuttoned the jacket and pulled an envelope out of the pocket. "Wonder what this is?" he mumbled. He flipped the envelope over to the front. The writing almost caused his heart to stop.

"For Coltan"

Coltan's expression of shock concerned Ian. "What is it?"

He stared at the envelope. "It's from Brian... for me..."

"Who is Brian?"

"Natalie's father. The one who brought me to Jesus." His eyes quickly filled with tears he could not stop. "I don't know if I can read this, Ian. How could he have known?" He handed the envelope to Ian and sat down on the mattress. "Read it to me."

"It may be very private. Are you sure you want me to read it?"

"Yes. Read it."

Ian opened the envelope carefully and unfolded the notepaper. He began to read aloud, *"Dear Coltan, my precious son. If you are reading this letter, it's because I cannot be there to see you marry my daughter. I bet you didn't think I knew how deeply you love her. Let me assure you, it did not take any special psychic abilities to figure it out. Your love for her is in your eyes every time you look at her. I have seen it many times over the past few days, and I know in my heart your love for her is real and will be forever. It's written in your eyes, Coltan. It's written in the way you smile and light up whenever she is present with you.*

"My son, I want you to know how much our relationship has meant to me. I knew there was something very special about you the first time I laid eyes on you. You may think it was only my memories of my brother I saw, but that is far from true. I saw a young man who wanted something meaningful in his life. I saw a young man who had a heart full of love and hope despite all the hell you had been through. I saw your strength and your decency. Our Lord saw it first, for he created you. He brought us together to walk a stretch of the path side by side, you—the young man who only wanted to belong with a family who would love you, and me—a jaded old cop who needed a son to nurture. Coltan, you are my son. You are the son I always wanted. I hope I fulfilled the role of father, as well as friend, to you in our short time together.

"Bev and I will be there at your side on your wedding day—at least our spirits will be there, God willing. How could he say no to us? We are so proud of you, Coltan! We love you so much!

"We know you will take good care of our Natalie. We know our Natalie will take good care of you. God made you for each other.

"Our eternal love to you, Son... Our Precious Charles Coltan...

"We thank God for you!

"Our love to you forever, Brian and Beverly."

Ian folded the paper and replaced it in the envelope. He saw the tears spilling down Coltan's cheeks. "That's quite lovely," he whispered. "How they loved you, Coltan! The Lord 'as blessed you. Even your tears are blessed. Take comfort there, my friend."

Coltan sniffed and nodded. "They were what I prayed for. I miss them so much!"

"To be loved so completely," Ian went on. "To be loved as our Lord loves you. Such a treasure it is." He sat next to Coltan and handed him the envelope. "Would you like to be alone?"

Coltan pressed his hand onto Ian's wrist. "No, Ian. Stay here. I'm glad you're here. I'm glad you read his letter. I'm glad to share it with you. Stay with me." He wiped away his tears with the back of his hand and stared down at the envelope. "Do you believe in premonitions, Ian?"

"Yes. I've 'ad some, meself." He was thinking about his unexplainable connection to Coltan, to Coltan's physical suffering, how he had sometimes felt Coltan's pain from a distance, shared his symptoms. Coltan had been in his dreams long before Ian left England. In his dreams, Coltan had told him they were brothers and would soon be together. Ian had dismissed the dreams as simply dreams. However, once he landed on American soil, the dreams increased in frequency. He never mentioned it to anyone.

"Brian knew he and Bev wouldn't make it. He knew. He tried to tell me the last night we were together. I wouldn't believe it." Coltan opened the envelope and took out the letter, scanned the contents. "I wonder when he wrote this? There's no date."

"Does it matter?" Ian said. "Perhaps what matters is 'e found the time to write it. It was important enough to 'im. You were important to 'im."

More tears fell. Coltan wiped them away and said, embarrassed, "I must seem like such a whiny little wimp to you."

"No." Ian felt only compassion. "You're grievin' for 'im. I still grieve for my family. In the darkness, I weep. Only God sees."

"I'm sorry, Ian."

He felt it was time to confide his secret to Coltan. "I must tell you something."

"What?"

"About premonitions... We've met before." He told Coltan about the dreams, and about the many times he felt Coltan's suffering.

Although it was fantastic, Coltan believed him. That night Ian first tended to him in the hospital, he felt a strange sense of complete trust in him, as if they were already friends.

Ian continued, "You're still very ill. I have the headaches, too, the sudden dizziness. I also tend to drop things for no good reason. I take it, that's when you get the momentary loss of feelin' in your hands."

"I never told anyone about that!" Coltan gasped. "I don't want anyone to know."

"The time will come when you cannot hide it."

"How much time do I have?"

"Only God knows. I pray for you. We all pray for you." He sat down with Coltan and faced him. "Morris is workin' very hard to find a cure. God has delivered hope today, Coltan. Let me leave it at that."

"Delivered hope? How?"

"James has sworn us to secrecy. I cannot tell even you. Please don't ask me." He smiled briefly, a hint of encouragement and faith. "God has blessed you in many ways. I don't believe he will cut your days short. Have faith in him, Coltan. Marry your lovely Natalie and live your life. Try not to worry. We'll fight together when the time comes. We'll fight, and we'll win. We're brothers in Christ, you and I, warriors in Christ. God has made it so."

"That's good enough for me," Coltan said. "I'll make us some tea. We'll celebrate."

Ian smiled warmly, "There's much to celebrate, ay?"

He returned Ian's smile. "You bet!"

NATALIE FOUND THE NOTE from her mother pinned inside the bodice of the gown. It was something she would have never expected to find there. She opened the envelope and unfolded the floral embellished paper.

"What's it say?" Carolyn prodded her.

Darla took her arm and led her to the little table in the corner dining area of the tent. "Leave her be," she told Carolyn. "Give her some privacy."

Carolyn realized her error. "I'm sorry, Nat."

"Forgiven." Natalie returned her attention to the note. She wondered how long ago her mother had written it. Maybe it had been years ago. Natalie figured her mother probably assumed she would be next to wear the beautiful wedding gown; that she had planned to pass it on to her daughter. Natalie anticipated the note would say something to the effect of congratulations with some marital advice thrown in for good measure. However, once she began to read, she realized it was all that and more.

"Dear Natalie: If I were still alive to attend your wedding, you would not be reading this letter. I would have put a different letter in your hand along with something borrowed and something blue. Along with my apology for not being here on the one day you would need me most (except the birth of your first child), I had a million other things to tell you. Sorry, kid – there could never be enough time or paper to tell you everything a mother would want to tell her child. Below is my condensed version of what your grandmother (Dad's mom) told me. Did I ever tell you Dad's mom was more a mother to me that my real mother? Maybe I did."

Natalie stopped reading for a moment. She recalled a brief

conversation in which her mother had mentioned that. She smiled and continued reading.

"Here's a succinct version of the advice she gave me. 1- Always listen to what he has to say. 2- Always listen with your heart as well as your ears. 3- Give him plenty of private space and private moments. 4- Avoid smothering with mothering! 5- Prepare his favorite meal once a week, and season it with all your love. 6- Let him keep the danged remote! Have a second TV. and remote that is just for you. Problem solved. 7- Expect imperfection. Every prince has his frogginess. 8- Explain PMS to him and assure him your behavior is not his fault and will not last forever. 9- Live life together, but seek out separate interests in order to continually grow in maturity, mind and spirit. 10- Note birthdays and anniversary on the calendar and place it where you know he'll see it, too. 11- Give him YOU for his birthday. 12- Rub his feet at the end of the day, even if they stink. You can always wash your hands. 13- Make all financial decisions together. 14- Forgive him his trespasses, as he forgives yours. If he doesn't forgive your trespasses, remind him what God says about forgiveness. Then, forgive him for hesitating to forgive you. 15- Once in a while, reminisce together about the first time you met. 16- Tell him all the wonderful things about him that made you love him in the first place. 17- If something breaks, don't expect him to be a magician. Some men are handy around the house, some are handy with other things. I guess what I mean is, appreciate his weaknesses as well as his strengths. 18- Don't expect him to have all the answers. 19- Don't expect that you will have all the answers. 20- When neither of you have the answers, bring it to God. 21- Pray together at least once a day. 22- Study your Bibles together at least twice a week. 23- Say grace at every meal. Thank God for each other along with that saying of grace. 24- Argue constructively and never tear each other down. 25- Never, ever, go to bed angry. 26- Make love often and don't be afraid to experiment with each other. 27- Learn his body and teach him your body. 28- Take a bubble bath together once in a while. 29- He takes

priority over your friends. 30- Display a united front for your children (don't let the kids play you against him and vice-versa). 31- Tell him you love him – and mean it! 32- Cherish him. 33- Never, ever, compare him to your Dad. 34- Above all, cherish God, cherish Him together.

"I'm sure there's a bunch more I've forgotten to list, my sweet Natalie. Whatever you don't find here you'll find in your Bible. Make it a habit to bring your concerns to God.

"One other thing, Nat. I know the man at your side will be Coltan. Your father and I both figured that out days ago. We know you love him as much as he loves you. The more we saw you together, the more we realized how perfect you were together. Coltan's presence in our lives was not by chance. God created you for each other. I don't know what the world will be like in the coming years. The only thing I do know is you will both be okay as long as you're together.

"Your father and I love you both with all our hearts, and we will love you forever.

"One last thing, Nat. I know you want to be a soldier. Please consider also the knack you have for medicine. You would make a splendid doctor. Please think about it. Whatever you decide, I will support you from here in Heaven.

"Dad and I will be at your wedding. You will not see us, but you will feel our spirits smiling upon you and Coltan.

"May God bless you and protect you all your days! Love Always, Mom.

"P.S. If you found our wedding rings in the nightstand, that means I couldn't find the time to clean them before I put them in the box with your gown. You know how things have been lately! I'll get to it soon, in which case I'll cross out this paragraph! Dad and I want you and Coltan to have the rings, no matter where you find them."

The letter was so like Mom, practical, humorous and unsentimental. She had used three different pens, obvious by the different shades and point thickness of ink. The handwriting also varied from casual to hurried. Natalie knew without a doubt Mom had worked on the letter during breaks at work. The only thing Natalie could not ascertain was the date her mother wrote her letter. Mom had forgotten to enter the date. For all Natalie knew, Mom may have completed the letter a few days before she died.

She wondered about her mother's premonition of her and Dad's death. Apparently, it had been strong enough to compel her to write the letter. Mom had never mentioned it to her, had never warned her. The image of her mother's death came back to her, and she quickly brushed it away. That was not how she wanted to remember her.

Natalie gazed lovingly at the photograph of Mom and Dad on their wedding day. They appeared so happy and full of hope. The world had been different then. There was still hope in the world at that time. Natalie wondered if that same happiness and hope would be on her face and Coltan's face, regardless of the world outside.

She set down the framed photo and put the ring boxes on her lap. She opened the black leather box first. It held her father's wedding band, a simple gold band with a tiny diamond in the center. She flipped it in her fingers to read the inscription inside. There was no inscription. Her mother's ring was a pair that joined together to create the appearance of one solid ring: a solitaire diamond engagement ring and a second ring that had a cluster of two diamonds in a vee shape at the center. When the two rings were placed together on her finger, the diamond on the engagement ring filled the indented space above the two diamonds on the wedding ring—a perfect coupling. The rings fit her marriage finger perfectly. Natalie wondered if Dad's ring would fit Coltan.

Carolyn had given in to the urge to peek at the gown and accessories in the box on the table. "Look at the little pink and blue flowers on the crown of the veil," Carolyn said to Darla, "Look how pretty!"

Natalie folded the letter and put it back in the envelope. She kissed the images of her mother and father and returned the photo to the box. She missed them. Yet, there were no tears, not a hint of sadness. Her heart filled instead with love and happiness for them. She silently thanked Mom for her letter. After a moment, she removed the rings and went to place them in the little powder blue satin box. She paused and checked for an inscription. Like Dad's ring, there was no inscription.

"Don't people usually inscribe their wedding rings?" Natalie pitched the question more to Darla than to Carolyn.

"We didn't inscribe ours," Darla said.

Carolyn begged Natalie, "Let me see the ring!" Natalie put both ring boxes in her hand. Carolyn opened them and admired the rings. "Oh! They're beautiful! Are you and Coltan gonna wear them as your own?"

"That's what Mom wants," Natalie replied. "I guess."

"Do they fit you?"

"Yeah."

"Try on the gown!" Carolyn said excitedly.

"I know it's too big," Natalie replied.

"We can take it in," Darla reminded her. "Go on, Nat. Put it on. Let's see."

TREVOR INTERRUPTED Morris in the lab. "Any results?"

Morris jumped, startled at the sudden intrusion. "Don't sneak up on me! What do you want, Trev?"

He took the vacant stool next to Morris' at the lab bench. "Have you tested the dog virus on the mord virus?"

"Yes, I have." Morris peered through the lens at the slide. The DV, as he called it for short, was devouring the V-One, the mord virus, rapidly. The process was working much faster than he expected. "I still have to wait to see how long it takes for the DV to die. If it doesn't die, the kid's out of luck."

"How long will it take?" Trevor asked impatiently.

Morris, worn out from the many long days he had devoted to this project, did not appreciate Trevor's impatience. He shot Trevor a hot glare. "I don't know how long! Get off my back!"

"Sorry," Trevor said. "I'm sorry, Morris."

"I've been at this for weeks, beating my head against the wall because we didn't have all the pieces of the puzzle! Now we got it. Give me time to work with it!" He was so angry he was trembling. "Get out of here! Let me work in peace!"

Trevor hopped off the stool and made a hasty retreat. He would not set foot in the lab again until he saw Morris come out with a happy grin of triumph.

THE GATHERING IN THE chapel that Saturday was very small. That was the way Natalie and Coltan wanted it. Ian sat in the second row with Guffy, Isabelle and Dillon. Across the aisle sat Joe, James, Franks and Franks' wife Rina. Jill came in with Reston on her arm and, after they signed the guest book, they took a seat together in the row behind Joe, James, Franks and Rina. Joe's wife Darla entertained the guests by playing sappy love songs on the portable keyboard.

In the pastor's office, Trevor fussed over Coltan. He adopted the role of valet, and thoroughly brushed over Coltan's tux with a lint brush.

"Let me see those nails," Trevor ordered.

Coltan put out his hands and spread his fingers, "They're clean!"

"Good boy!"

"Jeez, Trev! I'm not some tobacco chewing hick, you know!"

He noticed Coltan's hands were trembling, "Are you nervous,

lad?"

"No. Why should I be?"

"Your hands are shakin'."

"I'm okay," Coltan said dismissively. He did not want anyone to know how weak he felt. The past few days, he had doubled up on vitamins to fight off the fatigue.

Trevor stood back and looked him over. The boy cut a handsome figure in that tux. The haircut and fresh shave helped, too. As he glanced at Coltan's face, he saw the paleness and glint of sweat. He wondered if it was just nerves or if Coltan had come down ill again. He held the tip of his tongue between his top and bottom teeth to prevent himself from commenting about it. Instead, he took a handkerchief from his pocket and dabbed the tiny beads of sweat from Coltan's face. He stood back for one more look.

"There you are, lad. A handsome groom!"

Coltan grinned. "I hope Darla remembers to play *Pie Jesu*. That's our cue, you know."

"She'll remember." Trevor assured him.

"Thank you for everything, Trevor."

"You're welcome."

"You've got the ring, right?"

Trevor chuckled, took it from his pocket and showed it to Coltan. "Try to relax, lad!"

He lifted one arm and sniffed his underarm, "Do I smell like sweat?"

Trevor laughed, "No. You smell fine. Put your arm down."

"Thanks for everything, Trevor!"

"You already said that."

IN THE PARTITIONED-off ladies' room, Carolyn straightened

the train of Natalie's gown. She came around the front and gazed lovingly at her best friend. "You look beautiful, Natalie."

"Do I smell like sweat?"

"You smell like *Giorgio*."

"Do you have the ring?"

"Sorry," she kidded, "I dropped it down the toilet."

Natalie erupted, "You did not!"

Carolyn laughed. She unpinned it from her sash. "It's right here!"

"Don't do that to me!" She glanced around the room and then through the open doorway, "Where's Mitch?"

"The little boys' room. He's finishing getting dressed."

"*Pie Jesu* is our cue to get in position. I hope he remembers that."

"He remembers."

"Of course, I remember," Mitchell stopped in the doorway and gazed at Natalie. She hardly resembled the gangly little tomboy he had seen grow up over the years. A beautiful, stunning woman looked back at him. When she smiled at him, his heart jumped a beat. "Natalie! Natalie, you are incredibly beautiful!"

She looked down for a moment and blushed.

Carolyn volunteered a well-known fact, "He calls her his *beautiful angel*."

His gaze remained fixed on Natalie. "How right he is."

Pie Jesu began. Mitchell swiped the bouquet of lavenders and pink roses off the little round table and set it in Natalie's hands. He offered her his arm, and Carolyn lifted the train of her gown. They would wait in the hallway until the strains of *The Wedding March* called them through the doors and up the aisle.

Coltan and Trevor took their places at the altar. The Reverend Walter Lewis walked respectfully to the center of the altar. He nodded to both men and smiled subtly to Coltan. Coltan nodded once and smiled back. Trevor could feel Coltan's joyful anticipation.

Darla began *The Wedding March*. Coltan and Trevor turned to face the doors, to watch the bride approach her waiting, loving groom. The guests all turned at the same time.

She gripped Mitchell's arm tightly. This morning, Doctor Quimby replaced the cast on her left foot with a thin ankle wrap-brace for that day only, so she could wear the satin pumps with her gown. The shoes, a half-size too big, caressed the rear of her heels with each step. As long as Mitchell did not forget and quicken the pace, the shoes would stay on and she would not gain infamy as *The Bride Who Tumbled up the Aisle.* Her left foot was very painful in the fancy satin pump. Her broken ankle strained against the brace for lack of proper support. She tried to lesson her weight on that foot, and it caused her to limp slightly. Her fingernails dug into Mitchell's arm.

Mitchell felt Natalie shift her weight against him. He sensed her tension. She whispered through gritted teeth, "Damned shoes!" It was only loud enough for him to hear. He supported her weight and balanced her. In a whisper, he advised her, "I gotcha, hon. Keep your eyes on Coltan's. Leave the rest to me."

Natalie locked her eyes into Coltan's admiring and love-filled gaze. His eyes would enrapture her throughout all her days, she thought, those beautiful dark blue eyes that melted her defenses and uncovered the exquisite loveliness of her soul. How she would always love him, love him throughout all eternity!

Coltan stood there, relishing the sight of her. He was hopelessly enchanted at that moment, the core of his being overflowing with love for her. She glowed with ethereal beauty, glowed with it from the inside out. He wanted to remember this moment forever, to remember her this way forever. He thought if a person could die from an overdose of love for another, he must be in Heaven at that very second.

He offered his arm to Natalie, and she took it. Through the

material of the sleeve of the tux, she could feel the firmness of his muscles. The memory of her first day riding with him in her father's truck flashed in her mind. She had admired his arms, admired the strength suggested by his lean muscles. She had wanted to caress his arms, even then. It still excited her to touch him.

Out of the corner of her eye, Isabelle saw three figures standing near the wall close to the altar: a woman and a man standing with Jesus. The woman had light, golden-brown hair. Her eyes were the same as Natalie's. Isabelle knew they were spirits, because she could see through them. The woman glanced her way and Isabelle caught her eye. She smiled and winked at Isabelle. Isabelle smiled and winked back. Then the woman watched proudly as her daughter approached Coltan and Trevor at the altar.

Isabelle returned her attention to the bride and groom. When Natalie took Coltan's arm, Isabelle felt her eyes sting with happy tears. Her eyes on Coltan and Natalie, she took Dillon's hand and squeezed it gently. Dillon glanced at her, smiled, and returned the gesture.

CHAPTER 5

It had been almost a week since Natalie and Coltan wed. She loved being married, and so did Coltan. Although being married had not changed their relationship in any way, it had given them a sense of permanency lacking before. Natalie had read him her mother's advice, and Coltan decided he would abide by it, too. As for her father's letter to him, Coltan kept that to himself as a personal treasure. There was nothing in it that would benefit Natalie, and he felt the sentiments there would only dredge up her grief for him.

There was another secret, as well, and he hated to begin his marriage like this. He continued to hide the symptoms of the increasing viral load in his system from everyone. In private, he downed extra vitamins and took painkillers to ease the distress that screamed from every inch of his body. The bouts of fever had increased in frequency and duration. The night before had been a rough one for him, and Natalie suspected his illness had returned. He made light of it, held on to hope the disease would run its course like a flu virus, and he would be well again.

His denial of his attempts to conceal the truth of his condition did not fool her. She had suspected it since their wedding night. It was the first time he used a condom with her, and he explained the doctors advised it to protect her from the "few lingering" viral cells found in his semen. Although he denied the state of his health had changed, she knew the truth. Before the sickness ravaged him, he could not get enough of her and their lovemaking lasted for hours. Once the virus took hold, it had destroyed his desire, and they had continued their relationship in an affectionate, yet platonic, manner.

However, it was not the lack of sexual intimacy that worried her, but his gradually failing health. In order to avoid stressing him further by nagging him about it, she chose instead to silently observe him and pray for him. She knew he was only trying to protect her through his avoidance of the issue.

Natalie awakened slowly and lingered in that comfy state between wakefulness and sleep. Beside her, Coltan lay facing her on his side. She turned over and gazed at him as he slumbered. He breathed so quietly she could hardly hear him. His face was completely relaxed, child-like in the peace of deep sleep. His pale skin glistened with a thin, even coating of sweat. At first, she thought he was too warm under the blankets, but when she caressed his skin, she found it was ice cold. His entire body was cold and damp.

She sat up halfway. "Coltan?" She framed his face in her hands. He did not respond to her touch. "Coltan? Come on, hon. Wake up."

"Huh?" He opened his eyes and looked at her. Her image was a blur. He blinked to focus better. It did not help.

"Are you alright?"

His first inclination was to wrap her in his arms as he did every morning, to hold her to him, kiss her and caress her. His arms did not respond to the commands of his brain. He tried to move his legs, but, again, there came no response. His muscles, even his bones, seemed to be burning from the inside out. He knew what this meant, and it frightened him.

When he spoke to her, his speech slurred, "Find the doctor."

"Oh, my God!" she gasped.

Somehow, he thought he could have prevented this. "I'm sorry, Natalie!"

HOURS LATER, HE EMERGED from sleep into a hazy state of

consciousness. The familiar scents of the hospital told him he was flat on his back in a hospital bed once more. The sounds of occasional beeping and the muffled hum of machinery told him he was in the Intensive Care Unit. His body was draped in a maze of tubes and wires of differing thickness that all led to monitoring equipment. He felt Natalie's hands holding his left hand, and he tried to focus his eyes to see her. In addition to Natalie's blurry form, four other figures surrounded his bed, two in white coats, and two in blue scrubs. The four were standing, and one in white leaned over him and laid a firm warm hand on his forehead.

"Can you speak, son?"

Coltan recognized Doctor Quimby's voice. He tried to answer him, but all he could muster was a soft groan.

"You're in the hospital," Quimby said. "We're doing everything we can for you. Do you understand?"

Coltan managed to whisper, "Yeah..."

"We've given you something for your pain."

"Can't move," Coltan said, struggling to form the words.

"I know," Quimby said gently. "You're very ill, Coltan."

"Am I dying?"

There was silence in reply to his question. He heard Natalie whisper, "Please, God... help him..."

"Do you want to try the V-One?" It was Morris' voice, but Coltan could not discern to whom he addressed his question.

"Yes," Quimby said, "Go ahead and prepare it." He sat down at the bedside and took Coltan's right hand in his. "We have something we think will cure you. However, there is some risk involved and no guarantee."

"Tell me," Coltan said weakly.

"We discovered the mord virus and the dog virus destroy each other when together in the system. The one thing we don't know is what it will do to you while they're at battle. You may develop symptoms of the mord virus for a while until the dog virus wipes it out. If that happens, Coltan, you'll be a danger to us. We may need to secure you to the bed until those symptoms subside."

The thought of it was appalling. "How long?"

"We don't know."

Joe had seen Coltan's scars and had long suspected a history of abuse. He did not like the idea of using restraints on Coltan. If Coltan had been subjected to that as part of the abuse, the use of restraints would bring the memories to the fore, which could cause a psychological breakdown. Joe thought there was an alternative, and he suggested it to the doctor. "Instead of restraints, couldn't we keep him under heavy sedation?"

"We could try that first," Doctor Quimby replied. "It's a good idea." He squeezed Coltan's hand. "Would you like to try that?"

"Could the—could both the—viruses kill me?" He struggled to clearly see the doctor's face. If he could see, he would know if Quimby was only telling him what he wanted to hear. As much as he tried to focus, his compromised eyesight failed him.

Quimby took a moment before he answered. "Coltan, the dog virus is killing you. It's taken over your entire system. Your organs are beginning to shut down, and the virus is already invading your brain. The V-One is our—your—only hope at this point."

He was grateful for the doctor's honesty. "What would you do if it was you?"

"I'd risk the V-One."

"The mord virus?"

"Yes."

He heard Natalie sniffle. She was crying. "Nat? Don't cry." He wished he could speak without slurring, and he hoped she understood him. "What do you think I should do?"

Her voice was shaky. "It's up to you, Coltan. I can't make this decision for you."

It was clear he had no other choice. "Let's do it." He tried to turn his head to look at Natalie. The paralysis had spread. "Natalie... I don't want you here for this. I don't want you to see any of this." It took an effort to raise his voice to the shortest person in scrubs whose blurred figure had come closer to his side. "Ian, take her out of here. Take her out of here until it's all over. Please, do it now."

Ian rounded the bed to Natalie, "Come along, Nat. For him."

"I want to stay with you!" Natalie protested to Coltan.

"No!" Coltan said hoarsely, "I don't want you to see this! Please, Nat... Do what I ask. Please!"

She began to sob, "Coltan! I love you! I love you! Let me stay! Please!"

"Get her out of here!" The strain caused him to cough and struggle for breath. It had spread to his lungs, and soon he would not be able to speak; sooner than that, he would find it difficult to breathe.

She lifted him and held him in her arms, kissed his face again and again. "I love you! No matter what, don't give up!"

"I won't give up," he replied between breaths and coughing. "I love you! Get out of here!"

Her sobs tore at his soul. In his mind, he kept apologizing to her as the sound of her crying became softer with the distance as Ian led her farther down the hall, farther away from him. He realized then his only sense remaining was his sense of hearing. His eyesight had failed to where all he could see was shadows and a hint of light.

"Did he agree to it?" Morris inquired.

"Yes," Quimby said softly. "Go ahead and inject it." Coltan vaguely felt the doctor's comforting hand on his forehead once more. "God bless you, Coltan. May God be with you; we'll be with you, too."

CAROLYN JOINED IAN in the hallway and they took Natalie outside. They sat with her as she smoked and cried. All they could do was take turns holding her. No words could ease her emotional torment. Dillon joined them a while later. He held her, too. He held her for the longest time and, after so long, he began to pray aloud for her and Coltan. Ian and Carolyn prayed with him.

Natalie prayed in her heart, begged, pleaded, cursed, and even offered her own life in exchange. Finally, she succumbed to another bout of helpless, angry tears. She thought even the angels had fled away.

IT WAS WELL OVER AN hour later when Ian returned to the ICU. Doctor Quimby, Morris and two nurses were in the observation station, monitoring the equipment readings and Coltan's response to the V-One. Trevor had taken a seat across from the bed and had his weapon loaded and ready for the worst-case scenario. Ian noted the grimness in Trevor's face. He went around the side of the bed and sat down across from Joe, who was placing a cold compress on Coltan's forehead.

"How is he?" Ian asked.

"Still conscious," Joe said. He leaned closer to Coltan, "Can you still hear me, Coltan?"

His voice was weaker now, so soft they had to strain to hear him, "Yeah. Is that Ian?"

"I'm here," Ian said and took his hand, "I'm here, brother."

"If I die, Ian..."

"No," Ian stated, "You'll live. Remember what I told you!"

Coltan could not remember. He brushed Ian's statement aside, "Promise me you'll look after Natalie. Promise me."

Ian did not want to give in, but if it made Coltan feel better, he would go along with it, "I promise. 'owever, we won't let it get to that, shall we?"

"I'm an ass-kicker..." He smiled at the memory of Natalie's complement.

Ian suddenly felt cold, and he crossed his arms over his chest and shivered. The room was warm and, at first, he did not realize why he felt cold until he noticed Coltan shiver. Ian glanced at Joe, "Do we 'ave another blanket for 'im?" Joe pointed at the closet. Ian got up and told Coltan, "I'll get another blanket for you, Coltan. Just a moment, now." He got it quickly and draped it over Coltan, "There you are. That's better, ay?"

"I want you to have my Bible, Ian."

"No..." Ian begged off. He did not want to hear Coltan talking like it was the end.

"I want you to have it! Give Dillon the pewter cross in my Bible case. I told him all about it..." he passed out for a moment and came to again with a jolt. "Dillon knows what it means to me. I want him to have it. Give my necklace and my journals to Natalie. Give her my music, too. She likes the music..." He drifted into unconsciousness, a merciful escape from the war beginning inside his body.

Joe and Ian noticed his increasingly labored breathing and his skin's cyanotic tone. At the same time, Doctor Quimby ordered through the microphone, "Start him on oxygen." The oxygen was at Ian's side. Ian hooked it up, placed the mask over Coltan's nose and mouth, and turned the release valve on the tank. The soft hiss through the mask joined the rest of the medical music in the room.

Ian stared at the floor, unable to cope with the sight of Coltan's dire and rapidly deteriorating condition.

Trevor appeared at his side. He put his arm around Ian's shoulders, and said nothing.

THE EARLY STARS TWINKLED in the dusk, oblivious to the turmoil on the blue planet far away.

In the Communications and Security Surveillance Room, Mitchell and Glenda watched the satellite feed on the monitor. They watched helpless and full of shock as UEF forces conducted mass executions by firing squad in front of the tennis backboard at Bonito Valle High School. The victims were men and women of different age groups. All were dirty and emaciated, as if they had been living in the wilderness for a long time. One of the executed was a teenage boy in a wheelchair.

Glenda radioed the report to James and abandoned the satellite view for the view of the compound perimeter fed by the many cameras Mitchell and his team had installed last year. She saw Natalie and Dillon curled up together against a boulder in the smoking section. Dillon was holding Natalie and speaking to her. Glenda typed in for a wider view and checked the troops guarding the perimeter. They were all alert and doing their job.

James radioed back he was increasing the number of guards by four, and had just ordered ten on alert at the hospital inside the compound.

Mitchell was curious as to the reason for the alert. "What's goin' on, James?"

"Didn't anybody tell you?" James asked.

"Tell me what?"

"They injected the Allen kid with the mord virus in order to save him."

"What?" Mitchell almost yelled it. He knew Coltan had not been well, but this was too sudden. Why hadn't Natalie informed him? Then he wondered aloud, "Is Natalie there with him?"

"She's outside." Glenda quickly told him.

James spoke at the same time, "The kid's at death's door, Mitch. Morris and Quimby are doing everything they can for him."

"So, why the troops on alert?"

"In case he turns."

"Over and out, James." Mitchell shut off his radio and stood, strapped it to his belt. He told Glenda, "I gotta go out for a bit."

"She's in the smoking section," Glenda called after him.

DOCTOR PROUST AND DOCTOR Macky joined Quimby and Morris in the observation station. Proust was a kid to Quimby, a former second-year resident from Bonito Valle Community Hospital who split the scene when the military sent soldiers to man the ER. Macky was in her fifties, a country G.P. who ran a small clinic on a now defunct reservation in the desert east of the mountains. She had made it to Alpha Base in the first small convoy from Montana.

Macky was anxious to see how the V-One would affect a patient who was already dying from the dog virus. She had seen many mords, had even killed a few, but she had never seen a dog virus patient until the first of the infected troops arrived at Alpha, and they had all died within days. Coltan was an anomaly, and she was determined to learn all she could through him in order to help others.

She asked Quimby, "How's the kid doing?"

"His viral load just peaked. He went through convulsions ten minutes ago, and came out of it on his own." Quimby turned on the mic and spoke softly to Joe, "Has he regained consciousness?"

Joe answered through his lapel mic, "No. But, he did growl."

"That's not good!" Proust moaned.

"What else?" Quimby inquired.

"He's broken out in a full-out sweat. Nasty smellin'! Smells like decay—a dead body." Joe hesitated and watched Coltan closely. "I think he's comin' around."

Ian backed up his chair suddenly when Coltan growled and

reached blindly for him. As soon as that happened, Trevor sprung from his chair and aimed his rifle at Coltan.

"Increase sedation," Quimby ordered.

"Yes, sir." Joe injected a ready syringe into the IV. He watched Coltan.

Morris grabbed his lab kit. "I want a sample of that sweat." He rushed quietly to the bed and removed a scraper and a small vial from the kit. Without a word, he donned a facemask and gloves, pulled down the covers, and scraped a small amount of the putrid liquid off Coltan's chest into the vial. When Coltan felt it and tried to grab him, Morris calmly told him, "Behave yourself!" and swiped his hand away. He stood back and instructed Joe and Ian, "You two better put on your aprons and gloves. Don't forget the face and eye protection." He pointed to the stack on the side table, "Do it now."

Joe and Ian promptly did as ordered.

He noticed Trevor with his rifle at the ready. "You can relax Trev. I've seen this before. They can't maintain a grip on their victim when they're this weak. As long as we don't get careless, the kid's no threat to us."

Trevor kept his vigilance. After what he had been through with the mords out on the interstate, after what he had witnessed, he would not trust Morris' opinion or anyone else's. If Coltan got loose and began to attack, he would shoot him. He would shoot him between the eyes and be done with it. He would end the threat of spreading the infection and end Coltan's misery with one shot. This was his assignment.

Morris took another vial and emptied some urine into it from the catheter bag. The urine was a greenish-brown color. He had to turn away to avoid inhaling the pungent odor of it. Morris left hurriedly with the samples for his lab.

Coltan growled and screamed, blindly reached out.

Trevor cocked the rifle, took a step forward, and steadied his aim. *One more outburst like that...*

"No, Trevor!" Ian begged. His words came rapid-fire, his northern accent growing stronger with his emotions. "He doesn't know what 'e's doin'! He's blind, weak, scared to death, I tell ya! Give the sedative time to work. I beg ya, Trev!"

"Do you think I want to?" Trevor tried to explain. "I've got orders, lad!"

Joe intervened, "Give 'im time, Trevor. This is the worst of it, right now. There's only two ways it can go from here. He'll either die, or he'll get better."

"Stand down, Mr. Rolardy!" Doctor Quimby ordered.

"I don't take my orders from you!" Trevor replied.

Coltan moaned and whined.

Ian looked away from Trevor and bent over Coltan. It seemed to him Coltan could hear and understand the conversation. "There now, Coltan. I'm here for ya. I'm not leavin' ya." He implored Trevor, "You were Best Man at 'is weddin'. 'e trusts you, Trev."

Trevor maintained his stance. He wished the others only knew how difficult it was to be responsible for the safety of all at the expense of one. If only they knew how much he loved Coltan, loved him as his brother. He would not pull the trigger unless there was no alternative.

Ian said, "'e's me friend, an' I love 'im."

"He'd want me to protect you, if it came to it." Trevor replied.

Coltan moaned and cried out, thrashed from side to side.

Ian felt the pit of his stomach twist inside him. Suddenly cold and weak, he sat down in the chair at the bedside. It was not fear that caused these symptoms, the symptoms belonged to Coltan and Ian was receiving them. An image of blood, pure, warm blood came to mind.

"'e needs blood," Ian said, "The viruses are eatin' away 'is blood."

"What?" Joe looked at him as if he considered him crazy.

"Give 'im blood. 'e needs blood. 'e's tellin' me!" He turned to Doctor Quimby at the observation station, "I can't explain 'ow I know it. 'e's tellin' me 'e'll die without it! Please—give 'im blood. 'e needs it now!"

Macky could see Ian was mirroring some of Coltan's symptoms. "Empathic...!" She exclaimed under her breath. Empathics were common at the reservation. From her experience with the patients there, she knew immediately Ian was for real. She faced Quimby, "I think you should listen to him, Doctor."

Quimby had also noticed the change in Ian. He instructed Joe, "Hook up the blood bag to the IV."

"No, wait!" Ian shouted, "Put some in a cup, first. He needs to taste it, to drink it. The rest 'e can have intravenously."

Joe eyed Quimby, "What do you want me to do?"

"Go with Ian."

"Are you nuts?"

Quimby became impatient and said sternly, "Just do it!"

Joe used a syringe to suck the blood out of the bag. He quickly emptied the syringe into a cup and handed it to Ian. "You be careful!"

Coltan screamed again and curled up in a fetal position. He shivered violently and sobbed to himself. His world was one of shadows, strange noises and painful hunger—literally painful hunger. His stomach raged and churned for want of warm, soothing blood. Additional bodily chaos threatened his sanity: Thumbtacks raced through his veins and arteries, fire burned through his tissues, razor-toothed worms chewed through his brain, and his brain was attempting to escape the onslaught by sliding out through his ears. This world was the world at the gates of Hell, and he was trying to crawl away from it.

He knew if he could crawl far enough away, his prey would appear before him in the safety of that place out of Hell's reach.

The prey, something blue and gentle as a fawn, juicy with warm, comforting blood appeared before him in the distance. Oh! How he wanted it! He wanted to sprint to it and capture it, but his legs refused to obey him. He was too weak to subdue and taste his prey, even if he could capture it.

Despondently, he curled up into himself and cried bitterly. When would the pain stop?

"It's too risky, Ian!" Trevor warned. He cautiously stepped closer.

Ian folded the covers over Coltan and fearlessly put his arm under his neck. He removed the oxygen mask and brought up Coltan's head so he could drink from the cup at his lips. "Drink this, my friend. It's the blood you need." He pressed the rim of the cup to Coltan's lips. Coltan smelled it, and he moaned with relieved anticipation. He sipped at it while Ian tilted the cup more as Coltan drank it down. When it was gone, Coltan whimpered and sighed, relaxed.

In the meantime, Joe hooked up the blood bag and it was now feeding into Coltan's veins. He observed his patient closely. The bluish tint slowly faded from his pale skin, and his face became peaceful. The shivering subsided.

Ian gently guided his head to the damp pillow and released his arm from behind his neck. He wrung out the washcloth and bathed Coltan's face and mouth. "There, now. That's better, isn't it? All better."

Coltan tried to reach for the fawn, to pet it gratefully, to thank it. His arms and hands were useless. A whisper hovered upon his lips, "Bless... Thank..."

"You're welcome." As he gently replaced the oxygen mask, Ian softly encouraged him, "Try to sleep now."

Trevor expelled the breath from his lungs and un-cocked his rifle. He brought the weapon down to his side. "He spoke to you..."

Ian's full attention was on Coltan, "Sleep and dream of peaceful green meadows. The hand of God shall protect you in your dreams. Remember, Coltan... *He shall give 'is angels charge over thee.* You told me about them, about your angels. Call upon them now. I call upon them, as well. Rest in them, my friend."

Coltan settled like a lazily falling leaf into sleep.

Morris returned to the observation station, very excited, with two full pages of test results. "His sweat and urine is nothing but dead cells. Both viruses are virucidal and cellulicidal. They especially attack blood cells. However, the good news is, the number of dead blood cells are much fewer than those of the viral. The treatment is working."

Joe cocked his head at Ian, "You were right. How did you know?"

Ian sat shivering, "I can't explain it."

Quimby grinned, "Great work, Morris!"

"I need to get new samples from him every half-hour to plot the progress of the virucidal actions as opposed to cellulicidal. If the viruses are dying faster than they can devour cells, Coltan's got a fighting chance. If it's the other way around, well..."

"He's been able to move his arms." Joe commented.

"That's a very good sign." He turned again to Quimby and the other doctors, "I need to test his blood again, right away. The last sample was an hour ago."

"We just started him on blood replacement." Quimby said.

"Is it helping?"

"It seems to be."

Joe stared at Ian. Ian looked away from him and closed his eyes. He was too tired to try to explain it all, even if he could. A moment later, Joe's hand on his shoulder brought him out of an unexpected doze. Joe whispered to him, "Hit the other bed and get a nap. I'll wake you if I need you."

"I'm alright," Ian said.

Trevor interjected, “Do as he says, Ian. You’ll be no good to us, otherwise.”

Ian cast Trevor a glare of warning, “I don’t want to awaken to a gunshot.”

“It appears the danger has passed,” Trevor assured him.

The bustle of many young voices pleading with soldiers and medical staff demanded their attention. Coltan’s Bible study group was in the hallway. They wanted to come in and perform a hands-on healing prayer for him.

Doctor Quimby approached the group and hushed the authorities. He found it touching, a loving testament to Coltan the boys and girls would risk their lives to perform a hands-on healing prayer. He spoke softly with the teens, “You can come in for five minutes only, kids, but you cannot touch him. Only Joe and Ian can touch him because they’re wearing protective clothing.”

Dillon stepped forward. “Can a couple of us join hands with Joe and Ian if they lay their hands on Coltan for us?”

Quimby nodded and smiled, “I think that will be fine, Dillon. Those who join hands with Ian and Joe must wear gloves.” He had reservations about Dillon’s health; his immune system was still weak from the chemo. “However, Dillon, I want you to stand near the door, away from any contagion, and you’re to wear gloves and a mask. Your immune system is still compromised. Do you agree?”

“Yeah.”

“All right, kids,” Quimby herded them in, “Be very quiet now. He’s sleeping.”

“Is he getting better?” Dillon asked.

“We think so.”

With respectful silence, they all chose spots and circled the bed while Dillon put on a mask and surgical gloves. They joined hands with Joe and Ian. Not one to be left out, Trevor squeezed in among the circle between Dillon and Carolyn. One by one, they lifted their prayer for Coltan to the Heavens.

Coltan heard the voices in his sleep. He dreamed an army of angels surrounded him and shielded him under their wings. The angels bathed him in light and relieved his pain. The angels poured their light into him and filled him with peace.

HIS FIRST AWARENESS was of a strong scent of antiseptic soap. His second awareness was the sounds of hospital equipment humming, hissing and beeping. Gradually, the remainder of his senses awakened. He felt comfortably warm under the blankets, and the sheets were soft against his bare skin. One of the tubes pasted to his chest tickled his neck as it wound behind him to the equipment on the wall at the head of his bed. He went to move the tube and realized two slim, warm hands wrapped around his hand. He tried to open his eyes, but he was too tired and weak to do so.

Natalie caressed his hand, kissed it, her smooth lips lingering there for a long moment. "You made it through," she said to him in a soft, gentle voice. "You'll be okay."

He folded his fingers around her hands and squeezed to let her know he heard her.

CHAPTER 6

Ian could barely see the cup of tea framed in his hands. The episodes of blurry vision had been occurring sporadically ever since Coltan regained consciousness. Ian was certain the cause of his impairment was due to his sensitivity to another one of Coltan's lingering symptoms. Somehow, Ian had managed to hide his condition from his coworkers, but tonight was the worst it had ever been, enough to cause him to seek solace in the privacy of the break room. If all went according to the usual pattern, his eyesight would return good as new within another five minutes or so.

He sensed Joe's presence before the man entered the room. Ian calculated it must be two in the morning, for that was when Joe habitually took a cup of strong coffee to get him through the rest of his shift. As expected, Joe went to the counter and poured a cup from the fresh pot Doctor Macky had just brewed

He turned in Ian's direction, leaned back against the counter and took a satisfying sip, mentioned casually, "Dillon's finally getting his own tent tomorrow."

"I thought you were all letting him live *here*," Ian joked.

Joe laughed softly. "So did he."

"Just for fun, you should send him a charge for a half-million pounds."

"Dollars."

"I keep forgetting."

Joe's tone of voice changed quickly to one of concern. "Are you okay, Ian?"

"Right as rain, chum."

"You look tired."

"I'm fine."

"Your eyes look funny."

This surprised him. "What... 'ow so?"

Joe paused to think how to describe it. "It's sort of like your focus is off. Did you used to wear glasses? Did you lose them?"

"I've never needed glasses. Don't need 'em now. Stop fussin' over nothin'."

"Grouchy, too..."

"Don't mean to be."

"It's a slow night. Go get some sleep."

"You need your smoke break. We need two on for Coltan."

"Natalie's with him."

Ian's vision began to clear. He sipped his tea and sighed with relief. However, he suddenly lost coordination in his right hand and spilled the cup as it tipped from his grasp. He gasped as the liquid rolled down his arm. "Fuck!" Just a quickly, he cast Joe an imploring glance, "Don't tell Trevor you 'eard me say that!"

Joe laughed again. "I didn't know you British used that word."

"We use 'em all." He began to sop up the tea with a towel. "We're not all right proper, ya know, not where I come from."

"Trevor said you were quite the *potty mouth* at one time."

"An' quick with me fists, too. Did 'e tell ya about that?"

"Said you were a tough little fart."

Ian grinned at the memory. "What else did 'e tell ya?"

"That's all." And, then an afterthought, "He loves you, you know."

"I know." He knew Joe loved him, too. Joe had given him a home, adopted him into his family, treated him as one of his own children. It was the first stable family experience Ian had ever known. He wanted to tell Joe how much that meant to him and how their love had helped him deal with the trauma of both his recent and distant past. He wanted to talk about it, but he couldn't. To give voice to his inner turmoil and then his gratitude for the Davidsons' gift of love to him would only bring his pain to the surface. He was not ready to reveal his pain, much less express it.

Joe already had many a glimpse into Ian's battles; he had heard the boy's nightmares, sometimes watched him toss and cry in his sleep. His wife Darla and his oldest son Jayjay, Joe Junior, had expressed concern over Ian's phantoms. That was why Joe gave Ian extra attention, took him under his wing, mentored him, brought him to work with him at the hospital. The work was therapeutic for Ian; he was too busy learning and caring for others to dwell on his own emotional wreckage.

He patted Ian's shoulder. "I'll go have a quick smoke, bugger."

"No hurry," Ian said. "I got me second wind."

After Joe went out, Ian resumed his work. He placed a supplemental IV fluids bag on the pole in Coltan's room and set about checking his vitals.

Still half-awake, Coltan immediately sensed his presence before Ian had begun to place the blood pressure cuff. He spoke just above a whisper so as not to awaken Natalie in the second bed. "You look, tired, Bro."

"I'm not tired."

"Have you had a break yet?"

Ian grinned. "Don't be a mother hen. I'm lettin' Joe get a gasper."

"Did you ever smoke?"

"When I was seven. Mum boxed me ears an' then made me eat the entire pack. That cured me. Cedric thought it was hilarious, me pukin' into the thunder mug."

"Cedric?"

"Me older brother."

"Did you get along?"

His expression became suddenly dark. "No. Got mean when he

drank. Took after Mum and Dad that way." He put the stethoscope to his ears, gave Coltan a stern glance. "I'd rather not discuss it."

"Did you drink?"

"I said I'd rather not discuss it."

"I drank. Not because I was addicted, but because it silenced my demons." Coltan waited for a response, but Ian offered none. Coltan took that as a sign even the subject of his own experiences was off-limits.

Ian removed the stethoscope and draped it around his neck, removed the cuff from Coltan's arm. "Your blood pressure is very low. Any vertigo?"

"Only when I sit up. How's the fever?"

"Low-grade. Are you still having trouble seeing?"

"It's better tonight."

"What about the episodes of paralysis?"

"Fewer."

"You 'ad one earlier."

"Momentarily. How'd you know?"

One corner of his mouth lifted in a wry smile. "You made me spill my tea."

Coltan had forgotten their link. "Sorry." After Ian replied with only a half-shrug, Coltan became serious. "Any idea how or why we're having this connection?"

"No."

"Who else knows about it?"

"Only the doctors. Doctor Macky is especially interested in it. She's seen it before. I confide in her."

"Has it gotten worse?"

"No." After a few moments of reflection, Ian added, "Actually, it's been less intense the last couple of years—the physical pain, anyway. The other stuff—the emotional muck—I don't know if it's you or me."

"Maybe it's both of us."

Ian gathered his instruments. "I have to check on Mr. Poole, now." He adopted an American Western drawl that made Coltan chuckle, "Ya'll get some shuteye, partner."

ISABELLE AWOKE SUDDENLY from a deep sleep. She rolled over on her back and stared at the canvas ceiling of the two-room tent she shared with Unkaduffy, mulled over what had caused her to awaken. It was something about Coltan, a thought of his, or perhaps a feeling, that he had inadvertently sent to her consciousness.

An image of wolves came to mind, a pack of wolves ruled by a female wolf. She was the only female in the pack of five, and there was one, particular, male wolf who stayed at her side. This companion was not her mate, although she wished he were, but a loyal and trusted friend she loved with all her heart. He was brave, full of humor and loved her with equal fervor. Of the remaining three males, one—the oldest one—seemed to be a soldier; the second was very young, gentle in his ways, and wished to be her mate. The third wolf was powerfully built, quietly courageous, and possessed spiritual wisdom. This third wolf watched over her and her companion, and he loved them both with a love beyond understanding.

As the image faded, she felt a strong impulse to go to Coltan's side.

She parted the curtain that separated her space from Unkaduffy's. He was sitting up on his mat, reading his Bible. He did not notice she had awakened and was watching him. She cleared her throat and asked softly, "Unkaduffy?"

He looked at her and smiled. "You're up early, Princess!"

"I gotta go see Kotin."

"Right now?"

"Uh-huh."

"It's too early. He's still sleeping. We'll see him later."

"No, Unka. He wants me to see 'im now. Okay if I go?"

Guffy set the Bible open upon his lap, gave her his full attention. "What do you mean, he wants to see you now? How do you know that?"

"He thought it to me."

"Thought it to you?"

"Uh-huh. Can't exp—puh... puh... pain it. Can I go?"

Guffy regarded her for a long moment, appreciated the earnestness of her expression, the sincerity in her voice. "Okay. But if he's asleep, don't wake him."

"Thanks, Unka!"

She arrived in her flannel nightgown and robe, sat down in the vacant chair at the right side of the bed. No one had seen her enter, and Natalie was sound asleep in the next bed. The room was almost dark except for a very dim light on the wall behind the head of Coltan's bed. Coltan appeared to be asleep. She gingerly stroked his hand, silently awaited his response.

He opened his eyes slowly, heavily, gazed at her and smiled. His voice came very softly and with much effort. "Hey, Isa."

"Aw you bettew?"

"Yeah."

"Did you dweam about da wolfs?"

Surprised and curious, he answered, "Yeah."

"Dat's okay. Day nice wolfs."

"Are we the wolfs?"

"I don't know." She leaned her face close to his and whispered confidentially, "I can see in da dawk. Can you?"

"Yeah. I guess it's a side effect of the virus, huh?"

She shrugged. The ability to see in the dark was a very cool thing, but she had kept it to herself knowing it was not a normal ability. If people knew about it, they might be afraid of her, think she still had the dog virus or the mord virus. She knew Coltan felt the same and would keep the secret.

"I want to thank you for saving my life," Coltan whispered.

"God saved you. Deezus th-smile... happy when he tink of you, Kotin."

"The same for you, I'm sure."

She grinned. "Yeah."

"How long did it take you to get well?"

"Don't know. Ask Unkaduffy. He knows. Maybe Unkabowis, too."

"Okay."

"Don't be cawood, Kotin. You be walkin' again. Ahms get stwongoo. You be good as new." She paused then with a thought. "Maybe da wolfs is angels. Could be, huh?"

"Uh-huh."

"Yeah... Angels."

CHAPTER 7

Mitchell, Glenda and Roger watched the satellite feed on the screen. A crowd had gathered at a park in Bonito Valle to listen to a tall, sturdily built UEF general deliver a speech. The three at Alpha Base could not hear the words, but it was apparent the general had enraptured the crowd. They thrust their fists into the air and pumped their arms fiercely.

James had received Mitchell's call to come view the unfolding events on their monitors. He joined Mitchell and his team and viewed the scene over their shoulders. The crowd and the mesmerizing general at the podium impressed him as an impending threat to all who had fled from the new slave masters. The sight of it caused the pit of his stomach to wrench in that way it always did when something bad was on the horizon.

"Who is this guy?" he asked.

"We don't know yet," Glenda answered.

"He flew in this morning on Air Force One," Mitchell said.

"This ain't the VP," James remarked worriedly. "I wonder where he came from? Do any of you recognize him?"

There came scattered *no's* in reply.

The general spewed another diatribe of what the Alpha crew assumed was unifying rhetoric. The arms and fists of the crowd punched the air again. As if on cue, the band on the stage behind the general took up their instruments and began to play. As soon as they began, uniformed troops marched out from stage left and stage right and marched down the steps into the crowd. The crowd parted for them, their arms and fists raised, their eyes intent, their twisted mouths shouting and chanting in support.

"I think we're in deep ca-ca." Roger almost moaned the words.

"PLACE YOUR TONGUE BEHIND the tip of your top front teeth," Dillon instructed Isabelle. "Let me see the tip of your tongue."

Isabelle smiled so he could see the tip of her tongue in the proper position.

"Now..." Dillon said, "Say *lemon*."

"Le...mon"

Dillon grinned and laughed, "You did it!"

She laughed, too. "I made a ehw?"

"You made an *el*." He took her hands and instructed her once more, "Say *el*. Tip of the tongue behind the teeth." He demonstrated, "El...l...l."

She tried again, "El...l...l."

"Whoo-hoo!" Dillon jumped up and clapped his hands. "You did it, Isa!"

"El!" She exclaimed. "El, el, el!"

"Oh! What the el!" Dillon shouted happily.

Isabelle's eyes grew wide and she pointed to him, "Ummm! You said..."

"I said *el*," he replied, and sat down on the dirt beside her. "Keep practicing your L's, Isa. I know you can do it. You just proved it."

"El...l...la... *cucaracha*!" She joked. "I teach you Spanish, Din."

"Dil...lon."

"Dil...lon."

He patted her back. "Thank you." He saw her fishing pole dip and dip again. "Hey! You got a fish!"

She rushed over and reeled it in. She held it up by the pole, the fish still attached by the hook. "It's biggew den yoze, Din!"

He shook his head and laughed again. Speech therapy would be a continuous work in progress when it came to Isabelle. However, she did consistently reel in bigger fish than he did. "Congratulations!"

She unhooked it and carried it to the cooler. "Awl add it to da uddoo ones." After she did that, she checked his line. "You got nothin', yet."

"That's okay. I'm patient." He leaned back against a boulder and took up his sketchpad and pencils. "You go ahead and re-bait your line, and cast off." He waited while she did that, and watched her sit down afterward on the grassy rise at the edge of the river.

She sat there in her faded dungarees, pink t-shirt and a straw hat she had borrowed from one of her many teddy bears, the pole in her hands. She stared off into space, daydreaming and enjoying the warmth of the waning summer.

Dillon observed her from a distance, feeling great love for her. She loved him just as much, and he knew that. God had finally delivered the one thing he desired and needed most, someone to love him with a pure kind of love, untainted by ulterior motives. He had wanted not only someone to love him in that way, but he wanted to be able to love them in return with the same unselfish purity. Dillon figured God knew how much he and Isabelle needed each other, and God knew they would heal each other's emotional wounds.

The only insecurity he felt anymore was in regards to his health. The doctors had done all they could; what they had done was bought him more time. He knew someday the leukemia monster would return for another battle. He expected the third battle would be his last. Some day in the near or distant future, his time would be up. Dillon did not want to go. Unlike the times before, he had a reason to stay around.

Without realizing it, Isabelle had assumed the same position as when he had paused in his sketching to give his hand a rest. He gazed down at the half-finished pencil portrait and resumed his joyful work. She was his favorite subject.

Once he finished, he wrote Isabelle's full name at the bottom of the sketch, and then signed his own name and the date at the bottom right corner of the paper. It made him smile when he glanced at her and saw she was still daydreaming as she supported the fishing pole in her little brown hands. At first, he wanted to show her the sketch, but thought instead to wait until later. Right now, he was enjoying the sight of her so relaxed and happy, the way a kid should be.

TREVOR BIT INTO HIS sandwich while he relaxed under a group of pines at the top of the hill above the Alpha Base compound. He was wearing his fatigues, and his always-loaded rifle lay resting at his side next to his binoculars. As he chewed the last bite, he took up the binoculars and scanned the clear, deep blue sky. The only things flying around were birds and the occasional butterfly. He anticipated with a dull pang of dread the silver and black machines, the demons of death and destruction, would soon fill the sky. He prayed God would protect them from these demons from Hell.

He viewed the area around Alpha Base through his binoculars, watched Dillon and Isabelle relaxing under dappled sunlight at the river's edge. The scene resembled a portrait of two country kids enjoying a summer day back in the times when summers were normal and life for children was relatively safe and carefree.

It caused Trevor to recall the summers of his own youth that he spent on his uncle's small ranch in the countryside far away from the hustle, bustle and congestion of London and all the other growing English cities. How he longed to return to that green pasture embraced by gently sloping emerald hills. How he longed to taste the damp air and breathe once more the scent of hay, alfalfa and livestock. How he longed to hear Uncle Nye's gruff voice and hearty laughter, and the weight of his fat, heavy hand upon his shoulder. Those summers were the best times of Trevor's life, and Uncle Nye the savior who understood Trevor's dissatisfaction and rebellious ways. Uncle Nye taught him how to shoot and fight. Above all, he taught Trevor to respect himself and instilled in him the determination to rise above his working class limitations.

During the autumn that followed his final summer with Uncle Nye, that dreary autumn his sister Julina lay near death in hospital, Trevor began to study people. En route on the Tube to the hospital, Trevor watched his fellow passengers—the poor, the up-and-coming, and the successful—to discover what set each class apart from the others. He listened closely to their voices, their dialects, their phrasing, the breadth of their vocabularies, and from that he was able to discern their educational levels, their troubles, dreams and aspirations. He watched how they interacted, and who commanded respect. Trevor learned much.

In particular, he learned about himself, how he projected himself to the world. He realized his accent and use of slang, vernacular and the nasal tone of his voice revealed his lower class roots. As he studied how the successful carried and presented themselves, Trevor became aware of his own body language: his habitual tough swagger and how his always-slumped shoulders contradicted the swagger and revealed his subconscious insecurity. So he worked diligently to replace his self-defeating traits with self-empowering traits. After a short time, Julina commented on the change in him, and her compliment encouraged him further.

Just after his seventeenth birthday, the doctors sent Julina home to die. As Trevor tended to her at her bedside, placed a fresh cool compress on her forehead for the thousandth time, she advised him to never stop learning and to never stop believing there was still good in the world.

It was on the final night of her life, the night he read aloud to her the final chapter of Revelation (after beginning with Genesis so long ago) that she took his hands in hers and inquired again if he would accept her Lord Jesus Christ into his heart. For some reason Trevor did not understand at the time, it seemed to him she clung to life only to complete that mission to deliver him into Christ's arms. He vacillated, delayed a few moments as he gave her another necessary injection of morphine. If he accepted Christ only to set her free, she would know that and would continue to linger. He had to decide for his own good, not hers.

They briefly conversed about what he had learned from reading the Bible to her, reminisced about their childhood experiences in the Anglican Church, the beauty of the rites and the meaning of the Holy Eucharist. Trevor confessed he only attended in those days because their parents forced him to, and the taste of the sweet wine at Eucharist was his reward for his compliance. Julina had always known and, that final night, they both laughed at his confession.

She kissed his hands, confided to him he was her *"favorite brother,"* and they giggled riotously at that because he was her only brother. As their amusement faded, she fell to silence and simply gazed at him with purest love. Her love filled him—he felt it fill the core of his soul. It was then he saw the light in her eyes, what he now recognized as the unmistakable Light of Christ, powerful and penetrating even through her glassy morphine clouded haze.

That was the moment he blurted out his desire to have her Light, and the sudden conviction her Jesus was indeed the Savior of the World. That moment he rested his tearful face upon her breast in surrender, released his pain and grief. They prayed together, prayed for a long time.

Julina held him to her even after they had exhausted their prayers. She did not want to release him. One other matter demanded his commitment before she could feel at peace.

"You must run the boys' shelter for me," she said in an

uncompromising voice.

"I'm not qualified," he protested. "Can never be."

"Pray, Trevor... pray for his guidance." She lifted her head only enough to place a soft kiss on his forehead. "God will qualify you. The boys need you. More will arrive, boys not unlike the boy you once were. You must be there for them. Trust... you must trust. God has shown me." She swallowed hard, grimaced and moaned.

He pulled away, stared worriedly into her wet face. "Morphine?"

Her voice came as a restrained sob, "No." She weakly reached her arms to him, and he allowed her to again draw him into her embrace. "I've made arrangement for you to assume leadership. Sell everything here, put it to the shelter. The staff knows of it. They'll help you." She became quiet, her attention diverted by someone only she could see. After a few moments, she replied to that *someone*, "Yes... I'll tell him."

He assumed she was hallucinating. "What? Julina...?"

"A boy will arrive soon. His path is yours. A tiny, pitiful thing he is... so angry... so utterly sad he is... an instrument of God. You will cross the water together." At this, she let out an exultant sigh and sweetly demanded, "Accept this path, Trevor. You must. Tell me you will. Tell me!"

Dumbfounded, Trevor gazed at her. She was struggling to remain in his world, even as the world beyond began to summon her away from him. He found his voice and said with deep conviction, "I will. Rest assured... I promise with all that's in me. I'll do as you ask."

She smiled, gazed upon him with a deeply loving and serene glimmer in her eyes. "Stay with me a while longer, Trev."

He was still in her arms when she took her final breath.

Four weeks later, Ian arrived at the shelter, wet, shivering and hungry; a tiny thing with rageful eyes and a world-weary voice whom asked for and expected nothing but a hot meal. Trevor knew instinctively he was the boy of whom Julina spoke. In the days that followed, Trevor and Ian took their first step upon their common path. That path would lead them across the water and into a new life on foreign soil in a new and frightening world.

In present time, Trevor set the binoculars aside and reclined against a tree trunk, allowed his thoughts to wander. He recollected that fateful day on the interstate, that day the course of their lives changed. Ian had still not fully recovered from the trauma of the attack, and Trevor realized he had not fully recovered, either. He still battled his guilt over the deaths of the boys in his charge.

They had clung to each other their first week at Alpha Base, but as they settled in and assumed duties, they relied less on each other. Although Trevor considered Ian his younger brother, Ian longed for a conventional family life and the emotional security of two loving parents. It was to Ian's favor when Joe and Darla Davidson, concerned for his well-being, wholeheartedly invited him into their fold. Once they adopted Ian, Joe assumed Trevor's place as Ian's nurturing parental figure. Trevor felt a twinge of jealousy over that. Back in London, Trevor and Ian had been almost inseparable. Trevor missed their talks and playful banter. A resolve came to him then to reconnect with the freckle-face boy who had walked from the streets into his heart.

CHAPTER 8

The sun was just beginning to set behind the mountain peaks as HAZMAT-suited UEF troops concluded their search and recovery mission in the ruins of Baker Creek. A young soldier wearily settled on the clinic's broken steps. He unzipped and removed his protective head and face covering, slouched forward and wiped sweat off his tanned brow. Being inside the HAZMAT suit was like living inside an oven. He unfastened the upper half of the suit and let it spill in accordion layers down to his wrists where the attached gloves ended the journey. He removed the hot gloves a finger at a time, pulled the upper layer of the suit off completely, and draped it in a pile around his hips.

A dangerous mist of chemicals still lingered in the tiny burg. The air smelled like a mixture of ammonia and rotting flesh, and it made his nose and throat itch when he breathed it in, made his eyes sting. He didn't care. He was too hot and too exhausted to care. In the back of his mind, he hoped there was still enough poison in the air to kill him. That's how sick he was of the whole damned thing.

He watched the troops continue their work. Some laid body bags upon the cleared two-lane street in the center of town. Only a few of the bags contained intact corpses, the rest contained dismembered, torn away body parts, all charred beyond recognition. From behind him, two soldiers removed what was left of the woman's body they found in the rubble of the clinic. He shifted to his right to give them room to pass, and they said nothing to him as they carried the body bag down the broken concrete steps and into the street where they deposited it with the others.

They had not found what his superiors sent them to recover. The soldier knew this would be unacceptable to the brass, and he dreaded having to call in his report. However, the sooner he called in, the sooner he would be out of here—he hoped. He reached for his radio and positioned it in front of his mouth. After a sigh and a subsequent pursed exhalation of breath, he thumbed the *on* switch and pressed the direct key for Command.

Lieutenant Han's irritatingly tinny voice caused the soldier to wince. "This is Han."

"Sergeant Cory Jones reporting in, sir."

"What's your report, Sergeant?"

"We've scoured the entire area, sir. She's not here."

Han sounded impatient, "Come back?"

"I said she's not here. Over."

"Scour the area again! Every scrap, every building, every outhouse! You got that?"

Jones shot back with equal, but controlled, ferocity. "We've been at this for three days, sir! None of the corpses are children, and we've found only one female corpse."

"Clausberg?"

"Appears to be. She was wearing the remains of a lab coat. Her name badge was all burnt up, though, so we couldn't read it. Ferguson got a scraping for DNA, got scrapings off all the dead."

"Has he tested the scrapings for the mord virus?"

"Yes, sir. All but two tested positive."

"Was Clausberg one of the two?"

"Yes, sir."

"Who was the other one?"

"Some guy in the jail cell at the sheriff's station." Jones had found the body, and the memory of it sickened him as much as the initial discovery. It still bothered him that someone had dismembered the poor bastard and no one found the amputated limbs. It bothered him because it hinted something even more hideous was going on here, and it had nothing to do with the Resistance's plan to overthrow the UEF. Jones paused and considered quickly whether to give the details. He decided Han would demand elaboration, so he plunged ahead. "And, sir? The guy in the cell—someone surgically removed his genitals and the lower half of his arms and legs. Even more bizarre, it looks like someone had tried to keep him alive."

"What tells you that?"

"The wounds had been stitched shut. There was an intravenous hook-up. I think they might have been using him as food for the mords. There was one other thing..."

"What?"

"Someone had killed him, shot him point-blank in the head. Maybe after the mords got loose, someone finished him off as a mercy killing before they got to him. That's all I can figure."

"Did you find any disks in the clinic?"

"Everything was burnt up or melted, sir. The records are destroyed."

"Have you found any evidence of a burn pit?"

"Yes, sir. We've collected some bone fragments."

"Any remnants of clothing? Children's clothing?"

"Not in the burn pit. There was a blue nightgown under a filing cabinet in what looked to be a nursery at the clinic. We found a scrap of a page from a children's storybook. That's all."

"What about a hairbrush? We could get DNA from the hair."

"I know that, sir. We found two plastic hairbrushes—both melted. We couldn't get any hair from them. Everything was melted."

"Well, we'll get something off the nightgown. Make sure you don't leave it behind!"

"Ferguson bagged it." Jones wanted to add, *"I'm not a fucking idiot, sir!"* but wisely held his tongue.

"Have you searched the surrounding area?"

"Yes, sir. We went into the forest, the creek, scoured the area along the river. There was nothing but dead animals."

After a momentary silence, Han mumbled under his breath. Jones heard the cussword, nonetheless. Finally, Han said, "Have you picked up any transmissions from that Jesus Freak camp up there?"

"No, sir. Do you want us to head up there?" Jones heard silence in reply. He gave it a few more seconds. "Sir? Over?"

A pop came over the radio, then another pop, some static. Han finally answered. "Negative. Collect the bodies and return to C-Base. Over?"

"Copy... return to C-Base."

Cory pictured the sneer that accompanied Han's order, "*With the bodies, Jones*!"

"Copy... returns to C-base *with the bodies*."

"What's your ETA?"

Jones hid his elation at finally leaving this place, "Twenty-one-thirty. Over."

"Twenty-one-thirty. Affirmative. Over and out."

Cory Jones clicked off his radio. For a millisecond, he considered going AWOL, pictured himself surrendering to the Jesus Freak guys and begging political asylum.

He glanced up at the shadow figure that suddenly appeared before him backlit by the waning sunlight. The figure saluted and awaited orders. Jones took a moment to glance over the collection of stuffed body bags in the middle of the littered street.

His gaze slowly returned to the silhouette, "Did you find her?"

"No, sir."

He punched out a weary breath. "Load the dead for transport to Base."

BETWEEN CLASSES IN the grade school classroom at Alpha, Darla Davidson smiled warmly at Isabelle. "How old are you, Isabelle?"

Isabelle glanced at Guffy in the chair beside her before she answered. "I don't know, ma'am."

Darla cast an imploring look at Guffy. "How old is she?"

"Five, I think."

She gazed thoughtfully at the earnest black-haired child, noted her small size. The girl returned her gaze, and Darla saw the fear in her eyes. In her peripheral vision, she noticed Isabelle nervously picked at the side of her thumbnail. The little girl was unaware of it.

"I can wite my name," Isabelle offered.

"Can you write other words?"

"Don't membew. I fooget... got... yots of tings."

"Did you always have a problem pronouncing words?"

Isabelle's brow folded. She was quite aware her diction suffered when she felt nervous, and she was very nervous at this moment. Darla Davidson was tall and thin and had light hair, just like Doctor Mean at the Bad Place. Isabelle knew Mrs. Davidson was a nice lady—Joe's wife, in fact—but she had developed a slight fear of women because of the mean lady doctor. It only made matters worse as Mrs. Davidson gazed upon her, patiently awaiting her answer. Isabelle swallowed and softly replied, "Don't membew. Din hep wiff dat. Teach me ehws – *els*." She chuckled at herself. "Din th-said it take time."

Darla cast this question to Guffy, "Who's Din?"

"Dillon," Guffy answered.

"The blond boy from the hospital?"

"Yeah," Guffy said.

At the same time, Isabelle replied, "Dat's Din... yeah. He hep me. Good guy." She grinned at the thought of him. "He's my fwend."

"Dillon started school yesterday," Darla said brightly. "Did you know that?"

"Yeah. He tode me."

"Does he like school?"

Isabelle giggled, nodded her head from side to side. "Uh-uh."

Darla sat forward on her chair, "Have you ever been to school?"

"I tink so."

"Kindergarten?"

Isabelle shrugged, looked to Unkaduffy for help. All he had to offer her was a reassuring smile. Isabelle looked away, glanced at the pictures of alphabet letters on the walls. She recalled the name of each letter, vaguely recalled drawing the letters, arranging the letters to make words. She gazed at the blackboard and tried to make sense of the simple addition and subtraction exercises Darla had written there. Another fragment of memory told her she once understood the workings of numbers. At this moment, the letters and numbers, the overpowering scent of chalk and books and children overwhelmed her. In response to her building stress, she compulsively picked at the tattered hem of her third-hand dress.

Darla persisted patiently, "First grade?"

The little girl's eyes welled and her face reddened. With a pout, she whined, "Don't membew. Don't know. I ain't dumb! Jus' don't membew!"

Guffy put his arm around her. "No one says you're dumb."

Darla found her sudden emotional outburst a cause for concern. Would the child puddle up like this with every frustration or difficulty? Would she be able to handle the discipline of the classroom, the interactions with other students?

"Missus Davidson," Guffy began gently, "Isabelle really wants to go to school. She wants to learn. We all think she's capable."

"I know what dat means," Isabelle announced. "It means I can do da wook. Huh, Unka? I can do da wook. I ain't dumb. I know thum tha...panish woods, too. Wanna hear 'em?"

This surprised Darla. "You can speak Spanish?"

Isabelle nodded proudly. "Sí! Mama an' Mawio taught me. Wanna know aw my names?" She rolled it all out with a flourish and no hesitation, "*Eee-sa-behw Rrrote-za Ma-rrria Rrod-rrree-kez.* My mama was bone hehw in Amewicka. Got fambwy in *Meh-hee-co.* I'm Amewickan, too. Bone hehw."

Darla grinned. "My goodness! You can certainly pronounce your R's in Spanish!"

Isabelle wiped her tears. "Dat's what we do! We woe da ahws. Put wavy ting ovoo ens, too! Make ens sound diffent. Wanna hear? *Ahhnn-yo!*"

Darla clapped her hands together. "That's beautiful, Isa!"

Guffy laughed with delight and patted the child's shoulder.

Isabelle grinned up at him. "Tode you I was weddy."

THE GARDEN WAS IAN'S little corner of serenity in the crowded bustle of Alpha Base, the only place where he felt some control over his emotions and environment. Lately, he had been picking up on the fear and mourning, the residual psychological trauma of some of his fellow residents. It was bad enough to be a human antenna that received Coltan's signals, but the additional baggage from the others was simply too much for him to bear. On his last shift at the hospital the night before, he defensively shut down his emotions, shut them down so tightly that he zoned out completely and went about his tasks in a robotic fashion. Joe finally noticed and released Ian from his shift four hours early. However, the respite provided little relief from the bombardment of psychical energy. After tossing and turning for six hours on his cot in the Davidson's large tent, Ian gave up and headed for the garden and fresh air. He had spent ten hours outside, and he had harvested every bit of ripe produce in sight.

Carolyn's shadow fell over Ian as he stooped over a large basket of tomatoes. He was so focused on this task he did not notice her until she spoke to him.

"You weren't at school this morning. Are you okay?"

He startled slightly. "Huh? Oh... hullo."

"I missed you at school."

He lifted the basket and placed it with the others on the cart. "They're slackin' on the 'arvest. Someone's gotta do it."

"They haven't been slacking."

He spun on her, his shoulders tight, and gestured with a sweep of his hand at all the baskets of freshly picked produce. "That so, lass? Look 'ere! T'is all ripe! If I waited for them, t'would all rot!"

She crossed her arms in front of her chest. "Well, don't yell at me about it! It's not my fault!"

Ian relaxed, felt sorry for taking it out on her. "Of course it's not your fault. Sorry, lass. I can't bear to see food wasted. Been without, y'know... It's only with God's grace we've got a garden 'ere at all. If we don't tend it properly..."

"I'll mention it to Franks."

Ian bristled. "*I'll* mention it to Franks!"

Carolyn cast him an understanding smile. "Suit yourself."

"I shall."

"I'll help you cart it to the kitchen."

"*Franks* will 'elp."

"Suit yourself."

He sat down on the dirt and rested his back against the side of the cart. She joined him there, and he didn't mind. Carolyn knew him well enough to lend him some quiet when he was like this. Although he had never revealed his most unwelcome empathic ability to her, she understood he needed his space more than most people.

The sun had almost set fully behind the peaks, and the twilight cast gentle shadows upon the small valley. Ian observed the beauty of it, drank in the tranquility. Due to his upside-down schedule, the dusk was his dawn, and he thought the setting of the sun was more beautiful than it's rising; the setting offered a tender peace, the shadows a comforting blanket.

"Vesper light..." he whispered mostly to himself.

"Vesper?" she inquired softly.

"Yes... God's kiss goodnight."

"That's beautiful, Ian..."

"It makes the blue sparkle."

"The blue?"

"On the bridge. Tower Bridge."

"You must miss it."

After a moment's consideration, he said, "I like it 'ere better. It's peaceful... this garden is peaceful—not the rest of it, mind you. Only the garden... and the valley." His eyes suddenly stung with tears, and he blinked them away, could not understand the reason for his melancholy. "I love the scent of the trees. You can't smell the trees in London—too much exhaust, pollution. So much pollution. The color of it browns the vesper light. T'is sad, y'know... what we've done to God's creation. This place is different. I think he hides it from the rest of the world the same as he's hidin' us."

CHAPTER 9

A small convoy of troops from Denver arrived with troubling news. UEF spies had compromised the Denver branch of the Army of Christ, and the UEF quickly destroyed the Denver base/refuge by air assaults.

Spurred on and worried by the silence from the other AOC bases, Mitchell tried numerous times to contact bases in the Midwest, on the East Coast and in Hawaii. The only base that responded was out of North Carolina, and they were preparing for a rumored attack by UEF Forces. According to their reports, the UEF wiped out many of their bases, and the dwindling numbers of survivors were fleeing to the few AOC bases still in operation. North Carolina advised Alpha Base to expect a second wave of refugees by late summer, and to expect UEF spies among them.

James called for a prayer meeting. After the prayers, he retired to his office and taped a *Do Not Disturb* sign to his door. He did not emerge until late the following day, and his face bore the signs of his unrelenting fatigue. He spent the next few days in hospital after suffering a mild heart attack. After another week, James returned to his duties, rested and ready for the inevitable battle ahead. He told Trevor he had "reinforced his armor."

DOCTOR MACKY CHEERFULLY greeted Coltan as she rounded the bed. "Hey there, handsome!"

"Hey there, gorgeous!" he playfully answered.

"How are you feeling today?"

"Not bad."

Natalie interjected, "Not bad means he can stand up by himself now."

Macky grinned at her and then redirected her attention to Coltan. "I heard you've done a little walking."

Coltan pointed across the room. "To the toilet. Thought it was about time to release Natalie from bedpan duty."

Macky laughed and quipped to Natalie, "You lucky girl! See how he loves you!"

"He'd do it for me," Natalie said confidently.

Coltan adopted a mock expression of disgust. "Hell, no...!"

"That's it! I'm gettin' a divorce!"

The doctor put her stethoscope to her ears, set about to check Coltan's heart.

"Why do you keep checking my heart?"

"To make certain Dillon's hair-stealing monster hasn't graduated to hearts."

He chuckled. Isabelle had told him about Dillon's pretend monster that lived under his hospital bed. The monster had since become an imaginary hospital mascot.

"Shhh!" Macky listened carefully and as she listened, she inadvertently laid her fingertips upon his bare chest.

Coltan loved to flirt with Doctor Macky, and he could not pass up this opportunity. "Are you copping a feel, Doctor?"

Macky giggled, her face blushed. She glanced at Natalie. "Is he always like this?"

With a secret she would love to reveal, she replied simply, "Only since last night." She glanced with a satisfied smirk at Coltan. It was now Coltan's turn to blush.

Macky immediately thought of Ian. Around three o'clock that morning, Ian suddenly mumbled, "Oh, man... not now!" and abandoned his stocking duties. He made a beeline for the personnel bathroom and did not emerge for a good ten minutes. At first, the doctor thought he had become sick, but disregarded that diagnosis when she caught sight of the glint in his eyes and, the most obvious sign to *those in the know*, the darkened coloring and swelling of his lips. She figured poor Ian was suffering the wild hormone ride that plagued every adolescent boy. Now, with this subtle revelation from Natalie, the doctor realized empathic Ian had absorbed some of Coltan's arousal.

Still in thought, Macky mumbled, "That's what that was about..."

"What?" Coltan asked.

"Nothing." She returned to business in less than a breath. "Be quiet so I can listen." His heart sounded stronger and its rhythm was normal, a welcomed change from the previous evening.

As she sat back and grinned at him, Coltan inquired, "So? Did the monster eat my heart?"

"He must be a vegetarian." She patted his wrist. "You're well on the mend, Coltan. Our miracle. What changes have you seen in your other symptoms?"

Besides being able to see in the dark, he could now hear far distant sounds, and his sense of smell had become so acute he was able to identify individuals simply by their scent. He decided these were not symptoms, but advantageous side effects of the dog virus. Like Isabelle, he intended to keep it a secret.

As far as symptoms were concerned, he was still exhausted and his legs remained very weak. At least, the transient paralysis had ceased and his eyesight had cleared. He replied succinctly, "Just tired, and my legs are still kinda weak."

"How's your appetite?"

"Increasing." After a thought, he added something he considered important, "I'm craving meat. Guffy told me that's normal. Morris said so, too."

"They would know." She noted it in the chart and said as she wrote, "I'm prescribing extra meat rations for you—red meat." As soon as she finished writing, she scanned the latest blood test results from Morris. Coltan's blood was still low in minerals, electrolytes and nutrients, and his white cell count remained elevated. She concealed her concern, and made a mental note to compare Coltan's chart with Isabelle's before requesting another blood draw.

"What do my test results show?"

"They show you're getting better." She patted his wrist again, stood and assured him, "You're doing very well. Try not to worry, okay?"

"Okay."

Doctor Macky retrieved Isabelle's chart and brought it with Coltan's into the office. A comparison suggested he was at the same point in his recovery that Isabelle was in upon arrival at Alpha Base. The low protein count and high white cell count compared almost exactly. The most current findings in Isabelle's chart provided encouragement; everything seemed normal.

Natalie tapped on the open door and peeked in, a worried look on her face. "Can I talk to you?"

Macky had seen this expression of concern on the faces of many family members. Their concern was usually over nothing. She nodded and gestured for Natalie to enter and sit down. "What's on your mind?"

"I'd like to see his test results."

"Why?"

"You saw something. I want to know what it is."

She flipped the pages to the lab findings section and turned the folder so Natalie could read it. She expected Natalie would not understand the terminology and ratios. "Feel free to ask me any questions."

Natalie studied the findings. "His proteins, B-Vitamins and iron levels are way below normal. His white blood cell count is elevated. The whites mean he's still fighting off an infection. Why are his vitamin levels so low when he's being fed IV fluids? I know you're giving him the vitamin-enhanced formula. What's going on?"

"There's still some of the dog virus in his system. Nothing to worry about. The virus is dying. These levels are normal for his stage in the recovery process. Where did you learn how to interpret the lab results?"

"My mother. I studied her books, too."

"On your own?"

"Mostly. Is Coltan gonna recover from this?"

"Yes."

"Is he contagious?"

"Yes, but only through blood and certain bodily fluids."

"Tears?"

"No."

"Sweat?"

"No."

"Semen?"

"Right now—yes." The alarmed expression on Natalie's face worried the doctor. "Did you have sex last night?"

"Not exactly."

"Not exactly?"

"I gave him a hand job. He asked me to."

"Did you wear gloves?"

"No."

"I hope you washed your hands afterward!"

"Of course I did!"

"Was it only a hand job, or did you stimulate him—"

"No. Just a hand job." Natalie took a deep breath and said very quietly, "That's what else I'm worried about. It wasn't normal. I mean—he couldn't get enough. He came three times, like a multiple orgasm. Guys don't do that!"

"Did he ejaculate each time?"

"Only the first time. But... it seemed like his climax was way more intense by the third one. And... it was a long one. He climaxed for over a minute—wouldn't let me stop—you know. That's not normal."

This was a new one for Doctor Macky. "Right now, I have no answers for you. I have to note this in his chart. I'll write it in *medicalese* so only the medical personnel will know."

"It's not like we have a choice."

"This may be only a transient anomaly, but an anomaly nonetheless. With him being our first and only male survivor of the dog virus, we have nothing to compare it to." The doctor sat forward and reached across the desk, took Natalie's clenched fists. "This is a concern—yes—but it could simply be that he..."

"That he what?"

"Maybe it was a sudden hormonal surge, part of the process of his system rebalancing. In the meantime, Natalie, I want you to wear gloves when you relieve him. Will you promise me?"

"Yes, ma'am."

"And practice additional precautions, also."

"Ma'am...?"

"Use a condom, seal the condom inside a glove and deposit it right away in the hazardous waste bin. We don't know how long the virus is viable outside the body."

"Oh... got'cha."

"I'll present this issue to Doctor Quimby and Doctor Proust when we meet tomorrow morning. I'm glad you told me. I'm glad you were honest with me."

DOCTOR MACKY FOUND Ian studying in the break room later that night. Deeply focused on his reading, he did not notice she had entered. It was not until she bumped the coffee pot as she reset it on the burner that the noise got his attention. She glanced at the book's title at the top of the page, and was not surprised it would peak his interest.

She read aloud, "*Rare Psychiatric Disorders: Case Studies through the Ages*."

"One can never learn too much," Ian said with an uncomfortable smile. "Did you know there were children raised by dogs who grew up acting like dogs? They actually thought they were dogs!"

"Yes. There were a few documented cases. I recall a particular one in France."

"That one's here."

"What about Empathics?" When he reacted with his brow furrowed as if he had been caught guilty of a crime, Macky added, "That's what you're really looking for, isn't it?"

He relaxed a bit at the compassion in her voice, "Yes, mum." His face became grim, and he gazed down at the page. "There's only one in 'ere. He committed suicide."

She took the chair across from him, took his chin in her hand to make him look at her. "Are you considering suicide, Ian?"

"Gosh! No, mum!" He tapped his finger on the page. "It scares me, is all."

"That's a very old book. When was it written – the nineteen-thirties?"

Ian flipped to the copyright page, read the date, "Nineteen-thirty-one."

"Many conditions classified as psychiatric disorders back then are no longer regarded as such. You're not crazy. You're simply more sensitive to the emotions of certain people. You're still picking up from Coltan?"

He sighed and shook his head, surrendering. "It's gettin' worse. I'm pickin' up others."

"That often happens to Empathics during puberty. It will subside. As a matter of fact, the ones I knew on the reservation had fewer episodes as adults. It will get better, Ian."

"I feel like I'm goin' bloody barmy...!"

"If you're willing, I can prescribe a low dosage anti-anxiety med for you."

"No, mum. I'd rather not. I've 'ad substance abuse problems in the past. I was an alcoholic at the age of seven."

"Seven? My god!"

"I'd rather you not post that in my chart."

"Why did you drink?"

"'Twas the family tradition, right 'andy, y'know." It was then his cheeks reddened and his chin trembled with the recollection. "I wanted to stop the pain, stop the terrors. I thought ghosts were battering me. The doctors and my family dismissed me as either daft or, uh—what's the word—*neurotic*. No 'elp there, mind you. So I got pissed, an' I stayed pissed. Who'd notice, ay?"

"If you opt to try the medication, we can control your access to it. You'll have to come in each day for one pill. That way you won't be tempted to abuse it."

"I don't want it. Just pray for me. That's all I ask."

"Have you told Joe about this?"

"No."

"Why?"

"I like workin' 'ere. What if he fires me?"

"He would pray with you—with *us*."

"I'm not ready to tell 'im. Please... leave it be, mum."

She took his hands in hers. "In that case, Ian... Let us pray, then."

CHAPTER 10

Over the course of five more days, Coltan's health continued to improve. The disease had taken a toll on his nerve endings, muscles and connective tissues, and the triple whammy of weakness, pain and neurological misfirings necessitated a longer convalescence. Doctors Quimby, Macky and Proust put Coltan on a light physical therapy regimen that he could perform while still on bed rest. The therapy had begun to show results, and Coltan's optimism and mood heightened.

His Bible study students visited occasionally. However, Trevor, Dillon, Guffy and Isabelle stopped by daily to offer encouragement. Whenever Dillon dropped in, he brought his goofy humor with him, and he invariably left Coltan laughing. It was Dillon's visits he looked forward to the most.

On this day, Dillon arrived with little Isabelle and both had drawn get-well cards for him. Isabelle proudly presented hers first, a crayon drawing of an angel sitting on a crescent moon and her misspelled words beneath, *"Anjles ar heling you an blesing you!"*

"I tot of da angel myseff!" she told him. "Din tot of da moon. Good, huh?"

"It's beautiful," Coltan answered. "You made a beautiful card, Isa. Thank you for thinking of me and making this for me."

"I ony make 'em fo' peepo I love, an' I love you, Kotin. You a good guy!"

"I love you too, Isa!"

"Okay, okay—before you get all kissy-face," Dillon interjected, "Here's my card."

Coltan took it and stared at the drawing. It was a sketch of a hand sprinkling a shower nozzle over a stick figure. The illustration made no sense until Coltan read the verse inside the card, and the verse made him burst out in laughter. He read it a second time, this time aloud:

"Roses are red, violets are blue. You need a shower. You stink like poo!"

As Isabelle cackled heartily, Dillon snatched the card out of his hand. "Wrong one, dude. That was for Isa!" He handed it to her, and her cackle gave way to a belly laugh. He took a second card out of his jacket pocket and gave it to Coltan, "This is yours, bro!"

Dillon embellished this card with a colored pencil drawing of Jesus shooing vicious dogs away into a forest. Inside, the verse read, *"Jesus chased the dogs away. Now it's safe. Come out and play."* In his own uniquely fanciful and exquisite handwriting, Dillon added a personal note, "*Coltan, I miss our fun times, your laughter and big-brother wisdom. Someone once said laughter is the best medicine. Let's keep the chuckles going for both of us! Love ya (in a brotherly type of way, you dope), Dillon and his band of merry mercenaries.*"

"Mercenaries?" Coltan questioned.

"Yeah," Dillon replied, "Me, Isa and Guffy!"

"Wehw da ahmy of laughs!" Isabelle added. "Huh, Din?"

"Yep. We don't shoot off guns; we shoot off our *mouths*!"

Isabelle nodded and giggled, "Uh-huh... yep!" She pointed to the IV fluids bag and asked Coltan, "Does dat got medsin in it?"

"I think so."

She regarded it thoughtfully. "Wish we could put ouwa jokes in dewh. Dat way you'd have 'em all da time!"

Coltan tapped his temple. "I have them here in my memory. All I gotta do is think of you and remember all the times you made me laugh."

With a wide grin of appreciation, she bounced up and gave him an enthusiastic hug, "You keep ouwa *love*, too, Kotin!"

He gently thumped his chest, "Right here..."

Dillon rolled his eyes in an exaggerated display, "You're givin' me diabetes!"

Isabelle ignored Dillon and whispered in Coltan's ear, "Can you still see in da dawk?"

"Yeah," he whispered back.

She pulled back and gazed confidingly into his eyes, mouthed the words, "Me, too." Once more, she whispered in his ear, "Can you sum... sa... mell aw da peepo, too?"

Another whispered reply, "Yeah."

"It's seeket," she cautioned, whispering.

"Okay."

Suspicious and feeling excluded, Dillon leaned forward in his chair. "What...?"

Coltan fibbed quickly, "Kissy-face words."

Dillon chortled. "Nausea..."

Coltan shot him a serious expression. "C'mere."

Dillon stood and bent next to him. "What?"

Coltan reached out his arms and pulled Dillon to him in a hug. As he expected, Dillon dropped his faux macho defenses and returned his hug.

"Faker!" Coltan amusedly told him.

From the doorway, a familiar British accent called to them, "Lovely to see some smiles today!"

Dillon pulled away from Coltan, embarrassed to be caught hugging Coltan. It crossed his mind that he feared Trevor would get the wrong idea. He quickly recaptured his composure and greeted Trevor welcomingly. "We're spreading cheer."

"Dat's ouwa job!" Isabelle added.

"I'd say that's an honorable profession!" Trevor claimed the one remaining chair and planted it next to Isabelle's. He leaned over to Coltan and heartily patted his arm. "You've some color in your cheeks, lad."

"They got me laughing."

"Right good medicine, that is!" With hardly a breath, he lightly punched Dillon's arm and said to him, "They should hire you on as our official Court Jester."

Isabelle piped up, "Jestoo sum-mells like poo!"

With a confused expression in his eyes, Trevor glanced at each in turn, "What?"

Isabelle gave him Dillon's card for her, "Weed dat. Din made it fo' me."

Trevor read it and laughed.

Dillon feigned umbrage, "Hey... I was totally serious! That was private!" He gave the girl a stern look of mock consternation, "How dare you share that with everyone! ...*Stinky*!"

Isabelle doubled over with giggles, which caused them all to laugh with her.

"Just for that," he warned her, "I'm gonna give you my pie at desert!"

She pointed at him and laughed harder.

Dillon inquired of Trevor, "Is there any pie left?"

"Only if you hurry."

Isabelle shot up, "Let's get it befow it's gone, Din! Day wan out last time!" She rounded the bed and tugged on his arm, "C'mon, Din!"

He stood and glanced apologetically at Coltan. "Shows where you rate with her, dude."

Coltan replied knowingly, "That's kids for ya—the belly first!"

"If day got extwa, we'll save one fo' you, Kotin."

Trevor interjected, "Ian already saw to it, lass. You go get yours."

With their absence, the room became blissfully quiet. Coltan and Trevor took a few moments to relax and enjoy the peace. Finally,

Trevor said, "They make a perfect match."

Coltan chuckled, agreeing. "Yeah..."

"It's good to see Dillon happy. It's good to see you happy. You feel much better, yes?"

"They said I might get out of here in a few days. They want to make sure I'm clear of the virus, first. As far as the walking goes, they're gonna loan me a wheelchair until I'm on my feet again." He suddenly felt chilled, and he pulled the covers up and sunk against the pillow. "Say... how'd Nat do in your class today?"

Trevor smiled, "She threw me to the mat four times. No one else has ever done that."

Coltan laughed softly. "She's a pistol!"

"I know you don't want this for her, but she'd make one hell of a soldier."

Coltan did not want to encourage that conversation. Instead, he focused sharply on Trevor as he sat there in his fatigues with that *I shouldn't have said that* look on his face. Trevor always dressed in fatigues although he was not really a member of the military force at Alpha.

"Were you in the British Army?" Coltan asked him.

"No, sir." Trevor almost laughed.

"Why do you always wear fatigues around here?"

"They're comfortable."

"Where'd you get your firearms skills and your fighting skills?"

Trevor laughed full out this time. "The firearms I learned from me uncle, the fighting I learned on the streets. You could say I was quite the ruffian in my boyhood days."

"Did you drink and stuff? Drugs?"

"I did everything! I quit it all when someone knocked the chip off my shoulder."

"Who was that?"

"My father."

Coltan laughed. "He must have been a great dad."

"When he was sober."

"How'd you become a Christian?"

"My sister Julina." He suddenly became very serious. "We 'ad many a discussion at her bedside."

"Her bedside?"

"She died of leukemia. I was with her when she died."

"That explains you and Dillon."

Trevor considered Coltan's observation. He did not fully agree. However, he never completely understood his affinity for Dillon, and he chalked it up to his former role as *rescuer of lost children*. After all, Dillon *was* lost, and Trevor could never resist a child in need of help.

Coltan persisted, "That's it, isn't it? Dillon's leukemia?"

Trevor sighed, "Dillon was a mess, a god awful bloody mess."

"So, it was more than that."

"He was like too many of the children I sheltered." He met Coltan's eyes then with a somber gaze. "I don't know what happened to the ones I left behind there. I suppose the sickness got 'em. I suppose the staff... they probably died of it too. I suppose the house is gone by now. The authorities probably torched it—I saw it on the telly here—they torched many of the buildings. They thought the buildings were full of contagion. I suppose the only thing left of that house is Ian's garden."

"Yeah? Ian had a garden there?"

"He took it over when he came to live there. It was a small garden at first, worked by the children and us staff. We didn't know what we were doing. The vegetables were puny, but good enough for meals. Once Ian got a look at it, got a look at how we tended it—or *mis*tended it—he took it upon himself to teach us how to do it properly. I tell ya, lad... that summer's harvest not only fed us, it raised a good deal of quid for our program. That garden made us self-sufficient, and it became a model for other similar programs. That's what we were doin' here in the States when the plague hit." Trevor managed a smile at the memory of their success, how the word had reached across the ocean and an American shelter invited them to come and teach them their fundraising methods that also provided their once despondent protégés social skills necessary for future gainful employment. "We were visitin'a shelter for runaways here in the States." He paused for a few moments, relished the memories of better days. "It was all Ian, y'know. Ian was the force behind it. God bless 'im..."

"How'd Ian end up there?"

"He came from a very violent home. One day he'd had enough, took to the streets. After a month of pummeling by every tough around, after losing his coat and his shoes, after starving and then after stealing in order to survive, he found his way to us. I'll never forget it. He was drenched from the rain, barefooted, filthy and bruised from head to toe. He told us all he wanted was a meal and some dry clothing. He barely spoke the words before he fainted dead away from illness and exhaustion. He slept for two days. In the meantime, we checked the missing children's registry. He was not listed. No one was looking for him. We found that incredibly sad. It took weeks for him to fully trust us, months to release his anger and his hurt. He was a tough little scrapper, quick with his fists and even quicker with his potty mouth. Oi! The language! We worked with him—all of us—even the other boys. One of them told us he had nightmares every night, fought off someone in his sleep. There was something strange about that."

Entranced by the story, Coltan prodded him, "What? What was strange about it?"

"Ian sometimes spoke French in those dreams. Cried out, fought for his life, begged for his life in fluent French. Yet, in his waking hours, Ian insisted he did not understand or speak a word of French.

It was all very strange."

It was not strange to Coltan. "Was there anyone there who could translate?"

"No. Our house matron, she understood some French. Yet, she could not make sense of Ian's ramblings when she listened in one night. She said it was not European French, but some other dialect, perhaps Creole, or something of that nature. Needless to say, we never solved the mystery." Trevor paused, thought more about Ian. "Over time, Ian had fewer nightmares and he began to interact more with the staff and the other children. He was such a little thing, only ten years old, yet he had the way of an old man about him, as if he had lived many lifetimes in his few years on this earth. I've never known anyone like him."

Coltan thought about how far Ian had come since his arrival at Alpha Base. He recalled the first time he met Ian was at the hospital. The boy Coltan knew was not the same boy in England Trevor described. "You must be proud of him."

"Very much so."

"Are you the one who brought him to Christ?"

"It was a group effort."

"How'd you end up working there?"

"Julina was the one who established the program and raised the funds for the house. After she died, I worked there to fill the void. I got so involved, so caught up in the needs of the children, I never left."

"It sounds like you were doing God's work."

"And then God brought us here, across the big water." Despite the time that had passed since Julina's final moments, Trevor still marveled at the accuracy of her prediction. He again fell into a brief silence, reflected on the chain of circumstances that landed him and Ian at Alpha Base.

"Did you leave family behind?"

"No. My parents died on the Tube; that terrorist bombing years ago."

"I saw that on TV."

"They were on their way to the hospital to see Julina."

"I'm sorry."

"My uncle Nye spilled over from heart disease." He snapped his fingers, "Like that. Gone in an instant. A good way to go, I think." Trevor then smiled serenely.

"Well..." Coltan said, "You got us, Trev."

"That I do." He roughly patted Coltan's arm, "You're a blessing to me, chum."

"Ditto."

"It's funny, you know..."

"What?"

"I sometimes consider us all—you, me, Ian, Dillon... We sprouted from tainted soil, and we've spent out lives fighting to overcome that soil. Yet, God has preserved us. Why?"

"Because us weak little seedlings have the determination—and the good sense—to lift our eyes skyward and seek his mercy. Like Ian with his garden, God knows what we need to make us strong, and he knows when it's time for the harvest." Coltan grinned with the idea, turned over on his side, and regarded Trevor with certainty. "Right now, he's tending the soil."

CHAPTER 11

COMES A BITTER CROP

The exhausted stragglers from the wrecked Army of Christ Montana Moses Base finally crossed the threshold into Alpha Base territory. Led by Sergeant Sam Vasson, who the troops affectionately called "The Bulldog," they had managed to salvage most of their jeeps and trucks during the long journey through the mountains. The same could not be said for the many soldiers who died en-route from injuries and chemically induced respiratory diseases suffered during the UEF air bombardment of the Montana Moses Base.

Once they cleared the Hot Zone and into the mountains where they initially felt safe, skirmishes with UEF scouts and overly zealous Patriot factions claimed more lives. Vasson did not begrudge the Patriots; he understood their distrust of any groups in uniform and, if it had been him in their position with only a limited knowledge of who their enemy was, he would have taken up his arms too. Once he was able to establish the identity of the Army of Christ troops to the Patriot factions, he received their trust, apology and support. The once warring sides came together to bury their dead and exchange news from the outside world. By the time the Montana Moses convoy reached the western side of the Bitterroot Range into Idaho, about twenty of the Patriot fighters, both men and women, had joined them. They spent the winter near the Idaho-Oregon border, his troops sprinkled in Patriot-dominated safe houses and secret camps hidden in the mountainous terrain. Vasson's troops had become low on rations and anticipated food would be an ongoing issue. However, that concern dissipated when their hosts opened their stores of harvested vegetables and preserved game meat. Far from the populated areas, the game was healthy and plentiful, free of the mysterious viral strain that had plagued the domestic pets and wildlife in the cities, suburbs and outlying small towns. The rugged mountain population, a loose community of fiercely independent One-World Order resistors, had long prepared for the reality that was now upon them. Without these secretive yet benevolent souls, the Montana Moses troops would have been *ess-oh-ell.*

Vasson led his troops onward in the springtime. He attempted to contact Alpha Base many times along the way and had no luck. The sergeant blamed it on the mountainous terrain and the fact that their radios, and all of their black market equipment, were the products of obsolete technology. By the time they reached the Oregon/California border, the batteries in their army surplus radios had become unreliable. Without radio contact to give him assurance, he began to fear the Alpha Base refuge no longer existed. Sam Vasson kept his worry to himself, although the rumors began to spread among the troops.

In the lingering heat of the afternoon sun, he halted the convoy at the edge of the northern trail that led to Alpha Base. He sat there in the lead vehicle, the engine sputtering softly, and gazed through the dusty windshield at the small and thickly forested valley below.

"What do you want to do?" The voice belonged to Raul Santiago, a survivor from the Denver AOC Base who joined up with Vasson's team after the UEF wiped out that base. Santiago was a tall, muscular ex-Marine who had spent his post-military years with the Border Patrol down in south Texas. Although Santiago was of Mexican descent, he had no patience or sympathy for the *"drug scum wetback criminals"* who played revolving door games at the border. He had even less respect for Blacks, Middle Easterners and all persons of Asian descent. Sergeant Vasson didn't like the guy, but he admired Santiago's strength and bravery. Of all the troops, Santiago was only one of seven who had any real battlefield experience, and it showed in his performance and consistency. Impatiently, Santiago fidgeted in the passenger seat, tagged on another question, "If it turns out anybody's there, how do we know if they're friendlies?"

"The code." Vasson shut off the ignition and extracted the key. "We're gonna follow procedure." He exited the vehicle.

Only two people in Vasson's convoy knew the code. One was Vasson; the other was unidentified for his or her own safety. The troops understood the reasoning behind the rule. When they saw Vasson walk away from the jeep, they knew he was going to use The Code.

Sergeant Sam Vasson found a good spot at a clump of charred fallen pines beyond his troops' hearing range. He tried his radio again, got a signal and intoned the secret code-phrase, "Jackrabbit bonny belle held a tea and thee." He repeated the phrase three times, as was the procedure.

He was delighted to hear James' familiar deep voice and inner-city enunciation. "We see you. Stand down. What's your penbro?"

Vasson knew "penbro" was a code that requested a password or special phrase that would identify the newcomers' AOC Base of origin. He gave James the code-phrase that identified his Base as Montana Moses and his name as Vasson, "Watch the snake and don't vacillate."

James came back, "Mother-in-law."

Vasson replied to the code with the code, "Naomi."

James tried to trick him, just in case. "Press."

Vasson rose to the challenge, "Grind. We don't press wheat, James. We grind it. Now, are you gonna let us in, or what?"

There was relief and humor in James' voice. "Welcome to Alpha."

DILLON USED A LARGE cardboard box as an old-fashioned television set from which to "broadcast" his latest entertainment for Coltan. Using a black and white photograph of a television advertisement from a 1956 copy of *Better Homes and Gardens Magazine* as a guide, Isabelle had drawn knobs on the box's face with a brown marking pen, and Dillon outlined a frame for the television screen and below that the words, *In Living Color, No Fooling!* Below that, Dillon copied the *RCA* letters verbatim to the original. On top of the box, he fastened two long wires with little aluminum foil balls at the tip of each as an antenna. He set the huge box on the floor across from Coltan's bed, and he and Isabelle parted the curtain on the interior of the box's "screen" and began the show.

In an exaggerated British accent, Dillon announced, "Welcome to *Uncle Trevor's Oh-Bloody-Ell Tour,* with your host, Trevor Rolly-Polly. That's me! Brought to you proudly by the esteemed BBC—the Bloody, Balmy Constituency of Language Manglers."

Coltan laughed, not because of Dillon's performance, but because Trevor had parked himself behind them in the doorway and was observing the two with amused curiosity.

Isabelle then announced, "I'm *Eesabew Rrroteza Marrria Rrrodrreeekez*, twanspwant fwum *Goo-aw-doo-wa-ha-wa!*" She had practiced that line for days to get it perfect.

"When are you gonna swallow them marbles, lass?" Dillon asked her, still in character.

"I'm waiting fo' dem to lose dehr favoo, like bubba-gum!"

"Are you gonna park 'em on your bedpost overnight?"

"No, silly! Dem mawboes is wound. Wound stuff'll just rrrr-owall off!" She then became very serious and regarded *Uncle Trevor* the way a child would in request of a bedtime story, "Say, Uncoo Twev... tew me again 'bout aw da twees in da English fowest."

"Oh!" Dillon exclaimed, "Such as the terra trees?"

"Uh-huh! An' da seck-wet twees..."

"And the lab-ra trees...?

"An' da sem-ma twees... Doze aw da dead ones, ain't day?"

Coltan stifled his giggling, while Trevor covered his mouth to keep from laughing aloud.

"Mustn't forget the dig-na trees," Dillon stated, "They keep the forest in tip-top shape, by Jove."

"How do day do dat?"

"They spread around lots of bullcrap to keep the other trees happy and well fed."

"Why?"

"Fill 'em with bullcrap and you'll keep 'em right jolly! All the dig-na trees in all the other forests of the world do it, too."

"Why?"

"Now... 'ow would I bloody know? All I know is that's what they do to keep the forest they way they bloody want it!"

Isabelle spit a marble out her mouth. It bounced and rolled under Coltan's bed.

"By Jove, lass!" Dillon exclaimed, "You're losing your marbles!"

"It lost its buddy favoo!" The little girl shot back in an exasperated tone.

"This calls for a ditty of celebration!"

"It ain't dooty! I washed it wiff my s'pit!"

"Not *dooty*, you daft wench... *ditty*!"

"Dooty, ditty...."

"We shall sing an Ode to the Marble."

"Wasn't dat on da top ten?"

"I do believe that was the *bottom* ten!" After Coltan's laughter softened, Dillon continued, "What the 'ell, lass... let's give it our best voice!"

At this point, they began to sing a silly composition about

marbles, a little demented masterpiece Dillon had written just for this show. By the time they got through the second verse, some of the hospital personnel had joined Trevor at the door. Their laughter only fueled Dillon's and Isabelle's enthusiasm. At the end of the song, their audience responded to their efforts with applause.

"I tink day liked it!" Isabelle said.

"They clapped because it's finally over, you dolt! Now, climb through and take your bow."

Isabelle scrambled through the television "screen" and faced her audience in the doorway. She grinned, curtseyed, and took her bow. This show biz stuff was something she could get used to.

CORY JONES OBSERVED the shackled victims of the mord virus from a distance. There were eight men in the group, six teenage boys, two teenage girls, two pre-teen boys, one tiny five or six year old girl, and five women. The group had been living in a gated estate at the posh west side of Bonito Valle, and had slowly been starving to death. Some of them were naked. With the exception of the youngest boy who was fully dressed, the ones who still wore clothing were only clothed from the waist up. Their emaciated bodies and extended bellies bore witness to their months of starvation. They were filthy; their lower portions encrusted with feces and blackened dried blood. The men had beards, and their greasy hair had grown long. Some of the women had patches of hair missing, and the bare spots were red and oozing puss. Every one of these tragic prisoners smelled as if they had swum in the sewer. Even from a distance, the stench was overwhelming.

Some of the adults had awakened into a hazy stupor, but were conscious enough to understand they were captured and in restraints. They struggled and tugged against the shackles. They hissed and growled at the uniformed soldiers who gaped at them with a combination of terror, rapt disgust and shallow pity.

Sergeant Cory Jones knew from experience the restraints were stronger than the restrained. Still, he took a couple steps back and casually readied his weapon, just in case.

One of the soldiers with the firing squad said with small concern, "The baby's awake."

Cory looked at the little girl. She was too small for them to shackle to the wall with the others, so someone had hogtied her and leashed her to one of the stalls. She gazed at each soldier in turn, whimpered, cried and growled.

"The dart shoulda killed her," another soldier stated.

"Damn..." the first one groaned.

The child then hissed and shrieked. The sound of it made their blood run cold.

In the next second she wailed, "Bwad...wee! Come! Hep me! *Mama...!*"

When UEF forces using heat-seeking technology discovered the group, they stormed the mansion and quickly subdued the infected with tranquilizer darts. The order to keep the monsters alive was a new one for the troops; in the past, the rule was to execute them on sight. However, the UEF discovered some of the infected, especially the young ones, had managed to retain their ability to speak and reason. This stirred the curiosity of the top brass, and they adopted the new practice of observance and interrogation before execution.

Only one in this group, a nine year-old boy, had been able to speak and form cohesive sentences. His speech at first came haltingly, as if he was trying to remember how to speak. His interrogators bribed him with a meal of freshly executed deserter, and baited him with excised portions of the unfortunate's flesh as a reward for each answered question. The child, between growls and hisses, ravenously devoured the food and demanded more. Once the boy understood the rules of the Answers for Food game, he answered all their questions but provided no useful information.

The only thing they learned was that the boy was the son of the owner of the house, some local hotshot who had struck gold with real estate and wise investments. The boy and his family, which included in-laws, aunts, uncles and cousins, had been asleep when a mob of infected overpowered the security guards at the gate and broke into the house. The adults and four oldest boys in the extended family managed to take up arms and kill most of the monsters, but not before getting bitten or splattered with the virus-laden blood. In the confusion, some of their attackers had invaded the second floor and found the children. As the children screamed and fought, the armed adults intervened and finished off the assailants. Unfortunately, all of the children suffered bites, and the adults that avoided the mordants' teeth had lacerations from the monsters that immediately delivered the virus into their systems. The boy estimated it took less than four days for all of them to *turn*, and they survived on the corpse of their only dead (by friendly fire) relative until that meat became too rotten to ingest.

"We found your kitchen and storage facility chock full of regular food," the soldier in charge told him. "Why didn't you eat that?"

The boy made a face of disgust. "No good!"

"The little girl with you—is she a relation?"

"My sister. Did you kill her?"

"Can she talk like you? Can she talk at all?"

"She tries." The sedation had finally worn off enough that he became more aware of his surroundings and his physical sensations. His arms and legs were sore from the bindings. He fidgeted, tried to wriggle loose the ropes that secured his legs and upper torso to the chair. The restriction angered him. "Lemme go. I ain't gonna do nothin'."

"What's your name?"

He stared at the uniformed man for a long time. The man was big, fat and full of juice. The boy drank in his scent, and his appetite returned anew. Of all the men who surrounded him, this fat one smelled most desirable. The boy licked his lips, and he could not control the brown drool that streamed down his chin or the soft growl of anticipation that rolled in his throat.

The big man stepped back casually, but his eyes revealed his fear at the child's suddenly predatory exhibition. "You're still hungry."

He tried to hide it. "No..."

"They always drool like that when..." He then stepped forward, ducked his chin and peered into the boy's eyes. "You can't control it."

"Yes I can!" Desperation...

At that moment, a young soldier entered the room and saluted, stood at attention. The fat man returned the salute. "What is it, soldier?"

"General Tadesco's mouthpiece said they've abandoned the program, sir. He said to keep looking for the allegedly cured Baker Creek girl. That's the only one he wants from now on."

He saluted the young man. "Dismissed."

After the soldier left, the officer turned to one of his fellow officers, one of lower rank. "Is Chadislaw in place?"

This man replied quickly, "Yes, sir."

"Did Santiago get there?"

"No word yet."

He returned his attention to the boy and gazed at him for a long moment. The child both frightened and fascinated him. He debated whether to keep this captive alive for his own personal study. After weighing the pros and cons, he decided it was not worth the bother or risk.

Once they completed their very unproductive interrogation of the boy, the UEF C-Base bigwigs ordered the boy sedated. They dragged him into the holding enclosure, what was formerly a barn, and shackled him to the wall with his diseased family.

Now the distasteful job of execution was in the hands of Sergeant Cory Jones and a small squad of his best marksmen.

The boy awakened with a start at his little sister's voice, her pitiful wail to him, "Bwad...wee! Come! Hep me! *Mama...!*" Upon discovering his captors had shackled him with the others, he immediately realized his situation. Over the noise of the captive men's growls and the tiny girl's screeching, he called plaintively to Sergeant Jones, "Haven't we suffered enough? We won't hurt you! I can control them! All we want is food!"

"Shut-up!" Jones called back.

"We didn't ask for this!"

Nobody asked for this, Jones told himself.

The boy persisted, "There's got to be a cure! You got the cure!"

Cory turned to the firing squad, "Present arms!" They brought their rifles up. "Aim!"

The boy broke into tears, sobbed out the words, "I'm only nine! How can you kill a kid? I could be your son or your brother! *Please...!*"

Cory noticed tears forming in the eyes of one of the shooters, a pimply sixteen-year-old kid. He gritted his teeth and hissed at him under his breath, "Don't you dare tear up on me, boy!" The young soldier swallowed and nodded, kept his wet eyes pinned through the scope. Satisfied, Cory Jones yelled the order, and his voice cracked with remorse, "Fire!"

The group went down fast with the hail of bullets. They hung limply by their shackled wrists, their bodies twisted in bizarre positions. The sergeant ordered a second round of gunfire, just to make certain none survived. Once it was clear their captives were dead, Cory dismissed the firing squad and waited alone for the HAZMAT team to collect the bodies.

As he stood there looking out onto the C-Base complex from the barn's wide-open doorway, he felt strongly someone watched him from behind. Cory knew there was no one else in the barn—only the dead. Yet, the feeling grew stronger, enough to send a chill through him. He tried to ignore it, but finally couldn't stand it.

As soon as he turned, his eyes locked onto the open staring eyes of the boy. When the boy died, his head had come to rest sideways upon the crook of his twisted-up shoulder and vertically restrained right arm. Frozen in this position with his eyes open, he gazed not into eternity, but into the tortured soul of his executioner. The pale blue eyes burned into Cory, compelling him to make peace with the child. He sucked in a breath and approached the dead nine-year-old. It seemed to him the boy's eyes followed his movement as he neared. He boldly stopped in front of the boy, less than six inches between them. The sad eyes regarded him despairingly, pleadingly. Something in the child's stagnant gaze suggested his consciousness still lingered there, as if the boy had one more thing to say.

Sergeant Cory Jones had seen a lot of horrible things since this mord mess broke, but this encounter unnerved him to his core.

Yeah.... Cory thought to the kid, *You were someone's son, someone's brother. You didn't deserve this, and neither did I.*

His spoken words came in a tender whisper. "I'm sorry, kid." Using two fingers, he lowered the boy's eyelids. "It's over; rest in peace."

CHAPTER 12

Isabelle had no idea what time it was, but she could tell by the dimmed overhead lights it had to be very early in the morning. She rested there on her back on her thin little mattress for a long time, entranced by the shadows the light created on the ceiling of the tent. One of the shadows resembled an angel with very large wings. Isabelle contemplated it, concluded it was a sign from Deezus to reassure her she was still safe.

Yet, she didn't feel safe. She didn't feel safe because the kids at school had teased her the day before because word had leaked she had once been a mord. One of the boys, Randy Davidson, asked her if she still wanted to eat people. Curious to hear her answer, the students within earshot of Randy's question gathered around her and demanded she tell the truth. Isabelle felt trapped in the midst of them, humiliated by their taunts and laughter. She responded to their threat by instinct, the residual feral instinct left behind in her brain by the dog virus; she bared her teeth and growled at them. In the next moment, she wet her pants.

Laughing at her and at the same time frightened of her, they all backed away. They pulled back far enough to get a glimpse of the spreading puddle of urine at her feet.

"She needs a diaper!" one of them giggled.

"Baby mord!" another taunted.

This prompted a chorus of "*Baby mord, baby mord*," from the rest of them.

Isabelle began to cry. Then she became angry. She bared her teeth and growled, stepped forward and pushed the closest one, Randy, pushed him so hard she sent him off his feet. The second he hit the floor, she pounced on him and slammed her fists into his face and chest, growling and snarling.

By the time her teacher Darla intervened, Isabelle had bloodied Randy's nose and earned the distrust of the other children. Darla called an end to recess and ordered the students into the classroom. She segregated tearful Isabelle to a desk at the rear of the room and summoned Guffy on her radio.

Dillon had heard the commotion, heard Isabelle's sobs from his desk at the corner next to the door of the adjoining classroom. He leaned sideways and cracked the door open enough to get a look at her. She was face down on the desk, sobbing into her arms, inconsolable. He heard Darla reprimand Randy, and then she spoke to the entire class about the dangers of rumors and the value of compassion. During the teacher's little speech, Guffy quietly entered the classroom and took the empty desk next to Isabelle, put his arm around her and whispered to her. At that point, the bell rang softly that dismissed the morning's classes.

Dillon tried to console her while Guffy held her in his arms as Darla Davidson explained what had happened. She ordered her son Randy to apologize to the little girl, only to get a smart-mouthed retort of, "She don't belong here!" Darla then did something no child would ever expect from her: she hauled off and slapped the boy hard enough to redden the side of his face. As Randy gaped at her in amazement, she told him, "Perhaps your father can talk some sense into you!" With that, she sent him out of the classroom to wait for her in the corridor.

Isabelle cried even harder into Unkaduffy's shoulder. "None of 'em like me!"

"That's not true," Guffy said.

"Day scawood me an' I peed."

"That's okay, honey."

Darla glanced at Dillon. "Would you take Isa out into the corridor and wait for us?"

Guffy regarded her sharply. "You got somethin' to say, you say it in front of her!"

"Please..." Darla said softly to Guffy, "It'd be better if we discussed this alone. She can come back when we're done."

"This ain't her fault!" Guffy stated.

"No one said that." She again referred to Dillon, "Wait for us outside."

Isabelle sniffled and pulled away from Guffy's shoulder. "I can go wiff Din." She looked at Dillon and saw the sympathy in his eyes. He reached for her, and she climbed off Guffy's lap and took Dillon's outstretched hand.

"We won't be long," Guffy told her.

She waited with Dillon in the corridor. Against the wall, Randy Davidson scowled at her, blamed her.

Dillon stared down the kid. Isabelle could feel his resentment boil up. She willingly released his hand as he took his first step toward the unrepentant little punk who had hurt his *Heartagold Eensybelle*. The girl anticipated Dillon would protect her, and he did not disappoint her. He placed his hands on Randy's shoulders and gently shoved him against the wall. With a blaze in his eyes Isabelle had never seen until that moment, Dillon stated through his clenched jaws a warning to the still-scowling Randy:

"Fuck with her again, you'll answer to me!"

The heat of his gaze and the rage in his voice was enough to cause Randy to tremble. There came no wise-ass retort, only a compliant nod.

Dillon then returned to Isabelle. He squatted and looked respectfully into her face. "If they mess with you again, tell me."

"Okay, Din."

Now alone in the tiny curtained-off room in the tent she shared with Unkaduffy, Isabelle thought more about Dillon and how she had come to love him. She imagined someday she would marry him and they would have lots of blond-haired babies. Dillon would make a perfect papa, just as perfect as her beloved Unkaduffy.

Dull pangs in her belly interrupted her reverie, and she rolled over on her side and curled up. The pains had started earlier that night, but had gone away. She did not mention it to Unkaduffy because she had experienced that pain before. It was the same dull gnawing sensation that dogged her during her early days in the clinic where Doctor Mean kept her strapped to a bed. They had forced her to drink some kind of thick liquid that tasted like liver, and that did little to ease the pain. The only thing that eased it was the special diet of *peep fing* Clausberg finally ordered Unkabowis to give her on a regular basis—that was before she had come to trust Unkabowis. Then one day Unkabowis stopped coming and Unkaduffy appeared and became her friend. Gradually, the pains stopped coming and Isabelle began to feel better and stopped craving peep fing.

Tonight, she wanted it. She wanted a meal of raw meat saturated in blood. The meat didn't have to be human like peep fing, just as long as it was raw and had lots of blood in it.

Unable to resist the increasing hunger pangs, she put on her robe and peeked through the curtain at Unkaduffy at his side of their tent. His snoring indicated he was deeply asleep, and she could sneak away without his ever knowing.

On the way to the kitchen the only people she saw was Trevor and Roger. Trevor was on night watch and Roger had just gotten off work at the Surveillance station. Their soft voices drifted to her as she ducked behind Dillon's tent as they passed, and she waited patiently for them to enter the television room down the corridor and around the curve.

Once she reached the dining room, she ducked under the gate next to the serving counter and easily made her way through the dark kitchen to the industrial size refrigerator. This is where they stored the thawing meat for the next night's meal. She silently prayed the big "cold box" (as her mother called it) contained a few platters of red meat. She opened the door and saw three platters stacked. The top platter was full of venison steaks covered over with plastic wrap. She lifted the wrap and pressed her finger on the top steak. It gave under the pressure of her finger. It had thawed enough to eat. After grabbing a paper towel off the prep table, she lifted the steak into it and carefully replaced the plastic wrap over the platter.

Isabelle could hardly wait another second to eat. The paper towel began to absorb the blood of the meat even as she squatted down between the boxes across from the fridge. She didn't want the towel to absorb all the blood, so she lifted the steak in her fingers and began to eat it quickly. By the fourth mouthful, her hunger pangs stopped and she felt much better. She hurried through the rest of the raw meat, for the longer she remained there the bigger the risk of discovery. Once the meat was gone, she devoured the blood saturated paper towel as well and licked the remains of the blood off her fingers and hands.

Sated and partially in a state of rapturous ecstasy, she hid among the boxes for a few minutes while her equilibrium returned. The taste of the meat and blood lingered on her tongue and the scent of it enthralled her. Yet, the guilt of her actions caused her stomach to twist, and she felt dirty, as if she had committed a horrendous crime. She worried she had not been cured of the mord virus. She worried she would someday smell the scent of some unsuspecting resident there at Alpha, find the scent appetizing, and she would stalk them in the night and—

Deezus, don't let me!

COLTAN DID NOT NOTICE the raised crack in the ancient hardened lava floor until the wheels caught it and the chair toppled. He spilled out and rolled onto his side where he came to rest in an embarrassed *what the hell just happened* stupor.

Above the laughter of some of the teens and children on their way to the dining room, Dillon's rapid footsteps and alarmed voice rang loud and clear. "Bro! You okay?"

Coltan sat up and peered around. The ones who had laughed were still laughing, although some inquired if he was okay. None offered assistance. Only Dillon seemed truly concerned, and that angered Coltan.

Dillon knelt at his side, lifted the wheelchair off his friend, and set it upright. He then helped Coltan up and guided him into the seat. With a humorous smirk, Dillon inquired, "Who taught you how to drive?"

Coltan laughed.

"That's better!" Dillon grinned and began to push the wheelchair into the dining room. "You ain't hurt, are you?"

"Uh-uh. I never noticed that crack before."

"Morris said it's new. He said something about aquifers, and expansion and contraction, something to do with geology. Hell if I know..."

"Is this place gonna cave in on us?"

"Been here for millions of years. I doubt it." He parked Coltan at their usual table near the entranceway. "I'll get our meals for us. In the meantime, don't be doin' any wheelies!"

Coltan chuckled. "I'll restrain myself!"

Isabelle and Guffy brought their trays to the table as Dillon hurried into the line. Isabelle scooted her chair closer to Coltan. "Day got ben-sin tonight!"

"Bensin?"

Guffy translated as he settled into the chair across from Coltan,

"Venison."

"Oh."

"An' appo pie!" She offered Coltan a forkful. "Wanna taste?"

"That's okay, Isa. Dillon will bring me some."

"Eat your pie last!" Guffy reminded her.

"If day wun out, awl save you summa mine. Okay, Kotin?"

"Thanks!" He gave her his warmest smile, and she readily reciprocated. She topped her smile with a wink, and he winked back.

"Din can make wunna his eyes woll awound. You oughta make him do dat fo' you. It's funny!"

Coltan laughed softly and then asked her, "Can you do it?"

"Uh-uh. He's teachin' me." She patted his shoulder for his full attention. "I can cwoss my eyes, doh. Wanna see? Watch!" She crossed her eyes for him. After his laughter trailed off, Isa said in all sincerity, "Din says we-ooh da ennertainment committee."

"He's right about that!"

"We-ooh wookin' on anover show fo' you."

"What can top the last one?"

She crooked her head to one side in total seriousness. "Din got yots of ideyoos."

"*Lots*," Guffy corrected her. He pointed to her tray. "Eat your supper before it gets cold, honey."

She settled into her chair and daintily placed the paper napkin on her lap. "We gotta say gwace, Unka." She waited until Unkaduffy and Coltan clasped their hands and bowed their heads. "Deezus, tankoo fo' dis' food. Peeze bess us an' aw da animooze. Amen. Oh, yeah! An' peeze bess Kotin an' Unkaduffy so day get bettew. Amen."

"That was a beautiful prayer," Guffy told her.

"I wanna wait fo' Din," Isabelle said. "Kotin ain't got no food yet."

Guffy set down his fork. "*Doesn't have any* food yet."

She grinned, swung her legs under the table. "Oh, yeah..."

"I thought her diction was getting better for a while there," Coltan said.

"She backslid once she started school. We think it's the stress."

"Da kids aw mean to me."

"Why?"

"Day tink I'm a biting peepo."

"What?"

Guffy cast Coltan a strange expression that Coltan took as a signal to abandon that subject. He then told Isabelle in his most fatherly voice, "That's all done with, Isa. Now, honey... I want you to eat your supper and stop worrying about the other kids."

"I'm waitin' fo' Din!" she reminded him.

"You don't have to wait," Coltan told her.

"I saw da kids yaff at you, too, Kotin, when you tipped ovoo."

"It must have looked pretty funny," Coltan reflected, "I laughed about it, too."

"I hood a noose say she was scawood a' you 'cause you gwowa in you sweep."

Coltan had no response to that other than surprise.

Guffy tapped her hand brusquely. "Stop it!"

She shot Unkaduffy a curious gaze. "Do I gwowa in my sweep?"

"No."

"How come Kotin does?"

Guffy regarded Coltan compassionately. "I'm sorry. She doesn't know yet what's okay to say and what's not okay."

"Is anybody else afraid of me?" Coltan asked her.

She shrugged her little shoulders.

Dillon set Coltan's tray in front of him and then his own in the next spot at Coltan's other side. There, Dillon pulled out his chair and sat.

"That was quick!" Coltan said.

"There was this redhead at the front of the line, a soldier. The second she heard me mention I was gettin' an extra tray for you, she let me in line ahead of her. Maybe she's hot for you, bro."

"That won't set too well with Natalie."

Isabelle interjected over Coltan, "Maybe she hot fo' *you*, Din!"

He cackled in response. "I seriously doubt that!"

"Isa, please eat your—" Guffy tried.

She pointed to Dillon's red *Peterbilt Trucks* cap. "When you gonna take dat off?"

He tugged gingerly on the short curly golden strands at his forehead that peeked from beneath the cap. "When my hair grows back longer." His hair had still not grown long enough to cover his ears, and he was self-conscious about his ears; the kids at school used to pinch his ears because they stuck out a little. His cap was just oversized enough to tuck his ears under the side rim so no one would notice. The cap flattened the little bit of hair that had grown long enough to cover the tips of his ears.

"I like dat one bettew den yo' ode one." She took a tiny cut of the venison and chewed it thoughtfully. It was overcooked, not enough blood to make it taste like it should. While she chewed, she stared at Dillon's cap. "My mama use ta make Mawio take off his hat at da tabew. Day wouldn't let him we-ooh it at wook, eedoo."

"Where'd he work?" Coltan asked.

"Bujja-Mot." A tiny dot of venison spit out her mouth. She wiped her mouth with the back of her hand. The soldier with pretty red hair caught her eye then, and she bolted up and waved to her. "Tanks fo' Kotin an' Din!"

The young woman on her way to the soldiers' table waved back and grinned. "You're welcome!"

Isabelle pointed at each young man. "Dis one's Kotin an' dis one's Din."

"I know who Coltan is," she said.

Coltan waved. "Hi, Jill."

"Kotin's maweed, but Din's not!" Isabelle informed her.

Dillon bowed his head and covered his mouth, said under his breath, "Aw, jeez-loo-eeze!"

She pointed at Unkaduffy. "An' dis one's Unkaduffy. He ain't maweed, edoo."

Guffy stopped eating and rested his forehead in his hands. His cheeks reddened. Coltan began to giggle.

"Come sit wiff us!"

Jill could see Guffy and Dillon were embarrassed. "Are you sure it's okay?"

"Come on over," Coltan said.

She took the chair beside Guffy and across from Isabelle and her two gentlemen friends. Spying Dillon's cap, she told him, "My dad used to work for them guys."

"Really?" Dillon thought that was quite a coincidence.

"Naw. I'm just bee-essin' you." She smiled and extended her hand in greeting. "My name's Jill."

He shyly shook her hand. "Dillon." Her grip was strong and firm. Undoubtedly, she could beat him at arm wrestling. He instantly felt like a wimp in her presence.

She looked him straight in the eye and tightened her grip around his hand. It caused him to tighten his hand around hers in response. She nodded slightly to tell him he had delivered what she wanted from him. "Natalie's mentioned you."

He glanced away from her at Coltan."Uh-oh..."

She released Dillon's hand and offered hers to Guffy as she greeted him, "Unkaduffy..."

He shook her hand firmly, "Guffy."

"You came in with Morris and little Isa here."

"Yeah."

"That was some nightmare out there in Baker Creek. You got guts, fella!" Met with silence, she felt a need to explain how she knew.

"I guess you don't remember. I was on the squad that brought you in and searched your belongings. Trevor was having a fit because we forgot the kid's bear."

"Uh-uh!" Isabelle protested. "I had Teddy wiff me! We didn't foogetim."

She realized Isabelle had misinterpreted. She decided that was just as well. The kid didn't need to know Teddy was once a suspect. She told the girl, "I'm glad you remembered him."

"Unkabowis gabe me Teddy!"

"He's a good guy."

"He gabim to me when I was sick wiff da—" She stopped herself just in time.

"You were sick, sweetie?"

"Not bad sick."

That was a close one, Guffy thought. Tonight he would have a talk with little Isa about the danger of volunteering information. In the meantime, he wanted to distract her away from conversation. "Your food's getting cold," he reminded her.

As Isabelle for once stopped talking and concentrated on eating, Jill leaned over and whispered into Guffy's ear, "I know about the virus. I was there when you and Morris were explaining it. I kept my mouth shut. Don't worry."

"Thank you," Guffy said softly.

She smiled supportively and slapped her hand upon his shoulder.

"Have you seen Natalie?" Coltan asked her.

Jill laughed. "Yeah... She's in the training room throwing Trevor to the mat. I think he likes it."

That made Coltan and Dillon laugh uproariously. Guffy responded with subdued laughter, as if he feared he could not control it if he gave it free rein.

Isabelle laughed with them although she did not understand Jill's pun. However, Dillon had a unique laugh, a cross between a cackle and a rolling series of snorts with a few *hee-hees* thrown in, and it was this that amused her.

Guffy *ahem-ed* to get her attention, twirled his index finger in a circular motion, signaled her to resume eating. She obediently dug into her mashed potatoes. In the next moment, she felt someone's eyes upon her. With her fork halfway to her mouth, she paused and glanced expectantly at Unkaduffy. He was looking down at his plate, preoccupied with cutting his venison steak. Her next instinct told her the eyes in question were across the room. Puzzled, she sniffed the air, glanced out to see who was looking at her. No one was looking. She concentrated on the familiar odor of predation and tentatively traced it as coming from three or four tables away in the area the soldiers habitually gathered. The scent then weakened and mingled with the many other scents in the room. It was impossible to pinpoint the source. She sighed in frustration. A sensation of subtle fear slowly rose up her spine. A foreboding heaviness in her gut followed. That meant something bad. If she had been in bed at that moment, she would have hidden under the blankets, lest the bogyman found her.

She decided she did not want to meet the eyes; what if the eyes dug into her soul and set up house there? They would see *everything*! They would *know* everything! With a new resolve to avoid the eyes, she set her fork down gently and stared at her plate. Coltan and Dillon's laughter enveloped her. Their deep voices reminded her she could count on them for protection. Her fear subsided. After she thought it over, she wondered if she was wrong and no bogyman was looking at her. Maybe she only imagined it.

Beside her, Coltan's laughter died and he wiped the tears from his eyes. Her appetite gone, Isabelle slid her little saucer with the sliver of pie to the edge of his tray. He turned to her inquiringly.

She stated very softly, "I want you to have my pie."

THREE TABLES AWAY, in the section routinely claimed by the troops, Raul Santiago stole glances at the little girl. Of all the children he had seen here so far, she fit the description, and was the approximate age. The portly balding man with her fit the description of the assistant assigned by Clausberg to care for the mord child in Baker Creek. Although Santiago felt certain these were the two the UEF sent him to capture, he decided he would not jump to any conclusions. There was plenty of time. He would use that time wisely, make contacts, friends; maybe romance that homely freckled redhead at their table and learn what she knows. He quivered inwardly with that thought, quivered in disgust. Instead, he would give that job to one of his girls—they could easily befriend her.

Santiago dug into his baked potato and glanced over at the girl's table again while he chewed. He zeroed in on the slightly built blond boy, a handsome young thing with striking Nordic features. What did the child say his name was? Dan? Ben? Steve? Whatever his name was, he impressed Santiago as a typical teenage country bumpkin, what with the *Peterbilt* cap, thread-worn t-shirt and limp, faded jeans. Something about the boy's posture, his gestures and expressions told the soldier something else about the boy. Maybe, once he settled in to life at Alpha Base, he would strike up a casual acquaintance with him; find out if his suspicions were correct. If so, the kid would turn out to be like a hundred other kids Santiago had known: insecure, needy, starved for attention, reassurance and acceptance... intimacy... protection. In the meantime, he intended to watch the boy and watch how others interacted with him. That alone would tell him all he needed to know about him. After that, he would decide if the boy was worth the effort. At this moment, it seemed he would be worth the effort; the little girl was certainly fond of him and he seemed to know the girl well.

And, then there was the boy in the wheelchair. He also seemed close to the girl. Santiago had many questions about this one. This older boy appeared too muscular and lean to have spent his life in a wheelchair. So, what was the story on that? Santiago stole another glance at him, noticed by his behavior and demeanor maturity beyond his years; his eyes projected compassion and wisdom that were beyond that of a boy his age. This one was a puzzle. This one had many stories and many secrets.

Santiago saw the child slide her plate of pie to him. He got the feeling she considered this boy a confidant—something about the way they looked at each other, how the boy tilted his face close to hers, gave her his complete attention when they spoke to each other. Perhaps... if the girl was the one Tadesco ordered him to find, the boy in the wheelchair knew her secrets.

The soldier beside Santiago elbowed him, asked him to pass the salt. He set the shaker between himself and the soldier, and resumed his meal. Even as he diverted his attention to his food, the wheels in his brain kept turning. The voices of his comrades melted together and became a loud, white noise hum outside his ruminations.

He expected this mission would be an easy one.

CHAPTER 13

James, Mitchell and Trevor reviewed the disks Morris had brought from Baker Creek. This was their third review of the information Clausberg and her friends with the Resistance had gathered, and the historical scenario that unfolded there still brought shivers up their spines.

The mord virus began as a global biological warfare tool to eliminate the parasites in the population. The parasites were the frail elderly, the chronically ill, the disabled, the mentally ill, the substance abusers and addicts, and so on. These people were a constant drain of both money and limited natural resources. They were useless to the upcoming new order of things.

At the same time the United Earth Federation with the cooperation of contacts in the United Nations road-tested the virus in an isolated corner of war-torn Rwanda, they conducted their earliest experiments in the United States on a large group of violent prison inmates from assorted prisons across the country. The inmates volunteered for the program in exchange for a chance to serve out their sentences outside the prison system in the relative comfort of the UEF's subterranean New Mexico compound. The scientists with the United Earth Federation presented the experiments as controlled medical trials to test the effectiveness of a new drug that would control violent tendencies. They selected inmates who had no surviving relatives and no friends contacting them from the outside. After all, their full intention was to execute their subjects once they were through with them. No one would miss them.

The initial results showed great promise. The disease spread rapidly, and the beauty of it was that the infected attacked others and infected them as well, creating a domino effect of new victims in very little time. However, there were two problems with the virus. The first problem was that the disease it produced was not a fatal disease in itself; it was only fatal to the victim who ended up completely devoured as a meal. The researchers learned this truth after losing the first two victims to the first group of five infected with the virus. However, the scientists rescued the second group of subjects attacked by the infected after the first bite or two. These subjects subsequently became infected. The second problem with the virus was it only made the infected victim hungry for human flesh, and only human flesh would do. As long as there was "food" available, the cannibal stayed alive. This was *bad* in the fact that the only way to cure the disease was to kill those carrying it; and this was *good* in the fact that the only way to cure the disease was to kill the infected. What the hell: a bona fide reason the public could get behind to eliminate a segment of the population; that would make it very easy to carry out the elimination without much, if any, moral protest.

The plan to introduce the virus into the bodies of only the targeted segment marked for elimination posed the next hurdle. How could they do it without infecting the rest of the population? Somebody suggested implementing a fake vaccination program. The dummy vaccine would consist of water for the "keeper population" and the deadly virus for the "parasitic population."

They tested this plan in Rwanda under the U.N.'s umbrella, and they used new emerging mutant strains of Ebola and Primate Polio as the excuse for the "vaccinations." The Rwandan experiment was a disaster. It was almost impossible to keep the superstitious subjects in the tiny village under control when it appeared to them some of their fellows had *died* and then mysteriously *resurrected*. They were too ignorant of medical science to understand the death of their tribesmen was only a brief coma, and the resurrection was the recovery from the coma. To the villagers, their family members and friends had died and had returned to life accursed and dangerous. Soon, the women began to hide their sick children in the cave of a spiritual elder woman who prayed and cast spells over them. It was only a matter of two days before the elder woman died as the main course and the children wandered off in search of additional sustenance once they had devoured every morsel off her bones. Subsequently, the UEF's conspirators at the U.N. and the World Health Organization spread the false word a rapidly fatal mutated form of Ebola had ravaged the village. No one suspected foul play when the villagers died en masse, and the whole place went up in flames.

The UEF rethought the issue and considered the ramifications of the same scenario in the civilized industrial nations of the world. Their sociologists and psychiatrists asserted that even in civilized populations there would always be those whose instinct to save their families would win out over the needs of the society as a whole. People would go into hiding with their sick and very dangerous relatives in tow. Unlike its human creators, the virus could not choose its victims. Without an antiviral agent to control its spread, the virus would become an all-out epidemic in very little time. Taking all that into consideration, the UEF ultimately abandoned the program and they destroyed the virus.

So they thought.

There exists one fuck-up in every clan, and the virus team within the UEF was no exception. Tyrone Flynn, a biological engineer with a pleasure-seeking personality and crushing financial debt saw the virus as his ticket to debt-free obscurity. He found a renegade megalomaniac named Carl Dunwalde who headed a large group of like-minded followers around the globe who planned to usurp the emerging UEF. Unleashing the mord virus upon the general population would be an ideal distraction. The UEF Elitists would be busy trying to maintain order during the inevitable panic and worldwide civil disorder, while Dunwalde's group massed for attack against them. Not only did Dunwalde pay Flynn handsomely for the virus, he brought Flynn on board to utilize his knowledge and experience with the virus.

After undergoing minor surgery to remove his identification chip, Tyrone Flynn was sure he was finally free and safe from the Ones in Power. However, if Flynn had given it further thought and had paid more attention to his superiors, he would have suspected the truth, which was that the UEF implanted all their personnel with *three* chips. It wasn't but one month into the spread of the plague when the UEF found him, tortured the information out of him, and subsequently put a bullet through his head.

As for Carl Dunwalde, they tortured him into revealing every bit of information about his little resistance group and their members. When the UEF finished with him, their goons hung him naked by his feet over a cage containing two cannibals and watched, laughing, as the monsters slowly and painfully devoured him over the next hour.

Flynn had actually done the Ones in Power a service of sorts. The rapid spread of the disease provided an opportunity to gather the populace together into manageable groups and house them in massive "rescue centers." The existing containment camps would serve that purpose. Originally, the containment camps were for use during times of widespread civil disobedience. Under priority status, the UEF rapidly converted the camps into rescue centers for the refugees, and one had to look long and hard to find evidence of their formal use.

Under these current conditions, with the people panicked, helpless and defenseless, it would be very easy to convert the populace into accepting the new order of things. Once they eradicated this mord virus mess, there would be a society to rebuild.

It would only work if the citizens committed their very lives and souls to the authorities; and the only way to guarantee their cooperation was three-fold:

One: protect them from the virus with a "vaccine" containing a REFEHL chip that would have to be administered once a year for life.

Two: convince them acceptance of the REFEHL chip is a matter of life or death—literally. After all, the chip would provide a record of vaccinations. In addition, the chip would have the capacity to identify the existence of any dormant mord virus cells in the body, thus making diagnosis and elimination of the carrier a snap, which would prevent another outbreak. Therefore, it would be mandatory for all persons receiving the vaccinations to also accept the chip.

Three: The institution of a new global virtual currency accessible only through a personal REFEHL chip that would monitor each citizen's financial transactions. The REFEHL would guarantee accurate records of every citizen's assets, and the adoption of one global virtual currency would simplify things with every citizen's financial history, source of income and account status recorded in their personal chip. Therefore, one could only access their personal finances via a scan through the chip which was more convenient and hack-proof than the portafones in use at the time.

What Flynn and Dunwalde did not know, and the general chipped population would learn too late is that the REFEHL also served as a tracking device.

The injection of the chips, which the UEF planned to activate later, began concurrently with the "vaccinations."

JAMES THOUGHT BACK to what little he knew about the evolution of the RFID technology. The chips had been around for decades. James had even had his Labrador chipped after he rescued it from the pound the third time it got loose. He had found the dog with only hours to spare before they would have euthanized it. The thought of coming that close to losing his beloved pet was enough to cause James to join the legions of other pet owners who took advantage of the technology.

When James joined the Marines, they injected an RFID chip into him and all his fellow soldiers at boot camp. In the military, you had no choice. They pumped everyone full of all kinds of mysterious shit, made everyone run a gauntlet of hypodermic-wielding military doctors for their vaccinations and God-knows-what-else. The chip injector was somewhere in that gauntlet and the next stop for the recruits was the chip activation center. They required James to divulge every bit of personal information about himself, right down to an admission he sometimes bit his fingernails when he was anxious. There were psychological tests, medical tests, genetic panels and blood panels, spit panels and semen panels. They didn't miss anything. All of that information went into the computer, and the computer fed the data into the chip and then activated the damned thing.

Just like a beloved pet, James's loving owners could identify, track down, and retrieve him should he ever stray.

When it came time to begin construction on Alpha Base, James learned his RFID chip and that of all the other ex-military on the project was still active. Someone got hold of a chip-reading scanner, and everyone found out just how much private information his or her chips contained. The most disturbing thing of all was the discovery that the Feds could locate anyone by satellite via their chip number. A retired surgeon on their team, an old guy who died during that first year of construction, taught them how to remove the chips. It was minor surgery, and chip removal became an immediate requirement once Alpha Base entered into its second month of creation. The chips dissolved easily in acetone.

Today, all Alpha residents were free of their RFID and the new REFEHL chips, and not a single person protested.

CHAPTER 14

Dillon handed his tackle box to Guffy as soon as they cleared the granite overhang outside the south entrance to the lava tube. "I'll meet you and Isa at our usual spot."

Guffy tucked the box under his arm and rebalanced his fishing rod against his shoulder. "You really oughta quit smokin', Dill."

"Someday." Dillon's reply was unabashedly insincere.

Guffy simply shook his head, took Isabelle's hand, and walked off toward the slope that led down to the riverbank.

Dillon glanced around for a soldier who had cigarettes. He quickly spotted a new face, a dark-haired young man of about twenty who was standing away from the others. The man had just lit up. Dillon zeroed in on his prey and loped over to him, presented his most charming smile and begged a spare cigarette.

"You can get your own down at the fourth level," the young man said.

"They won't give 'em to me," Dillon explained, "I'm too young."

The soldier analyzed him for a few moments. Once the man memorized his face, he glanced over the boy's slight build and then returned his gaze to Dillon's eyes. He ascertained the little beggar appeared younger than his true age. He also detected a worldly sophistication in the boy's demeanor, sensed he had already been places and done things no boy should have been or experienced.

"Ain't you afraid it's gonna stunt your growth?"

Dillon shifted his stance, scowled at the guy, growled under his breath. "Fuck you..."

The soldier smiled, loosened up his broad square shoulders and stepped closer to the boy. He was five inches taller than Dillon, wide in the chest and trim in the middle. His face appeared to follow the shape of his body, broad of forehead and narrow at the chin, a triangle shape that impressed Dillon as unusual in a man. As he leaned his chiseled, handsome face slightly nearer to the boy's, he replied to Dillon's brusque retort in a very soft and confidential voice, "Ugly words from such inviting lips."

Dillon had not expected that. He backed up a step and regarded the man with surprise. In the next breath, he recovered his composure and demanded nicely, "Spare one, dude?"

The soldier grinned. His teeth were white and straight, perfect in every way just like the stunning young man himself. With his dark brown eyes riveted to Dillon's amber eyes, he extracted a smoke from the pack and handed it to Dillon. He waited until Dillon planted the cigarette between his "inviting lips" before he struck a match, cupped it in his slender yet muscular hands and brought it to the tip of the cigarette.

Dillon leaned his head forward and accepted the light. The breeze came up, and he cupped the strong young hands that cupped the match. The soldier suggestively stroked Dillon's fingers when he straightened to take the first delicious drag. Dillon understood, and he cast the young man a brief reciprocal smile.

"I could get you a couple of packs," the soldier offered.

Dillon expected there would be a price. There was no need to discuss it, only to accept the solicitation. "I'm in tent twenty-seven."

"Ten o'clock tonight?"

He found the man attractive, desirable. As long as they kept things confidential and were careful, the arrangement would work out just fine. Dillon brushed aside his suddenly condemning conscience, qualified his acceptance of the man's offer and price as a business deal. He smirked wryly, "Ten's fine."

"What's your name?"

"No names."

The soldier smirked in return, gave him a subtle wink. "Good enough."

IAN TRIMMED AWAY THE dead leaves in the pumpkin patch and lifted some of the smaller of the pumpkins to examine the undersides. These were not the common decorative gourds used for Halloween, but the edible type intended for baking and cooking. As he feared, most of them were beginning to rot on the bottom because of the dampness. He fumed about it, silently cursed Franks for not taking his advice to curtail the irrigation. So far, they had lost a good deal of the produce to rot from over-watering. He had repeatedly warned Franks the mountain climate was not the same as the roasting conditions in the sun-baked valley below, and the vegetables did not need as much water. Ever the self-proclaimed expert on farming, Franks had only half-listened and then disregarded Ian's good advice. Ian knew what he was talking about; his years of gardening in the cool damp of his native England made him the real expert on the proper methods, procedure and irrigation needs of these crops. The climate during early autumn in the mountains was very similar to summer in England, especially when one considered the misty precipitation here that rose each morning from the nearby lakes and streams. Because Franks haughtily ignored Ian's concerns, most of the crop was nearly ruined. The condition of the rest of the precious produce fared no better. Because of Franks, their provisions for the coming winter would be sparse.

Ian rolled the last of the pumpkins onto its side and surveyed the damage. "Sonofabitch!" he muttered angrily.

"Can we save them?" Carolyn asked calmly.

He turned on her, his eyes wide, his face red with his rising temper. "They're rotted an' fulla worms! Save 'em for what?"

"If we pull them now, maybe we can—"

"We can do nothin'!" He leaned forward on his wet, muddied knees and slammed both his fists into the soil. "I worked my ass off for months, tendin' the seeds, doin' research, makin' sure it all got proper feed! All for nothin'! I told Franks! I told 'im! No one listens to me!"

She put her arm around his shoulders, "It's only Franks that doesn't listen."

He shrugged her away. "Not so! If any of the rest 'ad listened to me, they woulda done what I said! Instead, they trust Franks! They trust him 'cause he's older. I'm just a kid, y'know... don't know nothin'... *don't listen to 'im*! *That's* what! *Don't listen to the kid! He don't know nothin'!* Well, fuck 'em all. Fuck 'em, I say. Let 'em starve!"

"Well..." Carolyn reached for the basket and pulled it close. "I still say we can save them." She began to dislodge the ripest.

Ian gripped her wrists and pushed her away, "Leave 'em!"

Carolyn tumbled onto her side and landed on the basket, crushed it. She stared aghast at Ian. "You hurt me!"

"You're not hurt! I didn't push ya that hard!" He stood and bounded over to the cavern's small entranceway, began to call shrilly and loudly for Franks. In the process, he added some expletives to Franks' name.

"Stop yelling!" Carolyn shouted, "You're just gonna make him mad!"

He regarded her for only a moment, "You think I care, lass?" That moment now spent, he resumed his irate demands for Franks' presence.

Franks emerged from the cavern with a company of curious residents who had also heard Ian's furious yelling. Franks reprimanded him, not caring to know the boy's reason for his behavior. "What the hell is wrong with you?"

Ian faced him indignantly. "You bloody fuckin' bastard!"

"We don't use that kinda language here!"

"Ya ruined the fuckin' crop! I told ya 'bout the water!"

Franks approached him, prepared for the inevitable battle. "What?"

Ian sprinted to the patch and removed one of the rotten pumpkins. He threw it at Franks; hit him right in the face with it before he could duck. The saturated gourd exploded into a slimy, seed-weeping mess down Franks' skin and clothing. Ian screamed at him, "Tell me ya wanna eat that! Tell me that's good food! Tell me it's salvageable! Lemme hear ya, Franks!"

Franks stood back in shock, wiped away the foul smelling remnants from his red hair and stinging freckled face. For those moments, he was too aghast that Ian had dared to do such a thing to react defensively against his actions.

"Ya don't listen!" Ian continued, "I told ya an' told ya! Whadda I gotta do? Do I gotta quit the hospital so I can supervise ya? The crop's ruined! It's ruined! It's your fault, but they're gonna blame me!"

Franks sensed the small crowd of onlookers behind him, sensed their concern, heard some murmur admonitions of blame, while some others debated Ian's sanity. He observed Ian's irately trembling, battle-ready posture, his tightly clenched fists and equally severe clenched jaws. Ian's eyes had taken on a wild quality that was terrifying to behold. In response to the sight, someone behind Franks announced they were going to find Joe. Someone else suggested Trevor would be the better choice. Someone else, a teenage boy, concluded Ian needed to "get laid." That caused a few to laugh.

Ian bristled at the laughter. "You'll find it most amusin' when you're all starvin'! Fuck ya all! Fuck ya all! I'm done with ya!" He then grabbed the nearest weapon, a sturdy steel-tined rake and set about to demolish the garden in a hideous display of unrestrained temper. Expletives flew along with bits of rotting plants and produce.

Carolyn had lately worried over Ian's gradually deteriorating self-control, but she had not envisioned he would lose it like this. Everything in Ian's behavior, his unreasonable assumptions and unfounded paranoia was alien to the gentle and patient young man she loved. Mournful and unable to bear the sight of him like this, Carolyn dashed away in tears, pushed through the small crowd at the cavern entrance. The onlookers were so fascinated by Ian's tantrum they hardly noticed her. She ran as fast as she could when she reached the corridor, determined to reach Joe or Trevor before Ian did irreparable damage to the garden as well as some damage to himself.

As Carolyn made her exit, Franks hotly rushed over to Ian and attempted to wrestle the rake from his hands. His efforts resulted in a swift hard blow of the handle to his face. Seeing sparkles in the air and hearing a rush in his ears, Franks tumbled, collapsed on his side. His final awareness before he passed out was the sight of Ian's red-flushed face over his and the blunt pain of the boy's fists upon his cheek.

TREVOR HEARD A FAMILIAR noise. The sound was soft, from high up in the atmosphere. He scanned the sky through his binoculars, but could not locate the aircraft. Sans binoculars, he squinted and focused with his naked eye. The craft emerged from above a small puffy white cloud, the only cloud in the sky. It was near the horizon, at the place where the blue faded gradually into the lightest of blues. As it traveled eastward, Trevor saw it get a little bigger in his sight. Now that he had pinpointed the location, he brought the specs up to his eyes for a better look. The plane came into focus large and fat and slate gray, a no-nonsense, ready-for-business-you-mother, heavily armed transporter. It was impossible to know if the craft carried troops or supplies. Trevor mused it perhaps carried some VIP's with the United Earth Federation, for the logo on the side of the plane was theirs. It was too high up to be headed for anywhere in Alpha's corner of the State, and Trevor decided it was probably on a return flight to the East Coast from somewhere out in the Pacific.

His radio beeped at his hip. He set aside the binoculars and answered the call.

Mitchell informed him, "There's a craft at eleven o'clock."

"I see it," Trevor replied. "It's a transport."

Mitchell confirmed the owners. "UEF."

"Affirmative. Do you see any more?"

"Negative." His tone abruptly changed, "Joe wants you to meet him at the garden."

"What for?"

"Ian's having a meltdown."

WHEN TREVOR THREADED through the crowd of onlookers and reached the garden, he found Ian on a rampage. Ian had abandoned his assault of the garden and had shifted his fury upon a pine tree. With no regard or even notice of the shower of pine needles, Ian repeatedly struck the trunk of the tree with the now broken rake. The tree trunk was in a scarred and shredded condition, evidence Ian had been at it for some time. Nearby, Franks sat in the dirt and cradled his bleeding head in his hands. Trevor looked for Joe, but Joe was not there.

Trevor addressed the audience, "What happened?"

There came a chorus of *I don't know, beats me, he's just nuts, he just went nuts...*

"Where's Joe?"

"He went to get Doc Macky," a woman replied loudly.

"Or a straight jacket!" some wise-ass added.

Trevor turned away from them and observed Ian. The boy's tantrum reminded him of a similar outburst he had witnessed back in England at the boys' shelter. It happened during Ian's second week there, brought about by another boy's innocent teasing when Ian was collecting seeds from a discarded stalk of dead hollyhocks. However, that tantrum was mild in comparison to today's performance.

Trevor took a deep breath and approached Ian at the tree. Now close enough to see him clearly, he saw trails of sweat mingled with tears trickling down Ian's flushed face. Ian, so intent on venting his rage, did not notice Trevor's presence.

Trevor called out to him cautiously, his voice casual and non-judgmental, "Ian..."

Ian heard Trevor's voice although it seemed to come from far away. He ceased his assault halfway in, the rake poised in mid air to strike the intended blow. Ian had to take a moment, catch his breath, and allow the swirling cacophony of cries in his head die down to silence. Finally, the veil between his internal tempest and external reality lifted.

Trevor's voice came again, this time closer and with a hint of sympathy. "Releasin' some Irish, Mister O'Connor?"

Ian allowed the rake to fall with an exhausted and grateful *thunk* to the dirt. Now that he stood still, he realized he had fatigued himself to the point of complete surrender. He wasn't aware he had collapsed in a heap until his knees screamed pain under his weight when he legs refused to support him any longer. Dizzy, trembling and drenched in sweat, he remained there on his knees, afraid he would faint if he dared to stand. His gradual awareness of the small audience watching him caused him to acknowledge his embarrassing actions. Confused and humiliated, he wondered how he would explain himself.

Trevor squatted before him, his voice barely above a whisper and full of concern, "Did you spend it all, lad?"

Trevor's tone was comforting, not taunting, and Ian appreciated his friend's gentle tact. The voice belonged to the Trevor who ran the boys' shelter, the same Trevor who once told him no one would punish him for expressing his anger. Trevor... who had offered him safety and solace so long ago, so long ago that dark day when death beckoned and he almost took its hand.

Ian questioned himself, *Do I wish to die today?*

Out of the corner of his eye, he saw the people watching him. He felt their myriad emotions: disdain, fear, contempt, compassion... There was so much more—so much pain, grief, hopelessness. They tried to hide it but they could not conceal it from him, for he involuntarily soaked up their muck into his psyche.

"No wonder," he thought to himself. *"It's yours as well as mine. Dear God... why do you put me through this? What have I done to deserve this?"*

Isabelle's face suddenly appeared before him. She peered at him curiously through a thin hedge of perplexed eyebrows that plunged together above the bridge of her nose. In an instant, her expression changed to one of sympathy, and she whispered intimately to him, "Deezus says it's aw yose dis time, Ian. It ain't time to liff it away yet."

How could she know?

As consciousness slowly returned, he realized she was not a figment of his imagination. She was beside him in the flesh, bent over him, peering down into his face. Through weak, heavy eyes, he perceived his blurred environment as bathed in dim yellow light. At first, he could not fathom this new reality, could not figure out where he was. The odor of the place finally reached his brain, the familiar pungent scent of the hospital. He realized then he was flat on his back on a gurney and someone had placed a soft warm blanket over him. Under the covers, his bare toes caressed the top sheet.

Joe's voice drifted from the distance. "Isa, you shouldn't be in here."

Isabelle's face disappeared from Ian's limited range of vision. When her voice rang, it seemed as far away as Joe's voice. "He's okay now, ain't he?"

"Yeah. Let him sleep. Go on, now..."

"We aw pwayed fo' him."

"Good. Tell them I said thanks."

"Okay."

The dim light died away into darkness. He felt heaviness within his chest. Suddenly, the heaviness lifted and he began to feel a curious floating sensation that lulled him into a dull state of lazy euphoria. He heard a sound, something like a moan. It came from very near. He tried to see through the darkness, see who had voiced such a soothing tone of compassion, but the darkness pressed upon his eyelids and held them shut.

Rain...

Shhh...

"Oh, no... the plants will drown!"

The rain... a little louder...

Shhh...

Sweet... something sweet... a fragrance... summer...

Shhh...

Roses.

CHAPTER 15

The moment Joe emerged from Ian's room Trevor took hold of his arm to get his attention. "What happened to him? Will he be alright?"

Joe closed the door gently and moved into the corridor. Trevor followed him, as Joe expected he would. He had been dealing with Trevor sporadically for the past hour. The young man had been a pest, wanting all the answers right away. Joe could not give him any answers then, and he could give him none now. As Trevor persistently shadowed him Joe could feel his anxiety, and it was making him crazy. He turned to him and replied shortly, "I don't know what happened. Yes, he'll be all right."

"How do you know he'll be alright?"

"Jeez, Trev... Give me a damned break, will ya?"

"I'm responsible for him."

"No, you're not. He's not your kid."

Trevor's eyes narrowed. "He's been my kid for three years now. Don't you dare tell me I'm not—"

Since Ian's arrival at Alpha Base, Joe had grown very close to the boy. Ian had spoken often and glowingly about Trevor and their relationship, but Joe half-ignored most of it. He wanted to nudge Ian away from his past and into his present. Although Ian's present life at Alpha was not ideal, it was much better than the life he left behind. Joe realized, too, that he had become fond of Ian, and he felt a small measure of jealousy toward Trevor, felt vaguely afraid Trevor would reclaim him. Instead of facing the issue head-on, Joe dismissed it as not the right time for a conflict. Their common concern over

Ian's emotional turmoil mattered much more than that. Joe was unqualified to understand or diagnose the boy's mysterious behavior. "You should talk to Doctor Macky about him."

"I want to see him."

"Macky said no visitors."

"*You* were in there."

"I'm on staff. He's my patient."

"Has he said anything?"

"No." Joe steeled himself for the next question, but Trevor said nothing. Instead, a sudden expression of introspection crossed Trevor's face, and he looked down at the floor, folded his arms in front of his chest. Joe interpreted that to mean there was something Trevor suspected. "Is there something you want to tell me?"

"When our bus was attacked... he saw his friends die." Trevor sighed and looked up at Joe, his eyes sad. "That may have something to do with this."

Joe considered Ian's frequent nightmares. "Probably. All the kids are... saw things. My Randy—he's going through the anger stage right now. They all deal with it differently. Ian's one of those who bottles everything up. Maybe the bottle broke today."

"What can we do?"

"Hell if I know..." He stepped away from Trevor, but stopped briefly and added, "We don't have any answers yet. Give Macky a day or so to work with him. Right now, the best we can do for Ian is to leave him alone."

"*You'll* be with him."

"I have other patients."

"Let me sit with him."

"Macky said no. He needs peace and quiet."

"I'll be quiet."

"You'll be sitting there worrying about him. He don't need that."

Trevor clenched his jaws. "You're steamin' me, Joe!"

"What do you think is more important to me; his health or you being pissed at me?" He saw Trevor would not give in easily. He opted to give him a glimmer of hope. "Go back to work. If Ian asks for you, I'll come get you."

"He *will* ask for me."

"Then I'll come get you." Eager to escape their standoff, Joe offered no other comment. He turned away and headed into the break room where he could get a moment alone to pray for Ian and Randy.

CORY JONES SALUTED Major Standish and remained at attention. The major, a very overweight, box-shaped man, squinted at Cory from under thick and wiry black eyebrows. When he stood and saluted, Cory noticed a button was missing from the major's shirt. The rest of the buttons strained with the man's ample girth. Cory expected to see all the buttons pop off at once and shoot through the air like liberated popcorn.

"At ease, Sergeant." The major then sat, gestured Cory to do the same.

Cory sat down slowly in the chair facing the desk. While Standish perused the sergeant's paperwork, Cory glanced around the room. It had formerly been a doctor's office, and medical books still occupied every inch of the built-in mahogany bookcase. Most of the texts had the word *"Oncology"* in the titles. On an opposite wall hung a huge color poster, an illustration of the human lymphatic system. Even though this room was away from the wards in the east wing of Bonito Valle Community Hospital, the smells of medicines, disinfectants, urine and death lingered in the air. Cory sniffed, and then his nose itched. As he rubbed his nose with the back of his hand, he noticed a large blood stain on the carpet beside the expensive mahogany filing cabinet. The gray water/detergent residue streaks on the light beige carpeting indicated someone had tried to scrub the stain away. Upon further observation, he noticed the room was dirty and dusty. He attributed the dust as the cause of his sinus irritation.

Major Standish leaned back in his leather chair, propped his feet up on the executive style desk and lit a cigar. The soles of his shoes were worn smooth and had cracks in the leather. His socks did not match; one was dark blue and the other was brown. An image came to Cory's mind that each sock had holes in the toes.

Finished with his reading, Standish again squinted at the young sergeant. The kid reminded him of his own son, muscled yet lean, the face darkened by sunlight, the cheekbones pronounced, the chin square and strong, his expression serious and respectful. If it had not been for that asinine *friendly fire* incident, it would have been his son sitting there, not this young man who reminded him of the one he had lost.

Major Standish finally spoke after a second puff off his cigar. "You have a background in psychology."

"Not exactly, sir. I never finished school."

"How far did you get?"

"Twelve units short of a Degree."

He tapped the papers on his desk with his two fat fingers that held his cigar. An ash fell. He casually swiped it off. "Says here you also got high marks in medical subjects and also did some counseling."

"Some."

"Your father was a doctor."

"A veterinarian, sir."

"Did you work with animals, too?"

"I helped out at the clinic when I was in high school." Cory was certain all that information was there in front of the major.

He did not understand why the man was questioning him. He did not understand why they had transferred him to Major Standish's command.

Standish curled his legs off the desk and sat up properly in his chair. He then sat forward intently, his now forgotten cigar burning a long fat ash that threatened to drop at any moment. "Do you have an affinity for animals?"

"Yes, sir. I always have."

"What about people?"

"Sure. I mean—yes, sir. I was a medic before the army decided to make me a sergeant. I don't know why they did that, sir."

"We've had many casualties, and then there are the deserters. You know what they do to deserters."

Han's comment sounded like a warning to him. Cory replied tepidly, "Yes, sir."

The major cast him a knowing glint. "You prefer working with animals, don't you?"

After four failed relationships, the most recent of which cost him his life savings, Cory's answer, if he were to answer truthfully, would be *people suck!* However, he did not want to come across as a latent sociopath. "Sometimes."

"What were you planning to do with a degree in psychology?"

He had been asking himself that very same question. Actually, Cory Jones had an almost psychic connection with animals ever since he was a kid. This talent had come in handy at his father's clinic, and he pursued psychology only to compare the human psyche to the animal psyche. The professional applications for this knowledge were limited unless he went into animal research for some pharmaceutical outfit, which was out of the question since he maintained the belief all they did was torture the poor creatures in the name of science. Cory wanted nothing to do with anything that promoted cruelty towards animals. That brought him back to

Standish's question. He had no answer.

Major Standish pressed on. "Perhaps you wanted to be an animal psychiatrist."

Cory had to chuckle at that, it sounded so ridiculous. At the same time, he blurted, "If you'd seen what some of those poor bastards have been through...!"

Standish reclined in his chair, smiled at the young man. "That's what I wanted to hear."

"What is that, sir?"

"Compassion. Nobody gives a shit anymore, especially about animals."

"Sir?"

"My daughter worked for Gennamatrix Pharmaceuticals over in Oak Shores."

"I heard about that place."

"Yeah. When all hell broke loose with the mord virus, they all split and left the lab animals caged up to starve to death. She risked her life to go back there to release them. She thought at least they'd have a chance." Standish paused then for quite a few moments. He stared down at the papers on his desk. His chin quivered ever so slightly. After a short time passed, he noticed his cigar had burned a long ash at the tip. He flicked the ash onto the carpet, and then he stuck the cigar between his teeth, pivoted the seat of his chair sideways and gazed out the window at the ruined city below. Still peering out the window, he asked, "Do you smoke?"

"No, sir."

"Is this cigar bothering you?"

"My grandfather smoked cigars. I rather like the scent."

"Lena knows I'm smoking right now. She used to nag me to quit."

Lena could have been Standish's wife or his daughter. He guessed Lena was his wife. However, Jones chose not to voice his assumption.

"Sir?"

"I chose you for a reason, Sergeant Jones. Your psychological profile..." He paused again, finally reeled the chair around and faced Cory. "I can trust you."

"Sir?"

The major did not answer. Instead, he opened one of his desk drawers and took out a large bottle of European scotch, a rare brand sold only in specialty stores. The wording on the label was in Danish or German, or something—Cory was no expert on languages. The bottle's design was overly embellished and fancy. The band around the bottle's neck was unbroken. Standish produced two small glass tumblers from the same drawer and set them on the desk. He then opened the bottle and poured each glass half full. He slid one of the glasses across the desk to Cory.

He gestured at Cory with the two fingers that squeezed his cigar. "Have a drink."

SOMEONE SCRATCHED THE canvas flap of Dillon's tent, and then the voice he had been expecting came muffled through the material.

"Got your smokes."

Dillon rolled off his sleeping bag and scrambled on his knees to the entrance. He unzipped the flap and motioned the soldier inside. "You're right on time," Dillon told him as he ducked in.

The soldier produced two packs of cigarettes from his jacket pocket and handed them to the boy. "They're one-hundreds."

"Cool!" Dillon whispered as he took them. "Thanks."

The soldier sat up on his haunches and looked around the small tent. "So, this is your crib. Got it all to yourself, huh?"

Dillon stated, "For obvious reasons."

He smiled warmly at him. "It's not that obvious."

"How did *you* know?"

"By the way you blushed when I looked you in the eye."

"I blushed?"

"Yeah."

"Shit..."

The soldier laughed softly. "So did I. I mean... I felt it. I thought you caught it."

"Uh-uh." Dillon then went to his sleeping bag, sat and patted the clear space beside him. "Have a seat."

As he moved over and reclined next to Dillon, he pulled a small bottle of rum out of his other pocket, and showed it to Dillon. "I thought this would help break the ice."

Dillon cast him a seductive smirk, the same one he used for his customers back in The Day. Tonight, his feelings were genuine. "There ain't no ice here."

The soldier's expression quickly became serious. "How old are you?"

"Eighteen."

"Fuck you! Tell me the truth."

"I'll be sixteen in March."

"A Pisces?"

"Yeah."

"Scorpio."

"Oooh... a hot-blooded Scorpio." The imaginary light bulb clicked on over Dillon's head. "That's what I'll call ya. *Scorpio*."

He pointed at Dillon and chuckled, "Catfish."

"Catfish?"

"You remind me of a cat, and you're always going fishing. I've seen you out there lots of times. Used to think to myself, *there goes that cat fishin' again.* I wanted to talk to you, but there were always the others around. I have to be careful, you know."

"Fuckin' macho dudes..." He said it disdainfully in a quiet commiserating voice.

"Naw, not that. Just don't need the bullshit." Scorpio opened the bottle, took a hefty gulp and passed it to Catfish.

Dillon read the label. "Expensive..."

"Tagged it outside of Boise. We all took as much as we could carry." On impulse, he tapped the brim of Dillon's cap. "What'cha got that on for?"

Dillon straightened it. "Aw... I forget I'm wearin' it."

"Take it off."

"My hair's still growing back."

"Bad cut, dude?"

"Cancer meds."

"Oh." In the next breath, he added with a nervous laugh, "You ain't gonna die on me, are you?"

Dillon scoffed, took a swig of the rum. It was good and hot in his throat, and the flavor definitely expensive. He let it linger on his tongue before he swallowed it.

The young man persisted gently. "Let me see your hair. I know it's blond. I like blond."

Reluctantly, Dillon removed his hat, tossed it over his shoulder into a corner of the tent. He then ran his fingers through the varying length tresses to fluff it up. When he felt presentable, he turned to Scorpio the Soldier and said, "There."

Scorpio scooted very close to Dillon, close enough that their bodies touched. He gingerly framed Dillon's face in his hands, peered admiringly into his eyes. He noted the shyness there behind the cavalier gleam. Suddenly, the boy looked away as if he wished to hide the secrets within his eyes, stared down at the padded floor. The soldier gently lifted his face, made him surrender and return his gaze. He said nothing to Dillon. He admired the boy's face as one admires a beautiful painting, softly stroked his hair as one would a tiny vulnerable kitten.

Dillon was at a loss as to how to react. No one had ever regarded him in such an intimate, sincere and loving manner. And there was that enduring gentleness, too. This man did not seem in a rush to get down to business. On the contrary, he seemed quite content to relish the tenderness of the moment and the opportunity to savor and appreciate the beauty of the hardened yet innocent face in his hands. Dillon, once he recovered his balance, accepted the man's unspoken offering of something more meaningful than a casual one-night fling. Very slowly and cautiously, he inched his lips closer to the soldier's, waited anxiously for the warm breath that would escape from his parting and accepting lips. The breath caressed his mouth, and he hungrily went for it and docked into those welcoming lips.

CHAPTER 16

"'Twas nothin'," Ian said as he dug into his mashed potatoes, "I was overtired, that's all. An' Franks don't listen. Got fed up with it, is all."

"How can it be nothing?" Trevor countered, "When you can barely recall what you did out there?"

"I told ya... I was overtired. Quit fussin', Trev!"

They fell into silence. The din of voices in the dining room filled the void created by their time-out. Trevor could tell Ian was already beginning to lose his patience. Doctor Macky had warned him the boy would be touchy for a few more days, at least. Even the noise of the chatter in the room was enough to send Ian into a furious tangent, which would end with him shutting down for the next few hours. It had happened the day before and the day before that. The kid's nerves were as sensitive and erratic as downed live wires in a windstorm.

Coltan, Natalie and Carolyn had given Ian plenty of breathing space. However, Coltan struggled while it was much easier for Natalie to maintain a distance. Coltan inwardly felt much of Ian's problem was his uncanny empathy for others' emotional turmoil. Ian was particularly sensitive to Coltan's buried trauma. Yet, Coltan did not know the truth, which was Ian had been picking up the traumatized energies of *everyone* at the refuge. Coltan dared not question Ian for fear the boy would once more lose his temper.

Trevor gave Coltan a nudge with his elbow. "Pass me the pepper, would you?"

Coltan slid the shaker to him, snuck a glance at Ian out of the corner of his eye. Ian was contently digging into his meal, and he had created an invisible emotional barrier between himself and his fellow diners.

Carolyn sat beside Ian across from Natalie and Coltan. She watched Coltan cut through his venison patty with his fork. He divided the meat into cubes and stacked them into a neat pile slathered in gravy. She thought his habit of organizing his food was very strange. During their days in Bonito Valle, she had not known him at all and could only imagine the type of person he was and his habits. The Coltan she had come to know here at Alpha was entirely different from the Coltan of her conjecture. She had never imagined he could be so meticulously organized and so impossibly polite; no one who had seen him back in Bonito Valle the way he was then, all *Mister Scowling-Tough-Ass on the Harley*, would have taken him for the well-read, sophisticated gentleman sitting near her today. Yet, Carolyn suspected the person he projected at Alpha Base was a phony, and she expected the rough and tumble, coarse-mouthed, mean-ass sonofabitch who glared at her at the Dairy Delight would surface when he'd had enough—just like what had happened to Ian.

She observed the way he and Natalie looked at each other, the mutual love and respect between them. Often, they held hands or one would wrap an arm around the other, or one would bend closely to the other's face and whisper a sweet sentiment that produced a smile. Carolyn thought it was rather sickening, all their lovey-dovey behavior. Back in Bonito Valle, her best friend Natalie wanted nothing to do with the enigmatic boy they had dubbed *Harley Guy*. Now, he was almost all she talked about, all she lived and breathed. Natalie had changed because of him, and Carolyn privately resented it. However, to their faces she made it a point to be pleasant and friendly because she did not want to lose what little remained of her friendship with Natalie.

Ian eyed Trevor and said loudly to get his attention, "You know what I miss?"

"What, lad?"

"Bangers an' mash!"

Trevor chuckled. "Aye."

"An' blood puddin'!"

Carolyn wrinkled her nose at the thought of it. "Eeww..."

Trevor offered over her comment, "And a good stout ale!"

Ian lifted his cup of hot tea in a toast, "Here, here!"

Trevor toasted, "Back at'cha, lad!"

Ian laughed. "God save us!"

Natalie said, "I thought you liked us, Ian."

"I do!" He glanced sideways at Carolyn then and, under the table, took Carolyn's hand and gave it a squeeze. "Especially my good lass, 'ere, which nunna you appreciate!"

Coltan jumped in, "We do, too!"

Carolyn offered no comment. She was surprised Ian had detected her feelings of alienation, although she had never mentioned it. His attention to her private misery endeared him to her even more.

He gazed at her for a long moment, his love for her plain in his eyes. "You keep me sane, lass, an' I thank ya for it."

"Same here," Carolyn said softly.

Trevor's eyes grew big. "What? What here? Say, lad?"

"Nothin'. Shut yer gob."

"Bloody hell..." Trevor knew Ian and Carolyn had been sweet on each other, but he was surprised their feelings for each other ran so deeply. He wondered how he had missed it.

Ian turned his attention to Coltan. "She's been needin' more shelves for the library. Are ya up to it?"

Coltan had quickly recovered his ability to walk and his stamina had improved. "Of course, I am." To Carolyn he inquired, "Would tomorrow work for you?"

"That'd be great," she replied. "Are you sure you're up to it?"

"Yeah."

Natalie regarded Ian quizzically, "What about your garden? Could you use some more help?"

"On what? The beds I destroyed?"

"Well... yeah. Franks said you demolished the planter boxes."

"Franks can fix 'em. He owes me that much. Bloody ass..."

"Now, there, there," Trevor admonished him. "Franks is doing his best. He said he'll do it your way. What else do you want?"

Ian grinned mischievously. "His 'ead on a platter! Stubborn bastard..."

"You're the stubborn one," Trevor said.

"I bloody 'ell 'afta be!" He suddenly fell silent, felt a stranger's eyes boring into him. He turned sharply and zeroed in on the culprit, a black-haired, dark-skinned soldier at a table kiddy-corner to his. This was not the first time this evening the black-eyed stranger had inadvertently sent his curious energy upon Ian. Fed up and feeling quite testy, Ian addressed the soldier harshly, "Oi! What's with you? What'cha lookin' 'ere for? You got a problem?"

The soldier tilted his head and eyed Ian questioningly.

Trevor tapped Ian's arm. "Stop it, lad! What's gotten into you?"

"I'll tell ya what," he informed Trevor, "Been puttin' 'is eyes 'ere since we sat down. 'e's gettin' on me nerves, 'e is!" To the soldier, he called out, "What's your bloody problem?"

The soldier, Raul Santiago, narrowed his eyes at Ian.

"Oi!" Ian said with a chuckle, "Are ya deaf, chum?"

Carolyn did not like the looks of the man. Something about him made her blood curl. "Ian, please stop. Let it go."

"The hell I will! I think 'e been lookin' a' you. I don' like it."

Natalie tried to soothe him, "Ian... I think it's perfectly innocent. There's some new soldiers just arrived. I think he's one of them. I'm sure he doesn't mean anything by it. He's just getting used to all the new faces."

He hotly disagreed, "Yeah? You think so?"

Coltan added to Natalie's comment, "Don't pick a fight, Ian."

Overlapping, Trevor advised him, "No scrappin', lad. Why look for trouble?"

Ian leaned closely to Trevor, said very softly, "I don' like 'im. Don' like bein' watched."

In an equally soft voice, Trevor assured him, "It's nothing, lad. You're making it bigger than it is. What's gotten into you?"

Coltan remarked, "This isn't you."

"We prefer the nice, laid-back Ian we used to know," Natalie added.

Carolyn slipped her arm behind him, gently stroked his back. "Please, Ian... Don't be like this. You're worrying me."

At this, Ian reined in his combativeness, realized he had let his raw nerves get the best of him. He surmised the hostility he felt was coming from either the soldier who was his target or someone else in the room.

"I don't mean to worry you," he told Carolyn contritely. "I don't know what gets into me."

"Spend some time with me in the library after dinner," she suggested. "That kind of work always used to calm you."

He considered it, "Might be a good idea, seein' Joe took me off duty for the week. I been gettin' rather bored. What the hell... okay."

That was a relief to her. "Good. We can dig into another box. Who knows what treasures we'll find?"

It had been like a treasure hunt when he worked with her sorting books in his early days at Alpha. They had found some interesting items in the many sealed boxes of donated books and magazines. Someone had given a first edition of Robert W. Service's *Rhymes of a Red Cross Man*, and Ian had devoured the prose with eager enthusiasm. Once he had finished with it, he had passed the precious writings on to Coltan, who loved it so much he kept it for good in his personal collection. They had discussed the poems many times since then, and their discussions about literature opened up a whole new world to Ian. Even Carolyn, who did not like anything to do with the subject of war, found solace in the sensitive words of a man who had experienced both inhumanity and humanity at the front lines. She and Ian had sat up many a night between the rows of shelving, sipping tea and sharing their feelings about the verse. Often, she would insist Ian read the poems aloud to her. She loved to hear his voice and his accent, which, she told him, made the words come alive to her. He loved her rapt attention and the way she made him feel that he was important to her. Since he began work at the hospital, they had spent less time together, and Ian found he missed those times with her. He realized then, it was Carolyn who had helped him keep it together this long. Without realizing it, she had shielded him from the sometimes-gloomy energy inside Alpha Base.

In order to get well, he needed her. The others could not help him. Only she could help him. The discovery silenced the turmoil within him, and he felt his nerves calm.

At the other table, Raul Santiago cast a glance at the petite, dark-haired young British man who had wisely quieted the Cockney-accented boy's confrontational impulse. He had seen this man with the red-capped country bumpkin blond boy and the little Latina girl many times.

Santiago added Trevor Rolardy to his list of people to investigate. He thought he would make the young man's acquaintance directly instead of delegating it to one of his underlings. For the time being, he would wait patiently for the opportunity to present itself.

As for the gawky red-capped blond kid he code-named *Catfish*, Neville Langly had already gained his trust. It would be just a matter of time before the dumb bumpkin spilled his guts to handsome

Neville over pillow talk following a night of forbidden passion.

Santiago smiled inwardly. Soon, he would have the information he needed, and he could get the hell off this mountain.

AT BONITO VALLE COMMUNITY Hospital, Cory Jones followed Major Standish down the dimly lit hallway in the mostly abandoned third floor of the northeast wing. Standish stopped abruptly at a door with a plaque that read, *"Doctors' Lounge 4."* He removed a key from his pocket and unlocked the door, opened the door slowly.

"Lena...?"

Cory stood on his tiptoes to look over the major's shoulder as they stood there in the doorway. He heard a growl and a gasp, and then a whimper. The whimper sounded as if it came from a child.

Standish stepped forward and stopped again. "It's Daddy, honey."

Cory felt a chill shoot up his spine. He had an idea what waited in the confines of the lounge. When the major flipped on the light switch, the flickering florescent illumination verified his suspicions.

She was a dark-haired woman in her mid-twenties, average in height. At one time, she was obese, for her stretched-out excess skin sagged from her now bony frame. The flaps of skin that hung from her upper arms trembled with her fear at the sudden intrusion. She was barefooted and wore only a hospital gown and thin hospital robe to cover her backside. Her face and body were clean, though, not the mess of dirt, feces and dried blood Cory had seen on all the other mords. Even her hair was clean, although it was tangled and otherwise neglected. When she twisted her mouth and smiled, Cory saw her teeth were coated with months of crud—not a pretty sight.

The rank odor of the disease escaped the room with the sudden inversion of air from the open door. Cory felt vomit arise in his throat, and he struggled to swallow it back down, lest he hurl his breakfast all over the tan Berber carpeting.

"Jaddoo..." she said softly and with much effort to form the word.

"Yes, honey," Standish told her soothingly, "It's Daddy."

She stretched out her arms, folded her hands into the shape of a cup. "Foo...?"

"I fed you an hour ago, remember?"

"Dink wad?"

"Your water glass is at the sink. You know how to use the sink." He then backed up a step and to the side for Cory to come up beside him. When Cory took position at his side, staring at the woman, Standish informed him, "This is Lena. She won't hurt you. She won't hurt anyone. I had to hide her, you understand."

"I've only heard the diseased children talk, and just two of those..." Cory gasped.

"She's trying very hard to stay human." He stepped into the room. She tried to intercept him, her arms outstretched to hug him, but the makeshift shackle around her ankle prevented her from reaching him. She whimpered again, crinkled up her face in frustration. He soothed her, "It's alright, honey. I brought someone to help us." He put his arm around Cory's shoulders and introduced him in a bright, hopeful voice, "This is Cory. I want you to trust him and work with him. He's going to help you talk again, and he's going to help you relearn how to do all the things you used to do. He won't hurt you. You know I'll never bring anyone here who will hurt you. You know that, huh, sweetheart?"

Her brow furrowed as she attempted to pronounce his name. "Go-wee..."

"Cory..." Cory said slowly.

She smiled, licked her lips, smiled again. "Dansum..."

Standish grinned and glanced at Cory, "She said you're

handsome."

Just what he needed—a mord with a crush on him. Cory was not sure about this. Taming a mord was very different than calming a frightened injured house pet. Still, she seemed docile, and she appeared to have retained enough memory and common intelligence to be a good candidate for rehabilitation.

If rehabilitation were possible, Cory's success with her would jet him up the military's bureaucratic ladder to an esteemed position in their fledgling W1 Psychological Sciences Program. The program, aimed at retraining mords as grunt-work laborers and battlefield bomb detectors had been a rumor, but Cory had discovered through careful research the Program was indeed real.

He inquired of Standish, "Will she be part of the PS Program?"

Standish bristled at this. "She's my daughter!"

Cory slouched, looked down at the floor, ashamed of his insensitivity. "I'm sorry, sir."

"I want you to make her well!"

"I don't know if I can do that, sir."

"I want you to try."

She tugged at the shackle around her ankle. The chain was long enough to where she could reach the bathroom and the bed, but not long enough to give her access to the door. She sat on the floor and tugged again, lightly whipped the carpet with the slack chain. As Lena did this, her eyes were on her father, pleading. "Jaddoo... fee... Why?"

"For your safety," he lied.

She cast him a sadly accepting gaze, sighed deeply.

"Did you clean her up?" Cory asked.

"No. She does that herself. She uses the shower on her own, under her own volition."

"She doesn't brush her teeth."

"She hates the taste of the toothpaste."

"I can snag a couple tubes of dog toothpaste from a vet clinic. It's meat flavored with a touch of peanut butter. She might like that better."

"That makes sense," Standish replied hopefully. "There's a clinic two blocks down on Westwood. I'll give you a clearance card to give you free access around town." He paused thoughtfully, then said, "That is, if you're willing to accept this assignment, and you keep your mouth shut."

Cory glanced at Lena. She grinned at him and twirled a strand of her hair. He felt sorry for her and, at the same time, he was frightened of her. He hid his fear, considered again this duty could be his ticket up the ladder.

"What's in it for me?" he asked.

Standish suddenly glared at him. "Your life."

Cory felt his heart hit the floor of his gut with a sickening thud. "Sir?"

"I've already programmed in your Reffell chip. I'll be monitoring your every move. Try just once to fuck me over, I'll fry your chip. Do you understand?"

"What if I decide not to accept this assignment?" A dumb question realized too late.

Standish's severe glare and clenched jaws did not soften.

"I'll fry your chip."

IT WAS WELL AFTER TWO o'clock in the morning when Dillon awoke from a short nap. He turned over on his side and squinted at Scorpio's sleeping face. Unlike the previous men in Dillon's life, Scorpio did not snore. Hell... he didn't even talk in his sleep. Once he was out, that was it; he was as quiet as a corpse for the rest of the night. If not for the soldier's deep rhythmic breathing, Dillon would have been worried he had killed the poor guy with his ravenous sexual appetite. However, Scorpio was not much older than Dillon, five years at most, and he matched Dillon's energy and stamina between the sheets. Ah... to be young forever, Dillon mused.

He was hard again.

Dillon propped himself up on his elbow and petted his lover's dark hair. He leaned close and peered into his face, admired the handsome prince, hungered for him again. The prince would have to leave for the barracks soon, and Dillon wished he did not have to go. As if the object of his enchantment was Sleeping Beauty, he kissed his lips to waken him.

Scorpio awakened slowly, returning the kiss upon his lips.

Dillon kissed him a second time before he pulled away to whisper to him, "How about one for the road, sleepy head?"

The soldier opened his eyes and groggily stared into Dillon's. His grogginess was due to too much booze, and he silently regretted overdoing it. However, that was the only way he could endure this disgusting detail and maintain the charade. Santiago had promised him twenty joints, four cases of smokes, and twelve bottles of Jim Beam for his troubles. In the past, "Sans" had always come through, and Neville Langly had no reason to distrust him now. He was looking forward to collecting his reward. He thought he should tell Sans he also deserved an Oscar for his brilliant acting performance. Could Sans deliver that, too?

Thinking about Sans reminded him he had to return to the barracks before morning call. Sleepily, he asked the eagerly smiling boy who hovered over him, "What time is it?"

Dillon took his watch off the floor and read it, "Two-thirty-five."

"Shit!" Neville bolted upright, pushed Dillon off to the side in the same move. "I gotta go. Where's my clothes?"

Dillon gathered them into a pile next to the mattress. He answered with a triumphant smirk, "Right here where I dropped them." In the next breath, he suggested, "Let's go for one more. I got an all night sucker with your name on it."

Neville brushed him aside and reached for his clothing. Over his shoulder, he said to Dillon, "Jeez, Cat! Don't it ever go down?"

"Not when you're around." Dillon chose to ignore the soldier's reluctant body language. He sidled up behind the young man and wrapped his arms around his bare torso, caressed his skin, pulled him close in embrace. "It's at attention even when you're *not* around. All I gotta do is think of you, and that's all the time."

Unable to control it, Neville tightened up in Dillon's embrace. He felt suffocated within the boy's locked arms.

Dillon pressed his cheek to Neville's, whispered in his ear, "I love you, Scorp. I can't help it. You love me, too. I know you do."

Those were the words Neville had been dreading. For the past week, his little Catfish had become increasingly possessive and clingy. Neville took a moment and regained his composure. "Look, Cat... We gotta keep this casual. If anyone found out—"

"No one's gonna find out."

The soldier wondered how much longer he could keep up this ruse. It had been eight days, and he had not been able to nudge a single morsel of usable information about the little girl from the Catfish's ignorant mouth. All he could get out of the kid were words of devotion, not about the girl, but about him. This had proved more difficult than he had expected. He hoped maybe by tomorrow the boy would spill something usable. However, tomorrow would be too long to wait. He wanted this to be over tonight.

Finally, he thought of a good opener that would lead to a discussion about the girl.

"Aren't you getting up in a few hours to go fishing?"

"Uh-huh. Wanna go with us?"

"You and the kid, and that fat guy?"

"Yeah. Can you get the day off?"

"I'm on duty." He began to put on his socks, said over his shoulder, "That little girl sure seems attached to you."

"She's sweet. She likes everybody."

"What'd you say her name was?"

"Isabelle."

"She had a bunch of other names, uh... Rosa?"

Dillon chuckled. "Rosa Maria Rodriquez. There's a mouthful, huh?"

"Is that man, what's his name—Guffy—her father?"

Dillon gave him a perplexed expression, jokingly accused him, "You're hot for him, huh? You want that roly-poly guy?"

Neville played along, laughed softly. "Fuck you...!"

Dillon giggled, thought he'd delivered a good one. However, the vague feeling his little joke had bombed told him he needed another swig of rum. He found the bottle within the folds of the sleeping bag and took a long gulp of what little remained. He offered the one gulp leftover to Neville. "Here, dude."

Neville waved it off, preferred the little Catfish have it. Maybe it would be just enough to melt down his guard and loosen his mouth.

Dillon shrugged and finished the bottle. He watched Scorpio put on his uniform and then his jacket. "I wish you'd stay a while longer."

He tossed Dillon his pants and sweatshirt. "Let's go out and have a smoke. After that, I gotta go."

Dillon proved to be drunk enough to need assistance with dressing. After what seemed to be forever, they finally ducked out of the tent into the emptiness and silence of the main corridor that would lead them out the exit to the south side smoking area and gardens. With Dillon too drunk to notice and Neville too preoccupied with keeping him on his feet and quiet, neither noticed the man working security that observed them.

They assumed a facade of sobriety once they exited the cavern into the cold night air. Neville noticed a few soldiers on guard duty, one of whom was Santiago. He casually waved and greeted them while he led the boy to the smoking area where they sat among the boulders under a soft green light from the main trail.

Dillon shivered, wished he had worn his faux sheepskin-lined coat instead of the thin leather jacket.

Neville draped his arms around him, knowing they were in a spot where no one could see them. "You cold?"

Dillon nestled into him. "Not now."

"Who catches more fish? You? Isabelle? Guffy?"

"Isabelle."

"How'd you meet her?"

"She visited me when we were both in the hospital."

"Oh... that's right. You had cancer."

"And, she had the—" Dillon caught himself just in time, he hoped.

Neville exaggerated his alarmed disbelief, "Mord?"

"No..." Dillon dismissed it brusquely. "She had trouble walkin' 'cause she hurt herself on the way up here." He thought it was a good save.

"She seems fine now. She must've walked a long way. Poor kid. The kids got the worst of this mess, you know. I feel bad for the kids."

Dillon looked up into his face. "You like kids?"

"I love kids! I had three little sisters." It was a blatant lie.

"I had two sisters."

Neville picked up on the word, *had*. It offered good bait. "My sisters are dead."

"Mine, too." Dillon felt the sadness of their loss suddenly weigh upon him.

Neville took advantage of that. "I bet that's why you took to Isabelle, huh?"

"Yeah... She went through so much. They fucking tortured her."

"Who?"

"Those bastards down at Baker Creek. They fed people to the mord pusses. I saw it. Fucking bastards..." The final gulps of rum were enough to send him off on a second wave of drunkenness. He knew he was running his mouth, but he didn't care anymore. He wanted to express his anger about the cruelty in the world, so much of it he had personally experienced. He continued mournfully, "They fed my family to the mords. Can you believe that? They wanted to keep *them* alive instead of us!"

"Why?"

"Experiments. They experimented on poor Isa, too. Gave her electric shocks to keep her from attacking them. If it wasn't for Guffy, she woulda died. Or they woulda done worse to her."

Neville went in for the kill. "So, she *was* a mord."

He felt cornered and regretted his carelessness. There was nothing he could do about it now. "Don't tell no one. She's cured of it. She ain't dangerous, not to anybody. Really."

Neville held him tighter and cuddled him, just to keep his trust. The boy felt fragile and small in his arms. The soldier suddenly felt protective of him, and could not understand why. He blamed the vestiges of the rum for that. "I won't tell anyone."

"They don't know how she got over it and nobody else did."

"She doesn't seem to show any symptoms."

Dillon rested his head on Neville's shoulder, shivered again with the cold. He tried to remember what brought him out here into this bone-chilling night in the first place. Finally, he remembered. "You said we were gonna have a smoke." He sat up then and searched pleadingly into the soldier's face. "I forgot mine. You got one?"

Neville took two out of the pack, gave one to Dillon. He went to light it for Dillon, but the only match went out too quickly in the breeze. He had another matchbook in his pocket, but he feigned being out.

"I gotta get more matches," he told Dillon. "You stay here, and I'll ask that soldier over there." He pointed at Santiago. "Okay, Catfish?"

"For a kiss," Dillon whispered.

Neville kissed him and then strode over to Santiago at an isolated corner of the garden area. He spoke very softly so the other soldiers and Dillon would not hear him.

"Her name is Rosa Maria Rodriquez. She's the one from Baker Creek. The kid told me. It's all here." He took a tiny pen shaped disk recorder from the interior pocket of his jacket and slipped it into Santiago's eager hands.

"Good work, Nev." He casually slipped the recorder into his pocket.

"Got a book of matches or a lighter?"

Santiago produced a book of matches from the same pocket and handed it to him. "You had to get the kid drunk again."

"Shit..." Neville said softly, morosely, "The little fucker's clinging to me like ants on honey! Thinks he's in love with me. Thanks a lot, Sans!"

Santiago chuckled. "It could be worse." He gestured at Audrey Eastman over at the opposite corner of the garden, a thick, mannish, dirty looking woman. Most of the soldiers did not know she was a woman until she spoke. Even then, her voice was deep and her language coarse. "You could've had to fuck *that* for a week!"

Neville wheezed as he tried to restrain his laughter. "I'll take the kid. At least, he showers!"

"And, he *loves* you..." Santiago teased him.

"Fuck you, Sans."

Santiago abruptly became serious. "We might need you to run this down the mountain to base."

"Why?"

"Our radios aren't working right. Chadislaw says it might be the terrain."

"So I gotta traipse down the mountains, dodging wild animals and fucking mords to get that to base?"

"Could happen."

"Shit..."

"If we can't send out, we have to get the message to them somehow. Then we can grab the kid, blow this fucking place and be on a chopper out of here..." he snapped his fingers to make his point. "Go back to the Catfish before he comes over here. We'll talk it over tomorrow."

FROM THE SOFA IN THE television room, Trevor kept one eye on the doorway where he could view the main corridor and see Dillon return from outside. Trevor's temper was on low boil at this point, for he had already seen too much of the sordid side of life to believe anything other than his worst suspicions about Dillon's drinking buddy. He intended to confront the young soldier once Dillon had safely returned to his tent. He would confront the soldier and make it very clear if he continued to use Dillon, there would be severe consequences, and Trevor himself would deliver those consequences.

While Trevor silently seethed, the voices of the two military news anchors on the television droned on in low volume, something about another Islamic uprising in Madrid. The satellite footage showed fires raging amid the rubble of bombed-out buildings in one of the many business hubs in the city. The Islamic revolts had become so commonplace that they were hardly news anymore. Like so many swept involuntarily into the grip of global government control, the Islamists and like-minded Middle-Easterners were beginning to resist.

A related story came on that showed a similar scenario in the heart of London's international business district, only this time the protestors represented a cross-section of the British melting pot.

On the rocking chair closest to the television, Ian sat forward and watched the coverage with horror. The video cut to a segment taken earlier that morning of his countrymen fighting amongst each other as well as their oppressors. Homemade bombs and grenades flew back and forth and every other way. A young woman's head shot toward the camera lens, blown off her shoulders. Blood spattered on the lens, and then the video footage showed a skewed image of bloodied concrete.

Ian gasped audibly and began to chew his fingernails.

Alerted by Ian's gasp, Trevor looked at him and saw his distress, saw the wide-open eyes, the trembling shoulders and shaking knees. At once, Trevor swept the remote off the side table and thumbed the *off* button. The television died into darkness and silence. Ian continued to stare at it, continued to devour his ragged fingernails.

Trevor leaned sideways and gently backhanded Ian's shoulder. "You shouldn't watch that."

"I can't sleep."

"Small wonder, what with your viewin' 'abits."

Through his teeth that were busy nibbling another fingernail, he moaned, "There's no more 'ome to return to. I didn't see no one we knew... Did you?"

"No, lad."

"No dogs or cats, either."

"You never see dogs and cats during rioting."

"No..."

"Go to bed, Ian."

"I told ya... I can't sleep! Stop fussin' a' me! You sound like me bloody mum!"

Trevor gave up. He glanced from Ian to the doorway and into the corridor. Dillon had still not appeared.

Ian noticed and inquired, "Awaitin' your other boy, Trev?"

"My '*other boy*'?"

"The little queen."

Trevor did not expect Ian to ever say such a thing. It bothered him deeply to hear anyone make fun of Dillon. "Don't call him that."

"He's found a friend, y'know. I seen him visitin' late. Leaves by 'imself. Leaves the queen be'ind. They think we don't know."

"Have you told anyone?"

"Why should I spoil their fun?"

"You should have told *me*."

Ian smiled wryly. "So you could make a scene? What will ya do, Trev? Ya can't change what 'e is."

Trevor turned fully to Ian, gazed at him sternly. "He don't *know* what he is."

"*You* won't *accept* what 'e is."

"Do you?"

"Don't matter what I think."

"You think he's hopeless."

"Don't matter what I think."

"If I had thought you were hopeless, where would you be now?"

Ian thought about it, yet his stubborn stoicism lay just below the surface. After a long moment, he replied ironically, "I would be blissfully dead, 'appily out of this godforsaken world. In light of that, per'aps ya did me no favor."

His cool reply caused Trevor to shudder. Then, as if in rescue, his sister's words returned to him, her prediction he and Ian would walk a path together. Her prediction had been correct. With this in mind, he told Ian, "God has something different in mind for you."

"I think God's off gettin' pissed at a pub somewhere."

"Mind your tongue, boy!"

Ian ignored him. A familiar form weaving down the corridor

diverted his attention. With a lifted eyebrow, Ian thrust up his chin and said, "The little queen 'as found 'is way 'ome."

Trevor bolted from his chair and took surveillance from one edge of the doorway. He watched, dismayed, as Dillon ducked clumsily into his tent. The fact that he had returned safely and alone was of little relief to Trevor.

"I wouldn't confront 'im right now," Ian advised. "He's in no shape to make sense of anythin'."

"At least he's safe," Trevor conceded.

CHAPTER 17

It was a bitingly chilly night with a clear, starry sky. Dillon brought up the hood of his imitation down-filled quilted jacket when the breeze came up and stung his ears and cheeks. His fingers hurt from the cold, and he had left his gloves inside because it was easier to smoke without them on. Now, he regretted his decision.

He regretted that along with a few other things.

Neville sat across from him in the smoking section at the south end access to the lava tube. He dropped his cigarette on the dirt and snuffed it with his boot, then put the butt into his pocket to dispose of it in the interior trash bucket. It was the rule not to discard cigarette butts outside, and no litter, either. Tobacco butts and litter were a dead giveaway of humans residing nearby.

Neville stuck his hands into his jacket pockets and gazed remorsefully at the hurt boy across from him. "I'm sorry it's gotta be this way," he said.

Dillon did not look at him. "I thought you loved me."

"I've never loved anyone," Neville confessed. "To me, it was just fun. I thought you knew that."

"I'm in love with you."

"No, you're not."

This time, Dillon met his gaze. "I am, too. You're all I think about."

"That's *infatuation*."

"We don't have to end it."

"Yes, we do. If we don't, someone will find out. I don't need that."

"That's all you care about, that someone'll find out? What about me? Don't you care about what I feel? Don't I matter?"

"We had fun, Cat."

"Fuck you!"

"You'll find someone else."

"Yeah, right... finding a homo Bible banger in this place is like trying to find chow mien in a Mexican restaurant."

"There's gotta be others." Neville reached out and roughly patted Dillon's knee. "You're a good looking kid. I bet there's a lotta guys checking you out."

"Closet pedophiles. I don't want that. I don't want some dirty old man with a kid fetish. I want *you*, Scorp. I'm in love with *you*!"

"Cat, you don't know what it is to be in love. You're only fifteen."

"I've been in love already. I know what it is."

"Your boyfriend Evan was a rat and you welcomed his abuse of you. I don't call that love; I call that desperation. He took advantage of you and you allowed it because you were desperate for him to love you. If I had known about you and him before I slept with you I never would've let it get this far."

"You think I'm desperate?"

"I think you crave love, and when you think you've got it you hang on like grim death. That's bad for me and it's bad for you." He felt then he had said all he could to escape this situation as gracefully as possible. Now, all he wanted was to get out of the cold and into the warm barracks. He stood and took a step toward Dillon, bent and patted his shoulder. "This is the way it's gotta be, Cat. I'm going in now."

Dillon looked away from him. In the dim light, Neville saw the tears spill down the boy's cheeks. He felt terrible about it. If he had known the kid was starved for affection, he would not have accepted Santiago's assignment. It was bad enough the operation required him, a heterosexual, to seduce this boy in order to extract information. It was even worse that the boy had misinterpreted his sexual attentions as genuine love. That had not been part of the plan. Now, the little Catfish sat before him with his face awash in tears and his spirit broken. What a damned mess.

Coldly, Dillon said, "You told me you'd get me another carton of cigarettes."

"I'll drop them by your tent in the morning when you're at breakfast. I don't want to see you. Is that clear?"

"I want a bottle of booze, too."

"That'd be a bad idea."

Dillon sniggered bitterly. "Like you give a fuck..."

"I'm sorry it has to be this way."

Dillon still refused to look at him. He used the back of his hand to wipe the angry tears from his face. "As of this moment, we don't know each other. We never knew each other."

"That'd be best." He walked away.

Dillon snuffed out his cigarette and lit another one. He hoped he had already come down with lung cancer. He hoped the leukemia had returned. He hoped he would not wake up tomorrow.

He wished he could stop crying.

He did not know how much time had gone by, but he was on his fifth straight cigarette when Trevor took a seat at the boulder across from him. Even though Trevor mumbled something that sounded like a greeting, Dillon ignored him and stared into the dirt at his feet, the pile of squashed butts there.

"I see you're not hurtin' for gaspers," Trevor repeated.

"I ain't in the mood for you to be ragging on me," Dillon warned him.

"You've been crying."

"What's it to you?"

"It's everything to me."

"Fuck you, Trev."

"Have I hurt you?"

"Get outa my face."

"I know about your soldier." He said it gently, with a hint of compassion and worry.

"Who else knows?"

"Ian."

"Did Ian rat on me?"

"No." Trevor waited a few moments before he said, "Are the cigarettes worth it?"

"It was a business arrangement. It's over now." Dillon looked up at him, a stern expression on his face. "I got what I wanted, and he got what he wanted. Don't lecture me."

"He broke it off with you."

He smiled wryly, and with a fresh wave of tears stated bitterly, "That makes you happy, don't it?"

"I don't want you to return to your old pattern."

"Why, Trev? Why does it matter?"

"Because you're better than that."

"I'm trash. We throw trash away. I've been thrown away so many times. It don't bother me anymore. I know what I am. *You* can throw me away, too. I don't care."

"Your tears contradict your words."

He sobbed in silence. Finally, he gasped, "I love him."

"No, Dillon..."

"How would you know?"

"You just told me it was a business arrangement. Isn't the rule of the trade to never fall in love with your customers?"

Enraged, Dillon threw his cigarette away, sprung up and tackled Trevor. He began to beat him with his fists. It was easy for Trevor to overcome him and subdue him. In the blink of an eye, Dillon landed on his back and Trevor sat on top of him. Trevor gripped his wrists to prevent him from flailing at him. He said nothing, waited patiently for Dillon to exhaust himself.

Dillon finally gave in. "Get off my chest! I can't breathe!"

"Are you done, lad?"

"He wasn't a customer!"

Trevor kept the tone of his voice gentle, "Will you be calm? No more hitting?"

"Yeah." Trevor let him up. He sat up in the dirt, wrapped his arms around his knees and quietly sobbed.

"I'm sorry you're hurt, lad."

"I was stupid," Dillon whispered. "I was so stupid."

"You have real friends. Don't you realize it?"

"I got other needs, Trev."

"We all have those same needs. We learn to control them."

"You're so full of shit. I know about you and Suzanne. Hell...! You're fucking your shrink! What kind of self-control is that?"

"She isn't my shrink."

"It started off that way!"

"And I do love her."

"So, why don't you marry her?"

"She doesn't want that."

Dillon eyed him tauntingly, "Maybe because you're twenty years younger than her. You're young enough to be her son! Don't tell me about self-control and what's moral and all that. You don't walk your own talk."

Trevor became silent. Dillon got him with that one. His inference that Trevor and Suzanne's relationship was based more on sex than anything else was correct. To top it off, Trevor realized he had never been in love in his entire life. There had never been the time, the opportunity or the desire. He loved Suzanne, yes, but he was not *in* love with her, and she was certainly not in love with him. What right had he to tell the boy what was good and moral?

MORRIS COMPARED THE images of Rosa's and Coltan's latest blood draws on the monitors. Both samples were clear of the mord and dog viruses. The only curious thing Morris noticed was the strange microscopic egg-shaped, six-legged gelatinous creatures that swam languidly among the red and white corpuscles. These were antibodies, an alien species he had never encountered during his twenty-five-plus years as a pathologist, until he first discovered them in little Isabelle's blood shortly after he arrived with her at Alpha Base. Although the antibodies were strange to him, they impressed him as being *guardians at the gate*, for they appeared to be patrolling the blood for threats while they diligently nurtured and fed the new young red blood cells. He wondered if he could harvest these "good guys" to create a vaccine against the viruses.

Doctor Quimby studied the images on the monitor over Morris' shoulder. "What shall we call them?"

"*Guardians de Isabella*. GDI's for short. How's that?"

Quimby smiled and shrugged.

Morris shrugged and nodded in return, "GDI's, then." He turned the chair on its wheels and faced Quimby thoughtfully. "When Coltan was sick, I tried these antibodies from Isa's blood on his blood. It didn't work. Instead of attacking the dog virus, the GDI's ignored it. Yet, when we treated him with the mord virus, he developed these same antibodies. I haven't been able to duplicate that action in the lab. I want to try again. We need some mice or rats to test this on."

"I could ask James and Vasson to send a squad into the forest to find some."

"There's a lot of infected wildlife still out there. I wonder if we can bag something that's already infected."

"I'll have to talk with James about it. I don't know if he'll go for that."

"We'll both talk to him."

"HI, DANSUM..." LENA greeted Cory with a shy smile when he entered the small two-room suite. She was sitting at the edge of the bed, and she was brushing her hair. Her feet dangled a couple inches from the floor, one still sporting an ankle cuff attached to a long iron chain wrapped around the base of the toilet in the adjoining shower room.

"Your father said he brought you breakfast," Cory said.

She lifted the tray at the end of the bed and tilted it for him to see. "Aw gone!" She grinned and laughed. "He gib me fwies wiff bacon! Said... no peepo! I twy hod. No peepo. No bud. I do good, Cowee?"

He saw all the food was gone. "You did very good, Lena!" He took the chair next to the door and out of her reach. He removed some music discs and a small player from his backpack, and then set the pack on the floor. "I brought you some music."

"Woning 'tones?"

"Mick Jaeger..."

"Big nips..." She pursed her lips and made a fish face.

Cory laughed. "Yeah... he had big lips."

She looked at him straight-faced. "He dead now."

"Yeah. They're all dead."

"Nong time ago."

"Yeah."

"Got *'tay Offa My Cowed"* on dat?"

"All their greatest hits, and then some. Well over one-hundred selections on this one little disk."

"Day! You! Tay offa my cowed...!" she sang loudly. To Cory's amazement, she sang on key.

"Wanna listen to it?"

She scrunched her eyebrows curiously. "What ewse you got? I

nuv aw da ode muzik."

He picked through the small selection. "The Stones, Billy Idol, a really ancient Black Sabbath, some old Rap artists—"

Lena interjected, "I nike summa dem Rap. Daddy membooed. He hate dat!" She giggled.

Cory continued, "...a moldy-oldie Buddy Holly – Greatest Hits, mind you – Madonna: *The Legacy Collection*..."

"She dead now," Lena commented.

"Yeah... Lived to be an old lady, though."

"Dooty o' nady!" Lena exclaimed, laughing.

Cory laughed with her. "Yeah... She was a fun gal!"

"Nuvved kids."

"Yeah... loved kids."

"You got Deffindum in dere?"

"How could I omit them?"

"Day cwazy!"

"I read somewhere *Disturbed* inspired them."

She reminded him sadly, "Day aw dead, Cowee."

"Yeah." He came to the last disk on the stack. "And, the last one is a change of pace: Gregorian Chant."

Her face brightened. "Gowin chant?"

"Your dad said you liked that."

"Yeah... dat, too."

"Wanna listen?"

"Need bud dink."

"He brought you some this morning."

"Aw gone." She crooked her head to one side, regarded him thoughtfully. "Cowee? You weally aw dansum. Weally."

Her intense gaze creeped him out. He was certain he was more appetizing to her than handsome. He made a joke of it, "You're just trying to sweet-talk me, aren't you?"

"Uh-uh. You dansum. Mell good, too."

"I smell like food to you."

"Uh-uh. Wanna kiss you."

"So you can bite me." He grinned at her. "Huh?"

She laughed again… "Uh-uh. Bite *Madonna*! B-cup boobs! Just enough!" In the next second, she became serious. "She dead now, y'know."

"Yeah. I know."

"Kiddin' about dat. I'm on weg-goo-loo food. You safe wiff me, Cowee."

"Did you brush your teeth?"

"Uh-huh! Nook…" she lifted her upper lips with her fingers and showed him her teeth. "Aw keen. Did good job. Dog toofpaste good. Don't sit—ting—mowff."

"Good girl."

She gave him a slightly miffed expression. "*Woman*, Cowee…"

"Good *woman*."

"Bettoo." She leaned forward and reached out her hands. "Gib me payer. Hew music nater. Tanks fow binging."

He held on to the disk player. "Did you read your newspaper yet?"

She dug it out from under the covers. "Tadesco says mord awmose gone. Chips found some sick natoo. No new cases." She gathered the sections and stacked them on her lap, looked at Cory with pleading eyes. "Don't net Tadesco get me."

"That's why we're hiding you here."

"Jaddy kied."

"He cried?"

"When he ta… saw me. Boke hawt. I kie." She gestured impatiently for the player, "Gib me muzik. I take."

He stacked the disks on top of the player, balanced it and leaned forward with it for her to take it. "Don't try anything funny," he warned her teasingly.

She took the player and the disks, set them on the bed, and turned back to him. "What it goin' take, Cowee? It been two weeks. Hab I twied bite you?"

"I haven't gotten close enough. I don't want to tempt you."

She sighed in a frustrated manner. "I got seff contwo."

"I know you do," he replied sympathetically. "I admire that. You've been doing great. Still, I'd better keep my distance for a while longer. It's safer for me—and *you*."

"Net me hode yo' hand. I show you." She leaned forward and reached for his hand. "Don't be afwaid. How you gonna twust me?" He met her request with indecisive silence. She patiently persisted, her eyes full of sincerity. "I gib you kiss on hand. No teef, no bite. Pommis. You see."

"I don't know..."

"I'm not wide animoo."

He looked away from her to the floor, "Lena..."

"We gotta twust each uddoo, Cowee. We get twoo dis pawt, we moob on an' you hep me nearn an' memboo hooman way wiff no bite 'tuff. I wanna be nomo again. Hep me, Cowee. Tart wiff twust. I twust *you*." Again, she reached out her hand, and this time she wiggled her fingers to him as encouragement.

Cory analyzed her face, searched for hidden signs of intended deception. There was no deceit there, only one hundred percent sincerity. Cautiously, he stood and stepped near her, reached out his hand, touched his fingers to hers. Her fingertips were cold.

"Are you cold, Lena?"

"I'm aw-ways code."

"I'll get you more blankets."

"Aftoo hand hode an' hand kiss." She caressed his fingers. "See? Okay? Now, net me hode dis handa yose." He allowed her to lightly grasp his hand. His skin was warm. She found that a comfort. "You hand wome. Mowff, too." She deftly ran her fingertips over his, paused and paid special attention to the calluses there. "You got cowuff on fingoos. Hod wook, huh?"

"It's part of being a soldier."

"Bing hand to mowff now?"

He did not want to step any closer to her, for that would bring him inside the perimeter allowed by her ankle chain. What if she changed her mind and decided to bite him? "I think we should wait and take that step tomorrow."

She clasped his hand gently with both of hers, gazed up at him tenderly. "Twust, Cowee. I twust you, an' you got gun."

He couldn't argue with that. He took two more steps closer to her and hoped he wouldn't be sorry. "Okay, Lena. I'll trust you."

She carried his hand up to her face, caressed the back of his hand with her cheek. Her eyes fixed on his, she smiled and said, "Okay?"

"So far."

Lena shook her head, rolled her eyes and chuckled. "You posed to be bwave. Big bwave soldoo. You shakin'!"

All the years he had worked with animals, he had never shown fear with the aggressive ones. Today, this emaciated woman terrified him like no wild beast he had ever encountered. Yet, like animals, people responded better if they felt they were being trusted and could trust the person to whom they responded. Cory realized his nervousness could make her nervous, and that alone might cause her to nip at him. With that in mind, he took a slow deep breath and let it out, gave her a grin and encouraged her, "Help me not be afraid, Lena." He allowed her to move his hand to her mouth where she caressed his skin with her lips. It surprised him that her lips were so soft and warm.

"Kiss now," Lena said.

"Okay."

She kissed his hand very gently. The scent of his skin whetted her appetite, and her sudden hunger for his flesh both frightened and disappointed her. She resisted her growing urge to taste him, and she concealed her arousal. She gave his hand one more very gentle kiss. After she did that, she released his hand and grinned up at him. "Done! We did good. You go sit now."

He backed up and sat down in the chair. "What did you feel when my hand was so close to your mouth?"

"Happy you twusted me."

"Something frightened you. I saw it for a second in your eyes. Tell me."

She sighed and stared down at the floor.

"Trust," he reminded her.

She looked up bravely. "Mell made me hungwy. I fought it."

"Thank you for being honest with me."

"How we gonna fix dis?"

"I don't know. To your credit, you controlled yourself."

"Maybe I can't be fixed. Maybe you should put me asweep nike animoo. It'd be okay."

"I don't want to do that. I promised your father I'd do everything I could to help you."

"I talk to him. Might be bettoo fo' him to net me go." She bent and picked up her ankle chain in her hands, jiggled the chain to make her point, "Dis no nife fo' anyone."

"Let's give it more time," Cory suggested.

"I don't wanna niv nike dis."

"Listen, Lena... You've made it farther than anyone else who's been infected. How, I don't know. But you can still function. You've kept your faculties. You can reason, take care of yourself, read, talk—"

"Can't talk good," she interjected.

"With practice, you can. We can work on your speech."

"Den what? I caw you on phone an' say net's go out? You take me on ankoo chain to dinnoo somewhew, an' I odoo neg of waitoo?"

She chuckled at her own joke.

He couldn't help it; he laughed. She had a good sense of humor.

Laughing, she added, "Hode duh pices! Jus' gimme yo' neg, mistoo!"

"Oh, Lena..." He took a few moments to let his laughter subside. He appreciated her ironic humor and admired her courage.

"Yup," she moaned, "Can't take me anywhew!"

ISABELLE CROUCHED BETWEEN the large cardboard boxes in the pitch-black kitchen. She was almost finished with the raw venison steak she had stolen from the cold box. The sound of light and cautious footsteps caused her to stop chewing and listen closely. The footsteps drew nearer and stopped. She took a slow, silent breath of air in and smelled it to identify the owner of the quiet feet.

To her relief, it was Coltan. She poked her head around the corner of one of the boxes just enough so she could view him through one eye. He had stopped at the cold box. The light made her squint when he opened the door. She watched and waited, hoped he would find a snack to steal and be on his way. He stared into the cold box for what seemed a long time. She noticed his legs were trembling. That was very odd; Coltan was never afraid of anything. Why would he be shaking in his shoes like that?

"Please forgive me, Father..." He whispered it under his breath, but Isa could hear it loud and clear.

She continued to observe him, now more curious than anything else. What did he think he was doing that would make God mad at him?

He lifted the aluminum foil that covered the big platter. The foil made that familiar metallic crinkle sound, but very softly because he was trying to be quiet. In a few moments, he reset the foil around the edges of the platter. When he turned around and shut the cold box door, she saw he had a small slab of raw venison in the palm of his hand. He sniffed it and then he licked it. He closed his eyes and took a deep breath, slowly released the breath. His breath quivered in the air with his anticipation.

Isabelle pictured his breath as like the wings of a butterfly hovering over a flower before it landed.

Suddenly, his posture stiffened and an alarmed expression froze on his face. He jerked his chin up, and smelled the air with short sharp bursts of rapid inhalations. He stopped after a few moments and followed the scent with his eyes.

Isabelle ducked her head behind the box to avoid detection.

"Isa..." he whispered, "It's only me."

Cautiously, she moved and peered around the side of the box. Their eyes met.

"Hi, Kotin..."

He squatted beside her. "What are you doing here?"

She stared at the meat in his hand. Finally, she looked him in the eye and showed him what was left of her fix.

"Same as you."

"Does your stomach hurt, too?"

"Not anymore. It's duh bud in da meat you need. Dat makes it stop."

He was still whispering when he spoke. "How long after you got well did you start to get the cravings?"

"I don't know. It was aftoo I got hewh."

"Does Guffy know?"

"Nobody knows. Don't tewh no one."

He smiled at the absurd jeopardy of their situation, and at the humorous thought that simultaneously crossed his mind. "As Dillon would say, 'I'm not as stupid as I look.'"

She giggled silently.

He gestured with the hand that held the raw meat. "Is this gonna give us worms?"

She giggled again and shook her head.

"Well..." he said, "Down the hatch." It was small enough to fit in his mouth. He chewed it slowly, savored the blood that squished from the meat onto his tongue and teeth. When he was done, he licked the traces of blood off his fingers.

Isabelle finished hers, and cleaned her fingers the same as Coltan did. When she was done, she returned his complicit gaze.

"Will this happen a lot?" he asked.

"No. Just sometimes. It don't happen that much." She sat down Indian Style (as they called it at school), leaned her face close to Coltan for intimacy. "I can sneak you food if you evoo need me to. Okay?"

"Okay. Same here."

"Okay." Then she added, "God ain't mad at you."

"You sound positive about that."

"I am."

"You don't wanna eat people, do you?"

Her whisper came emphatically, "Uh-uh!"

"Me, neither."

"Maybe it'll go away."

"Maybe."

CHAPTER 18

It had been over a week since Neville broke up with Dillon. During that time, Dillon did his best to function. He concealed his emotional turmoil from the others in his circle, joked and laughed with them. He put together another "TV show" with Isabelle and performed it for the patients in the hospital at Doctor Quimby's request. They performed their skits in Dillon's handy cardboard box pretend television set, in *living color, no foolin'*. He chose *hypochondria* as his subject, and managed to stretch out the laughs with the pretense hypochondria was a genuine medical condition. Isabelle played the role of Nurse Ratchetset to his Doctor Painsinyourhead. To add to the authenticity, they also included some commercials for diarrhea and flatulence miracle cures. Dillon and Isabelle, now renown as the *Ennertainment Committee*, had the patients busting their stitches with laughter.

In the isolating silence of night, the Court Jester suffered in his private misery, wallowed in his tears until sleep finally claimed him and gave him respite. Tonight was like all the previous nights, and his anger had finally given way to acceptance, and the acceptance another bout of tears.

He had no idea his muffled sobs carried outside his tent until Carolyn whispered to him from the sealed entrance.

"I'm okay," he whispered in response to her inquiry.

"No, you're not," she said. "I've heard you every night this week. Let me in."

Reluctantly, he crawled on his knees to the flap, unzipped it and allowed her entrance. She ducked in and promptly sat on the floor, regarded him curiously and concernedly.

"What's wrong? What happened?"

"I don't wanna talk about it."

"It must be pretty bad to make you cry every night."

He sniffed and wiped his nose with his sleeve. "I didn't think anyone could hear me."

"My tent's right behind yours. We almost share a wall." She scooted closer to him and gently rubbed his back. "You've probably heard me crying a few times."

"Only once."

"Natalie still cries over her mom and dad, too. She saw her mother die, you know. You knew that, didn't you?"

"Coltan told me." He was relieved she assumed he was mourning for his family. That told him she had no idea about his clandestine rendezvous with Neville.

"You know what I hate the most?"

"What?"

"Not having anyone there to hold me. Crying into your pillow has got to be the loneliest thing in the whole world."

"Yeah..." More tears escaped. He wiped them away.

"You don't have to talk about it," Carolyn said. "But if you want me to stay tonight just to be here for you, I'd be glad to. As a matter of fact, I want to. I can't stand to hear you so alone and miserable." She continued to rub his back, do what she could to comfort him. After a long contemplative silence, she said understandingly, "I've lost track of the number of times I've been dumped. Seems as soon as they get what they want, they're outa here."

He stared at her dumbly. She had known about it all along.

"You didn't tell anybody, did you?"

"Hell, no. What you do in the privacy of your tent is your own business."

"How did Ian find out?"

"Ian sees everything that goes on around here. I'm not surprised he knew. Listen, Dillon, he never mentioned it to me. I never mentioned it to him. The way I figure it that was your own private business. I ain't gonna judge you. If you knew about all the stuff I did..."

He broke down again into a spell of miserable sobs. She put her arms around him and drew him to her.

"I hurt so bad," he told her.

"I know. In time, it'll get better."

CORY HAD WORKED WITH Lena all week to improve her pronunciation. She was eager to regain all the abilities and knowledge the mord virus had dulled, and her rehabilitation unfolded surprisingly quickly.

This morning he found her on her bed listening to her disk of Gregorian Chants while she read a note Cory assumed was from her father. She had showered and washed her hair, and she smelled vaguely of flowers. Cory knew the flower scent came from her shampoo. She had mentioned it was a favorite fragrance of hers back in the time when she led a normal life. Her first goal was to reclaim that normalcy.

Her second goal was to return to work in her profession as a geneticist. To this end, Major Standish and Cory brought her textbooks and research papers they found around the hospital. Lena spent her afternoons re-educating herself.

When he took his usual seat near the door, she folded the note, turned off the disk player and glanced at him, smiled and said, "How's the handsome hunka soldier doing today?"

He laughed and replied, "I just did a spread for G.Q. Magazine."

"I bet you'd look spiffy in a tux."

"The last suit I wore was to a friend's wedding."

"Did your friend make it?"

"She's dead. My friends and my whole family are gone."

"I'm sorry." Lena then thought about it, cocked her head, "On second thought, they're the lucky ones."

After considering her comment, he replied, "I gotta agree with that."

She brightened. A naughty smile warned him she was about to deliver another zinger. "I ordered room service for us."

He played along, as usual. "Really?"

"Yep. I ordered leg of waiter, and a Bloody Mary. They didn't have a Bloody Mary. I had to settle for a Bloody Susan."

He laughed.

"Then they called me back and said they were all out of Bloody Susans. I said, 'Well, what else ya got?' They sent me a Bloody Boy Named Sue. He was young and tender. Sorry I didn't save you some. I couldn't help myself." She shook her head ruefully and added, "That was the worst one I've come up with yet."

"You could've had a second career as a stand-up comic."

"Yeah. Out there on stage with my ankle chain. 'You've been a great audience; and *tasty*, too!'"

He let that one go with a brief chuckle, said seriously, "You've done well on regular food, Lena. Have you craved any human meat?"

"Once in a while." She put aside the newspaper and sat up at the side of the bed. "I want you to know, Cory, you don't smell like food to me anymore."

"That's a relief."

"More for you than for me." She grinned at him. "I can use regular toothpaste now, too. How about that?"

He grinned back at her, "Excellent!"

"No more dog breath!"

He laughed.

"Can I get this damned ankle chain off? It's chafing me!"

"What does your dad say?"

"He says it's up to you." She gave him her best pitiful pleading look.

He stayed silent, thinking about it.

"It's rusting from the shower! Eventually the chain's gonna rust through and bust, anyway." She waited for him to speak, but he said nothing. "Look, Cory... Do I really still impress you as some kind of monster that's gonna devour you? Look at me. I'm a weak, skinny, little-old-lady type of gal. Hell, even when I was fat and healthy, I was a weakling. I couldn't overpower a fly! They used to rib me about it at work." She suddenly made a face, feigned ecstasy, closed her eyes and moaned ravenously, "Mmmmm, ribs..."

He knew she was clowning again, and he chuckled. Cory reconsidered her request. As he thought, he unconsciously caressed the butt of his gun in the holster at his hip. Finally, he came to a decision and stood. "I'll get the key, Lena."

She sighed gratefully, "Thank you."

NEVILLE SLIPPED AWAY from Alpha Base in the middle of the night. Santiago had given him a map to follow that would allow him to avoid the surveillance cameras on his way out. It was a dangerous trek through the tangled underbrush, and sometimes he had to drop to his hands and knees to follow the deer trail in the dim moonlight, but he cleared the perimeter and found the south side fire access trail as the first pale light of dawn emerged over the peaks.

He was cold and his feet hurt. The fully loaded backpack Santiago had pre-set for him at the junction of the deer and fire trails proved to grow heavier as the hours passed. To add to his misery, his hands, arms, face, neck, chest and calves had begun to itch with exasperating frequency. No doubt, he had encountered some poison oak, a double-whammy, what with the endless assaults from the mosquitoes.

Giving in to his fatigue and thirst, he sat down against a boulder at the edge of the trail and swung the heavy pack off his shoulders. He set it down and opened it, found the canteen and took a long drink. Afterwards, he pulled down his socks and examined the rashes on both his calves under the illumination of his tiny penlight. As he did this, a couple of fleas popped off the bare skin of his right calf. He wondered how many fleas had taken up residence in his socks during the journey—probably a few hundred, by the number of bites. He quickly removed his boots and socks, shook out the socks, all the while wondering if the fleas carried the mord virus in addition to Bubonic Plague. Wouldn't that be his luck to die on this mountain from a bunch of plague-infected fleabites! Where was the honor in that? He angrily unlaced and shook out his boots, slapped them together upside down to dislodge anything else hiding within. As he did this, a wolf spider scrambled out of his backpack and blindly used his bare outstretched foot as an overpass. Neville shrieked, dropped the boots and sprung up, did a panicked jig in an effort to shake off any other unwelcome hitchhikers. No additional creatures flew off him during his dance, a small relief to him. Neville had never been an outdoor kind of guy, and he was particularly terrified of spiders.

In the back of his mind, he recalled Santiago knew this, and that was likely why he sent him off on this particular mission in this hellish wilderness. The bastard had a sadistic sense of humor. Neville could picture him laughing with his butch pal Eastman over it.

The howling of wolves in the distance reminded him not to linger very long. When a pack of wolves even closer replied to the distant pack, he decided it was time to get moving. He sat down and gave his socks one final shake-off before he put them on. They felt rough on his feet, and they made him itch. He disregarded the itching as psychosomatic and tried to ignore it as he put on one boot and began to lace it up.

Something stepped on the dead leaves behind the boulder.

Neville froze and listened.

Something breathed... panted...

He smelled something that made him think of a wet dog.

My rifle...

He glanced from side to side, found it at his left. He leaned and reached for it.

The pack dived onto his back and his head, all claws and teeth, salivating growls and putrid hot breath. The dew on their fur chilled his neck. Their weight pushed him down on his belly. They tore through his parka with their claws, tugged at it with their teeth. One or more of them got hold of the hood and ripped it down, pulled the parka off his shoulders to reveal the thinner material of his uniform. Teeth penetrated his shoulders, the back of his head, his cheeks, his arms. He tried to reach for his rifle, but two of them had pounced between his body and the weapon. One of them kicked the rifle away with its hind feet, as if it knew that was what he was reaching for. The other went for his throat. He felt the sharp pain there, felt the teeth penetrate his windpipe. The air he gasped in escaped through the massive hole that opened up when the wolf ripped the tissue away with its teeth. In his panic, he flailed at his assailants, tried mightily to roll over into a defensive position. The more he fought back, the more persistent and ferocious their attack. They tore through his uniform, bit and chewed his legs, buttocks, back and arms. The one at his throat dove in for a second bite, and this time it locked its teeth in a death grip and proceeded to lick and suck the hot spurting blood.

Neville's final thought as his life faded away was a humble acceptance that he deserved this fate and, with that acceptance came an even humbler apology to God.

"WE CAN GET COLTAN TO build us some cages," Morris told James, "There must be some leftover materials somewhere around here."

James tapped the eraser end of his pencil on his desk as he searched his memory. "I think there's some chicken wire down in the fourth level. That wouldn't do. It's too weak and the holes are too big. You're talkin' mice, rats, maybe a dog—if you can find one—right?"

"Joe said there were a lot of stray dogs."

"That was months ago," James said.

Morris settled on the idea of rodents. "We could triple up the layers of chicken wire, make the holes smaller that way."

James tapped the eraser down a couple more times, thinking. "How secure is that live virus you got?"

"We got it sealed in four containers, one inside the next. We keep it in the freezer. The freezer's locked. I'm the only one who has the key."

"If one of your rats or mice gets loose," James sat forward intently, "We're looking at an epidemic here. To me, it's not worth the risk."

"They won't get loose."

"You can't guarantee that."

"The possibility that I can create a one-shot vaccine, or cure, is worth the risk."

James wouldn't budge. He mused his friend Morris was becoming the stereotypical Mad Scientist. "You've already got a cure for the virus."

Morris was getting frustrated with James' lack of vision. He recalled how Coltan had suffered through the effects of the introduction of the mord virus into his system to cure the dog virus.

He considered the fact that Coltan was still slowly recovering, and it pained Morris to see the once-robust young man struggle through everyday tasks. "Look, James. That cure we got put that poor kid through hell! If there's another cure that wouldn't do that, we should explore it."

"He's getting well. Better every day."

"You have no idea what it did to him."

"He hasn't complained."

"It ravaged his system! He almost died! He's still having problems with his coordination and his eyesight. He suffers nightmares, relives the hallucinations in his sleep. Of course, he hasn't complained to you. You're not a doctor. Why would he tell you?"

"Are you sure he's clear of the viruses?"

"Yes."

"What about the Rodriquez girl?"

"Her, too."

"Does she have any lingering symptoms?"

"No."

"Have you asked her?"

Morris sighed with frustration. "Yes. Once a month we take a blood sample from her. We ask her then. She said everything is fine. The only lingering disability she has is with her speech and memory. That could be a pre-existing condition she's always struggled with. None of us know anything about her past, so I can't positively attribute that to the viruses."

"Some of the mord kids displayed that same speech defect. I know because I came across a few."

"Is that so? Isa's the only child I've dealt with that had it." He reconsidered that with a vague memory of a three year-old boy patient at the clinic. That child's speech pattern had been virtually undecipherable, but Morris had attributed that to the typical speech pattern of a toddler. The boy had died a few days after capture, and Morris had shut the memory away. "No, wait... there was a toddler, a boy. He died. He didn't live long enough for me to study him."

"Trevor told me the boys with him who died, their speech had slurred just before they slipped into a coma."

"That was the stroke symptom phase of the disease."

"How long did it take Coltan to recover his speaking ability?"

"About two weeks."

"Was his speech pattern like Isa's?"

"The first five days. He was so frustrated and humiliated about it he stopped trying to talk for a couple days after. Finally, with Natalie's encouragement, he started talking again, and his pronunciation improved rapidly. It was like a stroke patient, only he recovered faster."

"Is there any chance he and Isa could have a relapse?"

"The virus is gone."

"I've heard of viruses that hide in the body. Herpes, for one. Chickenpox—my grandmother had shingles from it. What if the mord or dog viruses do the same thing? What if they're hiding?"

"All the more reason to find an alternative cure."

James reclined in his chair and thought about it for a long time.

Morris poured them another cup of hot tea, compliments of Ian's indoor garden. As he sipped the tea, Morris watched James and thought about Ian, considered the boy's uncanny ability to feel the hidden emotions of others. He toyed with the idea of using Ian as a radar system of sorts to hone in on Coltan and Isabelle to monitor their emotional and psychological patterns for any otherwise undetected changes. Morris considered taking the proposal to the boy.

Finally, James sat forward and said, "You'll have to bring it in front of a committee, a diverse group consisting of medical, military and lay people. Fair enough?"

"Sure... Fair enough."

Four days later, the committee voted no.

CHAPTER 19

"That's nuts!" Coltan blurted when Morris gave him the news.

Morris pressed the cotton ball to Coltan's vein, and secured it with tape. While he set the vial full of blood in the vial keeper, he lamented to Coltan, "They think it's too risky. You know, they even suggested I destroy the viruses. I talked them out of that when I reminded them that's the only cure we've got."

"Screw them. I'll make those cages for you."

"Forget it, Coltan. If they find out, we'll both be out on our asses."

"They wouldn't do that."

"I don't want to find out." He rolled a stool in front of Coltan seated at the blood-draw station, sat and gave Coltan his full attention. "You know what they say about biting the hand that feeds you."

"Is that supposed to be a mord joke?"

"No."

He shook his head disdainfully. "You can't get away from bureaucracy..."

"Hey... at least it's still a democracy in here. Try to live out there..."

Coltan chortled. "Shit..."

Morris grinned at him. "Our future pastor is not supposed to cuss."

"Sometimes I can't help it." He unrolled his sleeve over the bandage and said, "How do you deal with the frustration?"

"I drink..."

Coltan laughed. "Nuh-uh!"

Morris chuckled, "No... I'm toughened-up from years of dealing with red tape. It comes with the territory. Eventually, things work out."

"What if we get sick again? What if the cure isn't really a cure, but a treatment?"

"Are you having any symptoms?"

"No." He qualified the lie with his belief his enhanced senses were a side effect of the virus, not a symptom.

"Has Isabelle mentioned anything?"

"Not to me. She seems fine." *Oh, oh... Thou shalt not commit false witness.*

"She has a heightened sense of smell."

"Well, yeah... We all know about that."

"What about you?"

"Somewhat."

"What does that mean?"

"My sensitivity has increased."

"What sensitivity?"

Coltan surrendered, "Okay, okay! Like her, I can detect odors, scents from far off. I can separate the layers and individually identify them. I don't want people to know about it."

"Have you told Natalie?"

"No."

"Why?"

"She'll worry. She's been through enough."

"That's understandable. However, you should have told *us*. Now... is there anything else you're concealing?"

"No." *Yes, I sometimes snack on raw meat late at night.*

"How is your strength and balance? Still improving?"

"Yeah. I'm doing fine."

"What about the nightmares?"

"I haven't had one in a week."

"Are you still growling in your sleep? Has Natalie mentioned it?"

"She said I haven't growled in my sleep since I left the hospital."

"I'm going to ask her," Morris warned.

"Go ahead. I'm telling you the truth." He propped his elbow on the counter, leaned sideways and rested his forehead in his hand, rubbed it with his fingers, closed his eyes tiredly. "Are we done?" He lifted his head and gazed pleadingly at Morris, "Can I go now?"

As Coltan gazed at him, Morris caught a glimpse of something strange in his eyes, something that produced alarm in addition to curiosity in his acute instincts. "I want to check one more thing." He opened a drawer and pulled out a penlight.

"What?"

"Have you had any more trouble with your eyesight?"

"My eyesight's fine."

"Any hypersensitivity to light?"

"No. Can I go now?"

"Just relax." He rose and flipped off the light switch, used the light from the penlight to find his way back to the stool. As soon as he sat, he turned the penlight off. "Let's just sit here for a minute and get used to the dark."

Coltan did not like dark rooms. Bad things happened in dark rooms. He felt himself begin to tremble. His throat tightened with anxiety making it difficult to breathe.

Morris heard his labored breathing. He quickly ascertained what that was about. "It's okay, Coltan. Nothing bad will happen. We have to have darkness for another thirty seconds. Just thirty seconds."

"Turn on the light!"

"Hang in there."

He began to panic. "Turn on the goddamned light!"

Morris lit the penlight and shined it in Coltan's left eye. "It's alright, Coltan. I need to check out your eyes. This will take less than a minute." He watched the pupil shrink in response to the sudden intrusion of brightness. However, the pupil did not shrink into a pinpoint as the human eye does; instead, the pupil closed into a slit, as if someone had closed the curtains on a window. Morris found the same result in Coltan's right eye. He crossed to the wall switch and turned on the main light.

Coltan sat there trembling on the stool, the color drained from his wet face. He had folded his arms over his lap and had clasped his hands tightly together, so tightly the skin of his knuckles had turned white. His eyes were closed, and he was rocking himself on the stool, a childish attempt at self-comfort.

For a moment, Morris pictured a small, terrified boy in place of the young man. He sat down slowly on the stool and observed Coltan's posture, the parts of his body he was trying to protect. Joe had mentioned the scars, and Morris had seen them for himself while Coltan was down with the dog virus. No one had to explain to him what the boy had suffered in his life. Morris silently cursed whoever had done it.

"We're done, Coltan. You're okay."

Coltan emitted a very soft growl. It was so soft, Morris was not certain of it until the sound of it continued for a few more seconds. He feared Coltan would suddenly break and attack him. He did not know what to do, what to say, how to react. In light of all that, he decided no reaction was best. Morris sat there very still and very quiet, waited for Coltan's growling to subside and for Coltan to open his eyes and realize he was safe.

The growling ceased. Coltan's compulsive rocking slowed to a stop, and he finally opened his eyes and peered at Morris. Still trembling and short of breath, he sputtered, "Get panic 'tacks. Dark..."

"I didn't know that," Morris replied sympathetically. "I'm sorry."

Coltan sighed, rubbed his arms as if he was cold. "Are we done?"

"Wait until you stop shaking."

"I'm shaking?"

"Yeah."

He licked his lips. The muscles in his face suddenly went slack, and the blood drained from his face.

Morris recognized the warning signs of a faint. He placed his hand gently on Coltan's shoulder. "Slowly lean forward and rest your head on your knees until it passes." He guided Coltan as he did as instructed. "You'll be fine in a minute."

"Did I growl?"

"Yeah."

"I'm not cured, am I?"

"Let's give it some time."

"Tell me the truth, Morris."

"The truth is I don't know."

There came a knock at the door, then Joe's voice from the outside, "Morris?"

"Come in."

Joe opened the door. His worry was obvious as he thrust a vial of blood into Morris' hands, "Macky wants a c.b.c. and chem-seven, *stat*!"

There was no label on the vial. "Who's the patient?"

"Ian. He fainted."

WHEN COLTAN CHECKED on Ian, he found the boy reclined on a gurney in the triage area. Joe was at his side, guiding Ian's trembling hands as he tried to sip from a glass of water. Joe appeared as pale as Ian, and twice as worried.

"Take it slow, bugger," Joe said gently.

"I'm alright, now," Ian replied.

Over at the counter, Doctor Macky jotted notes in Ian's chart. She paused only long enough to tell Ian, "I want you on bed rest for the next two days."

Ian sighed, perturbed, rolled his eyes to display his displeasure with Macky's over-protectiveness. "There's nothin' wrong with me. I stood up too fast, is all!"

Joe admonished him. "Don't argue with us."

"There's nothin' wrong!"

"Ah..." Macky exclaimed playfully, "Self-diagnosis! When did you graduate medical school, Mister O'Connor?"

Ian continued to self-diagnose, find reasons for his faint. "We're all cooped up in 'ere all the time! A lad needs fresh air an' exercise. A brisk game of football! That's what I need!"

"You go out there and play soccer," Macky advised, "You'll be joined by a team of mords or sick wildlife."

"Let 'em play!" Ian joked. "Send for Trev. He'll tell ya. We 'ad our own team once, challenged the lads from the Salvation Army shelter. Tough little bastards, they were! Me an' Trev, scrappers we are, gave them boys a run for their quid. We did. We sure did. Trev'll tell ya! Trev is the best coach in the world! Takes a scrapper to teach a scrapper, I say. Earned me bloody respect, I tell ya. Where is 'e? I'm tough, ya know. 'e'll witness to it, 'e will. Send for 'im."

Joe took the chair next to the gurney, patted Ian's shoulder and regarded him in a perplexed manner. "You're babbling. Stop it."

Macky inquired seriously, "Have you been into the meds, Ian?"

"I should say not! I don' like 'em. I told ya so." He finally glanced across the small room and saw Coltan in the entranceway observing him. "Yo, Coltan! Tell 'em I'm okay. 'Twas your fault again, was it not?"

"Undoubtedly," Coltan replied.

Joe shot a confused glance at Coltan, "What?"

"I almost fainted in the lab when Morris was drawing my blood."

"Why would that make Ian faint?"

Coltan approached the bed, leaned his face close to Ian's, "Jeez, Ian! Haven't you ever told him?"

Joe's voice rose up an octave, "Told me what?"

"I'm a freak of Nature," Ian moaned.

This did not answer Joe's question. He shot a glare at Doctor Macky. "What do you know about this? Don't give me all that crap about patient privacy, either!"

"I guess we all better pull up a chair," Macky said.

Ian and Coltan spent the next hour explaining their empathic link and describing the horrible details of their shared pasts. Joe had a difficult time believing it; he had never heard of such a thing. Macky offered her experiences with the Empathics on the reservation where she ran a clinic, explained the process and duration of the strange condition, assured Joe Ian's ability and its accompanying symptoms would subside with age.

The details of the abuse Coltan had suffered, and then Ian's description of his experience as Coltan's telepathic receiver of the effects of the abuse horrified Joe. As their conversation drew to a close, Joe gained a new respect for both boys and an awed admiration for their strength in battle to overcome the effects of it all.

"What, if anything, can I do for you?" Joe asked Ian.

"Quit fussin' over me!" Ian stated.

To Macky, Joe inquired, "Is there any treatment or medication for this?"

"Anti-anxiety meds," she answered, "But he won't take them."

"I spent the greater part of my child'ood pissed," Ian explained.

"Pissed?"

Macky translated for Ian, "Ian is an alcoholic."

Coltan laughed at the irony. He high-fived Ian and said, "Dude! What was your beverage of choice?"

"Anythin'! Even cold medicine!" He laughed casually about it.

"Why are you two laughing about it?" Joe again, perplexed again.

"Because it's funny," Coltan answered.

Morris entered then with Ian's lab results. "Everything looks fine," he announced to Macky.

Ian requested sweetly, "May I leave this bed, now?"

Macky took his hand, "I'm going to admit you for tonight so you can have some peace and quiet."

Petulantly, he moaned, "Bloody 'ell..."

Feeling responsible, Coltan offered, "Could I stay with him awhile?"

Astonished, Joe spat, "Hell, no!"

Ian crumbled into a fit of giggles, pointed to Coltan and told him, "You should've expected that, chum! I love ya, though..."

CHAPTER 20

The cloudburst sent a sheet of fat heavy drops onto the windshield of the military issued officer's sedan. Cory set the wipers to high, and that barely helped enough for him to view the road. Beside him in the passenger seat, Major Standish rolled the window down a crack to de-fog the inside of the windows.

"At least the heater works," Cory remarked with a wry grin.

"Piece of shit...!" Standish grumbled.

Cory slowed, prepared to brake for the roadblock ahead at the Oak Shores junction. The roadblock was now a permanent fixture here, with a newly constructed covered structure containing two pairs of booths in each direction of the two-lane road. Only soldiers manned it, not toll takers. Just like at the last checkpoint, they would scan his and Major Standish's chips. "Time to roll up our sleeves again."

Standish turned to Lena in the backseat, "Nothing to worry about, honey." He and Cory were both wearing their uniforms, and that had helped things go smoother.

She wrapped Cory's official UEF teal wool coat closer to conceal the hospital gown she wore underneath it. Daddy had done all the talking last time. Once they verified his identity and he introduced Lena to them as his daughter, they did not scan her chip. She and the two men were not certain if the scanner could really pick up the presence of the virus off the chip as the public were led to believe, but they were taking no chances.

Their vehicle was the only one on the road into Oak Shores. Cory pulled up to the toll-taker's booth and pressed the brake. He rolled down the window and greeted the soldier in the booth, a pimply kid no older than sixteen with eyes that projected hopeless resignation.

Cory stated more as a cheerful greeting than a sincere inquiry, "How ya doin'?"

The soldier did not return his smile. He saluted Cory and pointed the scanner at him. "I need to scan your ID, sir" Cory obliged him. Afterward, the soldier asked, "What's your business in Oak Shores, Sergeant?"

At the same time, another soldier at the passenger side booth immediately recognized Standish's uniform as that of a major. This older and seasoned military man promptly stood erect and saluted. "Good morning, Major! I must scan your identification, sir."

The major offered his wrist to the soldier for scanning but otherwise ignored him to answer the first soldier's question. He leaned over Cory at the driver's seat, "I'm taking my daughter to her apartment to retrieve some clothing." He then turned his head and nodded at Lena, said to the soldier, "This is my daughter Lena."

The kid nodded his chin at her. "Good morning, ma'am."

She smiled and replied brightly, "Good morning, soldier."

Following procedure, especially because the major was present and could report him for being remiss, the soldier informed Lena, "I need to verify your identification, ma'am."

Standish lowered the tone of his voice, glowered at the soldier. "Is my word not good enough, Private?"

With trepidation, the green kid explained, "I beg your pardon, sir, but procedure requires that I—"

"Oh, alright!" Lena began to roll up the sleeve of her coat. Her father was on the verge of staging another one of his contemptuous hissy fits. Her embarrassment over his behavior far outweighed the risk of the soldier discovering her condition. She fully doubted the scanner would pick up the virus in her system. "It's alright, Daddy."

"It is *not alright*!" Standish boomed. He vented at the soldier, "How dare you challenge a superior officer!"

The boy trembled. "Sir, I'm just following—"

"What is your name, Private? Scan your chip for me!"

"Sir?"

"You heard me!"

"Sir, it's procedure! I have to scan her!"

Lena sighed loudly. "It's alright, Daddy!" She leaned over the top of Cory's seat and presented her left wrist out the window. "Scan away, sir."

He glanced hesitantly at the major, "Sir, it's the rules..."

Standish made it clear he was peeved as he acquiesced, "Do your job, soldier."

"Thank you, sir!" He scanned her chip quickly. The reader did not pick up all the numbers. The soldier realized that, but he did not want to re-scan her for fear of further inciting the major's wrath. He glanced at the reader, pretended there was data there. "All clear. Thank you, ma'am."

"You're welcome." Lena sat back and gave him a smile. She had caught a glance at the reader and saw it had reported an incomplete read that the soldier promptly erased with a press of his thumb. If he knew that she knew, he did not indicate it.

He ducked back into the booth and emerged a second later with a small green card. He scanned the card, then scanned Cory's chip once more. That done, he handed the card to Cory. "Give this to the guard here on your return, sir." He saluted Cory, "Good day, Sergeant." He ducked down a little to make eye contact with Standish, saluted him, "Good day, Major."

Cory shifted into *drive*, pressed the *up* button for the window as the barrier arm rose. A few raindrops landed on the armrest as Cory cleared the structure's shelter. At least the rain had lightened. He looked at Lena through the rearview mirror, a commiserative yet humorous glint in his eyes that she acknowledged with a tight smile.

"That was easy," Lena joked.

"Are you feeling alright?" Standish asked her.

"I'm fine, Daddy." She had not craved human flesh in over a week. Her memory and speech had improved significantly. The only strange things she noticed, and she kept this to herself, was an enhanced sense of hearing and smell, and the ability to see clearly in the dark.

As of yesterday, an additional ability emerged; she was now able to read her father's mind. This morning she learned he intended to eliminate Cory as a witness to her condition, and he planned to fry his chip once they returned to the hospital in Bonito Valle. That discovery did not sit well with Lena; she had grown fond of Cory, *very* fond of him.

"When you get to Crows Perch Road, take a right," Standish instructed Cory. Over his shoulder, he said to Lena, "Not long, now."

"I hope the place is still standing," she said. Until they reached the outskirts of town, she would have no indication of what to expect. The countryside looked much the same as she remembered, miles of barren fields between the low hills, an occasional billboard advertising a defunct fruit stand or coffee shop. At least the rain had nourished the fields, their verdant hue so much prettier than the dry amber of summer.

She smelled the stockyard long before the stench reached the nostrils of her companions. Lena observed it closely as they passed it. Soldiers milled about the stalls, and a small group of them stood guard at the gated entrance.

She asked her father, "Did the government take over all the ranches and farms?"

"Yes."

"Stores?"

"Yes."

"Schools?"

"Yes." He let out a deep breath, looked sideways at her and explained, "It was necessary. We're still under a state of emergency."

"How long will it be this way?"

"I don't know."

Lena looked away from him. When he said, "I don't know," what he was thinking was, "*It'll be this way from now on.*" Behind that thought, he felt perfectly content, even slightly powerful, as if he would somehow benefit from these conditions.

They had managed to poison him, too, with their oppressive intentions disguised as altruism. *For the good of the people.* Somebody said that. She could not recall who said it.

"Crows Perch Road," Cory announced. He slowed and hung a right.

Up ahead, the skeletons of charred buildings poked up against the murky slate sky. They looked like mute sentinels awaiting orders. Cory slowed the vehicle and gawked at the sodden corpse of a man that hung suspended from a traffic light at the Central Street intersection. Someone had nailed a large sign onto the body that read, *LOOTER!* Birds had pecked at the exposed flesh of his head, face and hands. One of the eyes was nothing more than a pecked out hole, while the remaining eye stared down at them.

Lena cringed and hid her face in her hands. "Oh, my god...!"

Cory grimaced. "Don't look at it, Lena!" He then glanced at her in the rear view mirror and saw she had turned away, curled up against the passenger side door with her face cradled in her hands. He felt sorry for her, and at the same time, he felt protective of her.

He stole a look at Standish. The major stared coldly at the dead man as they passed below him. Cory wondered if he would cast that same cold look upon him if and when he decided to fry his chip. The thought of it sent a chill up Cory's spine that settled and reverberated in his ears.

Standish pointed. "Take the next left at Wellspring."

The turning arrow light, accompanied by a traffic enforcement camera, was red. Like a good citizen, Cory stopped in the turning lane and waited for the light to change.

"What are you doing? Let's go!" Standish ordered.

"It's red," Cory said.

"Fuck that!"

Cory pointed at the camera, "The authorities will fine us!"

Standish blustered petulantly like a spoiled child. "We *are* the *authorities*!"

"Okay..." There was no traffic. Cory accelerated and made the turn.

Wellspring Avenue was a mixture of shops, liquor stores and small ethnic cuisine restaurants. They passed a bar that was open for business. The front door was open, and the upbeat music drifted loudly from the dim interior. Military vehicles, jeeps, and a few civilian cars filled the parking lot to capacity. On the wet hood of one of the jeeps, a teenage girl was on her back, her skirt pushed up to her thighs, a soldier thrusting his business between her exposed legs.

Jeez... Cory thought to himself, *in broad daylight, yet!*

Lena's voice came deeply, unusually foreboding, "My building's two blocks up on the right. Pull into the second driveway."

They passed a church at the left that had burned down. The only clues that it was once a church was the metal cross that lay toppled over some charred roof beams, and a shattered sign in the parking lot that still contained the partial words, *"ing New Adven urch"*.

Wide-eyed and dismayed, Lena exclaimed, "They burnt down my church!"

"It was contaminated!" Standish said.

"Contaminated?"

"A bloodbath! The infected stormed it!"

Suspiciously, she demanded, "What about Gennamatrix?"

He answered matter-of-factly, "There was a battle there. It's demolished."

Plaintively, she inquired further, "What about the animals? They didn't catch them, did they?"

"I don't know."

She read the opposite answer in his mind. She stared down and bit her bottom lip, hid her welling tears from him. Maybe some of them got away. Lena could only hope.

Cory slowed the vehicle again. "Which one is it?"

Standish answered for Lena, "Blue Oak Manor. The next driveway."

They pulled into the cluttered lot after Cory carefully maneuvered around and then between three vehicles that had collided and partially blocked the entrance. It appeared there had been an explosion of desperate, panicked activity there. Abandoned suitcases, baby strollers, stray shoes and tattered clothing, dropped purses, broken portable radios, and discarded disabled portafones littered the driveway and parking lot. Shattered glass and broken pieces of red plastic tail light covers glistened upon the wet pavement. Most of the vehicles appeared to have been smashed from the outside. Some had collided and were sitting in the same spots where they crashed into each other. Doors were open on some, exposing the bloodstains on the rain-saturated fabric inside. A rotted corpse of what used to be a large dog lay splayed along the property fence. A couple of cat carriers sat upright under an oak tree near the fence further up toward the first block of units.

Lena focused on the cat carriers. The carriers were intact, their little doors gaping, and there were no visible bloodstains in what little she could see of the interiors. Someone had opened them and let the cats run off. She hoped the cats made it.

Her father again gave instructions to Cory, "Pull up over there in Lot D. Her carport number is nineteen, the fifth one on the left."

Every two-story unit that faced the lots had broken windows at the ground floor. The cream-white stucco walls were pock marked with bullet holes. There were no doors on the lot side of the units. As Cory parked the car, he spotted a wide brick walk a few carport spaces up from Lena's. A white lattice arbor covered in thick brown vines of some kind quaintly invited entry. Cory assumed there would be a courtyard beyond that, and the front doors of the units faced the courtyard.

Standish opened his door and set one foot outside the vehicle. He pointed at the arbor, "It's through the courtyard."

Lena sighed resentfully. Daddy acted as if she could not speak for herself. Suddenly, she felt Cory's eyes upon her. She caught his gaze in the rear-view mirror. He smirked and winked at her. She grinned at him in return, flattered he understood her humiliation.

"Pop the trunk," the major told Cory. "I'll get our weapons."

The door to Lena's apartment had been kicked-in; they had expected that. The doors to all the other apartments were in the same condition. Inside Lena's place, someone, perhaps a small crowd of looters, had swarmed through and helped themselves to her belongings. In the process, they had strewn aside what they didn't want, and many things were broken.

Lena noticed her television was gone. In light of the fact there was no electricity and only one television station had broadcast during the peak of the crisis, she exclaimed in her usual humorous way, "What'd they think they were gonna watch on that? Good lord... people are idiots! They should've invented a virus that would've just taken out the stupid people."

"Maybe they were stupid enough to leave us some food," Standish said on his way to the kitchen.

To Cory, Lena said, "I need you to help me bring my suitcase down."

He followed her into the bedroom. They had to climb over the mattress that blocked the doorway. Muddy footprints of varying sizes and sole patterns, plus a few canine footprints on the mattress impressed Cory as some type of bizarre artwork. He recognized the pattern on some of the footprints as belonging to military footwear. It did not surprise him. Cory ascertained from the evidence people had explored the apartment recently, since the panic and evacuations in the area had taken place during the summer when the weather was dry.

Just in case a squatter or mord remained behind, he readied his weapon and pulled Lena back by her arm. "Let me check it out first."

She laughed softly, "Good grief! If anyone's still here, they can have the place."

He trudged over the mattress to a clear spot on the carpet by the open closet. "Doesn't it bother you that someone did this? Don't you feel violated?"

"I was already violated by the worst!" She rolled up her sleeves and showed him the teeth imprints on her arms. "Stuff is just stuff—I don't care about it." She crossed to the closet and began to rifle through the already rifled-through clothing on the floor. "At least they were considerate enough to leave the door open for me... Ah! Let's see here." She lifted a couple of sweaters and a pair of jeans. The jeans were obviously too big for her since her involuntary weight loss. She tossed the jeans over her shoulder onto the floor, "I can swim in those, now! These sweaters are okay. Who cares that they're too big now... Damn... I really do need some pants!"

"Can't you make do with any you got on hand?"

She sunk down to her knees and took Cory's sleeve, tugged it to tell him to do the same. When he kneeled beside her, she whispered, "You're in danger."

"What do you mean?" he whispered back.

"You didn't volunteer for this."

"For what?"

"Me."

"No. However, I'm glad I know you now. What's the danger?"

"Daddy's gonna fry your chip tonight."

He shivered at this unexpected news. Surely, Major Standish would have wanted him on board to assist Lena a while longer. Besides that, the deal had been to make Lena well in exchange for his life. Apparently, Standish decided to renege on the deal. "How do you know that?"

"I can read his mind. We gotta think of some way to *change* his mind." She resumed sorting through the clothing, found two pairs of sneakers and one pair of hiking boots. The hiking boots she had worn only once; that was the day she decided hiking was not her forté. "Well... shoes will always come in handy." She pointed upwards to the highest shelf. "Grab that suitcase for me, will ya?"

He grabbed it and brought it down, opened it for her and set it on the floor. "How can we change his mind?"

"Make him think he still needs you. I'm still sick, you know." She growled softly at him, followed that with a naughty smile. "I can stage a minor relapse—*minor*, I said; something that will necessitate your assistance. Maybe with my speech or reading, or maybe a behavior thing—something that requires the expertise of an animal psychologist."

Standish suddenly appeared in the doorway. "They left a few cans of asparagus and chickpeas. Do you want your microwave for your room?"

"That'd be handy," Lena answered. "Did they leave me any coffee and sugar?"

Standish narrowed his eyes at Cory. "What are you doing on the floor, Jones?"

Cory thought quickly. "The lock on her suitcase was jammed." He stood and walked toward the major, stopped just short of the mattress blocking the doorway. "Do you want me to take the microwave out to the car?"

"Yeah."

Lena suddenly scrambled backward on her haunches. "Oh, Cory! There's a spider!"

He rushed to the closet. There was no spider where she pointed. Recognizing it as a ruse, he stepped on the imaginary creature and squished it into the carpet. "There!"

She breathed a sigh of relief. "Thank you. I'm terrified of spiders." In the next second, she slowly brought her hand to her chest, panted a little, just a little so as not to be hammy. "Oh, my gosh... I don't feel so good."

Standish stomped over the mattress and made his way to her in three long strides. He knelt beside her and placed his arms around her. "What is it? Are you sick?"

She panted again, gazed confusedly into his eyes and growled softly.

Alarmed, the major backed off, stared at her.

Cory played along with her. "Now, Lena... Stop that right now. Fight it. You can fight it."

She closed her eyes and slowed her breathing. It was a very good performance, wisely bereft of melodrama. "I'm trying."

"You're human, Lena. Your human side is much stronger." He then took both her hands and gently rubbed them. "Look at me. Trust me..."

She gazed at him in a childishly dependent manner. "Please help me, Cory. I don't want to be like this."

"Are you craving meat? Blood?"

"No." She let out a quivering breath. "I think it's passing now. Don't leave me yet."

He continued to hold her hands. "I'm here, Lena. I'm not going anywhere. Do you want some water?"

"Yes, please..." She cast a pleading glance at her father.

Standish jumped up. “I’ll get it.”

They continued the performance until Standish was out of earshot and into the bathroom. They heard the rush of water out of the tap. Lena stifled her giggle. Cory smiled in return, gently patted her shoulder.

Standish was unusually quiet during the return trip into Bonito Valle.

Cory lived to see another day, and the many days after that.

CHAPTER 21

Dillon had laid out plastic tarps for them on the sloping bank at the water's edge. Isabelle and Guffy stood manning their poles and watching their lines submerged in the deep part of the creek. Coltan sat cross-legged on one of the tarps, patiently trying to untangle his line. Natalie had propped her rod between two boulders and taken a seat with Dillon on his tarp. Dillon had fallen asleep in a reclined position against a mossy boulder.

Jill guarded them from the mid-slope of the bank while they fished. She noticed Dillon had dozed off. He looked so stereotypically *Country* to her in his quilted red plaid jacket with his red *Peterbilt Trucks* cap positioned over his eyes and his mouth open just a little with the relaxation of sleep. He had covered his legs with his sleeping bag.

Natalie lit a cigarette and gave the napping boy an affectionate glance. She nestled against his side for the warmth and caught Jill's eye in the process.

Jill stepped forward quietly and commented softly to Natalie, "Isn't he just the cutest thing?"

Natalie grinned and stole another glance at Dillon. He was very cute with his suntanned cheeks and Scandinavian features. The wisps of curly blond hair sticking out from under the cap only added to his cuteness. His features had lately begun to morph into the predestined handsomeness of the man he would become. However, that process unfolded very slowly as if something within him had pulled back on the reins of his maturity to allow him to be a child a while longer. Now sixteen years old, Dillon still exhibited the reckless curiosity of the adventurous boy who never gave a thought to his inherent mortality. His face expressed his mischievousness and his good humor.

However, very close to the surface, Dillon's face—particularly his eyes—revealed a contradictory burden of pain. This pain was many-layered. Sometimes, Natalie had caught glimpses of some of the layers, the hurt of abandonment and his anger toward the cruel jocks that had abused him, also the simmering rage at the men who used him and promptly discarded him. Somewhere in all of that was the added darkness of self-loathing, a self-loathing fueled by his deep belief he was not worth loving and anyone who tried to love him would discover the monster within and throw him away as all the others had done. In contrast to all of that, whenever he grinned and joked his eyes glistened with hope that all his negative assumptions about himself were wrong. In those moments, the needy little boy emerged to clownishly charm his way into the hearts of others.

Natalie wondered if Dillon had any idea how many people here loved him, truly loved him, especially Isabelle and Coltan. While Isabelle seemed to regard him as a goofily fun playmate, Coltan drew to Dillon as one drawn to a lost puppy.

She then looked over at Coltan, appreciated the unique beauty of his face, a face that expressed a curious duality of innocent child and jaded adult, a face that bore the shallow scars of a life once offered to the Angel of Death. His face was full of stories and experiences, unimaginable pain and bitter disappointments. Yet, that same face reflected an inner peace and wisdom, a profound tenderness and compassion. He felt her gaze, looked over at her and smiled. His impossibly blue eyes caused her to melt inside with desire for him. As far as she was concerned, no one could ever be as handsome as Coltan.

She turned back to Jill and replied to her remark about Dillon's cuteness, "I can't give an impartial answer. I got that hunka gorgeous manliness over there." She raised her chin up at Coltan and gave him a smile.

Coltan smiled back and then resumed untangling his knotted line.

Jill watched him do that. She teased Natalie, "He's not much of a fisherman, is he?"

Natalie chuckled as she replied, "He's only out here for Dillon."

In his slumber, Dillon heard his name. He stirred and mumbled something, nodded back into sleep.

Regarding Dillon, Jill remarked, "He's been a lot quieter lately. Have you noticed?"

"Yeah."

"Is he okay?"

"As far as I know."

Isabelle called out excitedly, "I got anuddoo one! Look, Kotin!" She finished reeling it in and displayed it still hanging and struggling on the hook.

Coltan gave it only a glance. He could not stand to see any creature suffer. "That's a big one."

"Dis makes eight dat I caught today!" She began to unhook it, spoke compassionately to her catch, "I'm sowwy, fishy..."

Guffy called to her, "Good job, Isa!"

She grinned proudly at him as she carried the fish to the cooler. "Tanks, Unka."

Coltan asked Guffy, "How many have you caught?"

"Six. What about you? Any, yet?"

"Not a one."

Guffy was on to him, "Maybe if you used some bait..."

Coltan smiled as he stated, "I don't wanna ruin my flawless record."

Guffy shook his head with feigned exasperation at Coltan's absurdity. "Dillon knows about it."

Jill could not believe what she was hearing. She gaped at Natalie. "You mean, all this time, he's never used bait?"

"He doesn't want to kill anything."

Jill chortled. "Your husband's... man, I don't know." She took a few steps closer to Dillon, stopped and affectionately gazed at him. A smile crossed her face. "He seems right at home out here."

"Yeah. He likes being outside."

Isabelle closed the cooler and tiptoed over to Dillon. She got down on her knees, bent and peered upside-down into Dillon's slumbering face, whispered to him, "You still sleeping, Din?"

Dillon took a deep breath and mumbled, "Uh-huh..."

She giggled.

He lifted his cap, opened his eyes and crossed them for her. This made her laugh riotously, and her laughter caused him to laugh with her. His inevitable snorts and *hee-hees* followed as he tackled her and swept her on her back onto his outstretched legs. He tickled her belly and teased her. "C'mere, you! I got your tummy!"

She protested through her laughter, "No, Din! You'll make me pee!"

He continued to gently tickle her belly. "Don't you pee on me!"

"I will!" she warned him.

"No, you won't!"

"Yes, I will!" She continued to laugh, but her voice grew desperate and slightly angry, "Stop! Stop it, Din. I'm gonna pee! Weally!"

He stopped tickling her. "Go pee in the water. It draws the fish."

She didn't believe him. "Uh-uh..."

"Uh-*huh*!" he insisted. "That's my secret weapon."

"You pee in da watew?"

"When the fishin's slow."

"Uh-uh."

"Uh-huh! Really!"

She sat up and pulled the bill of his cap over his eyes, laughed at him. Under the cap, he made a funny face at her that caused her to laugh harder. He waved his hands in the air and exclaimed in a mockingly terrified voice, "I can't see!" She collapsed onto his chest in a fit of belly laughs. He hugged her and giggled at her.

Guffy observed them from the water's edge, smiled at the sight of them. It was apparent to him Isabelle was at her happiest whenever she was with Dillon. He thought it wonderful that she had found someone who still had enough kid left in him to appeal to her childish sense of humor. It seemed all the kids at Alpha found Dillon a riot. It seemed laughter was Dillon's greatest contribution to life at Alpha Base.

Presently oblivious to the others around her, Isabelle bored all her attention into Dillon's silly antics. She positioned her face directly in front of his and demanded, "Make yo' eyes woll awound fo' me!" He obliged her. With a fresh wave of laughter, she ordered, "Just do da leff one now!" He obliged her once more. She guffawed heartily and lamented, "I can't do dat yet!"

"You'll learn," he assured her.

"You da best at it," she stated.

"*You're* the best," he told her unequivocally.

She did not understand what he meant. "I can't do dat."

"You're the best of all my best friends."

She beamed at him, "Weally?"

"Yep!" He then glanced around at the others, saw he had their attention. In an exaggerated display, he brought his index finger to his lips and told her confidentially, "Shhh. Don't tell no one. They'll get jealous."

She giggled and rested upon his chest, "Day aweddy heawd you!"

"Man..." Natalie moaned, "I'm jealous!"

"Me, too!" Coltan pretended to be sorely hurt.

"Me, three!" Guffy added.

Jill plopped down beside Dillon. "I thought you liked me at least a little."

Dillon made an exaggeratedly thoughtful face at her. "Yeah... A little, I guess." In truth, he liked Jill a lot, even if she *could* beat him at arm-wrestling. Like him, she used humor to get through the drudgery of life in hiding. An added plus was that she didn't care that he was gay.

"Well," she joked, "A little is better than nothing, I guess."

Isabelle volunteered, "Din likes you a whole lot, Jill. He tode me!"

Dillon swept off his cap and lightly slapped the child's head with it.

Jill laughed and pointed at Dillon, "Busted!"

Isabelle snatched the cap away from him and put it on her head. "It's mine, now."

He suddenly realized he had exposed his sparse re-growth of curly blond hair to everyone. As if that wasn't bad enough, they could see his protruding ears, too. He reached for the cap, "Gimme."

The little girl teased him, pulled back out of easy reach, "Uh-uh."

"What beautiful blond hair!" Jill exclaimed.

He gave Isabelle an *I'm not kidding* look and retrieved his cap from her. To Jill, he replied, "Shut up about my hair."

"I was giving you a complement."

He quickly secured the cap into place, and he immediately felt better. It then occurred to him she had not mentioned his Dumbo ears. He figured she said nothing because she was too polite.

Dillon addressed the entire group, "How many fish have we got?"

Guffy answered, "Fourteen."

"Does that count mine?"

"I haven't checked your lines yet." Guffy trotted over and reeled in one of Dillon's lines. Dillon had attached three hooks to each of his lines. Guffy found exhausted victims on all three of the hooks. He began to unhook them. "That makes seventeen."

Natalie rose and reeled in Dillon's second line. This one also had three. She called over, "Twenty."

Dillon asked her, "Did you catch any?"

"No. I gave up."

He called out to Coltan, "I suppose your record stands unbroken."

Coltan looked up from his line-untangling project and grinned at Dillon. "My record stands!"

"We need more than twenty," Dillon announced.

Jill said, "Franks and his crew are over in the south inlet. Reston told me about an hour ago that they had caught twenty-seven."

Dillon was shocked and very envious, "Twenty-seven? What are they using for bait?"

"How would I know?"

Isabelle offered her own theory, "Maybe day all peed in da wattew."

Everyone laughed at that.

Back to business, Dillon nudged Isabelle off his lap and threw off his sleeping bag. The thought of Franks' team outdoing him was more than he could stand. As he rose to his feet, he proclaimed, "We're going for at least forty!"

Guffy sputtered, "Forty? That's impossible!"

Dillon took his first rod off the dirt where Guffy laid it. "Are we gonna let Franks win?"

"I didn't know it was a competition!" Guffy protested.

"It is now!" Dillon flipped open his tackle box and bait kit and chose the best he had. As he began to select some lures, he turned bossily to Isabelle and ordered, "Dig us the fattest worms you can find!" To Natalie, he commanded, "Go to the kitchen and beg some liver and scrap meat from them."

"They use that for fertilizer," Natalie reminded him.

He was undaunted, spurred by his competitiveness. "Get it before Ian gets it." He turned to Coltan, demanded sharply, "Stop messin' with that line. Cut it off and re-set it. Bait it. Quit bein' such a weanie! I'll reel the bastards in for you!"

Coltan was astounded at Dillon's suddenly obsessive manner. "Jeez, Dill... calm down."

"I'll calm down when I see those rods bob up and down!" He tossed Isabelle the little garden spade, "Go to that shaded muddy area over there and start digging."

She caught the spade and said enthusiastically, "Okay, Din."

Natalie got to her feet, "I'll see to that liver..."

Dillon started to bait his hooks. He glanced over at Guffy, who was on his way over for bait. "Guffy... I want you to triple-hook your line. Let's show them guys who's boss around here!"

Guffy grinned, encouraged by Dillon's determination to beat the competition. "Let's put four hooks on."

Dillon smiled, glad for Guffy's support. "Now, you're talkin'!"

Isabelle paused as she began to walk away, turned thoughtfully to Dillon. "Would you bait my line and cast out fo' me, Din? You can gimme a triple hook, too!"

Dillon waved her off. "Will do! Hurry back with those worms."

With the group now off in three different directions, Jill couldn't decide whom she should consider priority for guarding. The three men were now together at the water's edge, little Isabelle was now a good ten feet away from them near a curve at the creek, and Natalie was already up on the trail en route to the lava tube. She weighed her options and made a decision.

"You guys keep an eye on Isa. I'm gonna accompany Natalie back to the tube."

"She's armed," Dillon said matter-of-factly.

Coltan did not want Natalie to go alone, armed or not. He told

Jill, "I appreciate that, Jill. I'll watch the kid."

Coltan reluctantly baited his hook and strolled over to the area where Isa crouched, digging for worms. He cast out and then propped the rod inside the hollow of a broken tree limb. With the rod standing securely on its own, Coltan squatted down next to Isabelle.

She appeared to be taking her work very seriously, and she had already filled her little plastic beach bucket with seven worms. She used the spade to spoon some soil over the worms to keep them moist and protected as Dillon had shown her. In the process, she uncovered some more worms when she peeled a layer of moss off the mud.

"Dehw's lot of wooms hehw," she told Coltan over her shoulder. "Can you smell dem, Kotin? I can."

They smelled strongly of earth, rotted plant refuse and stagnant water. "Yeah," he said, "I can smell them."

"We can find'em easy dat way." She paused and took a deep breath of the air, closed her eyes, tasted the air, then opened her eyes again and focused on a pine tree directly across from her at the opposite side of the creek. "Dehw's a possum in dat twee."

Coltan sniffed the air, caught the gamy odor and followed her gaze. He saw the opossum, a small furry gray mound curled up sleeping on a high limb. With his enhanced visual acuity, he was able to see details of the creature. "He's a little skinny. Just a kid."

Isabelle continued digging and collecting worms. "I don't smell his mommy."

"The boys go off on their own. It's the rule with possums."

Her voice became soft and confidential, close to a whisper. "Do you tink da Biting Peepo do dat, too?"

He thought that was an odd question. "I never thought about it. Why do you ask?"

"Haven't you evoo smelled dem fum da uddoo side of da

wivvoo?"

He was shocked. "Uh-uh. Have you?"

"Yeah. I tot you smelled dem, too."

"No..." Her revelation frightened him. "Do they know about us?"

She stopped digging and focused entirely on Coltan. "About all da peepo hew, oawa just about you an' me?"

"All the people."

"Yeah."

"You and me?"

"Yeah. Day know."

"Are they going to attack?"

"Day cawood of us. Summa dem aw dyin'. Da west is too sick ta eat peepo no mo.'"

"That sounds like they're all dying."

"I guess..."

"Are there a lot of them?"

"Can't tell. Next time you go to wivvoo side, you sniff and tew me what you tink."

"Okay. Let's not mention this to anyone. No sense scaring everybody."

She gazed at him and grinned. She then pretended to lock her lips and throw away the key.

CHAPTER 22

Trevor found a soccer ball among the many items in the Free Store cavern. It stirred memories of home, memories of the boys' shelter and all the fun they had when they competed against the Salvation Army, Saint John's Retreat and the other children's shelters around London. Eager to bring some semblance of normalcy to the youngsters at Alpha Base, Trevor assembled teams and used the small glen below the lava tube as a soccer field.

Ian, ever the scrapper, took to the game with his usual fervor. It was the first time in a long time that Trevor saw joy in Ian's face.

A squad of twelve troops from Sam Vasson's regiment served guard duty around the perimeter of the pine-enclosed glen. Among the troops, Raul Santiago kept a vigilant observance, not for dangerous predators, but for additional information to relay to the UEF's Bonito Valle Base. He kept an eye especially on the lean, blue-eyed young man who he had first seen in a wheelchair. The boy now appeared healthy and muscular. The young man, whose name Santiago learned was Coltan, took to the game with ease. He exhibited a cat-like coordination on the field and stealthy awareness of the activity around him. Santiago found that very interesting, and he wondered why the teen had not entered Alpha's military.

The petite, dark haired girl Santiago had learned was Coltan's wife, head-butted the ball across the field with unexpected ease. Like her husband, she had a solid build, displayed a healthy but not bulky musculature. She was swift on her feet, unabashedly competitive. At one point, her husband had to take her aside to remind her it was just a game.

At the sidelines, the Little Catfish watched and cheered with the little Latino girl at his side. Santiago guessed the boy was not the athletic type, but one of those who preferred to watch. The Catfish was short and small-framed, had a gawky, loose build so typical of young teens on the cusp of physical maturity.

Santiago wondered about the boy, wondered if he missed Neville Langly, missed the young soldier's physical attentions. At this moment, the Catfish gave no indication. If Langly's abandonment had indeed broken his heart, as the soldier had told him, the boy hid it well.

This brought to mind his concern over Langly. Santiago had been unable to establish radio contact with him. Two weeks had gone by. Surely, the young soldier had reached Bonito Valle by now. Yet, there had been no communication from Bonito Valle Base, and no indication they knew Santiago and his two fellow spies had made it to Alpha Base. There had not even been a surveillance chopper for him and Eastman to signal.

Most likely, the UEF had not been able to communicate because the mountains and the conflicting wireless technologies interfered with their signals. Although the UEF had the latest technology, Santiago was stuck with the antiquated digital radios, and the satellites often scrambled the signals and bounced them back to point of origin when the digital equipment failed to read and respond to the new language.

It was just another of many frustrations for Santiago. If not for the fact the powers at Alpha Base would relentlessly hunt him down and execute him like a rabid dog, he would have abducted the girl and fled the scene in a stolen vehicle.

He cast another glance at the little girl sitting with the gawky Catfish. If he tried to deliver the mord child to Bonito Valle, would the Catfish try to save her? The thought of it made Santiago scoff inwardly. The little bumpkin was a mere child himself and certainly not hero material. Yet, the boy seemed to garner the girl's admiration. The two of them impressed Santiago as mutually protective and emotionally dependent upon each other. Rarely did he see them apart.

Suddenly, the soccer ball flew right at Santiago's face. He darted sideways and caught it in one hand, and then wondered why he didn't simply move aside and let it land in the brush behind him. The soldiers near him broke out in laughter. He grinned, embarrassed, tossed the ball up and caught it again as the petite British man in fatigues scampered over to retrieve it.

Trevor reached out for it. "Thanks for the save!"

Santiago said nothing in response; he tossed the ball to him.

"Have you ever played?" Trevor asked him.

Santiago shook his head, stepped backwards a couple of steps. He did not want to draw attention to himself. Behind him, Audrey Eastman laughed at him, slapped her fat, mannish hand against his shoulder blade.

An idea came to Trevor. "Perhaps a game of civilians against you troops some day!"

Eastman cackled and said, "We'd ream you!"

Trevor grinned at her. "Is that a challenge, then?"

Santiago turned to her and whispered, "Don't encourage him."

At the same time, Ian called out impatiently to Trevor, "Come on, man! We're loosin' the sunlight! Gimme the ball!"

Not wanting to spoil Ian's fun, Trevor trotted back to the field. He set the ball in Ian's eager hands, then broke for the sidelines where he settled next to Dillon on the grass. He shouted to Ian, "Give 'em hell, lad!"

CORY BROUGHT LENA A selection of trousers and jeans, plus a

full-length tweed winter coat. She tried on the coat. It fit and made her feel elegant.

"Back when I was a tub, I could never find this style in my size," she commented.

She had regained a little weight recently, and her slack stretched skin accommodated her gain well. Her goal was to gain another ten pounds and maintain her weight at that level. Now that she was on a healthier diet, she expected that would be easy.

"That coat looks great on you," Cory said.

"Where'd you find it?"

"In the doctors' lounge down on the surgical floor."

"Only a surgeon could afford it!" Her eyes sparkled with her good humor. "Thanks for thinking of me."

Cory had found himself thinking of her a lot lately—most of the time, in fact. Although Lena was not an attractive woman by society's standards, she had an inner beauty that Cory found desirable. For the first time in his life, Cory looked beyond the physical and saw the lovely treasure within.

She settled at the edge of the bed and hugged the coat around her. "I want to go back to work. I want to find out why I survived this and others didn't."

"There's a small lab on this floor," Cory recalled. "It looks like it hasn't been used for anything but storage. Who knows the story behind it."

"They probably intended to rent it out to an outside specialist. Hospitals were starting to do that to bring in extra revenue."

"When you worked at Gennamatrix, did anyone there mention any research around the mord virus?"

"Not to my knowledge. But then, I was concentrating on genetically engineered pharmaceuticals and didn't pay much attention to what the rest of them were doing. We only compared notes when a project called for it. My work had nothing to do with viral agents."

"Who used the lab animals?"

"All of us. We had animals assigned to us, kept in separate areas so as not to contaminate each others' research." She paused and searched her memory for anything unusual she had observed with the animals. "After they abandoned the building during the evacuation, I freed all the animals. I don't remember seeing any that were actively sick with anything. However, there were a few cats and rats in the Oncology Research lab that had various types of cancer. I euthanized them because they were suffering."

"Do you think you might have been exposed to something that weakened the mord virus?"

She thought long and hard about that. A fleeting fragment of memory came. She considered it, but dismissed the possible connection as unlikely. Still, she offered it to Cory. "I remember Doctor Clausberg was researching an air-born contagion discovered in a tomb in Peru. She had isolated some dogs in a sealed room and pumped in the contagion. I don't know if it was viral or bacterial..." With this, Lena became very quiet as she rethought her initial assumptions. A shadow of concern rose from deep within her and darkened her expression. "In my hurry to release all the animals, I completely forgot about that. I went right into that room and freed the dogs."

"They weren't sick?"

"They seemed... lethargic. Otherwise, they appeared healthy. Now that I think about it, a healthy dog caged for so long would have been jumping up and down at the opportunity to get out. Dammit! I wonder if..."

"Clausberg is dead," Cory informed her. "Her name was *Reneé* Clausberg, right?"

"That's her! She's dead?"

"The UEF smoked her lab up in Baker Creek. She died in the

explosion."

"She had a lab up there? Doing what?"

"Research on mords."

"That bitch! That explains where she disappeared to. She stole a bunch of our equipment on the way out. They saw it on the surveillance footage the next day." Her sudden anger gave way to unanticipated hope, "Do you think I was exposed to something in the kennel?"

"It sounds feasible."

She stood and removed her new coat, traded her slippers for a pair of sandals. "I've got to find out! I need that lab! I have to give Daddy a list of equipment and materials I'll need. He'll put through an acquisition order. I have to talk to him right now!" She bounded over to Cory and flung her arms around him in gratitude, "I don't know what I'd do without you, Cory!"

NATALIE AND COLTAN had made love well into the wee hours of the morning. His sexual appetite had increased tremendously and he achieved orgasm as many times as she did. Although his new ability to experience multiple orgasms was a concern, something unheard of and deemed abnormal for a man, Natalie had no complaints.

Now, Coltan was sound asleep, exhausted and exquisitely satisfied. When he awakened later that morning, Mister Dolce would be at attention, eager for another round. That had been the pattern ever since Coltan regained his vitality, not that Natalie minded.

Yet, so many orgasms affected her much differently than it affected him. Instead of exhausting her, as it finally did Coltan, the pattern of arousal, release, arousal, release left her body energized. As a result, Natalie could not fall asleep.

She finally gave up on the idea of sleep, gave her sweet lover a tender kiss on his cheek, and went in her thickest, warmest robe and slippers to the smoking section outside the south entrance. She found Dillon sitting alone there, bundled in a parka she recognized as belonging to Jill. Natalie whispered good morning to him and sat down on one of the old lava boulders.

Dillon gazed up at the clear starry sky and took a deep breath of the crisp air. "I love it up here," he remarked dreamily.

"It's pretty," she replied.

He lit her cigarette for her, and then he lit one for himself.

"It's awfully late for you to be out here," she remarked.

"Sometimes I wake up after a couple of hours."

"Is that something new?"

"No." He chuckled to himself. "I think it's the result of too much partying back in The Day."

"Do you miss those days?"

He didn't have to think long before he decided. "No."

The tone of his voice hinted the memories brought him some pain. Natalie opted not to question him about it. She knew enough about his past to tell her his partying days were not as much fun as he thought they would be. She changed the subject with the most obvious thing, the fact he was wearing Jill's parka.

"Jill's a good friend, isn't she?"

He grinned when he looked at her. "Yeah... She's one of the few people here who's not trying to change me."

Natalie tugged the sleeve of his borrowed parka. "I take it she's off duty tonight."

He glanced over the parka, laughed softly. "This is warmer than anything I got. I don't care if I look stupid in it."

"You don't look stupid in it."

"I said I don't care." He grinned again and winked at her.

"You're silly."

"Whatever."

"Have you been okay?"

"Yeah. Why?"

"You've been more serious lately."

"No, I haven't."

"What was all that about the forty fish? You acted like the world would end if you didn't bring in those forty fish."

"Coltan said I'm Alpha's best fishin' guy. I ain't about to let someone upset my *esteemed position* here!" He gave her another smile. There was sadness behind his smile.

"If there's ever something wrong, and you want to talk to me about it, I promise I'll keep it confidential."

"Thanks."

She took a guess at what he could be hiding. "Are you developing a crush on Jill?"

He laughed. "Hell, no...!"

"Truth?"

"Do you and Coltan think that just because I'm now a Christian, I've miraculously lost my taste for men?"

"Well... no!"

"Jill's a friend." He suddenly bristled at her. "If somebody thinks different..."

"Whoa, whoa! No one's said anything. I just wondered if—"

"You wondered wrong!"

"Alright... I'm sorry."

"Sorry I'm still a fag?"

"No!" She stared at him incredulously. "What's gotten into you? I love you the way you are, Dillon!"

He regretted he had overreacted to her well-intentioned inquiries. It was difficult for him not to be defensive after so many years of being the target of ridicule. "You're a good friend to me, Nat.

I didn't mean to snap at you."

"Forgiven."

Dillon grasped for an honest explanation for his behavior. He didn't want to reveal his short-lived affair with Scorpio, but he felt a need to cast blame on some obvious circumstance just to satisfy her worried curiosity. "I think I'm missing my freedom."

"We all are. Coltan moans a lot about getting away on his Harley."

"He had a Harley?"

"Yeah. He crashed it on the way up here. He was sick and he passed out."

"Oh, yeah... I remember. I heard the doctors talking about him. They thought he was gonna die at first."

"Yeah..."

"Can his bike be fixed?"

"No."

"Bummer..."

A soldier approached them, a large, fat-bellied man with a slight limp. He had an unlit cigarette between his lips, and he paused in front of Dillon, bent and asked for a light. Dillon gave him a light. As he did so, the soldier gazed at him, peered intently into his eyes. The intensity of his gaze made Dillon feel violated. It was clear to Dillon the man had used the light as an excuse to scope him out, learn if his suspicions were correct. Dillon extinguished the match and dropped it in the dirt.

"You can't do that," the big man reminded him. "No litter."

Dillon bent and retrieved the match, put it into his pocket. He looked away from the man to Natalie, took her hand in his and gently squeezed her fingers. She regarded him confusedly.

The soldier caught her puzzled reaction to the boy's gesture. Inadvertently, she had confirmed his suspicions. "Thanks for the light, kid." He smirked knowingly at Dillon and sauntered away.

Once he was out of earshot, Dillon snarled softly, "Pervert!" He clung to Natalie's hand, even after the soldier left them.

"How do you know?" Natalie asked.

"Experience."

"Has this happened a lot to you here?"

He pulled away from her, dropped his cigarette and snuffed it in the dirt. After a few moments, he answered, "No..."

This time, she took *his* hand, "If anyone gives you any trouble, tell us. I mean it. You're not alone anymore."

"I'm not gonna run to you every time some pedo-pervert makes a pass at me!"

"This isn't Baker Creek, Dillon. We're living in close quarters here. You have a right to be safe."

"I can take care of myself; I always have." He solemnly shook his head and stared down at the dirt. "Man... you and Coltan and Trevor..."

"We love you."

He remained silent for a long time. Finally, after thinking about it and accepting the fact that they truly did love him—even though it seemed to him they wished to change him—he mumbled, "I know."

"Do you love us?"

"That's a stupid question. Of course I do. What makes you think I don't?"

"Nothing makes me think that. What I want is for you to realize it's okay to love someone. It's okay to love us."

He did not understand what she meant.

She explained, "Unlike the people in your past, we'll never turn you away. We'll never hurt you. I think, in the back of your mind, you expect we'll hurt you. Because of that, you might be afraid to acknowledge the love you feel for us. If that's so, then you're denying yourself of a great joy in life."

She was correct. All this time he had been afraid to completely open his heart to them. Once, so very long ago when he viewed the world through a child's heart, he possessed joy. That joy was snatched away one day, and the pain of its sudden loss was a pain beyond the comprehension and endurance of a child. From that day forward, Dillon resisted any offering that would help him recover that joy. He feared the pain should it be taken away again.

Even with Isabelle, he protected his heart, resisted the urge to love her with complete abandon. Like his sister Tina, someday she would grow up and decide she did not need him anymore. She would grow up and discover he had less to offer her than she once assumed. She would recognize him as the weak, damaged, empty shell he had concealed under the costume of a clown. She would leave him and forget she ever loved him.

Oh, God... He did love his *little Eensybelle*. He loved her with everything in his being. The realization stung him, filled him with fear. He had set himself up for a fall. How had he dropped his guard so easily? How soon would it be when she abandoned him for someone more worthy of her love?

Dillon wiped away the unexpected and uncontrollable tears that suddenly rolled down his cheeks. He hated himself at that moment, hated his weakness, hated his vulnerability.

Natalie placed her arm around his shoulders. She had not expected him to cry, and the depth of his misery was not only tragic to her, but also frightening. "Do you want to know what we really think of you, Dill?"

"No."

"I'm gonna tell you anyway. We think you're a Keeper. Get used to it."

CHAPTER 23

Cory drew Lena's blood, five vials of it. From the lab doorway, Major Standish watched with subdued interest as Cory placed the dressing over the puncture wound in her vein and comfortingly smiled at her. Lena's eyes glistened with a tenderness Standish had never before seen when she looked up at Cory. The major had never expected his daughter and the young Sergeant Cory Jones would bond in this manner. He expected Cory to treat her like a test subject. He expected Cory would view her as all the men in her life before him, like the homely girl she was, the girl who sat rejected or ignored while the others burned the dance floor. That is what Major Standish was accustomed to when it came to the sad state of Lena's relentlessly lonely existence.

Ever since she was a child, Lena was an overweight, socially inept outcast with an unremarkable face and an even more unremarkable personality. However, her personality blossomed when she started college, spurred by an initially half-hearted attempt to fulfill required credits with an elective in the Arts. The elective she chose was Drama 101, which she thought she would float through for credit only in lieu of a grade. To Lena's amazement, she took to the stage like a horse to alfalfa, and she discovered she could make people laugh. She quickly adopted this newfound talent as her shield and sword. Still, she was ostracized by the glamorous sorority gals, and the artsy-fartsy students dubbed her "dangerously unconventional" because of her brilliant intellect. Yet, her humor drew some of the male students to her. The homosexuals particularly liked her because she was sexually non-threatening and she knew it. There was nothing pretentious about Lena Standish. She knew she was no glamour girl and she accepted it wholeheartedly and even harvested that fact for her spontaneous entertaining monologues.

Her brother Winslow had served as additional material for her "act." Through some injustice of genetics, Winslow inherited all the good looks and social graces. Everything came easily to Winslow, even death. Lena had privately joked to herself that Winslow never knew what hit him when the stray bullet pierced his brain, and he was probably very surprised to learn he was dead. Somewhere in the ethereal-sphere, Winslow was still asking angels to verify the truth of his early departure. More than likely, he was bargaining with God to roll back the scroll of time and give him a do-over.

That fantasy earned her a stinging slap one day when she made the mistake of joking about it to her father. She never spoke of Winslow again, and her father never apologized for his show of temper.

At this moment, her attention was on Cory. He was now her official lab assistant and trusted confidant. At her request, he abandoned the barracks for the doctors' sleeping quarters in the room next to hers. They spent their evenings playing chess and Scrabble, and talking movies and music. They dined together in the hospital cafeteria, and sometimes they ordered food to go for the express purpose of having a moonlight picnic on the hospital rooftop when it wasn't raining.

Yet, there seemed to be no romance between them—at least, not to Standish's knowledge. He had seen no fond caresses, no handholding, not even the subtlest of longing glances. Standish did not find that surprising. One day he looked closely at his daughter, tried to regard her not from a father's perspective but from that of a man, in order to gauge the likelihood of a man ever wanting her. When he regarded her in this way and gave it some thought, he found her to be rather repulsive as a woman. This conclusion about her lack of desirability gave him a strange sense of relief. She would never stray far from him, and she would always remain dependent upon him for the small amount of love that did exist in her life.

The major decided Cory Jones would never be attracted to her as a woman. Therefore, Cory Jones posed no threat to the major's curious position as *the man* in Lena's life. Additionally, he posed no threat to Lena's safety so long as he kept his mouth shut about her condition. For the time being, it appeared he did not intend to reveal the truth about Lena to anyone. It even seemed to Standish that Jones had become fiercely loyal to her and fiercely protective of her.

Nonetheless, Major Standish kept his radar on "high" and his fingers poised to type in the numbers to fry the sergeant's chip.

Lena observed her father, noted the combination of concern and disgust on his face. She assumed his disgust was in reaction to the blood draw, something that always made him squeamish. "Daddy, you don't have to be here for this."

He cleared his throat and asked, "How long will it take to get the results?"

"There's a lot to do. I can't predict. Some tests take longer than others."

Cory remarked, "We're still waiting on the centrifuge. They said they'd deliver it this afternoon."

Lena approached him, gave him a hug and peered up into his stern face. "Please, Daddy. I know you have other things to do. Go do your work and let us do ours."

From below, outside in the parking lot, voices and rifle fire caused the three of them to jump with a start. They raced to the window and watched four soldiers chase down a partially naked man. What remained of the man's clothing was in shreds, stained with blood and months of filth. His skin was sun baked and so encrusted with dirt, one would have been hard pressed to identify his ethnicity, save for the sparse patches of dirty blond hair at one side of his skull. When the subject turned, the three in the lab saw the terror in his eyes. They also saw the river of brown drool running down his chin and neck, the telling evidence of a mord on the prowl. The second round of bullets finally brought him down. Just to be certain he wouldn't get up again, one of the soldiers sent a final blast into the back of his head. The impact exploded the mord's skull and sent bio-hazardous brain matter flying.

"Jackass!" Standish bellowed. "We told them never to do that at close range!"

Lena backed away from the window.

Cory, still riveted to the scene below, said, "That's one hell of a mess to clean up!"

Standish shook his head ominously. "We'll be finding them for months...!

There came only a few seconds of silence between them before the disturbing noise of Lena's vomiting drew their attention from the scene below and reminded them a human being existed inside every mord.

ISABELLE ACCOMPANIED Dillon to the exam room for his check-up. She and Dillon knew from experience the examination would culminate with a blood draw to check for the resurgence of cancerous cells. Dillon cringed at the very mention of needles. His sclerosed veins protested with serious pain with the insertion of the needle for the blood draw.

Just like so many times before, Isabelle had him sing with her to divert his attention away from his pain as Morris sympathetically did his best to complete the procedure as painlessly as possible—a goal impossible to meet when it came to poor Dillon. The boy endured it bravely, sang a second verse with his Heartagold-Eensybelle while she gently caressed his cheek to provide him with a pleasant sensation away from the discomfort of the needle in his vein.

When he was done, Morris requested the two remain in the lab as he buzzed Doctor Quimby.

Quimby entered the room with a concerned expression on his face. "What is it?"

Casually, Morris replied, "I thought while we had Isa here, we'd give her that eye exam we forgot."

The doctor relaxed. Morris had informed him about the strange results he found in Coltan's eyes, and he wanted to learn if Isabelle displayed the same anomaly. He was glad Morris was on top of things.

Doctor Quimby squatted down to the little girl's level. "We need to check your eyes, Isa."

She nestled insecurely against Dillon. "How come?"

"Everybody needs an eye exam at least once a year."

"How come?"

"To make sure you don't need glasses."

"I can see fine."

"We still have to check you."

"Why?"

"To make sure you can see okay."

"Is it gonna hoot?"

"No."

She didn't trust that. Almost all hospital procedures hurt. She buried her face in Dillon's chest. "I don't wanna!"

Quimby and Morris sighed in frustration.

"Tell ya what," Dillon told her, "They can examine my eyes and you can watch. It really don't hurt. Wanna watch?"

"Okay."

Dillon confidently plopped down in the chair. "Make sure she sees everything you see."

Quimby grinned at him and gratefully patted his shoulder. He then shut the door and flipped off the light, plunged the lab into darkness.

Isabelle's voice seemed to come from far away in the endless space of blackness, "How come we got dawk? You can't see nothin'!"

Quimby switched on his penlight. "This is why. Come on over here and watch. Look what happens with Dillon's eyes when I shine the light in them."

She positioned herself between the Doctor and Dillon, watched curiously as Dillon's pupils shrank from big and round to the size of the head of a pin in reaction to the light. "Cool...! Is dat good? Aw his eyes wookin' okay? Aw day s'posed ta do dat?"

"Yes," Morris said. "His eyes are perfect."

Dillon joked, "You mean something about me is perfect?"

"Alla you is poofect, Din!"

"Okay, Eensy," Dillon said as he rose from the chair, "Your turn now."

Morris did not want Dillon to see it if Isabelle's eyes reacted the same as Coltan's. It was simply too weird and it would spook the boy. He instructed Dillon, "Go wait over by the door so she doesn't get distracted."

After Dillon obeyed, Morris and Quimby examined her eyes. Just like Coltan's, her pupils folded into slits. The two doctors masked their concern and amazement with lighthearted comments about how beautiful her big brown eyes looked under the light.

Quimby flipped on the room light. "All done! That didn't hurt at all, did it?"

"Aw my eyes okay?"

"Your eyes are perfect!" He lifted her off the chair and held her in his arms. "As a matter of fact, I'm gonna write in your chart that you got the most perfect and beautiful eyes I've ever seen!"

She laughed, flattered.

Once the kids left, Quimby and Morris discussed their findings over coffee in the break room.

"So, it's both her and Coltan. What do you make of it?" Morris asked.

"I've never seen anything like it. Did Coltan say anything about his vision since it's come back? Any changes?"

"He said everything is fine."

"Do you think he's lying?"

"Yeah."

"Has Natalie mentioned anything?"

"No. I don't think she's noticed anything different with his eyes. I mean... it's so... creepy. She'd definitely tell us about it. She'd be worried about him."

"I want him to return here for another exam," Quimby said.

"Not a good idea," Morris advised sternly. "The kid gets panic attacks when it comes to being alone in a dark room with a man. He almost passed out on me."

Quimby looked away sadly. "Good god... what people do to their kids..."

"I think we should wait, see what happens with him. Whatever he's hiding, he'll reveal it eventually—probably unintentionally."

"If he thought it was something that made him a danger to others," Quimby considered, "He would have come to us by now. We'll watch him. That's all we can do for now."

CORY AND LENA RECLINED against the wall at the heliport on the roof of the hospital. They sat very close together, huddled in blankets, drinking wine. The sky this night was cloudless and the moon was full.

Down below, the occasional crack of gunfire reminded them

the world would not be safe again for a long time. The troops had eliminated sixteen mords that week alone. It had almost become a sport to them, the thrill of the hunt, the satisfaction of the kill. They celebrated their victory at the Kona Hut Club, and the noise of their boisterous, drunken voices above the pounding base from the jukebox carried far into the night air.

Cory refilled his wineglass. He had a good buzz going from the first bottle he and Lena emptied, but the buzz was not enough to erase his condemning memory of the young mord boy he had executed months ago. The conviction haunted him that he could have saved the boy. Like Lena, he had retained the ability to speak and reason, had even tried to keep himself clean. Given enough time, the boy could have recovered, just the same as Lena was recovering.

"What are you thinking about that makes you so sad?" Lena questioned.

"A boy," Cory replied ruefully. "A mord who projected more humanity than those jarheads down there."

"He's dead, I take it..."

"They ordered us to execute him. He begged me for his life."

"Jesus..."

"If I knew then what I know now, I would've tried to help him. Maybe hidden him somewhere, taken care of him, like your dad did for you."

"Who ordered the execution?"

"Your father."

Chagrined, Lena stated bitterly, "That figures."

"I don't get it. That kid was like you..."

"He wasn't me."

"I wish..."

Lena spoke over him, "I hate him."

"Hate who?"

"Daddy. I love him because he's my father, but I hate him as a person. I've always hated him."

This surprised him. "Why?"

"He's always been very black or white, all or nothing, never a middle ground. He's a very cruel man. He drove my mother to suicide." Lena's face bore her hatred when she glanced at Cory. "Here's the rub: he blamed her, told us she was a coward, told us she didn't love us enough to stay around. The bastard didn't even cry over her. The way he looked at it, she didn't deserve any tears. She had gone AWOL, abandoned her troops.

"I'm not surprised he ordered that little boy executed. We're all expendable collateral— unless, of course, you serve a purpose to him. Right now, Cory, you're on the border between useful and expendable. Step carefully." She downed her wine and presented her empty glass to him, "Refill, please."

As Cory refilled her glass, he told her, "Your father saved you because he loves you."

"He doesn't love me. He never loved me. He's looking forward to his old age, expects I'll be a lonely old spinster eager to take care of him in exchange for his gratitude. That's what he's thinking about." She took a hefty sip of the Cabernet, and then said, "You don't seem very worried for your life, Cory."

"I don't really care for my life."

"Why?"

"Take a good look around! What's the point?"

"That's God's secret."

"I've never believed in God."

"Maybe someday you'll change your mind."

"I doubt it."

"Well, then... shall we throw ourselves off this roof? If anybody remembers us for any reason, it'll be for the mess we make when we splatter onto the pavement. Now, how's that for a memorable exit? Are you game, Cory?"

He laughed.

"I'll jump with you."

"Don't do that."

"Really! I'll jump with you. I'm sick of it all, too. The only good thing in my life these days is you. Without you..."

"Don't guilt-trip me."

Machine gun fire rang out.

Lena chuckled. "Sounds like they got another one. Either that, or they're shooting at each other." She sighed and nestled against Cory. "Makes you wonder who the monsters really are."

Without thinking about it he brushed his lips upon her forehead, gave her a kiss. She pulled back and gazed at him, confused.

"If you want to stay around," he said, "I guess I will."

"Why'd you kiss me?"

"I like you. Would you rather I slapped you?"

She laughed softly. "I guess an *I like you* kiss is better than no kiss at all."

"Would you like a real kiss?"

"You're drunk."

"So are you."

"We'll hate ourselves in the morning."

"We hate ourselves, anyway."

"If you were sober, you wouldn't have kissed me. If you really like me, kiss me when you're sober. Till then, keep those gorgeous lips of yours to yourself." She smiled at him, downed her wine, and then presented the empty glass to him. "Let's finish the bottle."

CHAPTER 24

Dillon stared entranced at the face of the man in the moon. It had been years since he took the time to appreciate the night sky and the constellations, and he had forgotten how peaceful it made him feel.

A breeze came up and chilled his skin. He gathered the material of Jill's parka and tucked it around his neck, brought up the hood to protect himself from the sudden freeze. At least tonight, he had remembered to wear his gloves, and he noticed the soldiers wore theirs, too. Because the soldiers wore their gloves, he didn't feel like such a wimp.

He lit another cigarette and dropped the match in the dirt.

A tall dark soldier stepped forward and reprimanded him, "Uh, uh, uh!"

Dillon bent and retrieved the match, dropped it into his pocket. He said nothing to the man, simply cast him a glance.

The dark soldier, Santiago, eyed the boy haughtily. The only time he saw the boy without the little girl was late at night when he came out to smoke. He detected anger in the boy's eyes, hopelessness in his slumped shoulders. Santiago took this to mean the Little Catfish was still grieving for his lost lover. He stepped closer to the boy and, when the boy looked up at him inquiringly, Santiago got a good look at his face. The kid had a beautiful mouth framed by full, pouty lips. He recalled Neville had quipped the boy gave the best head he had ever received in his life. Santiago wondered if that was really true. However, to find out would only complicate matters, and he didn't need any complications.

"What the hell do you want?" Dillon snapped, "I picked up the match!"

"You oughta be asleep at this hour."

"Who are you, the curfew police?"

Santiago chuckled, tugged his gloves up further on his wrists. If the rumors about the boy were true, the boy would know the meaning of the secret Santiago hid beneath his gloves. He relaxed his stance in order to lessen the boy's defensive attitude. "You're having trouble sleeping. A lot of us are having that trouble." Dillon met his platitudes with defiant silence. Santiago tried again, "I take it your parents died during the crisis."

Something in the man's eyes told Dillon he could not trust this soldier. He accurately interpreted the man's amicability as a put-on. "All of us lost someone."

"You seem very sad."

"That's none of your business."

Santiago did not expect the boy to be such a hard-ass. Outwardly, he seemed so little and timid. "A lion in sheep's clothing," he remarked.

"Leave me alone."

"Tough little shit, aren't you?"

Dillon's temper rose. "I ain't bothering you! Leave me alone!"

Again, Santiago chuckled to himself. If he wanted to, he could snap the kid's neck in half with one hand. Surely, the Little Catfish knew that, yet he maintained his hostile attitude. Santiago admired his bravery but pitied his stupidity. He decided to leave the kid alone with the moon and his misery.

"Fuckin' ay..." Dillon muttered under his breath. It was impossible to have a moment's privacy around here.

JOE ENTERED THE STOCKROOM and stepped around Ian who was re-stocking their dwindling supplies. He reached for a box of alcohol swabs. "There they are."

Ian sat cross-legged on the floor, neatly stacking cases of mattress protection pads on the bottom shelf. "We're starting to get low on things."

"There's more down in the fourth level. Don't worry." He rolled over the spare stool and sat down. "Mitchell said there's a snowstorm on the way." Ian did not seem to hear him. Joe still had trouble getting used to Ian's tunnel-focus problem, something Doctor Macky said was a form of ADD. "Have you cleared the exterior garden?"

Joe's voice finally clicked in Ian's head. "Sorry... What?"

"It's gonna snow. Did you guys clear the garden?"

"Yeah."

"How's your indoor garden coming?"

"Very well. By the way, Natalie's lilac bushes are beginning to grow. I forgot to tell her." Ian then smiled. "That will make her very 'appy. Remember when we found them when they brought her in? Remember? She had a branch tucked inside her jacket."

"Yeah, I remember."

"Fulla seeds..."

"Yeah."

"How could I not at least try?"

"Yeah. She'll be glad."

He looked up at Joe, smiled again. "Guess what?"

"What?"

"Doctor Macky says I should be a doctor. What do you think?"

Joe tapped his shoulder. "I agree with her!"

"Really?"

"Yeah!"

"Why don't you become a doctor? You could, y'know. Easily!"

"I put in enough hours here."

"Darla and the children..." Ian assumed. "You're a right good father, Joe."

Joe thought he had fallen short as a father. He was still worried about his second youngest, his son Randy. Randy had settled down some; the counseling sessions with Suzanne had helped tremendously. In spite of that, although Randy's anger had subsided, his nightmares had increased. Joe wished he could be there for him at night, but he was committed to work graveyard at the hospital because they were so short-staffed. Sometimes he regretted it.

Ian knew what he was thinking. "Per'aps you could request an earlier shift so you can be home with them at night."

"How do you do that?"

"Do what?"

"Read my mind?"

Ian laughed softly. "It's not readin'. I've come to learn your expressions. You get a look on your mug when you're thinkin' of your lit'el uns. You've a special look for Jayjay, another for Randy, and yet another for little Becka." He smiled perceptively as he added, "Not to mention that *very special* look ya get when it comes to Darla."

Joe blushed.

Ian stated as a reminder, "Such a blessin'."

"You're growing up too fast," Joe said.

"I was never young."

"That's what Trevor said."

"Trevor knows."

It was becoming awkward for Joe. He felt a strong urge to wrap his arms around Ian and tell him he considered him his son. At the same time, he felt such a sentiment would embarrass Ian. "Well," he said, rising, "I'd better get back to work."

Suddenly, Ian said, "Thank you, Joe."

"For what?"

"Your family." He then grinned and playfully backhanded Joe's knee, "Get back to work before I report ya for slackin'!"

LENA SET ANOTHER SLIDE under the microscope and viewed the strange centipede creatures that swam languidly in the drop of her blood. To her amazement, some appeared to be nourishing the red blood cells and then dividing them to increase their number while others appeared to be selectively eating some of the post-divided cells.

Cory entered the lab and set her special lunch order, wrapped in tin foil, on the little round table in the corner. "It took some fancy talking—medical gobbledy-gook that they didn't understand—but I got it for you."

She waved him over to the microscope. "Come see this."

He re-set the focus and peered at the alien world on the slide, the busy creatures there hard at work. "What are they?"

"Antigens, I think. Unlike anything I've ever seen."

"Are they products of the mord virus?"

"They have to be. Your blood doesn't contain them, but mine does." She crossed to the table and sat, unwrapped the foil from the small raw beefsteak and took a bite. Chewing, she asked, "Did they make you sign for this?"

"They were too busy."

"Were they suspicious?"

"I told them it was for cultures. Your signature on the order sealed the deal."

"Good."

He sat down across from her, unwrapped his cheeseburger, lifted the top bun to make sure they didn't forget the cheese like last time. He glanced at her, saw her take a second bite and savor it. "Is it good?"

She nodded.

"Must be," he said, "You're smiling." He took a small bite of his hamburger and said through his chewing, "I've been thinking. Perhaps the alcohol last night has something to do with the resurgence of your symptoms."

Lena did not reply. She had her own theory, and it had everything to do with her increasing attraction to Cory. Ever since he kissed her last night, she had wondered if he would be the one to finally overlook her lack of beauty and lovingly relieve her of her virginity. The more she fantasized about it and the greater her arousal, the greater her hunger grew for a taste of raw meat.

"I have a slight hangover," he remarked with a chuckle.

She smiled at him. "I don't."

"That figures. You must have a very strong constitution." After another taste of his cheeseburger, he inquired, "Do you like onions?"

"I love onions!"

"So, you won't mind that I have onion breath the next time I kiss you?"

She grinned and blushed. The few other men who had kissed her had only done so while they were too drunk to be repulsed by her homeliness. Here he was, sober, and he still wanted to kiss her. She surmised Cory needed glasses.

"You're blushing!" Cory teased.

"I don't blush." She finished the meat and went on to her salad.

He observed her as they ate in silence, appreciated the little nuances in her expressions as she took pleasure in her meal. During the last week, he had found himself more drawn to her, and he had begun to see the beauty of her features. She had the most alluring blue eyes framed by long curly lashes, and her eyes had a way of peering into him in the most flattering way. It seemed when she looked at him, she saw the person inside the handsome face instead of just the handsome face. The fact that she looked beyond the surface and perceived, even approved, the flawed man there appealed to his yearning for a woman who would love him despite his inner imperfections.

She reclined against the backrest of her chair and swept her hair away from her face. Seemingly from out of nowhere, she produced an elastic hair band and gathered her chestnut brown locks into a ponytail. That simple, innocent action of hers caused his heart to beat a little faster. He wanted to liberate her tresses and bathe his face in their softness.

"Don't tell Daddy about the meat," she said.

"Of course not," he replied.

"Do you think I'm getting sick again?"

"No. I think you're still in the process of recovery."

"You're not afraid of me?"

"No."

"Does your promise still stand to euthanize me if..."

"Yes. I love you enough to do what..."

She regarded him in a pleasantly shocked manner. "You *love* me, Cory?"

The reality of it filled him with the conviction that, for once in his life, his desire for her was much deeper and more real than what he had experienced with any other woman. "I do love you, Lena. God help me, I love you."

"Thought you didn't believe in God."

"Didn't you hear the *I love you* part?"

Of course, she heard it. However, she habitually dismissed those words as too easily said and too often insincere. At this moment, a part of her wanted to believe his words, but she had already put on her armor.

Cory's heart sank with her silence. "I guess I overstepped our boundary."

The disappointment on his face confirmed his words were

indeed sincere. Now, all Lena could do was accept the love he offered her and present her own love for him in return. She stood and leaned across the little table, planted a long, slow kiss on his lips. When she felt she had given it enough time, she pulled away from him and asked, "Was that right?"

He stood and drew her into his arms, pressed his lips upon hers.

CHAPTER 25

Coltan lifted the new bookcase and set it upright against the granite wall in the library. From the desk near the entrance, Carolyn admired his muscles. She hated that some of the old Carolyn from Bonito Valle still existed within her, the old Carolyn who found Harley Guy sensuously appealing. The former *biker boy* was now a mature, faithfully married man, and that was not going to change.

He turned and smiled at her. "I'll help you place the books, if you want."

His smile invoked within her an urge to surrender. She resisted it. "That's okay. Guffy's helping."

"I don't mind."

"That's okay."

There were still many boxes of books to sort and place. He could not understand why she refused his help. "Those boxes are heavy," he said.

"I've gotten used to it."

"Would it be okay with you if I looked through to see what's there?"

"Are you looking for something in particular?"

"The classics. Also poetry."

That surprised her. Coltan had never impressed her as the type who would like poetry. Back in Bonito Valle, he had never impressed her as the type who could read, for that matter. She pointed, "There's poetry on that rack over there."

"I've read all those already. Mitchell told me Walt Whitman

wrote some great stuff. Maybe there's some of his in one of those boxes."

She was not comfortable around Coltan. She feared he could sense her attraction to him, an attraction she now abhorred. However, Coltan was a stubborn guy, charming and persistent. Carolyn sighed resignedly, "Yeah… I guess."

He stepped over to the stack of boxes, lifted the top box and set it on the floor. He sat with it and began to remove the books one at a time as he read the titles. "Do you like poetry?"

"I find it boring. I do like the *Rhymes of a Red Cross Man*, though, when Ian reads it to me. That's one of your favorites, isn't it?"

"What do you like to read?"

"Porn." The flippant pun spilled out before she could stop herself.

He laughed. "Is there a hidden room where you keep that?"

"We don't have any porn."

"I didn't think so." He looked over a few more books and set them aside. "You haven't been at Bible study lately. How come?"

"I've been busy here."

"That's bullcrap…"

She sighed again in response, this time a little miffed at him.

"Is it boring for you?"

"No. I just get burnt out." She distracted herself with a stack of checkout cards to file.

Coltan suddenly laughed to himself and called out to her, "Hey! Take a look at this!" He held up an ancient text with a faded red cloth-bound cover. "C'mere…"

"What?" She settled beside him on the floor. He gave her the book. It was a musty old textbook from the early 1900's about surgical procedures. She thumbed through the illustrated pages and said, "Natalie'd get a kick out of this."

"That's what I was thinking."

Carolyn handed it to him. "Take it. You never know when she'll have to saw somebody's leg off."

He laughed heartily at that. "Sounds like you've been reading some Civil War novels."

"Not me. Ian."

"Oh." A French language title caught his eye. He removed the book from the box and looked through the pages. The hardcover novel, printed in Paris, contained French text. "Hmmm..." he said to himself. "Victor Hugo... *The Hunchback of Nortre Dame.*"

She exclaimed loudly, "You can read that?"

Coltan did not want to reveal to her his mastery of the French language. Somehow, it seemed pretentious to him, almost like bragging, to let people in on his secret. "It's a very famous story." He closed the book and traced the title on the front with his finger, "The words *Nortre Dame* gives it away. I'd like to check it out."

"Why, if you can't read it?"

"Just because."

Why would he want a book written in a language he could not understand? She shrugged at his silly lack of reasoning about it. "Okay. I'll prep a card for it."

The foreign language book in his hands gave him an idea. "Do you have any children's books written in Spanish?"

"Uh-uh. Who'd you want that for?"

"Isabelle."

"Can she read?"

"Guffy said she can. She has trouble remembering how to write and spell, that's all."

"She scares me."

"Why?"

"Sometimes she points her face up and sniffs the air like a dog. What's up with that?"

"Kids sometimes like to pretend they're animals. It's nothing."

"Guffy's trying to make her stop doing that."

Just for fun, Coltan did the *dog thing* and sniffed the air. He then gazed naughtily at Carolyn and stated, "You're wearing Chantilly."

He was right. That spooked her, and she slapped his arm. "Cut that out!"

Coltan broke out in a fit of giggles at her shocked expression. She could not resist laughing with him. He wound down and told her, "This is the first time I've seen you laugh since we got here."

"Well," she chided him, "The last time I laughed in front of you, you almost took my head off!"

He had to search his memory to understand what she meant. It finally came to him. "Oh, yeah... the Dairy Delight. You were laughing at me. You pissed me off."

"You were such a drama queen."

"It was a bad time for me."

"Fresh outa Juvy..."

"No... not that." He suddenly became crestfallen, stared down at the book in his hand. "You always thought I was trash. Everyone did."

"No, I didn't."

"Yes, you did. I once overheard you and Natalie."

He had caught her; she was guilty as charged. Now, she needed to atone. "I'm sorry, Coltan."

He thought about the memories, tried to consider their point of view at the time, tried to qualify that with how he appeared to people back then. As he was always inclined, Coltan assumed the blame. "I brought it on myself."

"No..."

"It was easier for me to let people be scared of me. That way, you'd all leave me alone."

"Why did you want that?"

"It was... easier." He didn't want to explain, didn't want to reveal the torment he experienced behind closed doors. It was nobody's business.

Carolyn had her suspicions, and she was certain her suspicions were correct. However, she sensed he did not want to revisit that frightening territory. She grasped for a fresh subject and finally came up with one when she spotted a Sci-Fi paperback on its side in the box. She removed it and handed it to Coltan. "Give this to Dillon. He loves Science Fiction. I promised I'd pull them for him. He's read all the other ones already. I used to hide them at the bottom of the book cart for him when I wheeled them over to the hospital for the patients. He sure was a little brat back then! Kinda likeable, though."

Coltan smiled at her, grateful she gave him an exit from their previous conversation. "I'll see to it. Thanks."

MAJOR STANDISH RAPPED on Lena's door. She awoke slowly to the persistent sound, recognized it as coming from her father's typically impatient hand. Still in that fog between awake and asleep, Lena slid from under the covers and pulled on her robe, opened the door.

Her father did not wait for an invitation to come in. Instead, he gently shoved his way past her and entered the room after giving her a brief hug. No sooner had he closed the door then he spotted Cory asleep in Lena's bed. The sight of him there caused the major's sense of violation to rise, as if the young man's sexual invasion of his daughter was an invasion to his own self. His anger at this followed.

"What have you done, Lena?"

"What do you mean *what have I done*? And... keep your voice down."

"I will not!" He crossed to the bed and backhanded the now-stirring sergeant's bare shoulder, "Get out of my daughter's bed!"

Cory awoke with a start. "What?"

Standish's face burned red with his anger. "How dare you!"

Lena set herself between her father and her lover. "How dare *you*, Daddy! You have no right to dictate what I do in my private life."

Finally awake enough to understand the gravity of the situation, Cory sat up and rubbed his eyes. Military protocol would have demanded he sprung to attention with a salute to the major, but Cory regarded Standish's unwelcome and unexpected visit as a personal matter. Because of that, he at first did not acknowledge the man, but instead wrapped his arm around Lena's shoulders and tenderly kissed her flushed cheek.

The major's face grew a darker shade of crimson when Cory kissed his daughter who, no doubt, was indecently naked under her robe.

Cory addressed his superior officer, the haughty father of the woman he loved, with disrespectful casualness. "Good morning, Major."

The major threw his question to both of them, "How long has this been going on?"

"Daddy, please calm down."

"I will not!"

"I'm a grown-up now! Or, haven't you noticed?"

He fumed at Cory, "How dare you take advantage of her!"

Cory regarded him with genuine sincerity. "I love your daughter, sir. I would never take advantage of her."

"What do you call this?"

Cory loosened up his stiff painful shoulders, the result of two people trying to sleep together in a twin-sized bed. To the major's question, he replied humorously, "I call this a need to move a double bed in here."

Standish made a fist and shook it at Cory. "Why, you... This is no joke, Sergeant!"

"It certainly isn't," Cory replied. "It also isn't the disaster you seem to think it is."

In his building rage, the major blurted, "Why, I could fry your..." At this point, he realized it was the wrong thing to say and the wrong way to deal with this situation.

"You will not fry his chip!" Lena demanded through clenched teeth.

The major restrained his temper. "I didn't mean that I would... I'm very angry with both of you. How could you let this happen?"

"Don't you want Lena to be happy?" Cory questioned.

"She is not well!" he boomed.

"I *am* well!" Lena countered.

Standish turned on her. "You could infect him!"

She cocked her head at him, a gesture he recognized as defiance. "I'm *well*." She then settled at the edge of the bed and gazed resolutely at her father. "You can't keep me attached to your hip for the rest of my life! I love Cory. He loves me. We've done nothing wrong. You have no right to charge in here like a pit bull and tear our throats out!" Her sudden satirical smile warned him she was going to let loose a quip. "Now, then, Daddy... Will I have to shoot you with a tranquilizer dart like you did me?"

Cory chuckled silently at her jest and inadvertent revelation. *So, that's how he smuggled her in here.*

Despite his anger, the major could not resist her humor. He laughed softly and seated himself in the chair at the desk.

"That's more like it," Lena said, mission accomplished. "Imagine that... two men fighting over me. Who woulda ever thought it?"

During the awkward silence that followed, Cory found his clothing on the floor next to the bed. Under the covers, he put his underwear and uniform slacks on. As he dressed, he glanced at the major. The major glowered at him. Cory cast him a disarming grin in response. The big man's expression softened.

Beneath his carefully measured cool handling of the major's ire, Cory wondered if the man would release him from his assignment as mord wrangler to the once ailing Lena. He wanted to continue his work with her, not for his original goal of advancement in rank, but for his new goal to restore her to health and full function. Cory's second conundrum was a very real fear: that the major would punch in his numbers and fry his chip. How could he prevent that? How could he persuade Standish he had only Lena's best interests at heart? How could he persuade this overly protective father he would protect her with equal, perhaps greater, fervor?

AS SOON AS DARLA DAVIDSON dismissed the grade school class, the children sprinted from their desks and ran, trotted or skipped out into the main corridor. Unlike the other children, Isabelle strolled out slowly and then waited at the entranceway for Dillon to emerge from the adjoining classroom. She was glad Dillon would be her escort today instead of Unkaduffy who was working at the library. She found it easier to talk with Dillon about the kid-issues that arose from being with lots of other kids.

Dillon strode over to her with a big grin and his outstretched hand. She took his hand and began to walk with him to the north end where they would have lunch. There was something on her mind, and she tugged on his hand to get his attention.

He stopped and squatted down in front of her so they could converse face-to-face. "What's up, Eensy?"

"Wandy pulled my haihw."

Dillon's face furrowed with concern. "Did he pull it hard? Did he hurt you?"

"Uh-uh. He did dis..." She gently tugged on a short strand of

Dillon's hair. "Just like dat. Den he pwetended he didn't do it when I looked at him."

"He did it nice and gently like that?"

"Uh-huh."

Dillon giggled and placed his hands on her shoulders. "I think Randy likes you."

"But he pulled my haihw!"

"He did that to get your attention."

"Why didn't he just tell me he wants ta be fwends wiff me?"

"Sometimes boys don't know how to tell a girl they like her. I bet he was afraid you'd tell him to get lost, so he tugged on your hair to test you."

"Test me why?"

"To see if you'd be mad or okay with it. Were you okay with it?"

"He didn't hoot me..."

"Did you smile at him?"

"I tode him to stop or I'd tell."

"What'd he do?"

"He said he didn't mean nothin'. Then he went back to his wook." In the next breath, she changed the subject completely. "Can we watch a movie dis aftoonoon?"

"What kind?"

"Singin' and dancin'. Wiff dat guy named Fed."

"Fred Astaire?"

"Yeah... him." When Dillon stood, she tugged on his hand again. "Will you show me again how day did dat wawtz ting?"

"Okay." He took her hands and guided her through the steps. Some of the people in the corridor paused along their way to watch them. Dillon waltzed her, both laughing with glee, up the corridor toward the dining room.

"You should wehw a suit like Fed's," she opined, "An' a taw hat like his!"

"A top hat and tails?"

"Dat'd look good on you, Din!"

"And a gown for you!"

She grinned big and laughed. "Yeah... like aw doze pitty ladies!"

He spun her a few turns, waltzed her further up the corridor. More people stopped to amusedly watch their impromptu performance. In the process, Dillon began to sing one of the movie songs to her to help them keep time.

He spun her again, right into Raul Santiago, shortly distracted by a soldier who called to him. Isabelle smacked dead-on into the tall, black-eyed stranger in uniform. The three of them came to an abrupt halt. Isabelle stared up wide-eyed at the man.

Santiago, although at first startled by the impact, recognized the child and surmised their collision provided an opportunity to warm up to her. He slipped his hands into the pockets of his jacket, knelt and smiled at her. "Hello there, *Bonita*!"

She replied shyly, *"Hola, señor. Lo siento."*

"Por que?"

"I wan into you."

Dillon eyed Santiago suspiciously. He took Isabelle's hand and gently urged her away from the soldier. He told Santiago, "Sorry. We weren't watching."

Santiago ignored Dillon. He grinned warmly at Isabelle, "Are you gonna be a dancer?"

She pressed her lips tightly together and considered it. "Maybe."

"What's your name, precious?"

She brightened at the familiar pet name he called her. "Unkaduffy caw me pwessis."

"But that's not your—"

Dillon pulled her away, "C'mon. You don't wanna be last in line, do ya?"

She glanced at Dillon eagerly, "Uh-uh!" As she allowed Dillon to lead her away, she turned back to the soldier and waved at him. "Bye...!"

Farther down the corridor, Dillon told her, "I don't want you to talk to him, Isa."

"Why?"

"I don't like him."

"Why?"

"I just don't."

"He looks kinda like Hectoo."

"Who's Hector?"

"Mama's fwend. Hectoo's dead now."

"Did you like Hector?"

"He was okay. Sometimes I didn't like'im."

"How come?"

"He put his hand down my panties."

Dillon came to a split-second halt and alarmedly stared down at her. "Did you tell your mother?"

She didn't seem the least bit bothered by it. "He tode me not to."

"How many times did he do that to you?"

"Ony dat one time. I tode him if he did it again, I'd tell on him. Mama an' Mawio ahways tode me nevoo to let no one touch me dere. I tode him I'd tell Mawio an' Mawio'd kick his butt!" She laughed with the memory. "Mawio *woulda* kicked his butt, too!"

"Did he ever try anything else with you?"

"Uh-uh. I tink I scawood him good! Aftoo dat, I didn't like him no mo."

"Did you ever tell Guffy about it?"

"Uh-uh. Why would I tell him? It ain't got nothin' ta do wiff him. Unkaduffy's a good guy. He's ahways been a good guy. He's nice to kids an' don't touch 'em bad." She then looked pleadingly at Dillon, "Don't tell him. He'd feel bad fo' me. I don't want dat. Duffy don't need no woowees. Don't tell nobody, okay?"

He saw wisdom in her reasoning. "Okay, Eeensy. As Trevor would say, *mum's the word, chum*."

"Mum's da wood!" She beamed up at him as if he was her personal secret treasure.

"If anybody here ever tries to do that to you, you tell me, okay?"

"Okay."

CHAPTER 26

Major Standish stood at his office window and peered down at the city three stories below. The wind had picked up in the last few hours. Like a whirling devil of destruction, it stripped the few remaining leaves off the trees and cast them swirling into the air and then down to the pavement. There was no rest for them on the pavement. They skipped, bounced and then soared again upon the crest of the wind, their ultimate destination decided at the whirling devil's whim.

Unlike the hapless leaves in the wind, Standish had the power to decide not only his own destiny but also that of anyone else in his unfortunate circle. It really screwed with his sense of security when someone tried to throw a match into his plans.

When it came to his plans for his daughter's life, the major had never considered that one day a man would fall for her. Men had always outright rejected her. Even the men at Gennamatrix barely noticed her and, when they did, it was because someone referred them to her to help solve a problem. Once they came to know her, they quickly grew weary of her endless quips and self-effacing humor. Of course, it didn't help that she had a tendency to prove herself smarter than they were. Many times as a result and mostly out of revenge for their bruised egos, some of those men utilized her knowledge and contacts for their own personal gain. Once they got what they wanted, they happily disappeared from her life. They left without even a *thank you* or *fuck you* card in their wake.

And then, out of the blue, Sergeant Cory Jones decided she was the woman for him. Under normal circumstances, this would have been unexpected; under current circumstances with Lena once (and possibly still) infected with the mord virus, his attraction to her would have been impossible.

What in hell was wrong with this guy that he would want someone as damaged as Lena? Perhaps everything was wrong with this guy. Surely, he was not in love with Lena. A man like him, with his looks, could have any model-type bimbo he chose. Lena had all the good looks of a withered rose. She had the personality of a tragic clown who cried behind the laughter. She was a loser. She had always been a loser. What did Cory Jones intend to gain through his relationship with her? How did he intend to use her to attain his goal?

Now that Jones had shown his true colors, Major Standish lost every ounce of the small amount of trust he once had for the man. In the major's cynical mind, Cory was just another in a long line of men who had used his daughter to further their careers.

All afternoon, as Standish watched the torturous journey of the leaves in the wind, he had been thinking about his daughter, thinking how she was so much like a leaf in the wind, hanging on to hope, only to be torn from that hope to drift once again on the whims of fate. Like the spent leaf of autumn, Lena was slowly dying inside, folding into her withering self as she alighted to the earth from which she came, the earth whereupon she would eventually crumble into a zillion obscure pieces and no one would ever know she once existed.

Good lord... there were so many Lenas, and all of them lived invisibly and died invisibly.

For a few moments, Standish mourned. He mourned not for Lena but for himself. He wondered how such a grotesque product sprang from such a magnificent seed.

That thought led him to wonder why he had gone to such lengths to save her. It would have been so easy to pop a bullet into her diseased-infested brain to end it all for him, as well as for her. Yet, she looked at him with those Bambi eyes and uttered the plaintive cry to him, *"Jaddoo!"* She had called for her daddy to protect her. That's what it was: she needed his protection, appealed to his need to control something—anything—among the uncontrollable circumstances, even if it meant she was the only thing he could control. That's what it was. It certainly was not his love for her; he never loved her. She was his daughter and that was all. A man had a responsibility to his daughter, even if she was a loser and possibly a product of another man's seed, as he always suspected. In his own responsible way, he controlled—steered—every aspect of her life. That's what his father had done for him. That's what a father was supposed to do, wasn't it? That's what a father *must do* for his daughter when she is crying out to him, *"Jaddoo!"*

Be responsible... Control the situation... Control the outcome...

The outcome.

Cory Jones would hurt her. She would shrivel up in tears and wish again to die, maybe even try to die. That's what she did the last time, the only time. Maybe this time, given her weakened condition, she would not come out of it.

Sergeant Cory Jones didn't care. All he cared about was the notoriety he would get from using her as his guinea pig. His research with her as a fully functioning survivor of the mord virus would jettison him up the ladder into the PS Program, the W1 Psychological Sciences Program. More than likely, he intended to present Lena to them as their latest experimental subject. She would go along with it because she loved the bastard and stupidly believed he loved her and had her best interests at heart.

He knew too much.

He was just like the others.

However, unlike the others, Cory Jones was a leaf in the wind. His destiny depended upon the whims of the one who had the power to control and decide. The Devil Wind had decided the leaf's destiny long before he dislodged it from the branch. After all, the leaf had completed its purpose, now it was time to complete its journey.

Major Standish took a seat in front of his computer, pressed the *Enter* key to awaken it from hibernation. The Master Tracking program blinked open on the monitor. Major Standish typed in the special numbers and symbols identification string for a particular Sergeant Cory Vanjensen Jones, former NATO Rank Code OR-5[4]. The MT program promptly displayed Cory's photograph and his personal, professional and biological information. Major Standish scrolled down to the bottom of the final page.

At the bottom of the page stood four boxes centered horizontally. The first box contained the word VERIFY, the second contained the word ARCHIVE, the third contained the word LOCATE, and the fourth box contained the word ELIMINATE.

Major Standish hovered the curser above the boxes...

IN THE LAB AT THE OPPOSITE end of the corridor, Lena scoured the illustrations and color photographs of the denizens of the microscopic world: the bacteria, fungi, cells, antibodies and viruses. These creatures, as Lena liked to call them, dictated the fate of the human race by their very existence. Lena had always marveled about how something so incredibly tiny could wield such extraordinary power. The mord virus proved to be a supreme being in the alien world of microscopic nations and serfdoms, a barbaric usurper of what had once been a natural balance of things.

In all the illustrations and photographs in this hefty textbook, she had not found anything within the order of antibodies or antigens that resembled the byproducts of the mord virus. Lena wondered if they were not actually antigens, as she suspected, but some new kind of creature that did not belong to the world inside the human body. She considered it was a microscopic animal, perhaps a parasite or insect.

She closed the fat textbook and set it at the clear spot on the table, being careful not to disturb the place setting of napkins and silverware she had placed there for lunch with Cory. She then rose and scanned the titles in the bookcase.

A title that referred to insects and parasites caught her eye. Lena removed the book and sat down at the table with it, opened it to the index page.

She suddenly felt nauseous. Pain—gnawing, burning—quickly followed the nausea.

She pushed the book away and bent at the waist in an effort to stem the pain, feared she would next need to vomit. A wave of heat that caused her to break into a sweat swept through her. Her mouth felt strange, felt heavy and tingly.

What on earth...?

Suddenly, a vision of a computer monitor replaced her awareness of the real world. She was sitting in front of a computer monitor, and saw the name CORY spread across the screen in giant red letters. Below his name, she saw four command boxes containing the words: VERIFY, ARCHIVE, LOCATE, ELIMINATE. The word, ELIMINATE, like Cory's name, was in giant red letters.

She smelled her father's scent, smelled it as if he was sitting on her lap.

She wanted to warn Cory, but he was down in the cafeteria on the first floor. He had been down there for the last twenty minutes, undoubtedly waiting in line to get the take-out lunch order for her and him and Daddy. Hopelessness overwhelmed her: What good would it do to warn him? It would take two seconds for Daddy to click on that ELIMINATE box, and Cory would collapse into a fatal episode of seizure.

Daddy! You bastard!

The feral instinct to protect what she believed was hers followed her rage. The savage impulse to destroy, devour and erase the threat to her loved one overpowered all her innate higher human characteristics of morals and reasoning. The mord virus rapidly regrouped in her brain, summoned by her overwhelming ire at the danger about to befall her and her beloved Cory.

Trembling, snarling and growling, Lena shot to her feet with fierce and direct intention. She took a steak knife from the table, decided it would do if she reached the bastard in time.

When Lena came upon the door to her father's office, she found it slightly ajar. Through the gap between the edge of the door and the doorframe, she saw her father at the computer, his back to her. He appeared to be staring at the monitor, vacillating over the command boxes. So focused on the adrenaline-fed intoxication brought about by his decision, he did not hear her stealthy footsteps approach, did not hear her tense breathing.

She stopped behind him, the knife ready in her hand.

He finally sensed her presence. He sensed it at the precise moment she grasped his forehead in her left hand, yanked his head back, and then brutally, deeply, savagely, incised his throat from ear-to-ear. There had not even been enough time for him to utter a sound. His warm blood spurted onto the keyboard. He gasped for breath, but all that happened when he did that was a gurgle of blood and trapped air bubbled up his throat.

She dropped the knife and then used both her hands and all of her strength to slam him backwards, chair and all, onto the floor. The scent of his life spurting and spilling out of him whetted her long-suppressed appetite for sweet human blood and flesh. Now, the desire to devour him replaced her desire to kill him. She threw herself upon him, ripped open the gaping incision on his neck, bent her face into the inviting, pulsating wet flesh and sank her teeth and her tongue into the feast. She tore pieces free with her teeth, chewed the flesh, savored the blood, swallowed it hungrily and dived in for more. As she did this, his body trembled and jerked. His legs, still bent at the knees over the seat of the chair, swung up and down in a marching motion, left, right, left, right, with his struggle. One shoe flew off and hit the wall. His convulsions were making it difficult for her to maintain a good grip with the vise of her teeth. She pounded her fists into his chest and growled at him to stop. As if he heard and obeyed her, he finally went limp. As soon as she swallowed her second helping, she ravaged what remained of his throat tissues for as much nourishment as she could get.

"Lena!" Cory's screeching voice coupled with the noise of a plastic bag heavily laden with full Styrofoam food containers crashing to the floor came at once into her fogged-in brain.

Don't stop me! Don't take my food! No, no, no!

She jerked up her head; shot him a snarling glare of warning.

This is MY food! Stay away!

Her father's blood and stray bits of his shredded flesh covered her face and clung to her hair. Her bared teeth exhibited the same. Brown drool rolled down her chin from the corners of her mouth. She snarled at Cory once more to keep his distance, and then she buried her face again into the feast.

Cory stood paralyzed for a brief time, watched her eat. At first, his mind refused to analyze and believe the grisly scene. Once the reality of it sunk in, and once he realized what this meant, his body began to tremble with grief and fear. Still, he did not move. Finally, some logic crept into his brain, and his military training kicked in with it. He took his handgun from his holster and cocked the trigger.

Lena heard the noise, knew what it meant. She gazed at him, first his terrified face, and then at the gun in his quivering hand. The rank odor of his fear drifted up her flared, bloodied nostrils. His fear renewed her appetite. She gazed again at his face, noticed the glistening sweat that sprang from his pores. His sweat impressed her as an inviting marinade, and she suddenly felt compelled to taste him. All she could understand by now was that he was food. He was not a living being with consciousness, feelings and a heart full of love for her. He was an appetizing meal, a benign thing that had no purpose other than to fill her belly and stop the burning pain there, satisfy her rage-induced hunger. Oh... how she wanted to lick the marinade and then sink her teeth into the delicious flesh!

"Lena..." he whispered aghast, "Why...?"

Slowly, she stood and cocked her head to one side. The words made no sense to her, and his voice was only an invitation to dine. She took a step toward him.

His voice struggled out of him bereft of breath, "Lena... I'm Cory."

Confused and curious, she again cocked her head at him. She did not recognize him.

With desperate hope to connect with Lena's soul, he peered into her dead eyes and tried again. "Talk to me, Lena. Say something."

She growled, cocked her head to the opposite side. Impatience came into her eyes. Suddenly, her eyes filled with the gleam of predation.

Cory then understood she was gone. Lena was gone. What stood before him was a monster. The monster had devoured her the same as it intended to devour him.

He aimed at her forehead. "I promised you." He pressed the trigger.

She crumpled to her knees and remained there on her knees for a few seconds before her body folded and collapsed facedown on the carpet beside her dead father.

Cory stared at her as his grief stirred within him. He tried to comfort himself with the fact he had fulfilled his promise to her. He had ended her suffering and had prevented her from killing anyone else. Well... almost anyone else.

He glanced at the soiled and mangled corpse of Major Standish still in a sitting position in the toppled chair. How strange he looked in that position, sitting while lying down. How strange the lake of blood upon which the chair floated. How strange... all so strange.

Cory looked away. He wanted to take in a breath, and he somehow felt the air around the two dead bodies was tainted. He stepped off to the side, turned away from the tainted area and sucked in the clean air he required. As he breathed in, his sight caught the rainbow colored geometric flowers swirling upon the darkened monitor screen. For a few moments, Cory allowed the hypnotic dancing display of the screensaver to suck him into its alternate reality. The brief respite gave him comfort.

Once Cory's mind cleared and he saw the screensaver for what it indicated, he wondered what the General had been up to before Lena ate him for lunch. He leaned and tapped his finger on the mouse to bring up the display. The name *Cory Vanjensen Jones* jumped out at him from various positions within the text. Curious, Cory stepped a bit closer, focused on the four command boxes at the bottom of the page:

VERIFY ARCHIVE LOCATE ELIMINATE

To his dismay, he saw clearly the line of the curser blinking upon the box that contained the ominous word, ELIMINATE. Now angry, and anticipating the Military Police would explore Standish's last activity on the computer, he rolled the mouse and directed the curser over the box with the word, LOCATE, and left it there.

He backed away and looked at Lena. He now understood what had triggered the resurgence of the mord virus in her system.

The faint ding of the elevator down the corridor told him the soldiers had heard the gunshot and were on their way to investigate. In a few moments, they would enter the room and see the bloodied dead, and they would see him with the gun still in his hand. Cory did not want them to shoot him, so he sunk down onto the floor and sat, slid his handgun away from him along the carpet to a spot near the door.

While he awaited the soldiers' arrival, Cory cast another look at the major. This time, Cory felt no sympathy for him. He only felt despise. However, his grimace of hatred became a wry smile of amusement when he saw the major's feet suspended over the edge of the upturned chair. The foot that had lost a shoe was dressed in a brown sock with a hole in the toe. The other foot still wore a shoe, but the pant leg had rolled up to expose the major's calf. The sock on that foot was black with a decorative gray diamond design on the top hem.

Lena would have found that hilarious.

CHAPTER 27

Coltan sat in the back of the gymnasium watching Trevor and Natalie demonstrate self-defense moves to the small class of teenage students. Simply for the entertainment value, Trevor let Natalie mat him again and again. The sight of such a petite woman repeatedly throwing such a muscular man to the mat drew hoots and laughter from the young students. Caught up in the performance, Natalie tossed in a few choice words to her opponent and encouraged the students to cheer her. Coltan laughed aloud at her overly hammy showmanship. All she needed was a cheesy *superhero* costume to complete the character.

When the class ended an hour later, Trevor spotted Coltan waiting for his "lovely ass-kicker-in-residence," who was changing out of her trainer's uniform.

"Would you like to learn a few moves?" Trevor offered.

Coltan waved him off. This disciplined type of warfare was not his thing. Coltan had learned an alternative form of fighting on the streets, and that learning had served him well.

Trevor was stubborn. "Show me what you've got."

"No."

"Afraid?"

"No. Tired."

"Bah!"

Natalie's voice drifted from the locker room, "Leave him alone before I drop you on your tail again, Trevor!"

Trevor and Coltan laughed.

"She's a lovely girl," Trevor said.

"Did she put that bruise on your cheek?"

"Yes. A little careless with her elbow." He settled into the chair beside Coltan. "I wish you'd join our class."

"I really don't want to."

"You've decided for certain on going into ministry?"

"Yeah."

"Well, then..." Trevor was impressed. "If that be your calling."

Coltan glanced over at the locker room entrance. Natalie was still changing her clothes. Her brief absence presented an opportunity for Coltan to have a confidential word with Trevor. "Has she mentioned any more about wanting to be a soldier?"

"Only once. It was during a conversation about her father." Trevor decided to tread carefully here, knowing about Coltan's history with Brian Danbury. "She's still mourning for him, as you are. I dissuaded her soldier talk by reminding her what it would do to you if something happened to her. She does consider that, you know. Having almost lost you a couple of times, she understands the hell it'd put you through. Therefore, I believe her soldier talk is just that—talk. A fantasy, perhaps."

"I think she still wants to please her dad."

"It would please him to see her happy. She would not be happy if she joined the military here only to follow in his footsteps, so to speak."

"I'm afraid it's in her blood, Trev. You see how she is."

"She's a tough one! However, I wouldn't be too concerned. Right now, the subject is willy-nilly for her. Tomorrow, she may fancy something completely different." Trevor leaned closer to Coltan and suggested in a confidential manner, "I would like to keep her on as my assistant and perhaps later recruit her as a trainer. How would that set with you, chum?"

"I'd be okay with that. Do you think she'd be satisfied with that?"

Trevor considered it. Natalie tended to approach everything

with single-minded enthusiasm. However, it could pose a dilemma if she viewed her position as trainer as a stepping-stone to eventual enlistment. At this point, she was still searching for a purpose, and it was too early to predict what avenue she would take. "I suggest you listen carefully to her musings and ask her what drives her toward certain things. If she understands her motivation, it will make it easier for her to reject or accept her ideas. Ultimately, whatever she decides will be her decision." He then chuckled softly and added, "Of course, women are notorious for changing their minds, aren't they? That's why we men almost lose *our* minds because of them!"

Coltan laughed, "You got that right! What the heck: after her hammy performance today, she might decide to join Dillon's fledgling entertainment troupe!"

IAN WAITED UNTIL MORRIS responded to his knock with permission to enter before he opened the door to the lab and peeked in. He waved the small brown paper bag for the Pathologist to see. "I've got the tea mix for you, sir. The peppermint leaves will quiet your stomach."

Morris turned away from the image on the monitor. He had been observing the actions of the centipede things for the past two hours. In those two hours, he had not learned anything new about them. He was frustrated over that and the refusal of James' advisory team to let him conduct further experiments with the odd antigens on live animals.

That frustration had caused Morris to suffer excruciating headaches and frequent indigestion. His belly was presently at it again, and another headache was beginning. He waved Ian into the room and appreciatively took ownership of the bag of tea leafs. "Is there anything here for my headaches?"

"Yes sir; two herbs. Let me know how it works for you." Ian then spied the centipede creatures on the monitor. His curiosity spurred, he approached the computer and peered over Morris' shoulder. "What's that?"

"Antigens, I think."

"So, that's what they look like."

"No. That isn't what they look like."

"If that's not what they look like, why do you think they're antigens?"

"I don't know. They don't behave like antigens, yet my gut says that's what they are."

Ian continued to watch the critters moving about in their little universe of microscopic soup. He was mesmerized. "How do they act?"

"They're nourishing and cultivating the red blood cells."

"Like tendin' a garden..."

"Something like that. But they're also doing something rather destructive."

"What's that?"

"They're dividing up the red blood cells to multiply them, and then they're eating some of the extras they created." Morris gave Ian a gentle shove to one side so he could get up from the chair. No sooner did he cross the small room to the sink and the counter that held his coffee maker, did Ian take ownership of the chair. Without a word, the boy spun the chair around and stared at the monitor. "Don't touch any keys!" Morris warned him.

"I won't." After a moment's silence, Ian remarked, "They look like bugs!"

"Yeah..." Morris filled the coffee maker with water and flipped the *on* switch. He was looking forward to that tea and the relief it would bring him. "Where did you learn about tea?"

"Me mum."

"Did she grow her own?"

"Yes." There was humor in his voice when he added, "Among other things."

"Veggies?"

Ian spun the chair around and wrinkled his nose, regarded Morris as one would a moron. "She 'ad a special crop in addition to our edibles. You're not that ignorant, Morris..."

Morris finally got it. He laughed to himself and explained, "I've got a really bad headache."

"It'll cure that."

Could it be what Ian implied? "What?"

"I included a very, very small amount. Too much would make your 'eadache worse."

Morris leaned back against the counter and inquired severely, "Do they know you're growing pot?"

"Yes, sir. They asked me to."

"Who asked you to?"

"The doctors. It's an ancient medicine, y'know. It has its uses."

"Are you smoking it?"

"Have you ever seen me stoned?"

"That doesn't answer my question."

"No, I don't smoke it. I don't bake it into cookies, either." He scowled at Morris, "Bloody 'ell..."

Morris grinned at him. "You've been hanging around Trevor too much."

Ian elected to stay with the previous subject. "Coltan told me a soldier at Baker Creek had given pot to one of the mords. Right calmed the bastard, made 'im docile. Did Coltan tell you?"

This aroused Morris' curiosity. "He never told me." Morris then glanced over at the monitor, considered the centipede guys. He wondered how they would react to a spot of tea laced with marijuana.

"Might be worth a try," Ian stated.

"There's no more mords."

"No, sir! What you were thinkin': the bugs! Or, per'aps the virus itself."

"Good grief, Ian...!" The boy was mad scientist material. The thought of it made Morris laugh aloud.

Ian thought Morris was laughing at him. "'tis not funny!"

"I'm not laughing at you."

"Then, shut your gob!" As an afterthought, he respectfully tacked on, "Sir."

Joe poked his head in the doorway. He frowned at Ian. "Did I just hear you tell Morris to shut up?"

"We were funnin' with each other," Ian replied with an innocent smile.

Joe knew how hard Morris worked, and he knew Morris hated interruptions when he was working. He suggested to Ian, "Mrs. Caventry in room eleven needs a fresh IV bag. If you'll get that, I can clean the wound and change the dressing on Private Phillips' leg."

"Which means you'll finally have a lull for a gasper," Ian concluded.

"You got it."

Morris intercepted Ian as he moved to leave. "Thank you for the tea, Ian. I'll let you know if it helps."

"You're welcome, sir."

Joe wrapped his arm around Ian's shoulders as they rounded the nurses' station into the ward hallway. "I appreciate all your help, Ian. I want you to know that."

"Do you think Morris will find a cure or a vaccine for the mord virus?"

"I doubt it."

"Why?"

"Morris is working under many limitations."

"Limitations...?"

Joe did not want to go into it. "When did you become so inquiring?"

"How else will I learn?"

Joe stopped at the far corner of the admittance desk. He placed his hands on Ian's shoulders and looked him squarely in the eye. In a low voice he cautioned, "Never talk about the mord virus within earshot of the patients, okay?"

"Yes, sir." Yet, Ian could not get the idea of curing the virus out of his mind. "I suppose Morris wouldn't let me work with him."

"The last thing he needs right now is a student." He then pointed his finger into the boy's face. "Don't forget you're still *my* student. You've a lot to learn right here with me. It'll be years before you'll have enough education to even think of working with Morris."

Ian's mood plummeted with his disappointment. At the same time, he wanted to kick himself for his foolish display of ego.

His abrupt change in mood, the boy's sudden shame was evident to Joe. Joe hoped he had not been too hard on Ian, for he never meant to be. What he wanted was for Ian to master the skills of a competent EMT and, perhaps later, move on to the process of becoming a Nurse Practitioner. Maybe, many years down the line, if they survived that long, Ian would become a doctor. To Joe's way of thinking, doctors would always be the most pressing need at Alpha Base. Joe decided to be very gentle and encouraging. "You're a smart guy, Ian. You've the heart of a doctor. We need you. We need your skill and your knowledge, as well as your passion. Don't try to rush your way through this. Someday, the only chance between me living and me dying might be in your hands. The same for Darla or my kids."

"Cripes, Joe! Nothin' like puttin' a lit'il pressure on me...!"

"If I didn't think you're right for this, you'd still be sorting books at the library." Joe stood back to give Ian some space and let him think about it for a while.

After he replaced Mrs. Caventry's IV fluids bag and Joe had gone on his long-delayed break, Ian still thought about it. He was not certain he wanted to spend the rest of his life interacting with patients. It was not that he was unsympathetic; it was that he was too *empathetic*. No one, not even Doctor Macky, knew how greatly Ian suffered when he experienced an empathic link to someone in physical or emotional pain. Ian reasoned that, if he was working with mindless, soul-less microscopic creatures and their kin, at least he would not be drawn into their suffering, for they did not experience suffering.

Ian again questioned the reason and purpose for his empathic condition. He wondered why God, despite his ceaseless petitions, refused to lift the curse.

RAUL SANTIAGO FINALLY emerged through the thick brush and tangled manzanitas onto the fire trail at the south flank of the mountain range. His night vision goggles, "borrowed" from the supplies room with a little help from Chadislaw, had helped him avoid many perils during his journey. He had come across a few small animals, mostly rodents and raccoons, many of which appeared to be sick. They moved about as if they were drunk, and their mouths were glistening with brown drool. To add to the pleasure of their company, every one of them smelled like rotting flesh. With the exception of one aggressive raccoon he had kicked to death, these creatures fled at the sound of his approach. Besides the animals, Santiago had to contend with the eight-legged denizens of the mountains. With fall being the peak time for the annual mating quest of the male tarantula, the soldier traveled with particular caution when the terrain called for him to crawl through on his hands and knees. There was little more disconcerting to Santiago than to inadvertently press his hand upon one of these furry and quite ugly creatures. No doubt, they did not relish the idea of encountering him, either.

It was with a great sense of relief that Santiago stepped onto the narrow clearing of the fire trail. Itching, sweaty and feeling soiled he brushed at his clothing to disengage any hitchhikers that dared to violate his person. While he did that, he scanned the sky, noted the positions of the stars, and quickly ascertained west was to his right.

Now satisfied he was free of hitchhikers, Santiago followed the trail west, the same route Neville Langly would have taken to reach UEF Regional Headquarters in Bonito Valle. Santiago had been worried about whether Langly had made it to Bonito Valle. If he had made it, the UEF would have made contact with their spies at the Army of Christ Alpha Base by now, and Santiago and his team would have already been out of there with the little mord girl in tow. But the Bonito Valle troops had not arrived, and this made Santiago suspect Langly had not made it down the mountain. Raul doubted Langly would have deserted the mission; he was too loyal to the UAF to have entertained such an idea. That left two possibilities: Langly was injured and sheltering somewhere or he was dead. Raul Santiago was determined to find out.

He followed the trail down the mountain. As he strolled, he kept a vigilant watch for animal threats as well as signs of human travel. There were few animals along the trail on this nearly moonless night. Occasionally, Santiago heard the faint hooting of an owl, the screech of a hawk, the spine-tingling howl of a wolf or coyote. Once, something black and small lumbered across his path. When he focused on it through the night vision goggles, he discovered it was just another horny tarantula looking for a girlfriend. He paused, slowed his pace and let the thing pass. *Yeecchhh...*

So far, there was no litter indicating a human traveler had come this way. Of course, Langly would have been careful not to leave any evidence along the route during his trek. Santiago tried to estimate how far Neville might have gotten before he was injured or delayed or whatever, if that was in fact what happened to prevent his arrival in Bonito Valle. With all his analytical brain cells working overtime to suggest a logical answer, Santiago finally gave up and lent his brain cells a rest. If he did not find Neville Langly soon, or at least some evidence to suggest what had happened to him, Santiago would have to turn back none-the-wiser and even more worried. Soon it would be dawn, and he had to sneak back into the barracks a good half-hour before first light. His journey to this point through all the treacherous terrain had taken him almost three hours. The return trip would take a little more than that because it was uphill all the way. Santiago decided he could spare ten more minutes before he had to turn back.

He pressed onward. A quarter mile down, he had to climb over the fat trunk of a downed pine tree that blocked the trail. In the process, the toe of his boot caught one of the jutting branches, and he tumbled onto his chest with his legs splayed behind him over the subject branch. His chin hit the dirt trail and the impact caused his upper teeth to bounce painfully upon his lower lip. He felt the sharp pain, tasted his blood, and spewed a string of hissed profanities into the night. He sat up and wiped the blood off his now-throbbing mouth with the back of his hand.

Something stunk. Something stunk like death times a thousand.

He adjusted the skewed goggles over the bridge of his nose and surveyed the quiet nocturnal world around him. The faint buzzing of insects drew his attention to a large fly-infested lump a hundred feet forward on the edge of the path. Santiago sniffed the air, traced the stench as coming from that direction. He assumed it was another dead animal, maybe a small deer or a mountain lion, by the size of it. He stood unsteadily and took a moment to get his bearings.

Finally deeming himself fit to walk, he stepped over the small broken pine branches that protruded from the trunk of the fallen tree that had tripped him. He made his way cautiously to the increasingly malodorous carcass at the edge of the trail. When he reached it, he covered his nose and mouth with his forearm and squatted before it for a closer examination.

The cadaver wore the shredded, bloodstained, mud-soiled remnants of United States Army combat fatigues. Tatters of the rest of the clothing lay scattered various distances circumferential to the body. The nearest article of clothing, a familiar military issue parka, lay almost flat. Santiago could see the narrow parallel tears that exposed the damp interior insulating down feathers, unmistakable evidence that identified a canine-type of animal as the culprit. The condition of the body told Santiago all he needed to know about the circumstances of the soldier's death. All Santiago needed to verify at this point was the identity of the victim, and he was ninety-nine percent certain it was Neville Langly. He held his breath as he bent closer to the bug-infested remains, lifted the frayed square of material glued to the corpse by the dried blood. The material was stiff and rough within the disgusted slight grasp of Santiago's fingertips as he peeled it up to get a look at the letters of the name printed over the pocket above the left breast. Santiago strained to make it out, identified the progressive letters V, E, A, N and Y. He then looked at what remained of the hair on the decomposing skull, concluded it looked like Langly's hair. The predators had nearly severed his head from his body at the throat. Subsequent cursory examination of the rest of the body revealed something had chewed off and taken away both legs and one arm.

Now satisfied he had learned the fate of his unfortunate underling, Santiago stood. He felt a strange sensation that he had forgotten something. He glanced around at the tattered clothing and the clawed-open parka. Something was missing. It came to him in a flash, and he shook his head and sighed to himself, scolded himself that he would forget something so important.

With time of the essence, he searched the area and finally found Langly's spilled backpack half under a manzanita bush. Santiago dumped out the contents and found the tiny recorder disguised as a pen. The recording of Neville's conversation with the young Catfish was their only proof the little Latina girl was indeed the mysterious survivor of the mord virus. Santiago stuffed the pen into his pocket. He then gathered and replaced the contents of the backpack, and tossed the pack down the ravine where it landed hidden among the dense brush.

He searched for Langly's firearms, but did not find them. Santiago deduced with an unsettling shiver up the back of his neck that someone had come this way, found Langly's remains and then salvaged his weapons before proceeding onward. Santiago hoped the wayfarer was long gone. He did not want a confrontation, for the echoing pop of gunfire traveled far upon the night air and the dips and valleys of the terrain. The noise would alert not only any armed refugees nearby, but it could also conceivably alert Alpha Base. In response, they would rally Vasson's regiment to go investigate. If that happened, Vasson would find Santiago missing, and then there would be big trouble—lots of questions, lots of outright lying and explaining to do. Santiago, on second thought, surmised he could use his Bowie knife to fend off and eliminate the traveler, should their paths cross, and providing there was only one foe and the stranger did not take a shot at him. Ideally, the stranger was far away by now, and that is what Santiago hoped and forced himself to believe.

Concluding he had done all he could do, Raul Santiago began his long laborious trek back to Alpha Base. As he reached the fallen tree that blocked the trail, he paused and freed his knife from its sheath at his hip; decided he would carry it in his hand for the remainder of his return trip.

With the failure of Langly's mission, Santiago had to devise an alternate plan. The most obvious alternative was to establish reliable radio contact. If Chadislaw proved unable to modify their radios to contact the Regional Headquarters in Bonito Valle, Santiago would have to come up with another plan to abduct the child and deliver her to General Tadesco.

Santiago thought about it all the way up the mountain.

END OF BOOK 3

Thank you for reading, "*Claiming Destination Book 3: Isa.*"
Independent authors rely on reviews to spread the word about their works.
If you enjoyed this book (or hated it), please leave an online review where you purchased your book.
If you would like to contact me directly, you can reach me here:
On Facebook: Colleen A Parkinson, Author

GOOD DEEDS GO AWRY, trust is shattered, and horror descends upon Alpha while the world continues its descent into madness in the final four books of this series:

Book 4: The Bitter Fruit
Book 5: To Move a Mountain
Book 6: Mister Death Shadow
Book 7: Desitus

Other books by Colleen A. Parkinson

The Finest Hat in the Whole World

"She's my heart, Gerry. Please don't take her away from me."

A life-changing gift arrives at Des Stewart's doorstep in early January 1917. Her name is Phena, and she is nine years old, troubled, temperamental, and desperately in need of someone she can trust. That someone is her Uncle Des.

This International award-winning novel has won the hearts of readers with its touching unforgettable story of healing, heartbreak and redemption.

Beneath This Hallowed Ground

(Previously titled, "Hell is in Me")

"*Hell is in Me is one of the year's top thrillers and is a must-read for horror and paranormal thriller fans,*" says The Best Thriller Book Awards

SMALL TOWN SECRETS can't stay buried when a volatile dead man pesters Quinn, an unwilling teenage medium, in this off-the-wall paranormal thriller. Adding to his upheaval, Quinn's new neighbor, Stephanie, enlists his assistance when she discovers one of her ancestors was murdered.

Sprinkled generously with black humor, teenage angst and deep characterizations, BENEATH THIS HALLOWED GROUND (*a revised edition of HELL IS IN ME)* is a unique and satisfying read for the aficionado of paranormal suspense literature.

www.ingramcontent.com/pod-product-compliance
Lightning Source LLC
Chambersburg PA
CBHW070844260626
47170CB00007B/2488

9798993369303